THE PATH OF THE TAPIR

a novel

Michael Jarvis

Brown Badger Books
Miami, FLorida

The Path of the Tapir
Copyright © 2020 by Michael Jarvis
All Rights Reserved
ISBN 978-0-9885389-7-9
Printed in the United States by Lightning Source, an Ingram Content Group

Cover design and illustration by the author
Author photograph by Beverly Visitacion

For invaluable editorial assistance, the author thanks Annie Smith

The Path of the Tapir is a work of fiction. The characters and incidents are products of the author's imagination. Any resemblance to actual persons, living or dead, is entirely coincidental.

For Beverly
And for Pedro and Hib

The animal shall not be measured by man. In a world older and more complete than ours, they move finished and complete, gifted with extension of the senses we have lost or never attained, living by voices we shall never hear. They are not brethren; they are not underlings; they are other nations, caught with ourselves in the net of life and time, fellow prisoners of the splendor and travail of the earth.
—Henry Beston

CONTENTS

1. In and Out of View • 1
2. Chloe and Peyton • 9
3. Forging Loose Alliances • 15
4. Images of Ellis • 19
5. Dead Ends • 24
6. The Path of the Tapir • 37
7. Boruca (Victor's Version) • 41
8. Labyrinth (Liz's Vision) • 47
9. Del Preet • 57
10. Backwater • 62
11. The Fourth Rider • 70
12. I Wouldn't Name a Dog Lucky • 76
13. Long Jimmy's Longing • 89
14. Half Measures of Wisdom • 96
15. The Zuniga Factor • 122
16. The Rain and the Little Devils • 132
17. Petrospheric Harmony and Balance • 150
18. The Bird's Eye View of Marco Vargas • 172
19. Babylon Sky • 178
20. Open World • 194
21. Major Mammals • 219
22. Accept No Pardon • 256
23. Ecocide • 285
24. Peregrinations • 319

1. In and Out of View

At first sight Phil Millege barely made a ripple. By all appearances he might have been another fisherman tourist—jovial, overweight, cigar in hand, affluent enough to be there. But he was alone, which made the reason for his presence more difficult to guess. And he brought no gear.

He didn't fish, didn't surf, didn't kayak or dive. He didn't hang out except to ask questions in a friendly yet provocative manner. He chatted with expats and locals alike and soon he was no stranger to Costa Rica's southern Pacific side.

In less than a week he made his first formal report to Dave Hiller, head of security for Progressive Palm Oil International—commonly called PPOI—the parent company of an agricultural conglomerate, headquartered in Raleigh, North Carolina.

> Regarding the recent deaths in Sierpe, which may have been accidental or collateral to an act of sabotage against property belonging to PPOI, the victims, two American female tourists not well known to locals, appear to have been acquaintances or accomplices of a

third party, an American male expat known to many in the region, and whose location is currently unknown.

Hiller's reply consisted of three words:

Find the fucker.

When Millege got to a restaurant with decent reception and could read the reply on his phone, he said aloud, "No shit."

A sandy-haired surfer named Long Jimmy leaned on the bar and one-handed the necks of four Imperial beers. He glanced at Millege and smirked. "You're with Aggressive," he said.

Millege paused in the relighting of his cigar. "Is that what you guys call the company?" he said.

"What everybody calls it," the surfer said, and took the beers and a bowl of ceviche to his table of friends.

Millege ordered another rum on the rocks and a whole fried snapper. A light salty breeze blew through the thatch-roofed shelter. Cars ran by infrequently on the highway like rogue sharks, or turned into the Pacific Supermarket next door and let loose snatches of music and conversation. The young bartender watched a soccer game on the screen up in the corner and kept an eye on the patrons and the passing perimeter activities.

A table of boisterous middle-aged expats drank and told stories, and Millege looked over at them and caught the eye of an attractive redhead, head cocked against her fist, hair spilling over her bare shoulder, mouth set wide in a bemused grin, eyes wet and sparkling. He thought she winked but wasn't sure. He figured she knew who he was. They all did by now.

On the way to his car he stopped beside the table of surfers. They continued to talk and joke as if he weren't there.

"Those two beautiful young girls burned to death,"

Millege said.

One of the surfers, his long brown hair in a ponytail, turned to appraise him. "What the fuck?" he said. "Are you a traveling counselor?"

"Burned to death in flames," Millege said. "Jesus Christ, can you imagine how stricken their parents feel? They want answers so they can understand their kids' last days. Wouldn't yours?"

"Dude," Long Jimmy said, "we're just having some beers."

Millege sat down on a bench at the adjacent table, put his hands on his knees and leaned forward. "I imagine you must have seen those girls around," he said.

"We see a lot of girls around," the ponytailed surfer said.

"Do you see a lot of dead girls around?"

"Some are pretty lifeless," the youngest surfer said. There was a snort at the table.

"There was a guy with them," Millege said, "just before they died."

"Like when they were on fire?" the kid said.

"He's gone missing," Millege said. "A surfer named Ellis. You probably know him."

"Not a surfer."

"Really? People say he surfs."

The kid shrugged. "Once in a while."

"You mean he isn't committed to the lifestyle," Millege said.

"Bird watcher," the kid said, pushing his long auburn hair behind an ear, grinning slightly.

"Nah," said the oldest, rubbing the unshaven hair on his neck, pushing his beard upward and then down, massaging his jaw. "That guy works with the Indians, man."

"In what capacity?" Millege asked.

"I thought he was running some nature tours," Long Jimmy said.

The kid smiled and nodded. "Yeah, he was into diving, right?"

"Muff diving," Long Jimmy said, and the other three laughed.

Millege smiled and looked out over the parking lot, observed a young couple leaving the store laden with bulky plastic bags and loading them into their back seat. He stroked his goatee a moment, then stood and got the bartender's attention and held up four fingers and made a swirling motion with his index finger toward the surfers. Then he held up one finger and pointed at himself.

"It's not about palm oil," Millege said, sitting again. "It's about two dead girls. Simple as that."

"Are you on a secret mission?" the ponytailed surfer said.

The bartender brought the beers over, handed Millege his rum and took the cash offered.

"I'd just like to tell those parents what happened to their kids," Millege said.

"No, besides that," the surfer said. "Are you on a mission to see all this wild land cultivated into plantations of nuts so we can have more lipstick and margarine and lubricants?"

"Boom snap," the kid said.

The four surfers clinked their bottles together and drank.

Millege sipped his drink and looked at the young men. The lean faces and long hair, the easy chuckles, the tanned arms and worn shorts, the tattoos and earrings, the sandals and open shirts, the woven bracelets and bead necklaces, the projected freedom, the casual air of simplicity and recreation.

"I don't get into the economics of it," Millege said.

"I'm looking for facts about an incident."

"Ain't nothin' simple," Long Jimmy said.

"I'll drink to that," Millege said. He stood and drained his rum and set the glass down. He took a card out of his wallet and placed it on the surfers' table. "Name's Phil Millege," he said. "Call me anytime if you think of anything helpful."

Jimmy raised his bottle. "Long Jimmy," he said.

Millege smiled. "Is that for Jimmy Long or the longboard preference?"

"Guess again, pilgrim," the bearded surfer said.

They all laughed and Millege walked to his car and drove off into the night.

The surfers left a little while later. At their table the bartender lifted the business card and put it in his pocket.

The next morning in Dominical, Millege ran into the attractive tipsy redhead from the night before. She worked in a shop that sold carvings and paintings and jewelry and beach dresses, and he walked in wearing shorts and sandals and a wide-brim camo hat and plenty of sunblock.

"You're really blending in," she said, smiling, "and I say that with just a touch of *sarcasmo*."

"Tough job," he said, "but someone has to do it."

A couple entered the store and she excused herself to attend to them. Millege stood studying an arrangement of masks hanging on the wall. A jeep rattled by on the stony dirt road and he could smell eggs cooking, and toast, and heard New Age music playing low in the store, seeping out of the walls, he imagined. It sounded like a pan flute with whale song interspersed.

"Nice, right?" she said, gesturing at the masks. "Boruca Indian. Locally made by tribal artists."

"This one's cool," he said, pointing at a half-man,

half-jaguar face in bright yellows and browns, with devil horns, a green snake entwined and descending like a vine down the human side.

"Taken by the jungle," she said, cocking her head. "Or so I imagine in my pensive moments alone in here."

"It happens," he said, glancing at her. "People end up staying longer than they intend."

She shifted in her sundress and looked at her sandaled feet, thought he might be asking about her circumstances. "I like the easygoing life," she said. "And the medical care is good too."

"All those freckles," he said smiling. "You have to take care. Get checked out."

"Oh, I do," she said. Her face and arms and chest were covered in a fine lace of spots, and she rubbed one shoulder as if to illustrate her care.

Millege tracked a pedestrian through the front window, a dreadlocked white male who passed the open front door. The woman turned to follow her visitor's gaze, and his eyes drifted down to her legs. More freckles—a uniform covering, he guessed.

"How's your investigation going?" she said. "People were wondering last night."

"Did you know the dead girls?" he asked. Off her pause, he added, "Chloe and Peyton."

She shook her head. "No, I didn't. I saw them once. They weren't here very long."

He nodded, his stomach growling. He watched a lizard on the windowsill extending its throat fan, thrusting its head upward, and felt a drop of sweat running down his backbone. "What'd you hear about them?" he said.

She turned at the coughing sound of a passing car, lifted her reading glasses on their chain and let them drop to her chest, studied his wide face, his hazel eyes, his thick lips pursed with a question. "I heard they were fairly adventurous," she said.

"Meaning what?" he said.

"Outdoorsy, athletic, all the usual stuff," she said. "Diving, hiking, surfing, ziplining."

"Fit and fearless?" he said, almost laughing.

She laughed. "Yes, I suppose so."

"And Ellis Hayden, the expat in question," he said. "Is he fearless too?"

"Why is he in question?" she said. She moved to the wall switch and turned the ceiling fan to a higher setting, came back, running her fingers through her hair.

"He was with them on their last day," Millege said. "Do you know him well?"

"I know him," she said. "He stopped at night in the rain once and changed my tire."

"A good Samaritan then," Millege said, looking her in the eye.

"He's a good guy," she said. "People like him."

"Super green, I hear," Millege said. "His viewpoint, I mean."

"Everyone's pretty green down here," she said. "That's why we moved here."

The music changed to reggae, and she moved in a subtle dance step to the front door. There were more people on the street, and she half wanted to step outside and get away from potential strife or incriminations or bad vibes in general.

He smelled incense and more eggs mingling with the sea air and motorbike exhaust. He watched her dancing and turning, her eyes closed, signaling an end to questioning.

"Helen," he said, and her eyes opened in surprise. "I enjoyed seeing you again."

"Likewise," she said. "I didn't know you knew my

name." Then she laughed and waved her hand. "Ah, my card," she said. "You're always gathering clues, aren't you?"

He shrugged and smiled. "Force of habit," he said. "And I'd like to take you to dinner."

"And dancing?" she said, winking.

"That too," he said, making an awkwardly comical move from foot to foot.

She laughed and said, "I think we've reached an understanding."

He walked to the door and squeezed her hand as he left. "I'll call you," he said.

She said from the doorway, "Be careful."

He looked back and nodded and gave her a thumbs-up.

As he moved down the street, she thought he looked surprising agile.

2. Chloe and Peyton

costa rica
peypad
To: Cheryl Paddington
hey mom, i've been trying to keep a regular journal and share things from it with you. not every place has internet but you understand. we are both still good having a blast actually. chloe is pushing her limits as usual but i'm used to it and keep her reined in when necessary. we love each other and this trip is only bringing us closer. we have checked off a few things on our activities wish list no injuries yet (lol) we're getting to know some locals both expats and ticos (what real residents are called). we have traveled down the pacific side and are finding less tourists and surfers than we did at first. you would love it here so fresh and clean and lots of interesting characters. pura vida everyone says, which means pure life. i think chloe has sort of fallen for this one guy we all went surfing and kayaking together. don't worry i haven't fallen for anybody. yet! but i like the guy too. he makes you feel lucky and special to be here

like you've entered a pure world that needs to be loved and protected. everyone here is trying to figure a way to live easily and peacefully and stretch their dollars as far as they can by working part-time back in the states or working the tourist angle down here such as having a shop or a bar or being a guide. chloe's friend does a bunch of things because he's so passionate about living here. he is also really handsome. maybe he has a brother who will show up soon. just kidding, mom. we are being careful and not too wild but it is just so natural down here. love to you and dad and paula and simon and snowball. xxoox, peyton

—

Chloe Summers lost her right eye at the age of nine. She was an adventurous child, and even after this family tragedy—which occurred in the backyard of their home in Vero Beach and caused her to withdraw for a time into sadness and bewilderment—she soon resurfaced and hardened her resolve and thickened her skin against the taunts of the cruelest older kids, wearing her patch defiantly and using her quick fists and smart mouth effectively. The story she told most often, when she acquiesced to someone's curiosity about this injury to such a lovely and athletic girl, was about her father, about his love for her and pride in her love of nature from the very start of her life. He doted on her and took her hiking, camping and canoeing and encouraged her constant engagement in regular backyard activities such as tree climbing and fort building and in organized games like softball, volleyball, field hockey, archery, and ultimate frisbee. She once jumped to her trampoline from their roof and broke her forearm, then perfected her flip while still in the cast. She developed a reputation for fearlessness, then lived up to it by pushing herself ever further, tackling any sport until she was good enough to announce her boredom or a new interest, and displaying that same attitude as an adolescent, driving boys mad with her early development, her boldness and her natural love of experimentation, all of which her parents tolerated and even endorsed, so glad were they to see her overcome the early disability that had scarred them all.

She had begged her dad to allow her to help care for an injured great blue heron he'd found wrapped in fishing line with a deep-sea lure's treble hook embedded at the base of its long neck and unable to fly or even walk well enough to get away from the blanket he threw over it. After the initial surgery, done with the aid of a naturalist friend, and during the attending of the wound and the careful feedings of minced fish, he kept the bird in a chicken wire enclosure while it healed and regained its strength. At first, he sternly resisted his young daughter's pleas to help, telling her that the bird was still wild and unpredictable. Then he began to let her watch as he fed the heron with a turkey baster, inserting it through the wire as she stood behind him. Before long she was kneeling beside him and soon after was staring intently, her fingers hanging in the wire, her face level with the bird's head. To her father's surprise, she lifted a wriggling lizard by the tail and offered it as a solid meal. The bird turned and instinctively jabbed at this living prize. Perhaps because of its injured serpentine neck and the girl's inadvertent flinching, the great bird missed the lizard as it plunged its sharp beak through the wire and lacerated the child's wide green eye.

Jonathan Summers wore his pride well ahead of his guilt and later told people his grown daughter was headstrong, a born leader, able to accomplish anything she wanted, and with a small laugh confided almost secretively that she intimidated most men, certainly those her own age and even those much older.

She adapted naturally to monocular vision, regained her depth perception well enough for any sport, her bravery and eye-hand coordination compensating for the ocular lack. Her first prosthesis was an acrylic shell that fit over an orbital implant and, like the braces on her teeth, both parts were refitted as she grew. By high school she had one made of cryolite glass, a real glass eye. "Look at me," she'd say, straight-faced, tapping the curved surface with the fingernail of her pinky, her other eye noting the reactions of potential suitors.

She laughed easily, did not yet seek a career, traveled while she found herself, got an allowance on the promise that she would graduate from college once she actually enrolled, still adored her dad and believed she was the epitome of the carefree lifestyle. She never whined and even as a child did not blame the bird.

—

Long Jimmy laughed. "Paddington," he said. "Isn't that a bear's name?"

Peyton laughed with him. "Pretty much," she said, "and trust me, it's a bear having that name. But I too am extremely cuddly. Ask anyone." With a broad wave she gestured around the open bar of Tortilla Flats and the beach road alongside, indicating everyone in sight. Tourists, locals, surfers, drifters, drunkards, dreamers.

"Well then," he said, and leaned toward the barmaid. "My dear Brigitte, could you say with certitude that this young woman is extremely cuddly?"

The blonde from France gave him a sly smile. "Ah, more than that," she said, placing two beers in front of them. She winked at Peyton as she moved away. "You watch that Long Jimmy," she said.

"You see," Peyton said, "everyone knows. Just like everyone knows you're long, Jimmy." She guzzled her beer and wiped her mischievous mouth. "Well, except me, I mean. I'm skeptical by nature, and I don't know for sure." Her dark hair fell about her shoulders, and she gathered a handful and shook it away, twisted it into a loose knot at her neck.

Jimmy examined the sweat beading on her neck and cheek, her profile, her lips, the damp, dangling brunette strands of her hair and, rubbing the crusted salt on his upper arm, felt himself stirring. He took a long cool drink, smiled broadly, and embraced the eternal quest for the twinned scents of sea and sex. "Take a look down here," he said, sliding the edge of his board shorts up his thigh a couple of inches. "Does that help your skeptical view?"

She glanced casually at his lap, stared for a long moment at the tight outline, the exposed swollen tip, then exhaled her whispered reply. "Pretty much."

—

My dear darling Chloe:
I write this with nowhere to place it or anyone to read it to. It is meant for you alone and I will keep it and add to it as if we are speaking through this journal. My heart is broken and my voice seeks your mind, your soul, your memory. You were always my girl, from day one and continuing until the end of time. I am struggling to make sense of and accept what has happened. The motels keep me busy as always but my mind wanders and my heart is not in the business right now and might never be again. But of course I must keep your mother and brother in mind and keep what's left of our family together and cared for. I know you feel my thoughts and

watch us still and will always be part of us. Your mother is a wreck but stays busy somehow and takes her long beach walks like before. Your brother is withdrawn and hides his feelings for the most part. He shrugs a lot and pretends he is tough enough to handle anything, turning away when he sees my tears or your mother's. The cat is still a self-centered asshole. She probably misses you but would never show it.

We are waiting for further word from the Embassy but the local police seem to be dragging their feet with regard to new information. For some reason the case is being treated as an accident with no serious ramifications. I had a call from the palm oil people who said they are investigating and wanted to send a man over to chat. That didn't sit right with me so we spoke on the phone instead. I can't tell you how angry I became trying to answer questions about my little girl, about your behavior and associations down there. I feel like they're looking for scapegoats, a way to spin this tragedy and paint themselves as victims, for their public relations and of course to help their insurance claim. I had to hang up and have been dealing with this anger ever since. I can't let this rest, my darling daughter, and I know in my heart you can hear me. I feel I will need to take an active role in this follow-up to ever have any hope of finding peace and closure. Not that I believe I will ever find closure, but maybe, hopefully, something similar. You deserve the truth to be known and I intend to get it for you. And for me, and for all of us here missing you.

Love, Dad.

3. Forging Loose Alliances

Gustavo Segura had been a bartender at Ballena Bahia Restaurant for three years and lately was also a part-time kayaking guide at Selva Tours. He often wrangled gringos at the bar into signing up because all they had to do was show up again in the morning to be driven in his minivan down to the start of the tour through the mangroves at Rio Coronado. If they expected to be hungover, he reminded them that they could sleep on the way down and that the exertion would soon sweat them clean. "*Pura vida, amigos!*" he said with both fists raised. But of course, sometimes they did not show up at all.

Stavo, as he liked to be called, considered himself a smooth salesman with an appraising eye, and he enjoyed pointing out to excitable visitors the white-faced capuchins, the long-nosed bats, the crab-eating raccoons, the boat-billed herons and scarlet macaws, the black howlers, the caimans and crocodiles, and the tree-coiled boa constrictors they frequently encountered.

Sitting in his van, he called Phil Millege two days after the investigator left his card. He recounted their prior meeting, and Millege, who was driving, said he remembered.

"I got a girl in Sierpe," Stavo said. "She has seen something for you to know."

"Okay," Millege said. "So she saw my reward notices, my posters."

"Maybe," Stavo said. "But I have also explain to her about this guy. You know, she works with me only."

"I understand you," Millege said. "You need to get your share." He pulled over and stepped out of his car at a roadside ceviche stand beside the beach. "How soon can you meet me there?"

"Tomorrow," Stavo said. "In the morning. I need to work at night."

"I'll be at La Perla at nine," Millege said. "That good for you?" He stood under the trees observing a closely aligned couple lying on the hood of a Hyundai, a brown dog trotting down the flat gray beach, the surf rolling in.

"Yes, amigo, we can talk more," Stavo said, a few raindrops splattering across his windshield and slow-hammering the roof. He closed his phone and cut the engine and grabbed his clean white shirt from the back seat.

—

The girl with the port-wine stain once attended The Dance of the Little Devils when she was a timid teenager. She lived in Sierpe with her family on a modest plot with some corn and a few chickens. Her father brought her to the Boruca ceremony with her brothers to see the marvelous masks worn by the parade of outlandish dancing demons bringing down the Spanish invaders of history, symbolized by one lurching participant wearing a brown balsawood bull mask and a bulky burlap costume, his defeat ordained by the indigenous devils who were simply real people respecting nature, telling creation stories, and living in peace in their hamlets and fields and forests.

The girl was enchanted by the little devils, the vibrant colors and animal faces, some of which were lifted to reveal the smiles and sweat of handsome human boys. With her own blood-marked face she often felt like she was wearing a scary little animal mask she could never remove. She became used to the stares and developed the ability to see truth and honor in people's eyes. She believed the Boruca boys, or at least one in particular, looked through the facial stain and saw her heart, her simple desire for a connection beyond family, her inner need for basic physical contact.

Late in the day her father and eldest brother, both purblind on the fermented corn drink *chicha*, inadvertently allowed her to roam at will, and with the older boy of her choice, a strong young native with a quiet disdain for the very parade he showed such prowess in, she let herself be escorted down a forest path to hear stories and be moved by the individual attention and by her own valence in this sudden exchange of attraction.

He told her the tale of the woman who fell in love with a snake at the river where she did her washing, how their repeated contact quelled the fear between them, how he caressed her face with his tongue and eventually coiled around her from legs to head and made love to her. How she became pregnant and the village chief became fearful of the brood of babies coming, and how the villagers built a fire and burned her to kill the birthing snakes, all except the one who escaped to Sierpe and became its namesake. The girl saw herself at this river, natant with desire and feeling her own face accepted and caressed, and when this boy Victor invited her to return to see the sacred falls and journey farther down the path into his world, she wanted nothing more than to go with him as far as she could. Sitting on a log, she accepted his kiss right then, kissed him back and felt her face burning with everything in the world except shame.

This is how, after a conch shell was blown and dancers descended from the hilly woods to taunt a bull who chased them through the village as the invader always did, and the flutes and drums and veracious devils countered the deadly conquistador and resisted its reach for a time, the relentless toro, a rampaging destroyer of nature, finally killed them all. And this is how the truculent forest devils combated evil spirits and resurrected themselves and found the craven bull as the spectators consumed tamales and chicha and cheered them on. And how a boy broke ranks and a girl fell hard while the toro was taken to the river and burned in effigy, the survival of a people reenacted as love hid nearby, erupting anew.

Liz was fourteen, Victor seventeen. A year passed before she was able to arrange another trip to Boruca. When the festival day finally came, with her heart beating in ceremony again, she learned he had left the village.

4. Images of Ellis

She looked after two houses owned by absent foreigners and had the use of a skiff belonging to one of the men. Her blemish kept her mostly apart, yet she was considered trustworthy. Children flinched, stared, made ugly faces, looked away. Adults often fostered an inner pity barely concealed. Liz Zuniga was twenty-eight, short and plump, resigned to her general exile among the more perfect. The dark bolt of birthmark descended from her forehead over her left eye and widened down her left cheek, a livid purple flame, shallot-shaped, the devil's one-sided raking curse, *la marca del diablo*. It was a permanent mask—stitched, burned, branded—of shame, evil, provocation, punishment, whatever the shallow-minded wanted to see. Everyone had a cross to bear, some more obvious than others. Perhaps as a consequence, or as a gift of balance, her penetrating, intuitive gaze peered deeper than most.

The Sierpe River wound through a vast green wetland like its reptilian namesake, undulating in width and depth, its surface flow shimmering with sunlit scales by day, its dark winding channels and tunnels foreboding at night, too many tentacles of water and mangrove to grasp, a labyrinthine landscape tangled and disguised at every bend.

In her boat, Liz searched for a hideout, a cabin on the water. Basic. Accessible. Yet unwelcoming. She knew this river world, grew up in it, had long explored its permutations and noticed its various dwellings. She meandered into offshoots of the great serpent, steered away from the main channel where almost all traffic ran the daily transport route between Sierpe and Drake Bay. Every dilapidated, out-of-the-way fishing hut belonged to somebody, but their consent was hardly required.

Ellis is here, she thought as she motored along. He's a squatter in this watery maze. Asleep, awake, trying to keep his panic at bay. A ghostly figure. Damp, morbid, languid as an eel, a wary runner inhabiting a tannic shack, with kingfishers rattling daily as in a recurring dream. She saw variations of his despair in her mind's eye. Saw silken feathers drop and drift. Drop and drift. Saw his fantastical floating fears too, nightmarish, understandably. She saw flashes of his imagined flight, his attempts at escape, his clambering away from big lizards, modern-day dinosaurs turning into birds, condor-size but more agile and cunning, gaining ground from tree to tree, leaping, shrieking, then silent, invisible yet present, always there. He awakened in a terror sweat, she knew, overcoming death again, standing and dripping at the edge of a window, a lank target in a riverbank cabin. She could see all this clearly with her eyes closed. She could construct a story that would become true enough.

Back in town she pried up and pocketed a handprinted poster tacked to a pole opposite the Baptist Bible Church. Then another across from the police station near the rental boats and tour agencies. In part, it read:

Missing Person, White American Male
36 yrs old, 6'0", 180 lbs.
Reward Offered - $$ - For Information!!
Please Help

The amount offered was unspecified, the words neatly printed in Spanish and English and taped to the page a photographic image of a lean, shaggy-brown-haired, suntanned man standing in front of a pale pocked wall like a prisoner before a firing squad. The phone number was not local, and no contact name was given.

—

His phone rang as Jon Summers stepped out of his Buick under the shaded drive-through of the Sunny View Motel. He stopped, noticed a housekeeping cart on the second floor, a sheet hanging over the railing, no personnel in sight.

"Hello?" he said.

"Jonathan? It's Ross Paddington. You got a minute?"

Summers looked into the office window and noted his desk clerk looking at him, then turned away. "Yeah, go ahead," he said, and walked along the breezeway outside the nearest rooms as Paddington spoke.

"Look, man, I know we're in agreement on this goddamn tragedy that something has to be done. I'm sick and tired of getting nothing new on this. My wife is going apeshit and I've had some thoughts on a course of action."

They had met before, sporadically over the years, the most recent time nearly a year ago at the presentation of an award Peyton was receiving, which

Chloe insisted they all attend. It was at the country club and the four parents had talked for a while in the bar before the program began. Paddington was retired NASA—strategic management—older than his wife and the other couple, drank bourbon, played golf, gave paid lectures to various civic institutions and organizations and spoke forcefully on foreign affairs, immigration, the declining state of the union, the financial markets, his family's long history of patriotic duty and the never-ending need for personal and national systematic house-cleaning and ass-kicking.

Summers tried to remember. Was it a scholarship she'd gotten? An environmental award? His mind was foggy lately. He looked at his reflection in the window of the empty room he was passing. A growing gut, long brown hair descending around a slack pallid face fallen into a morose glare, the usual loose khakis, old faded polo shirt, the whole image depicting the rut of sorrow he trod like a mule in a grinding circle.

Peyton's proud father, the likeable tyrant, was speaking again.

"For Christ's sake, man, are you there?"

"I'm here. Simmer down. We're in the same boat, man."

"Damn right we are. I'm locating a man to look into this. Privately. This jerk's all wrong, this shitheel your daughter decided to bring into their lives."

"Now wait a second," Summers said.

"I'm not blaming her," Paddington said. "The girls are young and adventurous and trusting."

"Were," Summers said. "They're not anything now except dead."

There was a slight pause. Paddington cleared his throat and took a drink, the clinking ice audible on the line. "I'm letting you know," he said, "that I'll be sending a man down there at my own expense. I'll keep you apprised of the results. This expat deadbeat is slinking around down there somewhere, shitting his pants. Or, more likely, his worn-out fucking bathing suit. I already know he was a protester, a dropout, a tree-hugging, anti-progress trouble maker. We'll find this bum and get some answers, some satisfaction."

"I doubt we'll be satisfied," Summers said. "I was thinking of going down myself, you know, to pick up the"—he almost said *teeth* but held back—"the ah, the remains, such as they are. Goddamn it, man. Fuck. Look, I appreciate the call, okay. And I'll be more than glad to chip in. Just keep me posted."

"Alright then," Paddington said. "Hang in there. And tell your wife—tell Amy—justice will prevail."

"She'll be delighted to hear that," Summers said, and hung up.

5. Dead Ends

Millege ended up in Boruca by a circuitous route, by spiraling, which was in keeping with his roundabout ways. He was prone to gathering as much local knowledge as possible, what seemed pertinent to the case as well as peripheral or esoteric information that was interesting to him and made him feel he could locate his target within a broader setting, using wider parameters, expanding the range of his own reliable instincts. Knowledge draws the net—this was his operating principle.

    He thought about hideouts—mountains, caves, jungles, obscure villages, communes—and what seemed most applicable to the subject, most likely to put him and Ellis Hayden on a collision course. Judging from the profile, Millege deemed it unlikely that the man had ducked, or was planning to duck, into Panama, figured it more likely that the man would ride out the heat of the initial focus and keep an eye on the local proceedings, or lack thereof.

    Sitting in his car in San Isidro, Millege studied his maps, tracing escape route ideas into the vastness and remoteness of the Chirripó and La Amistad

National Parks. He shook his head, muttering to himself in a two-sided conversation, arguing in favor of gut instinct. This guy would not want to be so far out of touch even if he was ultimately safer. Plus, daily survival would require more effort, and hardship would be a closer companion. No, he couldn't see it. Millege was leaning toward Sierpe—a wilderness world, yes, but near the subject's familiar territory—or somewhere even closer, a friend's hilltop home, for example, where supplies were simply attained and sources of communication readily available.

He strolled over to the *feria*, the fruit and vegetable market, a huge metal shed under which on each Thursday and Friday were assembled various fresh produce stands, assorted tables of jewelry, honey, used books, clothing, natural snacks, hot-food vendors along one side, and in whose adjacent parking lot could be found the trucks and vans of mechanics, artisans, and whoever else might be able to sell or trade goods or services.

Millege wasn't much interested in the market itself but gravitated to a rear corner where a gringo contingent congregated to sell hummus, falafels, cheese, chocolate, whole-grain muffins, New Age books, and a probiotic drink made with fermented vinegar and ginger, a sample taste of which he politely declined. He overheard two old expat hippies—granola-heads he had heard them called—talking about a sacred healing retreat in the nearby hills that one of them referred to as a tourist trap. Millege stepped closer, said hello and asked the name of the place.

"We're not recommending it," one man said.

"Just curious," Millege said.

"Circle Jerk," the other said. "Do yourself a favor and commune with nature on your own. You don't need a naval-gazing group to find your path."

"You've increased my curiosity," Millege said.

On the way out he stopped to peruse the jewelry offered by a young Tico couple radiant in their open friendliness and, buying several string-beaded gifts he thought might come in handy, asked them about the local spiritual retreat.

"Circle of Light," the young man said. He was tall and thin, with a sparse beard and multiple strands of leather and beads around his neck and wrists.

Millege handed over the money for his purchase. "Bright name," he said. "I heard it's a healing place, a forest sanctuary. What goes on there?"

"You know"—the young man shrugged at the obviousness of the ritual—"you take *ayahuasca* and a man sings to you all through the night." He smiled. "You become"—he made a gesture of expulsion, opening his mouth with his fingers moving away from it in a repeated flow—"sick, at the beginning."

"You mean purged?" Millege said.

The young man nodded. "Yes, this is the word. You become more with the nature and throw away your bad parts." He smiled and put a hand to his heart. "I don't take," he said, "but this is what I hear."

His wife nodded her agreement. "So expensive," she said, "but the visitors like to open their mind here." She smiled a lovely, benevolent, possibly mocking smile, one hand making circles away from her head. "They leave the earth and find the answer." Her brown eyes were playful. "For a short time," she said, "then everything is the same again."

"We call that tripping," Millege said, smiling at them both.

"Yes, we know," the man said, holding out a paper wrapping.

"Can you draw a little map for me?" Millege asked.

"I'm looking for a friend who might be there."

Twenty-five minutes later, as he neared Tinamaste, he spotted a small wooden sign with a faded yellow circle, and he drove off the highway ridge down a dirt road into rolling forest interspersed with patches of agriculture. He came to another circle sign and turned down a gravel track and entered a clearing surrounded by trees, a dirt track continuing ahead. He parked and walked out on a thatched-roof terrace overlooking a river some twenty yards below, the sound of rushing water reaching him as he stood at the railing.

He turned to find a young woman in a long draping white shirt and loose white pants standing at the entrance regarding him. Neither spoke, and the coursing river seemed to obliterate the need for language or purpose. He saw several large russet birds walking in the greenery across the clearing and waited for some prompt from the immobile young greeter who stared at him wordlessly while the onus of explanation settled and cast him in a cloak of mysterious authority.

"Circle of Light," he said, moving closer to her.

"What do you seek?" she asked.

"A lost dog, a lonely spider monkey," he said.

"Which?" she asked.

"He is a depressed and damaged man," Millege said.

"Why do you seek this man?"

"I have a question," Millege said, glancing over at the group of curassows strutting into the clearing. The girl looked over too. He saw her flaxen ponytail dangling down to the small of her back.

"The answer is love," she said.

"And love is truth," he said. He pulled a photo out of his wallet and moved closer, holding it up.

She stared at the photo, leaning slightly forward, hands held together at her middle. "No one I know," she said, meeting his eyes.

"It's a poor picture," Millege said. "But he would be at home here."

"Why would he?" she asked, her gaze direct, serene, confident.

"A chance to start over," Millege said, "to open up, to seek redemption."

"I think your journey's affirmation lies elsewhere," she said.

He admired the clarity of her skin, her facial structure, her prayerful demeanor, and nearly said something stark. "What's your name?" he asked.

"Dimaris," she said.

He guessed she was from the Midwest. "I enjoy your vibrations," he said without a smile. "May your life be fruitful."

"May you find peace," she said.

He walked to his car and looked back and bowed slightly.

She stood watching as the car climbed slowly out of the clearing.

Smoking a cigar with the windows open, Millege drove back to San Isidro and then south on Highway 2, passing small farms that gripped the foothills of the Talamanca range, the ridges and valleys, the changing patterns of uniform crops and irregular swaths of uncut trees, the manmade puzzles of utilized and unused land, cane fields and tractor carts.

He crossed the Rio General bridge, gazed at young women walking along the edge of the pavement in the shade of umbrellas, and the road was soon dissecting a rolling spread of enormous pineapple fields, spiked miles of monotony and monopoly, then a Del Monte packing plant, the roadside wall painted with slogans:

HERE WE WORK IN WORKER EMPLOYER HARMONY. LABOR PEACE = SOLIDARITY.

He turned north toward Buenos Aires, looking idly at pedestrians on foot and bike, at a flatbed pineapple truck full of green pebbled heads, a road crew squeezing cars into one lane, a pink house with laundry hanging, a white dog running roadside, a construction supply warehouse, and the thickness of a low ceiling, a shroud of clouds pressing downward on the distant hills, shadows sequestered like prisoners about to be released across a vulnerable land.

He was suddenly struck by doubt. A fool's errand, he thought, poking here and there, hoping to strike gold, to locate a single leaf in an entire countryside of identical plants. He drove around the few streets of the farm town noting the central park, the cathedral, the school, the agro stores, the cowboys, the bus station activity, and the indigenous outsiders in their colorful clothes and cartoon backpacks. He parked and got out, dropped his cigar stub and ground it into brown straw with his shoe. He closed his eyes and breathed deeply, feeling his corporeal self standing tentatively, aware of his excess weight and the overall clumsiness of his mission. He shuffled his feet and threw a right jab.

Tacking up a couple of notices, he attracted a great amount of silent attention. He perused the markets and small restaurants beside the bus station, looking at faces and collecting blank stares as he showed the random gringo's photo.

A mirthful old man, only partially shaved, sprouts of stubble both white and gray standing out in a patchwork of tufts as if a razor had been used without plan or mirror, entertained his query for a few moments as one plays with a child, first wrinkling his nose repeatedly at Millege like he was a large baby, then nodding at the pale picture and stroking his chin as if nearly certain of his recognition, but without spoken confirmation, perhaps due to the language issue.

Millege was annoyed and found himself thinking of Dimaris, the Circle of Light girl who had presented herself blandly dressed in excess material, devoid of form and passionless. In his mind, her body took better shape in a bikini, which would have been a more natural and earthy presentation, more like a river goddess, he thought, and he felt certain and strangely relieved that her slender figure actually possessed the feminine curves he imagined it did.

Strolling among the white-painted trunks of palms in the park as if he might casually stumble upon his foreign quarry lounging on a bench reading a paperback, he was suddenly aware of the large stone balls placed around the park, waist-high and rough textured but quite round, like perfectly formed asteroids, and he realized he had seen them elsewhere, depicted on signs like some sort of symbol of the region. The strange spheres of yesteryear.

After a late lunch of chicken and rice and beans under the airy pavilion of a clean spacious restaurant recessed from the dusty street, Millege investigated the only hotel in town, its unlocked rooms simple but pleasant, with a great open courtyard facing away from town, the first building two-story and the adjacent one single-story, with a barber's chair positioned in an alcove beneath the high metal roof that joined the two structures. Millege stooped to examine the dark hair clippings left at the base of the chair, idiotically he realized, while a curious dog, a midsize lab mix, watched him. No one else was around except the hospitable manager who sensed a potential customer for a few moments. But Millege just handed him a flyer and got back in his car and pressed on, fortified, back on track, covering ground on pure instinct.

At the signpost for Boruca he turned right and began climbing. A steep gravel road, no going back, no backing down, a metaphor, sure, but as real as anything. He was forty-eight, a former bail enforcement agent, twice divorced, now a private investigator sagging a bit in enthusiasm as he was in physical areas but up for the challenge, at least, the sheer improbability of the task itself. A chunky loner. With travel benefits. A trail of nonsense always in the rearview, up around the bend, in the air, falling like pollen. Cases sometimes seemed obtuse, but deciphering the causal mechanisms could yield genuine satisfaction. Otherwise known as the facts.

He stopped on the dirt road on the flat top of the ridge and got out to take in the views, a tangible reward only if you took advantage of it. Cows and small corrals, isolated houses, a great slate river bending through lowlands far below a sweeping high point panorama, receding greens and smoky blue ridges and ranges in colors muted with distance, a posse of cloud puffs riding shotgun. The Térraba, feeding and creating in partnership with its more southern lifeblood source, the Sierpe, the vast mangrove system known as the Térraba Sierpe National Wetlands.

Somewhere in there is the running man, Millege thought. Somewhere way down there, while he was up here on a field trip, a cultural outing, a soft recon, a drive in the country.

A blue sign. *Welcome to Boruca.* A store, some small concrete and wooden houses, open doors, two women on kitchen chairs weaving on back-strap looms in porch shadow, a man carving with chisel and club, black-haired children running up the rocky incline. A pair of light-skinned females in summer dresses in front of twin homestay thatch-roof houses watching the arriving rental car. Millege parked opposite, cranked the manual brake, stepped out, stretched his arms overhead, adjusted his floppy hat. A puppy sat scratching an ear in a doorway and a man stepped over it on his way outside.

"Gonzalez," he said, and shook the visitor's hand. Millege said his name and followed the man back inside. The elder offered a hammock with his hand and sat in the other one. The room was full of wood artifacts, shavings and scraps piled upon the earthen floor, uncarved blond balsa chunks, some drawn upon in red lines, mask designs awaiting transformation into scornful faces with long teeth and savage horns, the melding of devils and jungle cats, vines and trees and frogs and harpy eagles and snakes. The walls were plain planks, the space utilitarian and bright enough for work with the windows and door open. There was a tree-stump stool and a plastic chair and a low table color-crammed with jars and bottles of paint, a cup of brushes and several carving tools. Along the back wall a longer table held rows of frightful finished faces, lying flat, staring up into the ashen space above the loose rafter poles.

Gonzalez, his hair still thick and black, in open shirt and slacks and sandals, massaged a piece of wood, eyes crinkled at his guest, and said a few words in Spanish. Millege nodded and waited. A teenaged girl, a long-haired beauty in shorts and a sleeveless blouse, entered with a plate of stacked tortillas and a small bowl of pigeon peas and rice and offered it to Millege. He took one tortilla and thanked her and set it on his knee as Gonzalez continued to speak.

"Sorry," Millege said, "I don't understand. Can you speak English?" he said to the girl.

She smiled and stepped outside and whistled and he saw the shadow of her hand waving across the doorframe.

In a few minutes one of the other visitors stuck her head inside and Millege rose holding the tortilla like a validation of trust.

"I can translate," she said, crossing the threshold and greeting Gonzalez. A wispy blonde, green-eyed, early twenties, cheeks and shoulders sun-kissed.

"Thanks," Millege said. "My name's Phil. I'm just passing through. Mr Gonzalez said something to me."

"I'm Sydney," she said. "From Maryland." She asked Gonzalez to repeat himself and then said to Millege, "He just wondered about your purpose here. If you were looking for handicrafts. If you want to buy a mask."

Gonzalez watched Millege as he explained himself. "I'm exploring the area, my first time here," he said, "and also trying to locate a missing person."

She paused, then spoke to Gonzalez as he gouged his wood piece with the blade of a thin chisel.

Millege withdrew the subject's photo from his vest pocket and held it before the elder, who leaned forward and squinted, then handed it to Sydney, who studied it in the light of the doorway.

"Who is it?" she asked.

"American guy who was living in Uvita," he said, glancing at Gonzalez.

"And you think he's around here. Why is he missing?"

"That's the question," Millege said. "His name is Ellis Hayden."

Gonzalez spoke and she said, "He says many

visitors pass through."

"Yeah, it's a long shot," Millege said. "But I'm enjoying the region, meeting different people, learning about the country, the indigenous culture."

She translated and Gonzalez smiled and straightened. He carried his wood, the pale half-formed face, teeth unsharpened, eyes unopened, and stood in the doorway looking out. The brown puppy wandered between his feet and wobbled inside, sniffing the air. Gonzalez bent down and scooped it up, ears flopping and paws waving, and held it up in one hand and placed the back of the unmade wooden face against the back of its head so that they faced in opposite directions. He presented this double-headed creature to the visitors and said, "*Dos caras*," and set the puppy down and walked out.

The girl turned to Millege and said, "Two faces. I guess he means you."

"Okay. I've been called worse," he said. "Are you sure it's not you too?"

She smiled. "Well, I'm working on myself."

"That's good. I appreciate your help," he said. "Can we get a beer around here?" He rolled his tortilla into a tube and held it like a cigar.

They walked down the track together. She seemed to know everyone in the village. Millege kept slipping on the loose rock and catching himself like some vaudeville character practicing his routine, causing children to laugh.

"It must be tiring," Sydney said.

"What's that?" he said.

"Always looking for someone and showing their picture."

"It's a game," he said. "With consequences."

"Winners and losers," she said, waving to an old woman on her porch.

"Two girls died in a fire," he said. "About your age."

"Full disclosure," she said. "I did hear something about that."

"What'd you hear?" he said. They were coming to a crossroads with a Christian church on its own rise of land over the main road.

"Oh—" she stopped and looked down the descending road, taking in the thatch shelters, the corrugated roofs and red satellite dishes, the four matching schoolkids in white shirts, dark pants and backpacks, the bananas and palms, the thick green hillsides, the fingers of wood smoke reaching up from kitchens like signals of regularity. She made a sour face. "Oh, I guess that they were unlucky eco-warrior wannabes."

They walked down the slope to the Bar Boruca and Millege went inside and bought two Imperials and they sat on a bench against the outer wall.

"*Salud*," she said.

"Cheers," Millege said. "What brings you here?"

"I'm interested in the natural dyes the women use in their weaving."

"So it's that and the mask-making," he said.

"Well, they farm quite a bit, sustain themselves and their culture. That's what it's all about. It's not easy, you know, with everything against them."

"Meaning?"

"Well, I mean the big farms, the pineapples and coffee. Before that, the bananas, going back to the thirties. United Fruit Company. Now it's Dole, Del Monte, agrochemicals, contaminated water, soil depletion, the loss of family farms, the mistreatment of migrant workers. I could go on and on," she said.

"Go on," he said.

"Okay, how about the government dam down there that will flood out a shitload of their farmland and displace hundreds of their people."

"You sound like a warrior in training," he said.

She grinned. "Yeah, well, people are sympathetic, let's say."

"So no one really thinks it was an accident," he said. "Those girls."

"Palm oil is probably the worst," she said, staring at him.

"That's who hired me," Millege said. "Full disclosure."

"Really?" She made an exaggerated frown. "I thought it was probably his family or something."

"The same questions apply," he said, shrugging mildly.

She finished her beer and set the bottle on the bench. "I need to help with the cooking," she said. "Good luck in your quest." She stood and he rose beside her. They shook hands. He watched her walk away, the air cooler now, a few raindrops falling, the sounds of nature pressing in, he in his usual cocoon. He tossed the moist tortilla into the drainage ditch near a rummaging dog, wiped his hands on his knees and put a cigar in his mouth.

6. The Path of the Tapir

Paseo de la Danta. Peyton copied the translation into her journal. Baird's tapir. *Tapirus bairdii.* Largest indigenous land mammal in Central America. Biological corridor running roughly from Manual Antonio Park and the Savegre River south to the Térraba River and into Sierpe and the Osa Peninsula.

She and Chloe sat on the porch of their bungalow taking tea and fresh papaya while afternoon sun poured through the property's canopy of leaves and the small river they looked out upon sparkled in the open as a rippling of supple silver light. If it had been three weeks later, a rain shower might have been pounding the surrounding heliconia leaves and encasing the gutter chain in an undulating tube of solid liquid, the tumultuous sound and the gray opacity of the air obliterating the rock-strewn river coursing through the background.

It was the tail end of the dry season and rain was still in the future. Their timing, their actual presence there, was part happenstance, one occurrence in an alignment of disparate factors. If the Térraba Dam proposal had not been floating around like distemper among the Boruca and everyone else who cared about the natural state of the region. If PPOI had not recently grabbed another chunk of Sierpe to add to its empire of nuts, charting a path to monetarily and physically bulldoze a family out of its homestead. If the company's track record did not already include the cracking apart of an ancient stone sphere, one of the mysterious remnants of an indigenous ancestry which could have been rolled out of harm's way or transported to a museum and saved for posterity had care played a part. And if Peyton had not read about and fallen for Baird's tapir, the concept of a biological indicator species and a land corridor created and conserved for this major mammal in the neotropical landscape, a new world amalgamation of elephant and horse, a long-nosed, thick-skinned swimmer, a forest trotter, a grazing, slow-breeding herbivore, impervious to all comers except the adult jaguar, puma, and crocodile. And the adult human, of course.

But occurrences line up like dominoes, and the timelines of independent lives intersect without plan or reason and create an unwilled interdependence of human movements which could be likened to the trajectories of slow-moving electrons on uncharted and unstoppable atomic paths.

After dawn that morning, they had seen with binoculars a pair of otters waddling along the shore, then a show of basilisk lizards ranging languidly over riverine boulders, a mangrove black hawk, a toucan, several hummingbirds and flycatchers. Then they had surfed and eaten ceviche and contemplated a developed pattern of recreation and irresponsibility and its unsettling residue. This summer, they decided, they'd skip Bonnaroo and Burning Man, ease up on the festival scene, the ingesting of Molly and vodka, the cascade of raves.

The Path of the Tapir

"This is now my official mascot," Peyton said. She still wore her bathing suit bottom and a long-sleeved sun shirt and the warm moist air bathed and lubricated her scalp and skin and caused her laptop to slide on her thighs.

Chloe was leaning back, her chair on two legs, her head against the wall, feet up on the wooden bench railing, eyes closed to the music of peace.

"Which one, the mountain cow?" she said.

"They call it that in Belize," Peyton said. "Here, it's *danta*. Danta, danta, danta. Don't you love the sound of that word?"

"Very cool. Like Fanta. So you want to go hiking. See one."

"Yeah, pretty much. If we could get so lucky."

"I'm all about a serious walkabout," Chloe said. "We just need to find a guide who can get us in there and show us a good time."

Peyton reached out and slapped her friend's leg. "You're not referring to some low-key harmonious dude we happened to meet recently."

Chloe extended a foot and brought it up in a firm smack against the underside of Peyton's calf, shaking her leg, jostling her laptop. "Oh, baby girl," she said, "if you're out to track a shadowy jungle mammal, then I am too." She grinned and sat up, wagging her finger. "Oh wait, let's not forget your bar buddy, Mister 'Hey, by the way, did I show you my kosher dog' Longhorn."

"Apples and oranges," Peyton said. "My danta is not a stuffed animal or any kind of plaything. I'm making a serious statement here. A game changer."

They looked at each other, Peyton hardly smiling, the sunlight painting and unpainting the waving wide-leaf surfaces, the river breeze stirring through the porch and over their bodies with the water's murmuring flow as a serenade to sisterhood, an ongoing pact of strength and loyalty, the jokes a part of it too.

"Hey, Pey," Chloe said, her left eye direct, green, real. "I always got you."

"I know you do, Chlo. We'll talk to the dude. Maybe he is a guide."

7. Boruca (Victor's Version)

Millege returned to the hamlet of Boruca as the clouds rolled down the mountains and gathered dark in their seasonal conspiracy.

At the cooperative he met a courtly, kind woman named Melinda Morales who took him over to the museum and explained the meaning of the masks and the historical battles with the Spanish and the annual reenactment of the struggle called The Dance of the Little Devils, wherein the masked men of the village fought and defeated a single representative Spanish bull and thus remained an intact self-governing tribe of free indigenous people. As he listened, he realized he needed to find serious help as focused as he was upon a single goal, the missing bull who could be cornered, defeated, unmasked. He needed his own devoted devil, and he asked Melinda Morales if she knew of any man among her people who needed work but had no interest in mask-making or other regular tribal pursuits, who was more of a—here he struggled for the right word, fearing a misstep, an insult, as if he might be perceived as asking for a lazy man, an idle drunken Indian, a rogue element or a misfit with disdain for the usual routines of culture and community spirit needed to keep a self-sustaining minority together in difficult times—"a tracker," he finally said.

She regarded him in his camo hat, his white face and hazel eyes and restless hands, his unlit cigar a pointer in the air underscoring certain words, his dangling sunglasses, wrinkled shirt, khaki slacks and sandaled feet, his nearly desperate earnestness.

Children had gathered at the doorway and she shooed them away with a wave of her hand, smoothed the collar of her white blouse and gazed around the room as if seeking the root of his inquiry, the hidden source of a path she might wish to avoid. "To track what?" she asked.

"I meant to say guide," he said, smiling and rolling his eyes at his own foolishness, his cigar underlining the last word.

She nodded, her dark eyes quizzical, the deep lines at their corners radiating outward like etchings of symmetrical sunbursts. Her black hair, with undercurrents of gray streaks, gathered into a bulky bun at the back of her head. "There are many here who can take you to the sacred waterfalls," she said.

"I need to locate someone off the reserve," he said. "I want a strong, smart guide who would embrace a non-indigenous challenge." He paused. She pursed her lips as he was doing. "This is a specific job with excellent pay," he added. "If you know someone who might be interested." He handed her his card. "Think it over. Thank you for your kindness and consideration, Melinda Morales. Now I'd like to buy a jaguar-devil-snake mask and a nice colorful wall hanging any woman would love."

—

Fifteen months earlier, Victor Leiba met Ellis

Hayden at a meeting organized by Citizens Against the Boruca Dam, or CATBD, which Ellis immediately started calling TBD, correlating it to the American phrase To Be Determined, or Decided, uttered with a half smirk, which he felt indicated that something could be done to halt the project. There were already studies being conducted and meetings being held to include indigenous groups and wildlife foundations and societies and The Convention on Wetlands, which had designated The Térraba Sierpe National Wetlands a Ramsar site.

There were eco-tourists and nationals attending, small-time farmers, artists, foreign landowners and speculators, and one representative of the newly formed Danta Defense League, whose manifesto was short on details regarding membership, address, or donors but which characterized itself as a potent keeper of the Mesoamerican Biological Corridor. The rep was Hayden, though he remained out of the spotlight and preferred to observe as a young Boruca boy handed out his photocopied DDL pages. The logo was a drawing of a tapir in profile, its head lifted, long snout extended, trumpeting either suffering or victory, it was hard to say which.

Leiba was on his seventh beer, regularly stepping away to visit the bag hanging from his motorbike and reappearing silently with another can in hand. He seemed more of a perimeter guard, a bouncer, a scalper, than a participant. He was casually interested in the concept of the destruction of his culture and culture in general, the larger scheme of things inversely and adversely related to the notion of human progress.

He saw himself as a hawk soaring over the unbuilt dam, the valleys and trees and huts of the hamlet, the great river, the *Diquis* of olden days, barely swaying on his feet in the open air of the soccer field, hardly hearing the speaker in the tent but feeling entitled to be somewhere dark and wild.

He was invisible at night, now a soundless owl gliding over the future reservoir, the glistening water plane of the hydroelectric plant, and below its flat surface the upended disintegrating world he inhabited in that spacious drifting moment, the Boruca ground on which his boots stood and rocked, slipping on the under-slime of sodden logs, mud-coated thatch, and sunken swollen dogs.

"Where you been, man?" Oscar punched his buddy's shoulder.

Victor squinted at his old friend, arguably the only one left in these parts. "I ain't been anywhere," he said. "I been holding this can a long time."

Oscar hiked his jeans up and waved at a group of villagers looking their way. "It's all fine, folks," he said. "The rogue Indian ain't doing no harm at all."

"They talk about moving the dam?" Victor asked.

"Talked about putting it on the Rio General," Oscar said.

"Won't make no difference," Victor said. "One rio, then another."

"More people, more power, bro." Oscar gazed at the starry sky, let his eyes drift down to the glowing tent, the attendees milling about like moths. He walked over to the bike to get a beer.

A white man joined them. He had his own beer and stood nearby in his own space but he was with them. "You don't know me," he said. "I'm quiet in the forest. I climb trees and talk to monkeys without a word. I'm against the installation of more ziplines. I like treehouses singly but not as developments or hotels."

"What I'm asking myself," he said, "is do you need this. And then I have to ask myself, is it any of my business what goes on here." The two Boruca men looked at him and said nothing.

"The government wants to sell power to your neighbors. Yeah," he said, "Panama. Sometimes I go off on the corporate entities and wonder how you fight back. Other times I just want to shut the fuck up and have fun." He laughed. "Right now I'm at a crossroads, with very little beer. And no chicha."

"I once thought I could start a movement with two Indians and a piece of paper," he said. "Then someone told me they were now called indigenous people, or natives, and the best course for results was a relentless series of small, individual acts of courage."

Victor looked the man over. Hands in prayer around a can at his heart, unshaven face skyward, a starlight lover, bushy brown hair, thirty-something, lean, relaxed, an eccentric agitator. "Wet beers over there," Victor said. "On the bike."

Ellis looked at the men, glanced at the bike. "Cool," he said.

"Getting warm," Victor said.

Ellis smiled. "That's the path we're on, friend."

"The volcano will come," Victor said.

"Alright," Ellis said. "Let's drink to the ashes and the new earth."

—

A Boruca man, tall for his tribe, walked between the buses and entered the blue-tiled interior of Soda Acuario in Palmar Norte. Victor Leiba took a chair at a rear table facing the door and ordered coffee and breakfast. He seemed aloof and showed signs of day labor, his hands rough, his thick forearms so chalky with mortar and brick dust that his fingers appeared faded and colorless. He drank a glass of water, his black hair in a ponytail halfway down his back, his blank brown face unduly hard and lined for one in his early thirties. His coffee arrived and he took two sips, stood and went to the bathroom and washed his arms and face. When he returned, another man entering from the street saw him and came over and took the seat across the table.

This man too was Boruca, indigenous-featured and also taller than average, with prominent nose and ears, wide down-turned mouth, deep-set dispassionate or private eyes, a solemn longitude of facial expression. He caught the waiter's eye and ordered the same as Leiba. Both men wore boots, jeans and well-worn shirts, and spoke English. Oscar Morales had a message to deliver.

"I heard from my ma," he said. "Unusual white man left her a calling card."

Victor drank coffee. "About what?"

"Finding a tracker."

Victor's senses picked up a new customer entering, people passing beyond, talking on the street, horns sounding, bus brakes hissing. "Track what?"

"A person. Off the reserve."

"What else?"

"Man said excellent pay."

The waiter brought their plates and they ate their eggs and beans and tortillas quietly, glancing up from time to time at the open doorway, maintaining a general awareness of the motions and mannerisms of the others in the room and around the buses in front and at the outside counter window where coffee and snacks were steadily served.

"Man's number," Oscar said, sliding a scrap of paper across the table.

Holding a rolled tortilla over the edge of the plate, Victor Leiba paused in the mopping of his beans and put the paper in his shirt pocket.

8. Labyrinth (Liz's Vision)

Millege was paying his check when his phone rang. He looked at the number, reached for the receipt and left his change, then stepped outside in front of the belching buses of Palmar Norte, put the receiver to his ear.

"Millege," he said.

"Whatcha got for me?" Hiller asked.

"I'm meeting a source in a little while. Best lead yet," Millege said.

"What the fuck is taking so long?" Hiller said. "It's a small country."

Millege rolled his eyes at a passing stranger, shook his head and mouthed the word *asshole*. "Lack of data," he said. "Lack of witnesses."

"I put you on based on past success," Hiller said. "Now I'm wondering if your methods are outdated. Obsolete. Calcified."

Millege waited for more adjectives. "I have my ways," he said. "It's a process that sometimes takes some time."

"We don't have time," Hiller said. "What we have is a lack of closure. I don't need crying parents creating a disturbance that won't lie down. I need to give them a sense that this is wrapped up and done with. That means the culprit coming forward to face the music. We don't know what the law down there is doing, and we can't depend on them making an example of this clown. But we do need to put this behind us, close the caskets, satisfy the insurance business and move on. You get me?"

"Loud and clear," Millege said. "A few more days and I'll have him."

The line went dead.

He drove on to Sierpe and through the town to the water at the end of the road. He got out and stood at the edge of the river, gazing at the other side, the dense calamity of green, a lone dock with a few boats, the water curving out of sight in both directions. He read the tour signs again, looked over at the meeting place, the restaurant La Perla, the transport crowd gathering, saw no sign of Gustavo, no reason to continue without spending real money. He hadn't found anything solid, no clues or tips, no enemies. Just vague acquaintances.

Millege was sitting at a table by the water drinking coffee when the minivan pulled up. He watched the bartender spot him and head over. He stood, and they shook hands.

"You want coffee, breakfast?" Millege said. He motioned for the waitress.

"Okay," Stavo said. He was wearing creased jeans and a spotless white polo shirt, proud of keeping a neat appearance. His hair was short and gelled, his clean-shaven face radiated an earnest swagger.

"Where's the girl?" Millege said.

Stavo glanced at his watch, then nodded at the river. "She comes."

They ordered eggs and bread and beans, and it

came out quickly and they began to eat. "You know our guy," Millege said. "He's a customer, probably a good tipper. Maybe he's a friend of yours."

Stavo considered the implications of these statements. He sipped some water and cleared his throat. "Yes, of course," he said. "Many people know this guy." His hand over the table waved a negative disclaimer as he frowned. "But this—these dead." He shook his head, staring at Millege. "Too much," he said.

"So you like him but you want the truth exposed," Millege said.

Stavo hesitated. "The truth and be fair," he said. "The girls, the two dead, they were very nice."

"I heard they were sexy," Millege said, keeping his eyes on Stavo.

The young man nodded. "Yes, very pretty, very nice."

Millege pulled out a cigar and rolled it between his fingers. "I wonder if he was fucking both of them," he said. "What do you think?"

Stavo hesitated, considering this an unnecessary insult to the memory of the deceased women. "They did not speak of this," he said.

"No, of course not," Millege said. "I was just speculating. Why do you think they went with him? That night."

"He trick them," Stavo said.

"Tricked them. How?"

"Some story," Stavo said. "To make a big action against the company."

"What if it was their idea," Millege said, "and he just went along with them, went along with their dangerous plan. Maybe he just drove the car."

Stavo frowned again, wagged an index finger. "No," he said, suddenly strong in his conviction. "This guy—

he want to make some trouble."

Millege sat back and crossed his legs, aimed his cigar at Stavo. "Did you ever hear him getting angry, talking about making trouble?"

Other people entered the covered patio, and Stavo looked around and out at the wide water where an approaching engine could be heard. He leaned toward the older man. "This guy was waiting," he said. "Living easy and always waiting."

"Waiting for what?"

"Waiting to get his soldiers."

Millege stared at the river. "Let's hope your girl has more than that."

Stavo got the call, and they walked past a tourist group lining up outside the restaurant for the boat taxis to Drake and then down to the dock where the girl waited in a Carolina skiff with the engine running, her face in shadow under a wide hat. They stepped aboard and Stavo pushed them off, and they motored out to the middle of the channel so Millege could look back at the waterside town and gain a new perspective.

"Cut the engine," he said, and Stavo made a throat-slicing motion to Liz.

Millege observed the concentration of buildings and boats bunched together, the only place around for supplies, the daily transport boats being fueled, the silent world all around, the vast mystery behind mangrove walls.

He looked at the girl and saw her defiant stare, her facial stain, his eyes taking in her short solid body, small scarred hands resting on the wheel, the curves under the damp T-shirt and the tight jeans, the stained sneakers.

"Hello, Liz," he said.

"Hello, sir," she said.

"Do you know our little lost boy Ellis?"
"What, sir?"
"Do you know the man we're searching for?"

She felt the crimson glow in her firemark even as she shook her head.

"You know the story," he said. "Two girls are dead, and he needs to say what he knows. Right? And you want to help me find him. For the girls."

"Of course," she said.

"Okay. Show me where you think he is."

She turned the boat downriver, Millege in the forward seat and Stavo standing beside her at the console. They passed the ferry landing and kept to the center of the wide curving course, circumventing the floating clumps of hyacinths and leaving the little town behind. The sun bore down between drifting clouds, a few homesteads and docks were scattered here and there, a cow pasture with palms, a palm grove, then jungle dominated the shore.

They were ahead of the scheduled taxi boats and passed two drifting fishermen and another major artery. In both directions they were isolated as she made their mangrove-creek turn. To any onlookers they would have appeared to be a local couple taking a solitary visitor for a ride.

Within moments they disappeared into the mangroves, the vessel slowing through the dappled wilderness water, the looped roots receding in every direction, the way ahead presenting a repetition of view, an eerie welter of forms seemingly incompatible with human habitation.

Millege stood and turned to face them. "The man has to eat," he said.

Liz slowed further and looked at Stavo, then throttled down to idle and the boat began to turn in the narrow channel. "What, sir?"

"So far from town," Millege said. "He needs things to live. Food and water."

"Not so far," she said.

Millege looked at them both, turned back around and waved her on.

They approached a shoddy dock with a short boardwalk tilted upon roots leading to a shack somehow balanced among mangrove trunks.

"Like this," Liz said.

There was no boat, no sign of occupation. Millege studied it anyway as they cruised by. "A real hugger-mugger house," he said.

"What, sir?"

"Nothing," he said. "What else you got?"

"Maybe this guy is buying food," Stavo said. "Taking his boat."

Millege looked back at the property, telling himself to be more inclusive. "Alright," he said, "let's land, take a look."

He pulled himself up a wooden ladder and stood at an angle on the old dock and noted the webs and mold and tree debris and called it the longest shot of his career. Stavo stood beside him and pointed out a boat-billed heron in the branches overhead. Millege squinted at the bird and rubbed his eyes and shook his head. "Stay here," he said.

He moved carefully up the walkway, paused near the shack and listened. A few reverberating birdcalls, insects, a vast stillness undulating. No sound from the great Sierpe. He walked behind the building and stood looking out at repeated trees drawn in gray and green shapes eternal. No outhouse, no fish-cleaning table. He peered in the gritty back window, its screen warped and debris-filled, saw in the dimness a table, chair, lantern, cupboard, cooler. No sink, no water. No clothes visible. No cans, bottles, jugs, boxes, paper.

The Path of the Tapir

The door was padlocked.

He stepped around to the other window, saw nothing more except dead wasps and lines of ants and dark streaks of haphazard mold, moved away and stood with eyes closed, trying to see his man here. He went back to the landing.

"Let's go," he said, and climbed down into the boat.

Stavo followed and pushed them off as Liz started the engine.

They puttered back toward the river, Millege at the console beside them. "That's a day camp," he said. "Not for overnight, not practical. Okay?"

"I feel something, sir," she said.

He looked at her face, her mark, her eyes hidden behind sunglasses. "Say it," he said.

"This area," she said, with both men staring at her.

Millege adjusted his jungle hat, wiped his neck, inspected a wet collection of gnats on his fingers. "She feels things," he said to Stavo without sarcasm. "She feels our monkey."

Stavo nodded in solemn agreement, sweat showing through his shirt.

"Me, I'm thinking someplace closer to town," Millege said, "the other direction, a house share, someone helping with groceries, a roommate, a friend, a dog, a more normal life, just mostly out of sight. You understand?"

They were entering the river again. She shook her head and pointed downstream.

"You're thinking he moves around, changes places." Millege said.

"Maybe, sir," she said, turning the wheel. "I will show you more."

He placed his hand on the console between them. "Look," he said, "I need a sighting. Not a feeling, a sighting." He turned away and took his seat.

They motored to a homestead on the north side of the river, perhaps a half kilometer farther west. The place had no dock at all, just two posts near the bank, no boat moored, the house set way back, nearly hidden among trees, the collapsing remains of a shed closer to the bank, wood debris scattered between house and river. Millege didn't like it, ruled it out without landing.

The next place was on the same side, almost a kilometer farther on, appeared to be more of a camp, with several similar shacks close to the bank, multiple banana thickets, laundry hanging, a dugout along the bank, no dock, a small blue-canopied motorboat secured at the bank, a place with a clear community feeling. Millege couldn't picture his man risking his anonymity there. As they sat idling a boat full of orange-vested passengers passed them, all of their heads turning at once—as if this too were part of their tour—to observe whatever had halted the progress of and now occupied the three idlers. Some of the tourists waved. Millege shook his head at Liz and she steered them out through the wake of the other vessel and turned back the way they'd come.

They made a left into a major channel off the river, heading into pure wetlands, away from primary visitor traffic, the busy passage to the coast, to Drake Bay, Caño Island, Corcovado. No one up here but deep mangrove tours, possessed fishermen, scientists, occasional explorers. White-faced monkeys.

Would the guy actually stay this far in here? Could he? Millege imagined a week's worth of groceries, fuel, a generator, night noise, night vulnerability, no neighbors, a trap if you're approached. And then what, a shootout? Not likely. Plus bugs, animals, solitary insanity.

The next place was newer, more substantial,

tucked into a cove off the tributary. They motored inside as if curious, lingered in a slow turn. A boat at the dock, no sound but water licking around their own transom. Millege took a close look. Intrepid 245, twin Evinrudes, good condition, probably somebody at home. He stared at the house, the tin roof, the rain barrels, the windows, his senses open to any flutter of motion, a sound, a smell, a reflection, studied the boat again, knowing its cabin, galley, and head, a spare room right there.

"Let's go," he said, motioning back to the river.

Back in the primary stream he directed them upriver and asked for the idle. No one in sight, the heat settling in, humidity a transparent drop cloth. As they drifted, he pondered. Insects crossed and skimmed the surface. Maybe this whole area was too impractical as a hideout. He turned to Liz Zuniga.

"Why should our guy be at that particular house?" he said. "Why do you say this?" He held her shoulder with one hand. "Has someone said something? Have you or anyone you know seen him?"

She looked at him, looked at Stavo sitting behind her. She wanted to feel respected, trusted, useful to this project. She wanted a reward for her work, her unusual instincts, whatever they thought of them. She had always been different, her mind too, not just her stained heart, her tainted face.

"I can't explain, sir," she said. She touched her temple.

Millege looked up at white ibis winging over the river, their garbled honking passing and receding in flight, some language only they understood.

"Is it like a dream?" he said.

She frowned, shook her head. "Like an eye," she said.

"An eye," he said. He looked at Stavo and then

down into the river. The shifting, running current, sunlight striking slivers of loose river grass, a school of tiny translucent baitfish, the shimmering, slippery hints of the larger life below. When he looked up, she was holding her small backpack and digging inside. She withdrew her hand and showed him her open palm.

He stared and then bent forward, and Stavo stood to see this thing.

A small glob settled like a spilled egg, a melted white globe, green center gone wide, partly puddled and solidified again, a distorted stare into nowhere. He reached out and lifted it and examined its smooth manufactured surface. Warped discolored glass, green iris, false pupil spot, an amoebic misshapen eye blackened along its rough irregular edge.

"Where did you get this?" he asked.

"The burn place," she said. "The girls."

"Are you kidding me?" Millege looked at Stavo for help.

"She is from Sierpe," Stavo said. "Her family. She can go there anywhere and look." He nodded. "I ask her to pass by that place."

"Fuck me running," Millege said.

"Please, sir," she said, her hand outstretched. "I need it."

He studied her anew, then placed the glass gently in her small palm.

9. Del Preet

Ross Paddington called his old friend Mason Dunn and they met midafternoon the following day at the Vero Beach Country Club. Dunn was a former colleague at NASA, an air commando in his younger days. They got drinks at a table in the pub.

"I appreciate your input," Paddington said. "Cheryl's been going out of her mind on this. Things are at a standstill. The fucking palm company sent some guy, an investigator we're told, but we don't get updates. They made overtures of goodwill at first, pure bullshit to appease us, and now a state of limbo has been reached. The missing person"—he swirled his bourbon with its swizzle stick—"does not generate much noise. No priors, no recent credit card trail, no appearances. Here's what we have," he said, sliding a manilla folder across the table. "Old stuff, demonstrations, charity donations, eco-group memberships."

Dunn lifted his glass and drank swallows of beer. He wiped the edge of his mustache, a clean-lined salt-and-pepper ridge, with his index finger.

"No terror indicated," he said.

Paddington frowned. "The fire was the big move," he said. "All roads lead to this monumentally fucked-up act killing our kid."

Dunn opened the folder and flipped through the pages. He closed the folder and sat up straighter. He looked out at the patio for a moment, the golf course beyond, the stately, ordered world on view in a few squares of glass. He was dressed smartly himself, crisply casual, his trim fitness clear to see, his gray hair thick and close cut, as military as ever, his bearing steady and strong, his blue eyes intimidating for an average-size man.

"Look, Ross." He smiled kindly at his older friend. "I can put a man on this with one call." He slid the folder back. "He won't need this crap or anything else from you once you give the go-ahead. He doesn't need an emotional reason. He's a professional." Dunn let that assessment sink in for a moment.

Paddington nodded and Dunn continued.

"He'll find your man by any means he deems necessary, but he won't collaborate with police or any other interested parties. He works solo, and the fee is the only thing he's interested in. You read me?"

"I read you," Paddington said. He drained his bourbon. "Special Ops."

"Close enough," Dunn said. "The end result can go two ways. Either you want words, a confession, let's say. Or no words. Ever. Just gone. And a confirmation of that."

The older man took a deep breath and looked around the room, his eyes passing lightly over the other members leading their own miserable lives apart from his. His gaze settled on his formidable friend. "No words," he said.

"Of course if you wanted poetic justice, he could go the same way as yours did," Dunn said. "If you've become the poetic type in your doddering," he added with a wry smile.

Paddington smiled tight-lipped and shook his head. "Just gone," he said.

—

The man landed in Panama City and rented a car with a false American passport and a bogus company credit card. He was tall and lean, in his early forties and light on his feet. He carried a duffel and a black backpack and wore aviator shades. He drove out of the city chaos to Santiago and had a meal, then continued to David and got a room. The next morning he drove to Paso Canoas, turned in the car, cleared Immigration and walked across the border into Costa Rica, where he rented another car and drove the short trip to Ciudad Neily. There he booked a room at the Hotel Andrea for a night.

Later, he drove up to the Mountain View Restaurant and toured the grounds, noted the butterflies, squirrel monkeys, toucans and coatis, and took shelter as rain poured fast and loud and masked the forest and the view over plantations and the Osa Peninsula. Night fell with trees dripping, the air cooled further as he ate salmon tartare on the terrace overlooking the twinkling city below, the dark gulf, the relentless Pacific.

In the morning he showered and shaved and got a call and went down to the hotel's open restaurant. He ordered coffee and waited, dressed in tan cargo pants, a short sleeve blue linen shirt and running shoes. A dark-haired man approached, a clean-cut national, an independent contractor, ex-military.

"Del Preet," he said as the American rose to shake hands.

"Reymo, my man," Del Preet said, "good to see you." After that they spoke Spanish.

Reynaldo Elizondo set a nylon messenger bag on the seat between them and once they'd ordered breakfast, delivered his report on the subject.

"No yield on the skip trace, no digital footprint, current cellphone records nonexistent, probably using a burner now. Ministry of Public Security files gave up copies of the passport photo, fingerprints, A2 visa, resident status as a *rentista*, a small investor (partner in a surf shop, later sold), medical-exam results, clean bill of health at the time, proof of income, bank account in Portland, Oregon. Last known residence in Uvita, cottage rented from Grady Gordon, American expat, permanent resident. No wife or children recorded for Hayden. Canadian girlfriend exited the country a year prior. Occupation listed as guide service."

Del Preet examined the contents of the bag. Maps, subject docs, Gerber lockback folding knife with a three-inch blade, Springfield XDS 9mm handgun, extra magazine, waistband holster, ziplock bag of ammo.

"Hasn't left the country," Rey said. "Legally."

"What's the status of the investigation?"

"Technically an open case, but after visits to the suspect's residence and the questioning of known acquaintances, the assigned manpower has dropped. The terminology being used is accidental death. Could be politics too. Company said to be downplaying the story, possibly to kill it, bury any public fallout."

"Any other interested parties?"

"Insurance people came and went. "One gringo from PPOI is looking around. Internal ops for security."

"Somebody's seen our man," Del Preet said as their breakfast arrived.

"*Buen provecho*," Rey said.

"Likewise, amigo."

In his room, Del Preet wrote a list of friends and acquaintances, went online and searched the landlord, former girlfriend, former business partner, Portland family and connections, social media cross-references, outdated background on the subject, his dormant website, email and phone contact info.

He drove north on Highway 2 toward Sierpe listening to a meditation CD called *Mindful Moments*, a series of stress-reduction exercises centered around breathing and visualization.

10. Backwater

The rubbing alcohol was gone. What now, boat fuel? His leg burned, a sprinkle of aliens imbedded high in his left thigh, a series of wood splinters no doubt deeper than he hoped, not having had an X-ray to see the fucking extent of the injected damage or anyone handy enough to extract them right here on the premises. Squatter's rights? The wounds were small plugged holes under a gauze wrapping, infection starting to leach inward, the surrounding skin tender, the red surface spots expanding like ink stains.

Food needed too, and rum. A few books that suited his taste might be considered a luxury. Ellis laughed silently, making do with the library at hand. When he could even relax enough to follow words on a page.

The shelter, the enchanting water-walking trees now a damp, dripping prison he needed to leave. Pushing his luck this far was no plan. Take the risk, get fixed, be gone again. He hobbled to the window, squinted through the edge of the blinds, saw nothing beyond light and lunacy, heard his wary breathing, his mind ticking, looping a scene over and over, the fire that sears the soul.

The Path of the Tapir

—

On the outskirts of Sierpe a car passed acres of African palms, their massive kernel pods clustered in oversize orange bunches, the deep spaces between the rows receding in tunnels of gloom that clouded in the distance. The car stopped on the shoulder adjacent to a community field bordered by a collection of colorful, old wood houses, remnants of the United Fruit days. Del Preet sat in the car across from the burn site and waited to attract attention. A pair of flop-eared oxen stood yoked together at the edge of the scorched ground, motionless before a rusted metal wagon, staring at nothing discernable.

A young woman in a tight red T-shirt approached from the north on a moped, and he got out and walked into the road. She slowed and tried to go around him but he moved in front of her and she stopped, placing her sandaled feet on the ground and revving the high-pitched engine in protest.

Del Preet held up his hand and apologized in Spanish. "I need help," he shouted. She shrugged with open hands in question and looked at his vehicle. He glanced behind him and saw a car coming through heat waves. To his left, two field hands were emerging on foot from the shadows between the palms.

He gripped his face and shook his head as if in great pain. He conjured images of interior flames illuminating the seams and cracks of a maintenance shop, an assortment of tractors and tools and oxcarts seen in the dancing light, an unforeseen explosion, a cave-in, the vandals themselves unable to escape their own minor target, moans and strained cries issuing from within the buckling walls, the yokes and leather bindings burned and crumbling in the crackling orange inferno, the twisting machinery, the thick black smoke and the trapped choking girls, their screams and desperate coughs, their temporary friend stumbling to the car, his flight down the long dark road. Past a witness?

The car stopped in the road. A middle-aged man and woman got out and left their doors open as Del Preet screamed, "My girl, my girl!" He whirled around to reveal his anguish as the field hands neared and he pointed at the charred earth. "Is this the place? Is this where she died? Oh my god!"

He staggered off the road into the dirt and the rubble of black charred scraps. "I never should have come," he said as tears ran down his face. "I never—"

The woman on the moped took off as the couple followed the distraught foreigner. They met the field hands at the edge of the burned earth and the four waited as the man wept over the blackened ground, bent forward, his hands on his knees, his shoulders heaving with the physical release of emotion.

"How horrible," the woman said, and the men watched and agreed in silence as the man straightened and looked around as if he had lost his place and was surprised to see them there too. "I'm sorry," he said. "Forgive me."

The woman gripped her husband's arm and he stepped forward in his fedora and faded pants, his sad worn face showing his commiseration, his wife speaking behind him. "God bless you, mister. We are sorry for your heavy loss. May His son watch over you."

Del Preet wiped his eyes, his streaked face, sniffling with his head bowed humbly. He shook the man's hand and thanked him. Thanked all of them with his hands pressed together in prayer.

Several people had gathered and stood watching way back near the houses across the road. One man began walking toward the scene. The field hands stood quietly in their straw hats and muddy rubber boots, machetes hanging idly from their dusty hands, wondering about this poor weeping stranger as the sun poured down upon them all and the oxen stood as dazed as ever.

"What can you tell me," the man said, "about her last moments on this earth? What happened in this place?" He looked at each of them. "My baby girl," he said, his face an ugly mask of anguish, his hands open for help.

The man in the fedora put a hand on Del Preet's shoulder. "It was late at night," he said quietly. "Who knows why they came." He looked at his wife and she nodded. "Something happened," the man said. "The fire started. Maybe it was a game. Maybe they were smoking. An accident."

"An accident?" Del Preet said. He looked at the place where the building had stood. "What about their friend? What happened to him?"

Everyone was silent. A breeze stirred the tops of the tall palms and their fronds waved weakly, innocently, the heat stifling dissent. Del Preet heard low croaks and rustling sounds from the trees and saw a man from the houses crossing the road. The field hands seemed paralyzed.

The volunteer approached the group raising his hand slightly to the other locals as if he knew the state of the situation, had been expecting this day to come. He was poor but his hands were clean, his face deeply lined and solemn, his beard gray, well-trimmed, his authority displayed with dignity.

"How can I help?" he asked.

"Can you tell me, sir, what happened here?" Del Preet said. "For the sake of my dead child. For my pitiful grieving wife."

"Of course," the man said. "I live there," he said,

pointing at the houses. "I was awakened on that night by a sound. I didn't know what it was but I went outside and saw the flames and knew it was an explosion. I ran closer and saw a car parked there." He pointed to the roadside beyond the rubble. "I ran to get help and when I looked back I saw the car driving away."

"Which direction?" Del Preet asked.

"That way," the man said, pointing north.

"Did you see the driver?"

"I was too far away."

"So you don't know if the driver was alone."

The man shook his head.

"Did you see anything else?"

"Only the fire. We did not know about the deaths until later."

"Did anyone else see the car or the driver?"

"I don't know," he said. "It was very late."

"What kind of car was it?"

The man looked over at Del Preet's SUV, a black Nissan X-Trail. "Like that," he said, "but not so large."

"Like a little pickup?" Del Preet asked.

"Maybe," the man said.

"Was it gray?" Del Preet asked, his manner crisper now.

The man frowned, looked at the others listening to this car talk. "Dark," he said. "Maybe red. Or green."

Del Preet turned back to the man in the fedora. "You said maybe it was a game. What kind of game?"

The man put up his hands and his wife said, "Only rumors, sir."

"What rumors?"

She shrugged and pulled at the hem of her blouse.

The man from across the street spoke. "Against the company, sir."

"The company," Del Preet said. "The bad guys, the

evil corporation."

"They make work here," the man said.

"Yes, yes, work that prompts young people to play games that kill them."

There was silence, and then the man said, "Your daughter, sir?"

"Thank you for your time," Del Preet said, and walked toward his car.

The man said, "The blame is like holding a fish underwater, sir."

Del Preet paused and turned this slippery sentence over. He waved without turning around and got into his car and continued south.

—

Millege drove out of Sierpe with Stavo following in his van. He passed the Nueva Jerusalem church and a school with painted tire planters and a toucan mural and a roadside restaurant with a woman mopping a tile floor around a prone cat. On his right, he saw a stretch of the lazy brown Estero Azul, a branch of the Sierpe River, then a few faded houses, pink and blue and ocher, amid almond trees and bamboo bordering a soccer field situated opposite endless rows of tall African palms.

He passed an eighteen-wheeler laden with netted palm-nut clusters and jerked back in his lane just ahead of an approaching vehicle, a speeding black Nissan. He looked across at the passing car, saw the face of the other driver—white skin, close brown hair, pilot shades—as that driver turned to see him, and felt a flash of intuition or professional recognition like a jolt to his system. He stared into his mirror at the rear of the receding car, saw Stavo's minivan pull around the truck, block the view, and fall in behind him again.

Millege pulled over at the burn site. Okay, his blue Rav4 was now known. He could switch it out. Or was he being paranoid? Stavo parked beside him as the palm company truck blew past in a gritty roar, the driver eyeing them.

When they got out, Millege said, "I thought we should revisit this place."

"It's good," Stavo said. "Can maybe learn something new."

They kicked around the debris in the area where the shed had stood. Millege kept picturing the glass eye, looking for teeth or jewelry or bone. He didn't know. Chunks of wood and rubber were here, splinters of this and that, tire fragments that left unholy marks on your fingers, ashen crumbs, the metal pieces already towed away somewhere. He heard a whistle and saw a field hand watching them from the trees. "What?" Millege asked Stavo. "Was that a comment?"

Stavo beckoned the man over as he walked toward him.

Millege watched them speaking and kept scouring the dirty ground. "What'd he say?" he asked as Stavo came back.

"He says the father was here."

"Who, the priest?"

"The father of the girl."

Millege looked up at the field hand, glanced over at the distant houses, and back at the empty road. "Which girl?"

"One of the dead ones."

Millege stared down the road. "Was he driving a black Nissan?"

Stavo put the question to the field hand and Millege heard the answer.

"How can you know the car?" Stavo asked.

"We're done," Millege said. "Thank the man."

They were outside their vehicles when the field

hand, still in the same spot, shouted his last remark.

"What was that?" Millege asked.

Stavo turned to face him. "He said the father was not the father."

11. The Fourth Rider

Del Preet cruised the waterfront, the marina, the side streets of Sierpe, stood at the ferry crossing gazing across at the continuing road, entered the Bar La Esquina and stared into the defensive faces of the few patrons without a word, then sat outside on a concrete table in the park across the street consulting his notebook as if he might be contemplating the purchase of the establishment or the town.

He drove north to Palmar Norte and then on to Uvita and stopped for a roadside coffee as the mountain clouds delivered their daily summer deluge in this tangled region where tropical elevation fell abruptly into the coast. He continued upward on a muddy hillside gravel road, the sun dropping toward the blue horizon and sending its late rays through a profusion of wet leaves and showers of sparkling drops released by chattering birds taking wing in advance of the coming dusk.

He saw the sign for Whale Tail Vistas, its aqua logo a breaching humpback, which the place advertised you could spot during two thirds of the year while savoring your favorite cocktail. At the turn into the property, a *Perro Bravo* sign warned of an aggressive dog, or dogs, and another sign stated that entrance was prohibited, meaning wandering sightseers were not welcome. The drive was splendidly embraced by frangipani and red ginger and all manner of thriving heliconia. He leaned out of his window to identify a small furry gray body and found that it was the corpse of a baby sloth, as yet unmolested.

Twelve years ago Grady Gordon had visited and fallen in love with this country. On his second trip, following a divorce and the sale of a heating-oil company in Tennessee, he discovered the southern Pacific zone and purchased three acres of hillside jungle. On his third trip he hired a crew and carved a driveway and built a house and the first of four *casitas* he envisioned in his master plan. In the following dry season the construction was completed and the rental cottages kept the plan going as others like himself came down and stayed for days or weeks at a time. He was sixty-nine now, healthy and content with the simple formula for late success and joy he espoused and embodied.

He was trimming a few fronds away from the gazebo terrace from which guests could enjoy the ocean view when his dogs barked and he heard a car crunching gravel. Generally guests parked down beside their cottage, so he set the clippers on the table and wiped his hands on a towel. His brown dogs, local midsize rescues he named Bella and Lucky, moved toward the vehicle and he called them to a halt. The sun was bathing the yard in a yellowish glow.

Grady wiped his face as a man approached, probably to inquire about the place, he figured. The gardener and the cleaning girl were gone for the day. He watched the man striding toward him, looking around as he came up the slope, a nicely dressed professional type, possibly an investor in search of information. If so, he wouldn't be the first. This investment was easy to admire.

Del Preet took in the clean air and processed the profuse and standard vegetation, the hoots of trogons, the afternoon sea breeze, the hot light behind the owner up here with his animals, framed as an aging overexposed picture by thinning backlit hair standing like a baby bird's new head feathers, his long nose lifted, his vacant dream world before him, his guests absent, maybe roaming the coast, taking their happy hours elsewhere.

"Mr Gordon," Del Preet said, stepping up under the gazebo roof.

"Afternoon, friend. How can I be of service?"

Del Preet bent down to scratch the heads of both dogs as they smelled his pants at the knee. "Sweet spot on earth," he said. "A good place to die."

Grady squinted at the man. "Beg your pardon?"

"When the time comes," Del Preet said. "We never know it, do we?"

"What's your business, friend? Your name."

"My name's not important. Let's talk about your tenant Ellis Hayden."

"I find your tone offensive," Grady said. "And I don't provide personal info."

"Put my tone at the top of your list of worries," Del Preet said. "If you don't have a list, now would be the time to start one." He straightened and stood observing the other man.

"Now look here," Grady said. "I don't know who you think—"

"Shut it and listen," Del Preet said. "This is a day you'll long remember. This is a line drawn in the sand of your life. Forgive the quaint imagery, but something about the country touches me as it does you. That may be the only thing we have in common so let's move along. You need to pay attention and answer my questions to the very best of your ability with nothing held back. I hope you understand exactly what I'm saying because if you don't, you will rue this day. That is an absolute certainty."

"You're threatening me," Grady said.

"You're a bright man," Del Preet said. He gestured at a chair. "I want you to be comfortable and never have to see me again. Or it can be the opposite."

The older man gripped the top of a metal deck chair, more for stability than with the intention of sitting. His hand trembled slightly so he held it tight. The dogs stood watching him, sensing an imbalance, a disturbance.

Del Preet smiled at the dogs, looked past the man at the wide horizon, glanced around at the lush property as if forming vacation memories. He pulled out a chair, metal scraping on the stone terrace, and sat. The dogs turned to him again. "You have a nice life here," Del Preet said, looking up at Grady. "You don't want to upset it needlessly." He linked his fingers across his chest and leaned back. "One day you'll find your dogs gone. Vanished. You won't be able to reach one of your friends. Let's say, for example, it's Helen. You won't be able to sleep. Your stomach will hurt. Your days will be filled with dread. You might dream of extreme pain, or you might find actual bullet ants in your bed."

A wave seemed to hit Grady as he remained standing. He missed some of the words of the stranger as sounds began gapping out like missed beats in a corrupted recording. He grew light-headed and saw floaters in his peripheral vision, started drawing deeper breaths as he mechanically pulled out the chair. Helen? he thought. He sat heavily, legs wobbly, and looked at the other man, entoptic squiggles vibrating up in the trees and on the ceiling of the gazebo.

The man held Bella's head in his hands, was stroking her between the ears.

"We love our dogs," Del Preet said. "But they are a nighttime nuisance for someone who wants to visit unannounced. Not their fault, they run on instinct. Like you're doing now, holding onto self-preservation. Listen to all those little frogs and insects cranking up to their nocturnal volume. Great for sleeping. Unless you're afraid those natural sounds are masking those of an intruder. Then all bets are off, right? You just lie there with your eyes open. Waiting."

Grady couldn't figure out what to say. A few words assembled in his mind, but they would not be aligned in any sensible order. He felt like he was hallucinating. He rubbed his eyes and swallowed, the breeze chilly at his neck. He needed a drink. He needed to wake up. He moved his fingers absently over his pants pocket, feeling the outline of his cell phone.

"There's no one to call about this," Del Preet said. "Honestly, it would just get worse. You have to see it as a private matter. You're not at fault here. You just happen to know something that I'm insisting you share." He waved his free hand around. "Whatever you call this—paradise, freedom, tranquility, Grady Gordon's wonderful expat life—" he patted his knee and Lucky smelled his hand and looked under the table at his owner, "you certainly don't want to lose it. It's really that simple. If I leave unsatisfied, this will all be gone for you. And I mean gone."

The older man just sat staring at him. In disbelief, horror, paralysis. Motion was necessary. The sun's receding orange glow was slipping into purple spreading sky as dusk loomed and grew. Wings rustled overhead and the wild croaks and piping whistles rose higher into the evening's texture and the stars appeared and then became larger pinpoints of bright, uncaring beauty, nightly testaments to unfathomable truth.

Del Preet stood. "Let's get a drink and take a look at Mr Hayden's lodgings. You should probably feed these beasts too."

Grady sat looking up at him, blinking at sliding floaters, darkness.

"That's your only play here," Del Preet said.

The older man stood unsteadily and the stranger gripped his upper arm and they moved to the pathway and down the slope, the dogs following.

12. I Wouldn't Name a Dog Lucky

There were shrimp on a square white plate at a table by the infinity pool. Pasta with clams was coming, along with an artichoke salad. A glass of pinot grigio sat sweating crystalline drops. A long slice of papaya meat rolled in the shape of a cinnabar rose garnished his plate. Fuck Hiller. Millege was going for a fuller experience.

The peaceful hotel was nestled on a hillside in Ojochal. His spacious room featured hardwood shelves with stone sculptures and an outside shower boxed by bamboo. It was an airy secluded sanctum.

Dining room doors open to the night, rattan couches propped with botanical print pillows, lounging areas under a dark sky in the cool hill weather, serene green lighting cast under palm fronds waving. A steady sea breeze pushing through treetops, nocturnal caresses from the great roiling Pacific. A retreat he couldn't fully fall into.

Still, it would be sweet to bring Helen up here, he thought. Sip some fine wine, tell stories under a tropical moon. His own ringtone startled him.

He regarded the unknown number and answered.

"Hello."

"Millege," a deep voice said.

"Go ahead."

"You left your card with an old lady in Boruca."

Millege paused, thinking back. "I did," he said.

"Then we should talk," the man said.

"I need a badass assistant with no worries," Millege said.

"No worries," the man said. "Work is work."

"Do you have wheels?" Millege asked.

"Got wheels."

"Excellent. Let's meet in the morning in Palmer Norte. You know the Soda Acuario?"

"I know it."

"Let's meet at nine."

"Okay," the caller said. "I'll be the solemn Indian dude."

Millege smiled. "Outstanding," he said.

—

She was reading in bed, glasses low on her nose, a novel on her lap, a tumbler of red wine on the bedside table, hearing her neighbor's dog barking faintly among the nocturnal noises and feeling dense night air drifting through her open windows. She was taking a sip when her phone vibrated on the table. She saw Grady's name and flipped it open.

"Evening. What's up?"

"Helen? Helen, are you alright?" His voice sounded strained.

"Why wouldn't I be, Grady? I'm reading in bed. What's the matter?"

She heard his breathing, nothing else. "Grady?"

"Listen now," he said. "Don't be alarmed, but you need to keep this private between us. You hear me? Are you alone?"

"Yes, I'm alone. What are you talking about?"

He was breathing loudly, then drinking and swallowing.

"I had a visitor. He wanted to know all about Ellis."

"Was it that investigator guy?"

"Helen, I don't know who the fuck this guy was. He told me not to call anyone. And now I'm calling you."

"Calm down, Grady. He's gone, I assume. He doesn't know you're calling me. Right? And he won't know. This is completely confidential."

"You have got to promise me. This guy was fucking intense."

"I promise. Of course. Take it easy." She took another sip of wine. "This doesn't sound like my guy. Do you want to come over here? Are you hurt at all?"

"No. No. I'm just shook up is all. It was fucking nerve-racking." Grady paused and then went on. "He mentioned your name. I thought you should know. I mean, he knew things about me, Helen."

"What?" She felt a slight shudder in her spine and set her glass down. "Why would he mention me?"

"Nothing specific. Just a way to impress me with his knowledge. With his threatening manner."

She sat up straight and looked at the windows. "He threatened me?"

"No. No. I'm just saying your name came up. As a reference point."

She threw the cover off and stepped into her flipflops, listening to her environment, the phone held away from her ear momentarily. "Reference point?"

"Yes, he wanted me to know that he knew about my life. That's all."

"Jesus, Grady. What else did he say?"

"He's looking for Ellis. He wasn't fooling around either. I had to tell him something. I had no choice."

She sighed into the phone and walked slowly through her living room, scanned the windows, the door, the illuminated part of the yard, her kitchen knives.

"What do you want me to do?" she said.

"Get in touch with Ellis, give him a heads-up."

She felt exposed, standing in the middle of the dark room. "I really need to get a dog," she said.

"Did you hear me?"

"Yes, I heard you. I'll reach out."

"Tonight," Grady said. "Leave a message, something."

"No name, no ID, no badge?" she asked.

"No. Nothing. American, maybe six two, around forty, short brown hair, fit, clean-shaven."

"And he actually threatened your life?"

"He threatened my whole way of life."

"What does that mean?"

"You know what he said to me when he left?"

"What?"

"He said, 'I wouldn't name a dog Lucky.'"

—

The call went straight to voicemail.

"Ellis, this is Helen." She paused, hoping he might pick up, wondering what sort of state he was in. "Helen Prentiss. Look, I just got a call from Grady. A guy came looking for you tonight. No name but he impressed Grady with his seriousness. You should move on. The guy's American. Forty. Six two. Short brown hair. Also, there was another guy a few days ago. Chunky, sort of goofy, said his name was Philip Millege, working for Aggressive. He's asking around but seems less of a threat." She stared at her feminine reflection in the dark window glass, listened to herself breathing into the phone, still tenuously connected.

"Be careful, honey. Call me if you need anything. Anything at all. Delete this message, okay? Please."

The Path of the Tapir

It was becoming a regular stop, a breakfast crossroads that Millege liked at first bite and Victor practically called home. The grinding buses, the careening street life, the nearby highway of rolling potential, the passengers and the Palmar Norte passersby. You might run into anyone.

Millege talked over toast and coffee, provided the background. Victor listened, his rough hands folded, his eyes attentive and dark, his long hair pulled back, his solid presence fitting the laconic image Millege expected.

"I was told our man worked with the Indians. Among other things."

Victor showed no reaction. "Could be," he said. "Many pass through the village—sightseers, artists, weaver girls."

"Doesn't matter," Millege said. He looked around again, checked the people inside and out, the young counterman glancing their way.

He looked directly at Victor. "A new player has entered the game. I don't know who hired him, but I need my back watched. That's your function."

The smooth Borucan waited a beat, impassive, either unimpressed or unconcerned. "Protection," he said.

"Essentially," Millege said. "But more than that." He sipped coffee, tried to signal for more. "I need local help, with language, with everything. I need another set of observant eyes and a man who can handle himself."

"A man who carries a weapon," Victor said.

"That would be useful, yes. There are unknown factors at work here."

"Not your average job," Victor said. "Or wages."

"Not at all," Millege said. "We're both making a decision as we speak. Is this a guy I want to work with? Is there a balance conducive to success? Will this be fun and educational?" He laughed. "I just threw that last one in for my own amusement."

"You're expecting a conflict," Victor said.

"We're after the same target," Millege said. "A conflict could be expected."

Victor looked out at the street, the passing fray, the stream of tedium, his known prospects lying ahead like potholes. "Tell me how this can work," he said. "Tell me a cash number."

The waiter brought more coffee and stood silently as he poured and neither customer spoke. When he left, Millege wrote a number on a napkin and pushed it across the table under his middle finger with a casual dramatic flair.

"Dollars per day," he said. "We'll go together in my car most of the time. Other occasions, you might have a separate job and meet me later. One fuckup and the deal is stopped cold. That's just the way it is. Wheels and a phone and a bad fucking view of anyone bothering me or preventing me from doing my job. We think, we talk, we act, we improvise, we get results. Any questions?"

Victor folded the napkin and pocketed it as a contract. "You armed?"

"I have some matches," Millege said.

"Planning to burn the target?"

"You never know," Millege said. "Might have to smoke him out."

—

Ellis turned off the house lights and stood at the front door and opened it and listened to the predawn world outside, the soft natural stirrings, the plops and rustlings and birdsong near and far, the low honks and high keening cries. He heard a faint, distant engine somewhere out on the Sierpe.

Leaving with his backpack, he closed the door and limped out to the dock, the sky crawling gray over the trees behind the house. He dropped his pack into the Intrepid and unlooped the stern line from its cleat and tossed it aboard. Wincing, he stepped down into the boat and put the key into the ignition and turned the engines over. The deep rumble was startling and he hastened to lean forward on the bow and pull the boat up to the forward cleat and free himself from this place. He pushed off and looked behind and reversed into the stream, cast a last look at the dark house and then throttled forward, running lights off, his eyes squinting into black undulating water, the big river just ahead, daylight exposure coming, another evasive move needed.

At the intersection of channel and river he slowed, checked his phone by habit. No service. Not anywhere around here. He was too isolated. No way to know if he had been warned already.

He could go back into Sierpe and risk an encounter. Leave the boat at the marina, then buy a scooter ride to Palmar. Have someone meet him.

Or take the other direction, down the coast to Drake. Even more isolated. And what, leave the boat moored at anchor, swim in? Not cool. Or hole up at an expensive ecolodge? Then another boat onward. Where, the national park? Or get to the airstrip. Try to hop over to Palmar or Golfito or San Jose. Maybe get stranded waiting for a flight. Or get stuck with a charter rip-off.

He turned upriver toward Sierpe. Take the risk. It'll be early, barely light, pretty quiet. He pushed the throttle and flipped on the running lights, accelerating out into the wider river as it began to materialize into view, a ghostly white heron rising silently, banking over the treeline and out of sight.

The Path of the Tapir

At the Hotel Margarita, Del Preet woke before his alarm went off. He stood and listened and went to the bathroom, the tiles cool on his feet. He'd driven down the night before—waking the manager and paying extra for the inconvenience—to be in position to catch the first boat available. He did his abbreviated version of squats, sit-ups, push-ups, yoga stretches, ten minutes of meditative deep breathing, then showered, shaved, dressed and carried his bags out in the dark.

He parked near La Perla and took his backpack and waited to see which boat operation would open first, noting the small, quiet police station, a man staggering down by the park, a truck idling outside the Catholic church, its beams illuminating a dog in the rough street stretching each of its hind legs and shaking its head as if awakened prematurely.

He heard keys jingling and then a gate being opened, and he walked over to investigate. A man told him his employee Carlos would be there in fifteen minutes and could pilot a boat charter right away. Del Preet walked out to the end of the dock and stood listening as the world came into being.

The Intrepid rounded the bend into the waterfront view and slowed and drifted with the current, its lone occupant searching the shore from the middle of the river. He checked his phone signal and listened to Helen's message as a man stood watching him from a restaurant dock and another man behind him was bent over beside the console of a standard, single-engine, blue-canopied river cruiser. They stared at each other until the American observer turned and stepped into the rental vessel and spoke to its pilot, who then straightened and looked out at the idling Intrepid.

Ellis wheeled the boat around as he called Helen.

"Oh hey—" she said, her voice full of sleep.

"Listen, I just got your message," he said. "I'm in the river at Sierpe and the guy you mentioned is watching me right now. He's about to chase me in a rental boat so my plan just reversed. I'll beat them to Drake unless a problem pops up. If the timing works I'll hop a flight to Palmar. Otherwise—fuck, I don't know. Maybe a hotel. I'll call you from one place or the other. Thanks."

"Good lord," she said. "Be careful. I can pick you up in Palm—"

The Intrepid roared past the ferry landing and a man lounging at the shelter there stood up to watch the speeding vessel pass. Its captain kept to the center of the wide river as he pushed the throttle forward, hair flying back in a banner of flight. A few hundred yards ahead, three fishermen in a small open boat were pushed into the tangle of mangroves, and two of them threw up their hands and shouted and made rude gestures, taking notice of the boat's make and model.

The lone running captain caught their displeasure as he looked back, but his sense of self-preservation overcame all else. The twin Evinrudes had given him an instant lead, and his mind raced through alternative plans as the wind rushed by and he checked his gas and other gauges and scanned the river for snags and floating debris or anything at all that might disrupt his forward course. As he ran ahead, his mind ran backward too, examining the man on the dock and his possible motives and mode of operation.

Old Grady, his former landlord, had given him up—no big surprise there if the pressure was strong enough. But he couldn't understand why this bounty hunter, or whatever he was, had been standing in plain sight instead of watching surreptitiously and following his quarry to the marina to spring whatever he had in mind. This was troubling, like an announcement of intent, an act of intimidation which succeeded and now made the situation feel much more dangerous. Perhaps that was the point. Either that, or the timing of their encounter had simply been coincidental.

He considered ducking into a distributary, like the lone horseman in a western who pulls into a side trail until his pursuers pass, then doubles back the way he came. He preferred Sierpe, getting on the road sooner and vanishing inland, but could he chance a watery dead end? This brazen tracker gave him a bad feeling. What was his plan, kidnapping? Unofficial extradition? Was there even a bounty? Could it be basic revenge for whoever sent this guy?

—

Carlos Barrantes knew they couldn't catch the Intrepid and doubted his customer's pretext for the chase, even though it was well stated in Spanish. A debt owed and a stolen boat and a private handling of the matter? He figured this was simply a direct trip to Drake and the answer might be seen at the end. But if the boat was stolen, what would be the point of taking it to Drake Bay? He felt the American's silent impatience, especially when he slowed to reduce their wake. No, he wouldn't accept bribes to ignore the river rules he lived by.

Behind his shades and between the slits of his saurian eyes Del Preet watched the passing greenery, the sunlight flashing through mangrove leaves and rippling across the surface of the river as he breathed slowly and audibly into a state of near patience. He glanced at the profile of the stocky pilot, his pencil-line beard and silver loop earring and black hair gelled up into a short center ridge. The small blue-green hummingbird tattooed on his neck. Should be a peccary, Del Preet thought, which would better suit the man's appearance. He pictured his younger self grabbing and removing this man from the running boat, shocking him silly, his shaken form thrashing through the wake toward mangrove roots with rampaging fears of crocodiles and bull sharks spurring him onward like an animated hydroplane.

"What do you expect this morning at the mouth, the tides at the ocean?" he shouted at Carlos, who stood wide-legged and stoic at the console.

The local man gave his fare a glance and said, "No problem."

The weather was clear, and Del Preet watched four frigate birds soaring high ahead of them, indicating the sea. As the boat banked into the widest part of the river, Carlos pulled back at the approach of a private taxi from Drake, its pilot raising a hand as the two passengers, a middle-aged Norwegian couple, leaned out from under the roof.

"Don't stop," Del Preet said.

The two boats came abreast and idled so the pilots could talk for a moment. The Norwegians nodded at Del Preet, who stood impassively humming a tune to himself, almost smiling.

When they resumed the journey and no other vessels were in view Del Preet stepped closer to the captain and raised his arm in front of the man's face, pointing at the far shore. "Holy fuck," he shouted, and the captain instinctively pulled the throttle back. The passenger's right hand came around quickly and gripped his left wrist, locking the V of his elbow away from the larynx, his forearm and bicep in a chokehold at both sides of the man's neck, pulling him backward against the seat as his left and right carotid arteries were blocked. Carlos reached behind him as the grip tightened and he lost his footing and the blood to his brain. Del Preet turned his head sideways and pulled the man off the floor as he struggled, his fingers clutching at the attacker's hair and face, clawing wildly at the man's head and scratching his ear and cheek before his energy leaked away with the contents of his bladder and his arms fell wide to both sides as if he were floating or imitating a man crucified.

Del Preet rolled the unconscious body against the transom and put the boat on plane for the coast. He watched the rippling confluence of river and sea, the rocks to the south, the waves approaching in steady building threats and the calculated up-and-down line he needed to maneuver between and behind them, steering the boat's gradual rise and drop over churning crests and through smooth troughs to reach the open water. On the floor, Carlos bumped along with the boat's motion. He stirred and opened his eyes and lay breathing purposely and looking up at the man towering over him, the bleached sky beyond. Del Preet looked down and said, "Stay down."

Carlos saw himself as a boy in church, in awe of a visiting missionary, a tall stranger from the north with his worldly knowledge, his strange parables and warnings of the end-times. He touched his wedding ring with his thumb as the American squatted beside him. "Think about your wife's safety," the man said. "Give her a long happy life and never mention me to anyone. To you, I'm the Antichrist you never want to see again. Think of the future of your kids."

Spotted dolphins leapt offshore near Violin Beach as the boat pushed out of the turbulent mouth and turned south, parallel to the wild green wall of coastal palm and rising jungle. Off to the southwest, the island of Caño rose in a smoky plateau out of the vast Pacific. In another twenty minutes ridge dwellings appeared, then Drake Bay, a few *pulperias* and people and pieces of driftwood scattered across a beach stroked by rolling surf, home and lodge roofs in view up the hilly slope. A few boats rode offshore. In the distance, a larger vessel ran toward Caño. A nearby captain waved to the new arrival and Del Preet waved in reply. No Intrepid in sight. He turned the boat seaward and cruised out beyond the waves and continued south along the coast. At the far end of the wide bay he spotted a fancy lodge with its own cove and steered the boat into it, puttering in a slow circle as he examined the twenty or so similar crafts, mostly standard blue-topped transport vessels. Now he figured that he'd been tricked and turned the boat and headed back to the Sierpe.

When they reentered the river and were cruising up toward town and the dark sky accumulating above the shrouded spine of the Talamanca range, Del Preet began to sing an old western tune, high and raspy and steady as a migrating bird, his ludic voice remarkably sincere and tuneful, unconcerned with any possible appraisal by his audience of one.

> We were roamin' in the canyons
> Down where the eagles dove
> Passed by the Rocky Mountains
> On our way to the western coast

Sitting with his bruised back against the vibrating transom, Carlos Barrantes jounced and shook against the floor, his eyes closed, counting the loud minutes and praying fervently for freedom.

13. Long Jimmy's Longing

They lay in the humid afterglow of their physical wrangling, face up, side by side, frond shadows nodding on the wall like puppets in play, a residual tingling skipping from skin to lung to heart, the overhead fan's wobbly ticking intercut with interrupted sunbeams and waving window-side heliconias, the lazy buzz in the room erupting spasmodically in sensations like heat lightning.

Jimmy was watching the fan, breathing the scent of lilac lotion, feeling his condom shifting like loose skin. "So what's next?" he said.

"What do you mean?" Peyton said.

"I mean after you've checked off your tropical adventure list. It's just a vacation, right?"

"Pretty much. But I don't know—things are always changing."

"Are they?"

"They're not for you? Is it all just a parade of pussy, surf, and beer?"

"Hey, I gotta walk the big dog."

"Yeah, a good line. Walk it over here again. I'm just sayin'."

"What, like I'm stuck in a pattern? A prisoner of paradise?"

"I see you've totally thought it out," she said.

"I'm a wave rider," he said. "I'm still young and carefree."

"I get it," she said. "You won't be in the same rut when you're forty."

He laughed. "That gives me a little time for an audacious plan."

"Fuck," she said, "what's wrong with right now?"

He rolled out of bed and snapped the condom off, dropped it in the bathroom basket, grabbed a damp towel and wiped himself. Stood at the sink looking at her in the mirror.

"I covet the whale road," he said. "I stand upon the salt skin of the earth, fearing nothing, neither fish nor current nor wave. My pulse beats with the moon tide and the dolphin's heart, my mind's highway rolls over water into freedom. The open breaker lifts me into being, pushes me through time's guidance. I am the same as always, my parts formed in wind and sea and sand, my gliding life transformative, crystalized in pure seconds of perfection and grace."

She clapped slowly, four beats, and sat up. "So you're wanting to be a poet too," she said. The light on the door was mutating into an unnamed color.

"I went to LSU for a year," he said. "But the world was calling."

"Why'd you leave?"

"I got some money when my aunt died. Went to Puerto Rico to surf. Then ended up down here."

"And the money's going to run out," she said. "Sometime."

"You can only live cheap for so long," he said.

They ate chips and salsa and shared the last beer on the porch as the late light burnished certain trees in sections of modulating orange and the resident hawk fired its harsh cry above the river's cool comical gurgling.

Disregarding these natural noises, a silence soon descended on the porch, and Jimmy wondered if he should leave while he was ahead or wait for the inevitable shared shower and the assumed opportunity to fornicate in a slippery setting with this ripe young vixen. They definitely needed more drinks. The question was whether or not the postcoital atmosphere was favorable.

"You want to fuck me again, don't you?" she asked.

"Your psychic abilities are approaching normal," he said.

"And my dating skills are so transparent."

"Is this a date?" he asked, smiling.

"This is a meeting," she said. "We're brainstorming potential projects for the common good."

He shifted in his wraparound towel, repositioned his legs wider on the railing. "Now you're arousing me again," he said. "Something about the common good does it."

"Great," she said. "Now we just need a project."

"What are the categories?"

"People and animals."

"Shit, that's easy," he said. "People are the ones fucking the animals."

"There you go," she said.

"Harmonious interaction," he said, "despite a severe shortage of beer."

They heard a vehicle crunching down the drive and pulling in beside the bungalow. Laughter, doors slamming, then Chloe and Ellis stepped up on the edge of the porch and paused with a collective look of sly surprise.

"What are you naughty kids up to?" Chloe said.

Ellis moved forward lifting a bottle of rum out of a bag. "Yo, a local surfer dude. Don't answer that until I open this," he said. "Know your rights."

"Damn, dog," Jimmy said. "That's what I'm talking about right there."

"You guys know each other?" Peyton asked.

"Crossed paths a time or two," Jimmy said.

Ellis found orange juice and ice and mixed the drinks half-and-half and passed them around. He brought out two more chairs and they sat in a line, the men on each end, the porch a stage of characters now, the light dropping among the audience of trees awaiting the second act.

"My man here took me on a tour of Sierpe," Chloe said, "a land tour. We also brought some boxes of supplies to a family there. Old clothes and kitchen stuff."

"I've been collecting that for a while," Ellis said. "Needed to get rid of it."

"Yeah, of course you did," she said. "Turns out this Mr Zuniga dude and his wife have been living in an old wooden house at the edge of the community forever, they raised their family there. He's retired now but used to work for the palm oil company, I mean practically his whole life."

"He started out at the bottom of course," Ellis said. "One of the young machete guys who clears the weeds at the base of the trees so no snakes are hiding there for the next group of workers, the frond cutters, who go in ahead of the pod cutters."

"What pods?" Peyton asked.

"The seed clusters," he said. "The nuts, huge fucking orange clumps that weigh about a hundred pounds each. They hit the ground and some nuts break off and scatter, and women and kids gather those up. They've got teams doing different jobs during the harvesting process."

"So this sweet old wrinkled guy invites us in for coffee," Chloe said, "and his old wife sets the table with a cloth, and some neighborhood kids are peeking in the door while he tells us about his life's latest episode."

Ellis brought out a bowl of ice along with the bottle and the juice and refilled his and Jimmy's drinks and topped off the girls' glasses as Chloe continued.

"His house is really old and tilted. I mean you could set a soccer ball down at the front door and watch it roll to the back. Yeah, but get this. They are coming in to bulldoze it so they can add a few more rows of palms and squeeze more product out of the area. Can you fucking believe that? After the man and his family have worked and lived there all this time. One of his sons is a field inspector and another drives a truck for the company. Makes no difference apparently."

"Where will they go?" Peyton asked.

"I don't know, they'll get another house, I guess. But here's the thing. He's worried about his stone sphere. I mean it's on his property, which won't be his property much longer."

"What are you talking about?"

"There are these big stone balls around there. They're like a thousand years old and weigh tons. They're so mysterious that no one knows what they were made for. There's a park in Palmar Sur with a bunch of them lying around."

"They were discovered when United Fruit came in back in the forties," Ellis said. "Some were moved to a museum in San Jose, others to parks and private properties where people used them for garden ornaments. Some were destroyed during the creation of the banana plantations. Workers bulldozed them aside and busted them, and treasure hunters drilled them open or blew them apart with dynamite, thinking there was gold hidden inside."

"What's your guess on their original purpose?" Jimmy asked.

"Hard to say. Could be related to astronomy. Probably religious."

"They're like replicas of the moon," Chloe said.

"They probably couldn't think of any other shapes," Peyton said.

Jimmy laughed, spilling some drink on his bare chest. Then they all laughed and each burst triggered another and another until they fell into a rum-induced fit whose cascades drowned out the river.

Peyton took Jimmy by the hand and disappeared inside and the others heard the shower splattering and the disjointed words and groans escaping the window above them as the night sounds rose and descended like a carnival of peeps and staccato rasping and the jungle air enveloped the porch and filled their heads with fragrant entrancing scents that added to the combination of stark ardent cries and grew into vines of blind passion in the dark.

Chloe stood and Ellis kissed her silver navel stud and pushed the barbell with his tongue as she pressed his face into her stomach. She untied her bikini top and he gripped the fullness of her breasts and pulled them down to his mouth and she straddled him in the chair and settled and rocked herself back and forth in his lap, the chair scraping with her rhythm.

"Spank them," she whispered, and he did, the background shower splashing like rain roar encircling him in the darkness, the few fireflies out there seeming to defy logic in their winking movement through space and time, neither near nor far, sporadic spots across the palest starlight sifting onto leaves and the activities in this place running all together at once in a languid mosaic mix, details standing out from moment to moment, the eight-point star tattooed on her left shoulder blade, a compass face inside it, he remembered, his lips close enough to kiss it, some directional indicator appearing and unchanging except by her body's naked movement as she faced the night world, leaning over the railing, her spontaneity infectious, her warm wiggling bottom pulling him into her.

14. Half Measures of Wisdom

She pulled up along the edge of the Park of Spheres in Palmar Sur and sat idling roadside in her Corolla as he rose from a shaded bench and hobbled up the sidewalk and got in the back and reclined across the seat. They crossed the Térraba River in silence.

At the Palmar Norte junction she said, "Which way?"

"Up," he said, and she took the turn inland, following the river's winding course, climbing gradually toward the indigenous territories and the wild open southern heart of the land. She pulled around a truck, driving fast.

"Didn't know if I'd see you or not," Helen said.

"Neither did I," he said.

"What's hurting?" she asked.

"Splinters in my thigh."

"Is that from—"

"Yeah, there was an explosion."

"Got it," she said. "I brought my kit. We can pull over somewhere, maybe Buenos Aires. Where are you thinking of going?"

"Fuck if I know. There are bloodhounds on my

trail."

She turned to look at him. His eyes were closed, head resting on his pack. "Thank you for helping," he said.

He dozed through upland curves, rolling as if on a boat, imagining blind alleys and cul-de-sacs, the tangle of mangroves, his fingers occasionally twitching and reaching toward the floor like time-lapse roots.

Around Puerto Nuevo he cried out and woke.

Helen looked over the seat. "Were you dreaming?"

He sat up. "Being pursued," he said. "Stark raving terror as usual. I'm struggling through mangrove roots but somehow I have a good head start. When I look back there are these creatures coming, sort of a lizard-bird that leaps easily from tree to tree and keeps gaining on me. Finally I can see their faces, their beaks opening as they shriek and prepare to attack me."

"Good lord," she said. "How dreadful."

"Probably better than burning to death," he said.

"It's a recurring dream?"

"It is."

"But they never get you?"

"I always wake up just before."

"Good," she said. "That means you'll escape. One way or another."

He laughed, one note, and said, "You can't escape your own mind."

The rocky hillside rose vertically on their left. Bits of fallen rock lay in the road like warning shots. They crossed a smaller river that fed into the great Térraba meandering in and out of sight beyond the grassy screen and sunken villages on the eastern side, the highway a ribbon running between the close wall and the land sloping down to the wide river valley. At times the river vanished and then reappeared lower than before, vaster, muddier, with flat pastures alongside, or more distant, contained by green hills bordering its far shore, the whole landscape, the bus shelters with hanging banana bunches, the school flag pole, the jungle trees and riverine curves and shore stones, the cows, a contiguous scene unrolling as a pastoral canvas as they came upon it.

"Where should we go?" she said. "Everything normal looks surreal now."

"I'm trying to figure it out," he said.

He sat up and then lay down again as a vehicle approached.

"What a situation," she said. "How long can you run?"

"I don't know. It's never come up before."

"I'm sorry," she said. "I don't mean to speak of the unspoken."

"Let's stop at the Paso Real crossroads," he said. "Get a bite. Maybe you can work on my leg there."

She pulled in at the front of Restaurante Hilda but then drove to the edge of the building and parked between the restaurant and the little row of rooms next door, as if she wanted more privacy or might be thinking of renting a room but wanted to eat first. Trying to be discreet, she made them more noticeable. Near the entrance were two pickups, two cars, and parallel with the road, a big rig with its long bed full of tarped goods.

"This is crazy," Helen said. "I feel so conspicuous." Her red hair was windblown and she wore large sunglasses.

"It's a risk," he said. "No doubt about it. Truck-stop gambling."

Despite the rustic charm and shaded convenience of tables under a high-peaked open patio and cut-log stools at the long bar and the pool table and the rear view of a grand, tree-lined, full-size soccer field down below and the distant winding river even lower and the pleasant breeze flowing through the place, Helen brought the food out and they sat in the hot car in the dusty dirt lot eating chicken with rice and beans, antisocial suspicious gringos habitually watching the road for a malicious appearance, an absurd assault coming to breathe down their necks and snare them.

"Do you actually have a plan?" she asked. "Not that I want to know it."

He smiled. "I want to be able to run and keep running if necessary, to be healthy and quick and mostly out of sight."

"What about money?"

"Well, obviously I only have so much cash. After that will be credit cards, ATMs, alarm bells that signal where you're calling from."

"Then what?"

He looked over at the patrons inside, the regular rhythm of freedom and public appearances, the waitress behind the bar glancing up, seeming to look their way. "Right now I'm just free running," he said, "being alone all the time, sweating, having nightmares, not knowing what I'll need to do or where I'll go. How's that for entertainment, for paying the piper for that last dance when the barn burned down?"

She turned away and looked over at the rooms, the one car parked there. Then gathered and bagged their trash. "I guess there's nothing to say about that night," she said, seeking his eyes in the rearview mirror. "Unless you want to talk about it."

"There's no time for that now," he said. "We need to pick up the pace."

"And there's not enough room back there for me to perform surgery," she said, opening her door. "I'll get one of those rooms and they can think whatever they want about us."

"I'll try not to scream too loudly," he said, then reached for his pocket. "Here's some money."

"I'm not taking your cash," she said, and walked away.

She went to the restroom and washed her hands and coming out noticed the poster tacked to the porch post, a call for information on a missing person with an unspecified reward offered and an old faded picture of Ellis. She pulled herself away from it and walked as nonchalantly as possible through the dining area and motioned to the bargirl and asked about renting a room. Two men at the bar turned their heads to follow the inquiry as she was directed to a woman back in the kitchen who wiped her hands and asked the number of nights and number of people and handed over a registration card and pen while Helen floated in place, scratched marks that were words made up on the spot, and said she had forgotten her passport. The woman paused and then accepted the cash and retrieved a key from her apron pocket.

Ellis was sleeping when she opened the door. She drove the car a hundred feet, and they got out with their bags and entered the far room. She placed a towel on the lone bed and he removed his shorts and boxers and reclined with his feet on the floor. She placed another towel over his groin and pulled the single chair to the edge of the bed and opened her first aid kit beside him. She had been a nurse in the States, and she fell into care mode naturally, pushed his knees farther apart, leaned in to clean the red sores on his leg with rubbing alcohol. He flinched violently. She applied a lidocaine cream and he turned his head to see the front window and watched the treeline across the road and the white space above it, the faint permutations of clouds, breathing deeply and gripping bunched bedspread as she removed slivers of wood with tweezers and a hemostat. She hummed and sighed as she worked, and he saw a man donning a devil mask, firing shots in the air, coming up in a forest pool, water dripping from horns and fangs and flared nostrils.

With his thigh shaved and bandaged and taped, he slept, feeling mangled and feckless, his left leg elevated by chair and pillow, and its burns beating like birds on the wing. Her voice woke him.

"Someone's coming."

He roused himself and heard footsteps clicking outside on the concrete porch. As he sat up he saw a man pass the window from the direction of the restaurant, then the audible footsteps receded and ended as the man either stepped down to the ground or stopped walking. Where would he be going?

Ellis opened the door and saw a heavyset man in a ballcap, maybe a trucker, standing a few yards from the end of the building, facing the road with a phone to his ear. As they left and shut the door, the man looked back at them.

Over at Hilda's there was a different assortment of vehicles, a weird custom Civic hatchback with stars painted on its side, a dump truck, a couple of motorbikes, a commonplace crowd taking a common afternoon break, each patron an innocent deadly witness. Helen backed up to the edge of the road and turned out and, at the intersection, continued straight on Highway 2, in the direction of Buenos Aires, San Isidro, San Jose. Ellis sat in front this time.

It did not seem as if they were being followed. He directed her to turn off the highway at the Térraba sign toward Boruca and, after a few climbing curves, asked her to pull over and wait.

"Jesus, I'm all tensed up," she said.

"Let's just see if we're clear," he said.

"He is not going away," she said. "This man means to harm you, Ellis."

"What about the other guy?" he said.

"I don't know. He's much fuzzier, but I doubt he's going away either."

"After a while they'll give up," he said.

"You don't know that. You'll always be looking over your shoulder."

"Whatever happens," he said, "the wheel is in motion. Nothing can be undone."

"But we can influence the future," she said.

"I'll be another mammal in the forest."

"I never thought of you as a survivalist."

"Another major mammal," he said.

—

Vero Beach in May. Hot but the humidity far from full swing. A steady sea wind lofting pelicans in dawn formations, a loose blue tarp flapping over a backdoor scooter, the rhythmic rustling like the sheets in her childhood yard, a memory of her own mother smiling as she reached into the clothespin bag hanging on the line. Pleasant external factors, and memories, hanging on a taut thin line themselves, vanquished in an instant by a baby's cry or a gull's unintended mimicry. Any child, her child. A high cry, and the weight of loss nearly toppled her to the sand. Amy Summers leaned over and sobbed into the sea, her salty tears falling into the wave running over her feet, swirls of ache moving in and out of her like tides.

She struggled on, a shapely woman of bearing and strength, an eastern breeze drying her face, ruffling her hair. Your offspring should never precede you in death. An unpredictable, unspeakable crime of chance. She stood gazing at the horizon, the spreading silvery glow, the visual birth and pain of the new day. Windblown tresses still long and blonde, just beginning to acquiesce to strands of gray intermingling, her bright green eyes inflamed often now but striking like her daughter's. Bold cat eyes, wide and frankly fearless. "Heaven help the stranded mother," she whispered to the sea. "Forgive me."

At her turnaround point she knelt at the high-tide mark and with the gathered fingers of her right hand dug into the sand and wrote the letters that spelled her daughter's name. She stood and surveyed the word—C H L O E—and pronounced it to herself many times over, holding each shoulder with the opposite hand, wanting to send a signal. She knelt again and drew a heart below the middle letter, and then a smaller heart inside the larger one. She thought of the Cummings poem: *I carry your heart with me (I carry it in my heart) I am never without it.* When she stood again she felt light-headed and she closed her eyes and remembered their little girl before her disability, their precocious angel with the crooked smile, the fierce grin of determination, the way she marched with her fists balled up, taking on the world at age four.

When Amy Summers got back to the Sunbeam Motel, she saw her husband coming down the stairs to the parking lot. He looked up and saw her and waved. She waited at the back of the lot, absently noting the morning traffic out on A1A, the dozen or so cars at the motel, the retro sign Jon had had custom-made, its parallel beams of yellow neon luminously ironic at night. She stood removing particles of sand from under her fingernails as he approached.

"Morning," he said, consciously having dropped the word *good* from the greeting lately.

She nodded, smiling weakly.

"There's coffee upstairs," he said, needlessly.

These days she left their apartment for her walk before he was up and stirring in the kitchen. In her new life she was up half the night and tended to recline on the couch, barely dozing.

"What's with you?" she asked, reading his face.

"Oh, the usual research," he said. "I put a flight on hold for next week."

"Don't be ridiculous," she said. "She's gone, Jon."

"We owe her," he said.

"Owe her?" she said. "We gave her every damn thing, spoiled her after the accident, and now she's had another one and that's the end of it."

"We don't know all the details," he said, pointing his finger at her.

"And you think ruining someone else's life will help?"

"I just want answers," he said.

"None of it matters," she said. "Chloe always made her own choices. She died with her best friend. She had her last adventure. Period."

"I don't feel the closure," he said, turning away.

She closed her eyes and pressed her temples with her fingertips. Then stared at him again. "If you insist on keeping this case open you will make it impossible for either of us to move on. Why does there have to be somebody to blame? Chloe wanted to make a statement—talk to Cheryl and hear what Peyton told her, will you just do that? Don't turn it into a witch hunt. Why go after the survivor because he was lucky and she wasn't? Imagine how he feels now."

He frowned. "You act like you know how the whole thing went down."

"It doesn't take a genius to put the pieces together," she said.

"I didn't realize grieving could lead to such insight," he said.

"Try it sometime," she said, extending her arm toward the ocean's wide blue plane. "She's right out there. Your baby. Still fearless."

—

When Millege glanced at but otherwise ignored his phone vibrating in the cup holder, Victor turned to appraise the man's facial reaction, which was nonexistent.

Millege noted the look. "My boss," he said. "A real douchebag. Luckily there are plenty of dead zones down here." He laughed at his joke. "He thinks I think I'm on vacation." He looked at his passenger's blank face. "Douchebag is slang," he said. "Like fuckwad. Or dipshit. No question is too small."

Victor was staring ahead at the road, eyes shifting from side to side as objects or movement drew his attention, squinting slightly without sunglasses, appearing solid in the Rav4's passenger seat, his arm a thick vertical beam in the window's frame. Four horses seeking palm shade along the fenceline, large brown eyes seeming to meet his. A pair of scarlet macaws squawking over the winding Estero Azul, the small white Baptist church, the marina's round cove.

Millege spotted the Intrepid as soon as they got out of the car.

"Son of a bitch," he said. They walked over to the dock and Victor noticed a man watching them from the carport of the small office building. The Intrepid stood out as the dominant vessel in this modest marina. Out by the creek a couple of men could be seen working on a boat under a tarp supported by a bamboo framework.

"Son of a bitch," Millege said as he stood looking at the clean white boat with the twin Evinrudes. "It appears my girl was right."

"You sure that's it?" Victor said.

Millege gave him a quick pursed look, eyebrows raised, his full answer.

He stepped down into the boat for a minute and the office man stepped out into the light and headed over. The investigator saw nothing of interest and climbed out as the dockmaster neared. Millege raised his hand in greeting.

"Good day," he said. "I'd like to speak to the owner about a purchase."

Victor translated as the wiry dockmaster considered the two men.

He informed Victor that the owner wasn't in Sierpe.

"Maybe his friend was using the boat," Millege said, pulling the small photo of Hayden out of his shirt pocket. Victor again translated.

The man studied the photo for a moment and nodded.

Millege threw his hand up and laughed. "This morning, right? Isn't that just the way it goes. Missed him by hours," he said. He offered the dockman his card. "Please call me if you see him again. Muchas gracias," he said.

Not a word was spoken in the car until they reached the Térraba bridge between Palmer Sur and Palmar Norte. Millege spread and drew together his fingertips in imitation of a cast net closing. "I should've listened to Liz," he said.

"Where is she?" Victor said.

"She's ahead of us, making the San Isidro loop with Stavo. She's like a bird dog trying to pick up a scent," Millege said. He was studying the rearview mirror. "I'm not big on clairvoyance," he said, "but she did put the man in Sierpe." He looked over at his associate. "What do you think, a lucky guess?"

The sturdy Boruca man gazed toward the roadside foliage, his eyes fixed in place on the window glass so that botanical shapes streaked by in a screen of running green, and images in his drifting memory, triggered simply by the name Liz, seemed to project outward and fly alongside the car. He saw the young girl he met those many years ago, their private exploratory day in his village during that festival of little devils which proved to be his last. Her defiant red-marked face and his protective stance. Her yearning to connect with him for reasons he scarcely understood, the two of them outsiders and devilish actors themselves, her passionate and rare young kisses by the river meeting his amid the shouts of night revelers raining upon them like random admonitions.

He'd never seen her again, fighting later that night with several other teenagers who made fun of her, making a bloody spectacle of himself and them, leaving a stain on the tribe's annual display of pride. Possessing an innate anger at his own fate, he struggled with the constraints imposed by his stagnant culture, the limitations of the insulated local life that made him feel like a jaguar turning in a cage. He left the reserve at seventeen and dove deeper into troubles that dogged him for years, the twin night hounds of drinking and fighting, his physical efforts to break free of his heritage and himself.

Over the years, his anger was dissipated by physical labor, by bruises and alcohol, and now he sought to escape those clinging clichés too. Yet here he was, in dubious service.

"I don't believe this fucking guy," Millege said.

Without thinking, Victor looked back.

"Normally I'd say use the mirror," Millege said, "but this black Nissan motherfucker obviously doesn't care if we know he's there."

It was apparently true. About a hundred yards

back, the Nissan followed, dropping out of sight on curves and reappearing like a shadow, rippling over the road to match their speed.

"If he tracked us from Sierpe," Millege said, "he started out slicker." He focused on the rearview mirror. "Can you determine if it's just the driver?"

Victor turned around and watched the other car emerging from its river-like turns. "Looks that way," he said. "Plenty of black Nissans around."

Millege smiled. "I feel this conniving freeloader following," he said. "We'll stop at an appropriate place and see what the lazy bastard does next."

The twisting Térraba was often in sight, its pastures and sandbars, its convoluted route muscled by green hills beyond the river plain. To the north and east, isolated clouds rode over the higher elevations like guests meandering to an afternoon party. Invisible villages lay indicated by map names and thin spidery tracks branching off the highway.

"There are no rules of engagement," Millege said, then wished he'd kept the statement inside his head. He looked at Victor staring ahead. Could be more like him, he thought, not such a chatterbox. But then again, Millege considered himself a social person as well as a loner.

In Curré, he pulled over at the entrance to an indigenous school, a compound of buildings, a drooping flag. There were a few people outside and they noticed the waiting car, the two men remaining inside. A few minutes later Millege saw the Nissan approaching. As the car neared, it slowed and crawled past, and the driver's head turned to face them, the figure wearing an unpainted Boruca mask, the blond wood an elongated devil's face scowling at the two men. The car rolled past with the face staring back at them.

Millege looked at Victor, who remained expressionless, unoffended. "Everything just got more complicated," Millege said.

He stepped out of the car and lit a cigar and stood smoking while the villagers observed him. When they moved on, Millege lowered his window and drove slowly and smoked and talked to keep from feeling rattled. He asked Victor where he'd learned English, where else he'd lived.

"Mom sent me to her cousin in San Jose," the younger man said.

"Why, because you were in trouble?"

"Yep. Went to a missionary school there."

"So you became a Christian." Millege was smiling.

"I pretended. Met a church girl who taught English."

"Smart, that paid off well," Millege said. "Did you fall in love?"

Victor looked out at the river. "We got along," he said.

"No doubt," Millege said. "Was she American?"

"Yep. She went up to Managua to another school so I went too."

"Okay," Millege said. "International travel. How'd that go?"

"Fine. Went to Bluefields and worked construction, met some people. Miskito Indians and Rastafarians."

"What about the girl?"

Victor shrugged.

"She kept pushing Jesus," Millege said, "and you had enough."

Victor rubbed his chin and looked hard at Millege. Said nothing.

Millege glanced over. "We need to get some food," he said. "Let's hit that roadside place in Paso Real."

And there sat the black Nissan X-Trail, appearing

unoccupied among other parked cars and a passenger van.

"The fucking tree-shaker," Millege said.

A tall lean man came out of the restaurant and walked with a confident stride to the Nissan. He wore a ball cap and aviator shades and did not look at the blue Rav4 with the men sitting inside. He placed his package on the roof of his car and squatted in the dirt with his back to the watching men as if he'd found something and wished to keep it private. He appeared to be scratching at the ground. He stood and dusted his hands together and got into his vehicle and drove back onto Highway 2 in the northerly direction they were all headed.

They sat for a few minutes and then Millege said, "Wait here," and got out of the car. He stood holding his cold cigar and watching the restaurant, other patrons leaving, then walked over to where the Nissan had been parked. He stood staring down at the spot where the other man had squatted. There were marks drawn in the dirt, and he bent closer to see the meaning, squinting as the block letters coalesced into clarity.

SAVE THE INDIAN. CUT HIM LOOSE.

He straightened and dropped his cigar on the message and ground it around with his foot until the leaves were shredded and the words obliterated.

—

Tribes of the Talamanca. The phrase woke Long Jimmy Finn. Gray stain of dawn, walls washed in grains of texture, a humid bloom thickening the air, clothes strewn across the floor, books toppled, spread and curled like abandoned sandwiches, beloved board dinged in the corner, his bottles, tubes and tins—pills, creams, surf wax, supplements, rubbing alcohol, water, wine, dead tequila on its side—testifying to some kind of tropical apothecary. He stumbled to the bathroom, leaned against the wall with both hands to dangle his free cock over the toilet and loose a stream with eyes closed. At the mirror his slack haggard face stared him down with bloodshot vision. Tequila of the Talamanca. The bohemian surf-poet hung way over. Alone. Nauseous, but not enough to puke, praise be to Jah. Or *Jaja*, the Spanish laugh. No noise but a rooster, then Jimmy himself was the wavering cock of the walk, making his way to the beach, barefoot, shirtless, a dusty feeling of feathers in his mouth.

The salt air administered its tonic. He lay on the wet gray sand and wavelets sculpted his body's impression of itself. Adhesion and gravity held him quick as driftwood. Hair wet, his skull cooled, the metronomic surf clearing his mind, eyes shut to the lightening sky. All the natural clocks kicking in again. The breathing forest, the wakening brain, the stirring birds, the endless waves. The lack of plan totally untimed, the young years ticking by, the spiraling drain of the unfettered life, the crush of the unexpected name. Oh, pretty Peyton.

What does it take to wake you up, to change you? A whale encounter, another form of intelligence, its big rolling eye telling you something important, something overlooked, cracking you open to other possibilities, other points of view? Why can't you just imagine the impact? Intellectualize it. Breathe it in.

He rolled a quarter turn and lay on his side with sand-level sight, the world tilted and changed temporarily. He closed his upper eye. Saw wet round stones as hills or turtles, washed up fronds like iguana profiles linking tree to sea, the working diversity of the colossal biosystem, the deadwood logs tumbled up to the treeline, the great green rise of jungle, the myriad dissections unseen from this low angle—a vast opulence, no roads or wires or plantations in view.

He saw it walking in the distance, as if out of the sea, yet returning to the forest cover. A big brown mammal, long head and snout downward. Jimmy leaned up on one elbow, realigned his sight. An adult tapir strolling toward the trees. The animal stopped and turned his way, looking toward the prone man, its flexible nose lifting for scent, contracting in the air. He saw it searching for him, smelling but not seeing. If he stood it would trot into the trees and vanish, as it soon would anyway, ending this momentary meeting on a desolate shore.

The jungle creature turned back to its path and continued. Had it been walking in the surf before dawn? What for? Leisure? Curiosity? A footbath?

He wished he could follow it, see its wanderings in the canopied gloom, the river and mud baths, the plucking of tender leaves with its short prehensile trunk, like some smaller streamlined new-world version of an elephant.

When it was gone, he walked down the beach to see the tracks. Four toes in front, three in back, the impressions larger than his open hand. Peyton, he thought, your danta has come to me.

—

Enjoy the journey. Relax and renew. Del Preet focused on his breath without being told. Hands on the wheel, eyes ahead but taking in everything without judgment. The workers, the scratched yellow tractors, the spike piles of decapitated pineapples, the northern hills, the empty rearview. *Notice your jaw.* Yes, it's set and determined, yet not tight, not clenched, not locked. He pictured the face behind the calm feminine voice on the CD, cajoling him with tips from *Mindful Moments. Where is your tongue?* He narrowed his eyes, watching himself straying off message, lowering his head toward a yoga mat and then forward into her lap, a sensual cobra pose. *If it's at the roof of your mouth you must lower it.* Where shall I put it? he thought, picturing her serene smile, her closed eyes, the blissful tilt of her head toward the heavens, the long brown ringlets of silken hair cascading past her bare shoulders. *Observe the natural rhythm of breathing. Direct your breath to your belly. Allow your center to fill with fresh clean oxygen.* He pictured himself ballooning up through the sunroof and into the great space above the car while his essence remained slim and steely. He heard waves crashing gently, then strings and flutes, a peaceful cacophony of sounds falling like a vaporous avalanche through his mind to his ribcage, a violin weaving through his chest as the invisible stitching of a surgeon joining breath and body.

Give thanks to the breath of life. Yes, I am thanking the warrior as well. I am the unstoppable avalanche across the valley, seen but not yet heard, suddenly smothering my adversary's doubt-ridden life. He is a toad upon the road. My ribcage is his prison. My breath coats him and slows his lumbering moves, hinders his reaction time. He falters on the path, tripping himself as I breathe deeper. Each exhalation drains away my benign concerns and floats back to him, a cloud wrapping his fat fluffy head. Each wave reaches deeper into my body and purifies my mission. *Allow the wave to wash through you.* Yes, my astute beauty, my smiling sorceress, your modulation rejuvenates me.

"The visualizations in this recording are not intended to be used while operating a motor vehicle," Del Preet said, in sync with the narrator's sly voice.

—

Essentially Stavo was the driver, following the demonic girl's lead as she tried to intuit their way to the American fugitive. She spoke calmly and sometimes pointed to a turnoff, a place at the side of the road where she could step out and stand around, facing different directions for a while, often with her eyes shut, while he sat in the vehicle and thought about her, wondered how she managed life with such a defining mark, how she ever found a boyfriend or had sex, or what her childhood was like and how her parents had treated her, and her teachers and all the other kids, especially the meanest ones who thought nothing of harassing a dog or throwing rocks at a turtle or breaking the tail off a lizard. For a time, he had been one of those uncivilized kids, somewhere around his fourteenth year when he had undergone a growth spurt and made bad, indecent friends and sought to be seen as a risk taker, a daring braggart who backed up his boasts and insults with crude bullying behavior that was more reckless and inhumane than he rightfully felt inside.

He understood the concept of a team effort, appreciated the value of team spirit, of working together for a common cause. But he couldn't relate to this girl, his temporary partner, his coworker, his freakish fellow employee, the so-called scarlet charlatan. Couldn't honestly believe in her method of pursuit. He kept looking for ways to elevate his own position, make himself more valuable to the team, prove himself to their employer, Mister Philip Millege.

The truth was that he had misrepresented himself a little and now felt he was falling behind. He had found the girl, true, though she wasn't actually at that time *his* girl, meaning his accomplice or associate, as he had indicated to Phil Millege, as if he and Liz had an established working relationship. He had simply asked a friend at Rio Sierpe Tours for a local with a boat who knew the water well and would be free enough to guide off-hours custom tours. When he spoke to Liz on the phone, he said he was hiring her for an American but she would report to Stavo until their boss came onboard, literally, as in the moment they stepped into her boat in Sierpe and began the search in earnest. He told her she should not act as if she and he were meeting for the first time, but should be cool and speak only when necessary. Admittedly, he was shocked at the first sight of her face but then felt that this off-putting stigma might prevent her from getting too close to Phil Millege and could possibly work in Stavo's favor. And, to be fair, in a stroke of brilliance he had suggested that she take a look at the burn site to get a feel for the seriousness of the case. But it turned out she actually, unbelievably, found the girl's glass eye, and when she showed it to the boss Stavo saw instantly that she rose to the top spot on the employee team. Millege started calling her his little bird dog and treating her like the leader despite the fact that Stavo had brought her on and personally felt, he was resolutely sure, a greater desire to apprehend the criminal.

Stavo imagined himself as the guy who ran down the fugitive, who tackled him in a crowd of innocent, unsuspecting people, possibly saving countless lives when the trapped terrorist became frightened and desperate and finally completely unhinged and dangerous again. The man had shown these tendencies already and, in Stavo's mind, was a time bomb waiting to go off. The capture could be one of those moments when bravery is revealed and people see a hero where they had seen none before. It was a question of having the physical strength, the wits, the fearlessness, to do what needed to be done. Stavo gazed out the window at his short plump companion as she stared at the highway ahead, her hair blowing wildly in dark tangles like a witch in the midst of a spell descending from the wind, staring in the direction they were going already, toward a destination they would be getting closer to, wherever it was, if they were in the car driving instead of stopped here, doing whatever they were doing. Maybe the guy was just getting out of his parked car up ahead and they were missing this chance at a dramatic capture because the little carnival woman was feeling around in the air with the tentacles of her devilish mind.

True, it was a shared task, a group effort, but the takedown could be a spectacular act of individual courage, an explosion of innate powers he had honed and developed through the challenges a mature man faced and rose to accept and grasp, the culmination of a diligent period of awareness and deduction manifested and remembered as an amazing solo display of cunning and daring. Perhaps even historic in the recording and retelling to future generations. He pressed his palms together and increased the pressure until his hands and forearms and shoulders were vibrating with energy and power.

She got in the car and pulled back her wild hair and looked at him until he declined to return the stare any longer. He started the engine.

"What'd you learn?" he said, grinning, looking back to clear himself.

"Nothing about your unfortunate daydreams," she said.

In the car's silence with the wipers sluicing back and forth, she directed him onward with her hand toward Buenos Aires, and they left the highway and slowed to a halt in a line held up by road work and rain. Cement pipe sections were stacked beside the jointed yellow arm of a backhoe, or as Liz's father called them, industrial digging insects. Red soil washed over the road, and as their lane moved forward Stavo's worn tires spun and slid on the mud plane and his van took out an orange cone. Liz reclined her seat slightly and leaned her head back on the headrest, and he imagined her critical thoughts steered, as his were, to the practical necessity of using a 4x4 for a mission like this, not a coastal minivan best suited to the loading of babies and groceries.

They rolled slowly into town, scanning the sheltered storefronts and the observable residents moving along under umbrellas and plastic ponchos. Stavo suggested they call Phil Millege and get further instructions. They would need to find a room somewhere, or rooms, he meant, not believing they would be instructed to share, not with the business expense account of Phil Millege at their disposal. His eyes crept over to Liz Zuniga as she gazed out the passenger window, her facial blemish hidden at that angle, and he imagined her getting undressed, removing her shirt, pushing her tight jeans down over her hips and standing in her bra and panties as he casually drank some water and studied a map of the area while sitting by the window in the room's single wooden chair.

She faced forward again just as a car horn blared, and Stavo jerked the wheel to pull his minivan out of the lane of oncoming traffic.

"You should get some coffee," she said.

"Why not," he said. "I can call Phil Millege at the same time."

He dropped her at the bus station to use the restroom while he went to gas up the car and inquire about the gringo. She roamed among the people in the station's adjoining stalls, glanced at the produce and sweets and shoes, and then stood beneath a corner restaurant's overhang in her jungle hat and turned in a slow pivot to cover the two hundred and seventy degrees away from the building at her back where working men sat on counter stools watching as she cast her mind out into the rainy air. She felt restless in the public eye and closed her eyes to focus inward and outward. She rotated again, her senses circumventing the dripping trees, the pelted roof, the murmur of background voices, the whining motorbikes. She heard passing rubber boots squeaking evenly like windshield wipers, felt shopkeepers across the way accusing her. A car's tires over wet pavement made the staccato hissing of angry whispered voices. Then a suggestive whistle rose, drowned out by bus brakes. A dog crunched bones on the ground to her right.

She crossed the street, rain rolling off her hat, passed a lawyer's office on the corner, and walked the unpaved drive into the property of the town's only hotel, Cabinas La Flor. No one appeared to be there aside from the occupants of a couple of cars parked under trees in the far corner treating the place as a semiprivate meeting point. Her sensors spread, seeking out kindness, fear, friendship, truth, tension, masquerades.

Hello Liz, he said. Ellis seemed to have slipped out of the building on a layer of air, a trick of her mind. *How is your family? How's your dad doing?*

She frowned and scolded him in a mixture of Spanish and English. *You are too open here*, she said, gesturing toward the street, the town, as if he should be somewhere underground instead. *Men are coming.*

Who's coming?

Gustavo and Mr Phil.

Is Mr Phil nice to you?

She stared at the trees, clasping her hands together in irritation, then cast her eyes toward the office door, the dark window glass. *He is not a bad man*, she said, *but he doesn't stop. He is always looking, always pushing.*

Like a dung beetle, Ellis said, *rolling his heavy burden.*

She stood silently, not expecting a sensible analogy or explanation.

Are you scared? she asked.

I'm fine, happy to see you.

Her frown softened. She felt foolish to have left her umbrella in the car but not to be seen having this phantom conversation in the rain, her innate strangeness consistently protected within her fortified public walls. *We will stay in San Isidro tonight*, she said.

The three of you?

Mr Phil has another local man with him.

What about the other American? he said.

She hesitated.

Have you seen him?

She shook her head. *He is a shadow man.*

A shadow man, he said. *That can't be good.*

No, she said.

You need to be careful, he said, squeezing her shoulder. She looked up at him and he pulled her closer, hugged her and kissed the top of her head.

She stayed in this ghost embrace, arms hanging at her sides, her reddening face pressed against his chest, the sweat of his shirt mixed with the clean rain. She closed her eyes, trying to quell her roaming mind for these few warm, rare, unjudged moments.

"Can I help you?" The hotel manager had pushed open his office door.

"Oh!" she said. "No, thank you." She turned to leave, her face inflamed.

"Is someone meeting you?" he said. "You're getting soaked."

"Yes," she said as she moved away. "He's right across the street."

—

mas (more) costa rica
peypad
To: Cheryl Paddington
hey mom, we're still alive, sorry for the lack of writing lately. i developed a new passion and no i'm not talking about a guy or a band. lol.
seriously i've actually sort of changed lately. maybe i'm finally growing up. i can't even really explain it but i'll try. i guess i was open to change, as people say these days, just by being here with the jungle all around and the smells and sounds of this concentration of life, the incredible biodiversity that suddenly hit me and actually hit me in the form of one particular animal. here it comes - the danta (locally) aka baird's tapir (or maybe any tapir since there are other types in other parts of the world). wow huh? look it up.
anyway as hard as it is to believe, my eyes, and chloe's one (joke) have been opened in a new way. honestly this time i'm the leader and she's going along and i guess she likes the idea and the encouragement of our friend ellis, the expat guy i mentioned before.
mom, did you know that the 3 toed sloth descends to the ground to defecate once a week? yes i'm wondering how long this act takes too. lol. we have seen a few, not defecating but just hanging in trees. they have algae growing on their backs like green paint some ecowarrior sprayed to make their fur undesirable. not that anyone

wants sloth fur but they will kill jaguars and any jungle cats just to get their beautiful skins. pretty sick.

nature fact #2 - leaf cutting ants allow ten percent of the light to reach the forest floor. yeah you don't call orkin for that kind of bug benefit. everything works together mom.

all this kind of stuff is prompting us to venture into the jungle to see a wild danta. or try to i mean. not telling you this to scare you or make you worry but just because it's real and what we're doing now. a major seismic shift, right? lol.

not surfing as much but eating tons of fruit and rice and beans and maybe a few beers to complete the balanced meal. lol. seriously mom we are doing great and feeling really good about this trip. you will see a new girl when i get home. not sure when yet since we are embarking on new adventures to explore more nature and help the natural world survive the attacks people and companies inflict for their selfish greedy reasons.

love to you & dad & paula & simon & snowball, peyton

15. The Zuniga Factor

Leonardo Zuniga rose before dawn as usual and stepped out his back door and down the three wooden steps to the soft ground. He breathed the new day's air deeply and raised his eyes and then his hands in tribute to the greater world above. He liked the early stillness, the assorted chirps and calls that acknowledged his presence as he acknowledged the other random lives around his. He walked to the corner of his plot at the edge of the long brooding palm rows and stood before the stone ball he called his *luna piedra*, his moon stone, and placed his hand on its pocked and mottled surface, his daily communion with this puzzling inanimate object. He believed his ancestors had constructed the sphere somewhere up in the hills and had somehow rolled it down to line the road to their temple or pay tribute to the universe or had employed it for some such illustrious purpose. Whatever their creative reasons, the stone balls fit both into that prior cosmology and into his today, linking them through the centuries of time between. And though he believed the studies done by educated men and women, the experts in archaeology and antiquities, he also felt an unearthly connection to this gnomic symbol of space and time.

He steadied his small two-step ladder against the curve of the sphere and climbed up and leaned over it, spreading his thin arms wide and pulling himself on top of the great stone ball, stabilizing himself on hands and feet. He tucked his shoulder and rolled over and lay on his back and felt it crack as he let his arms and legs extend down the rough surface of the sphere. He faced the dark heavens and pictured himself traveling through them, the ball flying like a meteor with his body held firmly against it by the force of its movement.

He lay in this meditative position for long minutes of unchecked time, his body rooted to the earth and his mind loose in the sky, soaring up above the world and seeing the planet as one complete entity, the wondrous space photos he had seen in a magazine coloring his view of the blue planet in the cosmos, the only home anyone had ever known. Unless there were others far beyond the scope of his own thinking on the subject. Like in the movies.

Back inside, he put a pot of water on the stove to make coffee. The floor creaked as he moved to the bedroom where his wife slept. Her statue of blue-robed Mary stood watching over the room from her shelf in the corner but the figure did not provide him the comfort he got from his great round moon stone. Still, his wife remained a believer in the Sacred Mother, and they each tolerated their few disparate beliefs in the miraculous love they had forged and sustained during their forty-nine years together.

He sat on the bed and looked at her, his Isabel, in the pale light cast from the front room, her long gray braid splayed across the pillow, her creased and beautifully solemn face serene, her breaths soft and her eyelids beginning to flutter toward wakefulness. He held her hand and said the quiet words he repeated daily. "Thank you, my love, for waking again to be with me for another day in this life." He kissed her wrinkled hand and she opened her eyes.

In the kitchen she went about her tasks as if still asleep. As if she were moving through water, her smiles as brief as shooting stars. When their eldest son Roberto stopped by, he sat with his father at the table and quietly noted his mother's continuing distraction, her subdued nervousness over the coming move, her dissatisfaction as obvious as the banality of his arguments.

"She is only happy when she's sleeping," Leo said.

Isabel went on stirring a pot as if she hadn't heard.

"Sometimes," Roberto said, yet again, "we are the victims of progress."

Leo smiled and nodded. His son worked for PPOI as a field inspector, directly concerned with quality control over the raw material. "Progress knows no limits," Leo said. "Enough is a word with no meaning. Sometimes more forest must go, other times a house." He held his son's patient gaze, still smiling as if everything was simple to understand and explain and accept.

"I know I've said this before," Roberto said, "but a house is just a house."

"Yes," Leo said, "there is no soul or feeling to leave behind. And we can roll my big ball down the road into town. We'll get a couple of friends to help."

"Papi," Roberto said, "you can't take what you don't own."

"It sits on my land," Leo said.

"It's not your land now."

"I didn't sell anything. Your mother doesn't want to move."

"Let's not start that again," Roberto said. "I've told you I'll try to get a machine over here to move the stone to the edge of the common field."

"So football players can sit on it between games," Leo said. "Children can carve their initials in it and draw crude pictures with colored chalk."

"You can visit anytime you like. It'll be part of the community."

"But not us anymore."

"You'll be just down the road. You have to go with what's available."

"We can wait."

"Papi, there's no more waiting. You have to let me help you."

Leo walked out the front door and down the dirt road toward the playing field. He felt betrayed, his son taking money for him as if he were a child, holding it so the deal could be completed and his own parents could be ousted from their old homestead, one of the original United Fruit Company houses. Of course they were extremely fond of Roberto's wife and the three grandchildren, two boys and a girl, nearly grown now, but that didn't excuse the selling out of one's own parents.

His other son, Ernesto, the middle child, did not come around much. He worked for PPOI too, driving a delivery truck between the plantations and the processing plant. He said he was too busy to stop often, and when he did, he had little to say. He was polite but seemed to lack curiosity or the desire to improve himself. He was a mystery to his father and preferred the company of other drivers and childhood friends. He was divorced and childless and either unable to or uninterested in finding another wife. Nonetheless, Leo and Isabel had always treated their sons as equally as possible.

And then there was the little one, the unexpected third, the blemished princess, a late-in-life delivery plainly marked as special. Leo had always done his best to make her feel loved and cherished despite the taunts and teasing she had endured throughout her childhood. They called her the scarlet macaw, even though she was never a squawker, and this, along with the other hurtful words, had torn him inside and made her mother weep. All he could do was heap as much love as possible upon his treasured girl, take her everywhere he went and defend her honor with his life, developing a stony gaze that often disarmed the pitiful looks and careless comments before they were launched.

Liz would bring him books and magazines from the homes of the Americans she worked for. She fed his interest in science and history, helped him expand his mind with new discoveries and developments by translating as much as she could, by teaching him the English words she knew.

He stood alone in the grass field between the colorful neighborhood and the road into Sierpe, looking back at the line of old faded houses, their rusted roofs, the shade trees in between, some houses two-story and some pink, his pale green place over at the far northern edge, a creaky shack really, the smoky blue hills in the distant background. He was an old man now, his plight well known, standing in view of his neighbors and anyone passing on the road. Still, he felt strong, was amazed that he had lived here so long with the woman he loved, had raised a family and was now on the verge of leaving.

He watched as Roberto's car pulled out onto the road, his son's arm extended in a wave. Leo waved back and his eyes followed an empty palm nut truck pulling into the vacant area beside the maintenance shed across the way. He looked to see if the driver was Ernesto. As he waited, a small gray pickup turned off the road and traveled along the dirt track and stopped at his house.

Walking back, Leo saw a man and a woman emerge from the truck, and as he got closer, recognized the man, an American who had visited them once before and who stood waiting by the vehicle. The man had come with Liz the first time, had met her because he knew the owner of one of the properties she looked after, and was now evidently her friend. But this woman, Leo realized as he approached them, was a stranger to him.

In his tan trousers and white collared shirt and worn sandals, with his compact wiry frame and thin gray mustache, Leo looked exactly as he had when Ellis met him a few months before. They shook hands as Isabel came out, and Ellis introduced them both to Chloe. "She's a tourist," he said, upturning his palms in a show of helplessness, and they smiled at this.

The men unloaded several boxes from the truck's bed and brought them inside. Ellis and Isabel, she in her plain floral cotton dress and flip-flops, her braid hanging over one shoulder, began to go through the boxes, pulling out and separating clothes, kitchen utensils, books, and magazines.

Leo motioned for Chloe to follow him out back and they walked through the grasses and weeds toward the rows of tall African palms. Cicadas cut the warm air with their ratcheting buzzes and dragonflies drew aerial geometries from one high frond to another. A white hawk flew in a silent flicker, receding through the tunneled shade of the trees as if into a deep cave. At the edge of the grove the sphere looked to Chloe like a neglected sculpture. They stopped before it and Leo watched her face for a reaction. He noticed her artificial eye and she felt him staring at her as she placed her hands on the surface of the sphere and leaned forward as though she wanted to roll it. He felt a catch in his throat and his mind flooded with thoughts of his daughter, her facial disfigurement, his immense love for her, as this young foreign woman in shorts and sun shirt crouched and then leapt onto the great stone, scrambled to find her footing and stood atop it almost instantly, extending her arms horizontally in front and in back, knees bent, assuming a surfer's pose. She smiled down at him, green eyes shining, her long limbs lithe and strong, her athletic posture resolute and poised. She dazzled him, and Leo's eyes brimmed with tears.

"The Silver Surfer," she said, "on his new galactic ride."

He nodded without understanding a single word.

She lowered herself and sat atop the stone, crossing her bare legs and placing the backs of her hands on her thighs, palms up, her back straight, in another pantomime, her attempt to show that she appreciated his showing her the stone, that she liked it without needing language to express it, and could see herself meditating on it. "I'm kind of a show-off," she said.

Leo smiled and said in Spanish, "We are happy for your visit."

She didn't understand him but smiled anyway.

"You look comfortable and natural on the great stone," he said.

She stared at him and he returned the gaze and she said, "I feel you."

He looked back at the house. "The company will destroy our home and damage this great stone," he said. "Or they may transport it to the plant manager's yard."

He looked at the girl as she reached out for his hand. He stepped closer and took her fingers in his. "I don't know what's happening here," she said, "but I want to help the situation however I can."

"Your visit is a gift," he said. "You remind me of my daughter."

"It's funny," she said. "I feel like there's some hidden energy trying to find me. Just now. Crazy, right?"

He squeezed her hand once more and released it. "You like coffee?"

"I understand that word," she said. "Thank you, sir."

"You are both strong fighters," he said. "Always walking uphill."

The wooden table was covered with a blue-checkered cloth, cups and spoons were placed for the two guests, along with a small plate of cookies. From a dented pot Isabel poured hot coffee into chipped cups and set a glass bowl of sugar between them. She apologized for the lack of milk.

"Not important," Ellis said. "We are all here together. Please," he said, indicating the other chairs, but the old couple remained standing nearby, giving the Americans some privacy while still invading it, occupying some middle ground between deference and hospitality.

Chloe tasted her coffee and smiled at Isabel. "Good," she said, and then spoke to Ellis. "Just tell them I lost my eye at age nine, okay?"

He told them. Then stood with his cup in the open doorway looking out at the other houses along this communal stretch, some small kids walking on the dirt track and pointing at him. He saw a man in a hat crossing the playing field on a horse, the vast palm groves across the road defining this small world.

Leo joined Ellis at the door and Isabel sat with Chloe at the table.

"They say anyone can change the world," Ellis said. "One man, one woman. Working against giant companies. Do you believe that?"

"It's possible," Leo said. "She is a strong woman. Your girlfriend."

Ellis smiled. "We're just having fun. Nothing too serious."

Leo raised his hands in an innocent gesture, eyebrows lifting slightly, not prying, yet not convinced either.

"How is your daughter?" Ellis asked.

"She's fine, also a strong woman."

"She's cool," Ellis said. "I like her a lot."

They all sat together at the table and spoke of the injustice and uncertainty of the upcoming move, Ellis translating as much as he could. The three roaming children were soon heard giggling and seen peeking their heads in the door, playing a game like miniature spies, eager to know things and brag to others and innocently instigate the passing of gossip and rumors about foreigners and money and impending trouble.

"They're such beautiful real people," Chloe said as they got in the car. "And so helpless. It's a fucking shame they can be treated so callously."

"Same old story," Ellis said. "The only difference here is your personal connection. Knowing the victims," he said, watching in his mirror the old couple standing together in their modest tilted doorway.

"I think she must be very rich," Isabel was saying. "But she presents herself as humble and imperfect."

"I doubt she has trouble taking vacations," her husband said.

"And she must certainly be intimate with him," she said.

"That would not be surprising," Leo said.

They watched the truck turn out on the road and vanish. Isabel put her hand on Leo's bony shoulder. "I think Elizabeth was intimate with him too."

He looked at her, touched her cheek. "I hope so, my dear," he said.

16. The Rain and the Little Devils

The night was one mask, the rain another, the drumming on the roof a third, the drenched, hissing trees a fourth, layer upon layer of obliteration so solid he felt like a cocoon dweller. These worked both ways for adversaries, shielding each side from the other. On the dark porch he stood gazing beyond the pouring water screen through trees and over ravines and grainy hillsides toward the distant ridgeline of Panama. To his right he caught glimmers of light from another cabin, the nearest one he supposed, though the terrain made this assumption uncertain. Arriving as the rain began, Ellis had rented the simple cabin at dusk and in getting to it got a limited sense of the vastness of the property. Forgotten Valley. Seriously? he had wanted to ask. And then realized the B-movie name, plus the eco-space, suited him, at least in the short term. Which everything now was. Short term. He raised his glass of rum in a toast to the dark mask of night. He wouldn't be mingling at the bar, nor would he be forgotten, not in the short term.

He stood at the rail, an invisible target pouring another glass, and thought of the biological corridor he roamed within. Where was your old Jasper Johns target T-shirt when you needed it? Faded blue and yellow circles, the washed-out-red background, the collar frayed but the shirt soft and still striking. Jessie wore it and decided she liked it too, and he said, "Sure baby, looks great on you, everything does, including nothing." She was wearing it right now in some Vancouver bar, he imagined, girl and shirt both looking good. Or using it as her go-to pajama top, cotton panties rounding out her sleep ensemble. He drank, pictured the artsy target on his own chest, spread his arms wide and was on the mocking verge of yelling out *Take a shot then, motherfucker.*

The rain lessened. He saw the nearest lights more clearly, and then much blurrier, his night vision fuzzed with liquor.

Inside, he turned on the dim bathroom lamp and navigated by that, had his pocket flashlight for outside. Kept his glass full and the door to the porch open, the drips and frogs providing the soundtrack to his solitude. He had some crackers and cheese but wasn't hungry. He opened the kitchen cabinets and drawers out of curiosity, habit, sat on the bed under the ceiling fan, notepapers rustling on the table, pages of memory turning in his head. Spring mushroom foraging back in Oregon, bag of morels hanging on his back, dogs sniffing around, the moisture in the air, the spongy woods underfoot. The great breathing trees.

The bedside drawer damp-stuck, he yanked it open and noticed green particles spread like spilled spice, pinched a clump and smelled it. Weed. Someone left their shake, their bud crumbs. He drank, set his glass down, withdrew the drawer and knocked the leaf pieces into a corner—a good pipe-full, if one had a pipe—stood and wiped the dining table with the edge of his hand, upended the drawer and spilled its contents onto the smooth surface.

He poured another drink and stood studying the room, thinking of pipe options: foil, tin can, hollowed palm-nut chillum. And a flame, which the stove could provide. But a pipe? He looked in the barren fridge again. The drawers, the cabinets with minimal kitchenware.

He sat at the table making little sandwiches, a slice of cheese and sprinkled weed between two crackers. Took his plate outside and ate and drank until every crumb was consumed and leaned back for a while and nodded off for a few moments it seemed, then felt himself oozing into the environment, his body sinking in increments too small to completely fathom, the porch boards rising to meet him, his own audible breaths deeper and more pronounced, each an anchor keeping mind and flesh together even as they grew apart, the glass on the floor an object of art, separate and distinct, able to rise to his mouth as his jaw clenched and he chewed the residue of flavors in his mouth like cud, methodically, swallowing and gazing about in slow motion, a silent warped wizard of the night, seeing the bottle inside, a tannic elixir far away now, and wondering how to get it closer, swallowing harder in what felt like involuntary and purposeful actions at once, his body heavy and his mind's eye lifting like smoke, scanning around to look for torches on the trail, his head gaming him in a spiraling high.

He pushed himself erect, floating and then laughing as he took a baby step, then another, discovering with joy that he could walk freely, primitively, an ape upright and thinking, leveling out into action, saying aloud, "That shit is the shit." He laughed again, and added, "Well put, well said," and this made him laugh harder, gliding on air as he threaded the doorway and found himself inside, marveling at the simple beauty of the room, the perfect arrangement of the individual articles, the furniture, and then the dwelling itself in this dark countryside setting, nestled like an bird in a nest in a tree in a forest in a country in a continent in a planet in a solar system in a galaxy in a cosmos.

Fresh drink in hand, he landed on the porch and peered at the lights again, one minute obscured by waving trees, the next seemingly approaching. He squinted to see if they were actually moving, set his drink on the railing, leapt to the ground, found himself loping down the path, bare feet in the dirt.

Consider the path of the tapir. The dense cover, the shady gloom, the preponderance of leaf and mud and water in an overarching biomass. The rivers, the established trails, the smells of fruits and tender shoots, the agile solid steps, ears turning, proboscis periscoping in perpetual wariness. Thick hide, thorn and insect resistant, the brown bristled skin. The largest mammal around. In the dusk, in the river's cool comfort, you feel content and agile. A natural escape route. You can run along a river bottom like a hippo.

A shrill whistle. Another of your kind standing in the track, snout lifted. No other threat present. Competition acknowledged but no ground given. You mark your area and now your high-pitched squeaks let the other bull know he should move on. Both loners able and willing to use their teeth and jaws. A squeaking standoff, the other nosing around, head down, nut-hunting in the soil, then he drifts back into the bush and vanishes.

There is the nearby openness of a cattle ranch, the stench of that concentration of fenced beasts eliciting the instinct to circumvent. Constraints of the corridor perceived, often you walk in circles now. You push along the track, scenting for family and predator alike. Darkness deepens and your other senses guide you without the need to see well. Do you have some sense of the dwindling world, the squeezing advances on all sides, the thinning avenues weaving between farm and ranch, between the roads cut for wood, for the extraction of goods? You smell the machines, the hunters, the men and roaming dogs, as if the big cats weren't enough to jolt your jungle heart. And they are fewer too, the puma and the jaguar, so you all negotiate the patchwork land left, stumble upon the surprise of new clearings, foreign compounds, the eco-worlds built to be near the wild species, so guides can bring them close, the monkey watchers, the binoculared birders, to catch a mating exchange or see your deep footprints, to spy you between zones, trotting across a clearing, wallowing in stream-bank mud or swimming like a horse, trying to avoid their encroachment, seeking sanctuary among secondary growth and under culled canopies, running from earth-moving engines, the constructed interruption of rivers, while you become a more exposed version of yourself.

The clearest way into the universe is through a forest wilderness. So said Muir, Ellis remembered as he emerged from the wet woods, these words engraved in his mind. He watched the dimly lit cabin and reasoned it must be his. He felt his muddy hands and heavy tender feet, witnessed a giant blossom of bamboo spiked against the opening sky, the stars above his infinitesimal vulnerability down here on the ground.

He jogged across the clearing, a major mammal seeking shelter. Our best intentions backfire, our dark thoughts run rampant, our visions engulf us. The cabin seemed like a shed as flames erupted and he stopped in the open yard and relived a fire from this perspective, kneeling and then falling to his hands in an animal posture, wonder and freedom turning to sickness. He hung his head, his eyes dripping, the beautiful girls forever trapped and burning, beating their fists against the inside of his skull, the heat of their cries seared into the folds of his brain like brands with no removal ever possible.

—

Millege's unanswered phone went to voicemail.

I don't know where the fuck you've gone but you'd better get to a working zone ASAP. My man Felipe is expecting your call this week. Everyone down there is eager to wrap this shit pronto. In case you missed it I'm emailing you a story from yesterday's Courier, a rehashing of the original plus addendum. The reporter received a credible copycat threat to hit the main processing plant, which is really tipping your hand, obviously an amateur or a fake but nothing left to chance here. Once our arsonist punk is prosecuted and made to denounce his pissant, tourist-killing crime, we think things will settle down. Find him, secure him, take him in and make sure you see Felipe in person. Then you're done. Release your squad, send in your final report, get up to my office for the travel tally and debrief and let's put this fucking groundhog to bed. Tighten up.

Millege sat sipping a margarita in the bar of the Hotel San Isidro. He put his phone to his ear and played Hiller's message again. Victor stood at the tinted front door staring out at the highway traffic and the dusky sky, drinking a beer while rain clouds rolled in from the Talamancas. They were three kilometers from town, out among the auto-repair businesses, positioned defensively in a stand-alone, modest establishment next to a pharmacy, all but invisible in a corner room whose darkened door faced the entrance to the property and whose darkened windows looked into the adjoining restaurant. It was the sort of nondescript place with clean sight lines Millege felt would suit their target well. If he even came to this town.

"What's up?" Victor said as the first drops hit.

"Let's talk it over when the other guys get here," Millege said.

The restaurant and the bar were empty of other customers. It was nearly dark. Corralled by the small bar itself, the lone silent bartender struck the nonchalant pose of a bored connoisseur, leaning back in a burgundy jacket against a narrow strip of wall beside shelves of liquor bottles, arms folded across his chest. Victor pulled another metal table and two chairs next to theirs as rain hammered the pavement. A car turned off the highway, its lights raking the hotel's facade, then passed out of view along the side of the building. A few moments later a purple umbrella hovered along outside the restaurant's corner windows and was then collapsed and shaken at the door as its owner backed inside.

"Ah," Millege said, "our little bird dog is home." He tapped on the bar's window and she looked up at the dark glass and then at the adjoining door.

The girl entered, removing her floppy hat and unwinding her scarf. She slipped her backpack off and unzipped her wet jacket and looked at the two men as she came forward. She abruptly stopped, staring at the Indian as he stared at her, so still in the dusk light he seemed cut from stone.

"You two know each other?" Millege asked. He looked from one to the other as the tension held and neither moved nor spoke.

The fourth member of the team passed the windows in a running crouch, pushed inside the restaurant holding his small wet duffel and stood dripping at the door, his black hair plastered to his head, his white shirt stuck to his chest, his eyes wild, as if he had urgent news from the front. Millege tapped the glass and Stavo jumped, his suspicious gaze turning to the entire empty room before he focused on the door to the bar. He wiped his face and strode ahead. Upon entering, he sized up the bartender and the silent stranger behind Liz and then nodded to Millege and saluted like a soldier reporting for duty.

"Spit it out," Millege said.

Stavo shook his head and stood shivering slightly.

"Why didn't you share the umbrella?" Millege asked.

"I don't use one, sir."

"Really?" Millege looked at Liz for help.

"Not a purple one, sir," she said. "It's not macho."

Millege lifted his drink as if in a toast. "Do you want a margarita?" he asked. "It has a feminine name."

"Yes, sir, that drink is for either," Stavo said, still standing at attention.

"Glad we cleared that up," Millege said. "Check in and change and we'll have our meeting and eat dinner. Reception's right through the dining room."

Stavo turned on his heel, shouldered his bag and walked stiffly through the restaurant door.

In the manner of the two-faced god Janus, Liz looked forward and into the past at once, attempting to ascertain if a person's direct stare was due to the obvious reason or if they had met previously. She felt a twitch in her memory, saw youth in the lined face and somber eyes of the indigenous man.

"Liz," he said, and the room took on a bluish tint.

She seemed to tumble over a waterfall, her name in his mouth, her mind plummeting in space.

Victor took a long stride forward and caught her elbow as she leaned on the nearest chair.

She looked up at his face, reeling in the embrace of his presence as he took her hat and scarf, placed her umbrella on the table, and leaned closer. His name was inscribed in permanent marks in the catalog of her teenage years, the Boruca boy's position singular in the private jeweled box of her earliest and most precious erotic remembrances.

"Well, look," Millege said, "Victor should get us some drinks so we can celebrate whatever this is and get ready for our meeting."

Victor squeezed her small hand and trailed his fingers along hers as he released it. "What would you like?" he asked.

"Just water," she said. "Thank you, Victor."

His face took on a lopsided smile as he walked to the bar.

Millege looked at Liz looking at him, her lips tight, eyes sheepish, her face red beyond the regular red borders.

"You okay?" he said.

"Yes, sir," she said. "Only surprised."

"So you met Victor a long time ago."

"Yes. At the little devils festival in his village. We were kids."

"And you haven't seen each until now?"

"Never, sir."

"Wow, this does call for a team celebration. Sit over here," he said.

She moved to the table, glancing at Victor as he turned to see her.

Millege smiled. "Before we get all nostalgic and misty," he said, "let's focus on the job at hand. Where

The Path of the Tapir

do you see our swinging squirrel monkey?"

She paused, taking in the scene concentrically, seeing rings of reality expanding away from her, his hazel eyes and wide stubbled face, the cigar in his shirt pocket, his thick ringless fingers at the table's edge, her long-lost Indian boy with drinks in his hands, the bartender wiping, two cars parked at the rear, the rolling highway pelted by rain. She saw shaved swaths of hillside and the land rising upward to the cordillera and the rivers cutting down both sides to the seas and the drifting motions of clouds and the people coming and going like mice and the waking dream of Ellis in Buenos Aires that afternoon.

"He is not moving," she said.

"From where?"

"Back there."

"You mean the direction we came from?"

"Yes, sir."

"So you mean we overshot him or took a wrong turn?"

"I think so, yes."

Millege rubbed his forehead, then said, "Try again."

She closed her eyes, heard the drinks placed on the table, a chair scraped across the floor, smelled the lime and tequila, felt Victor sitting near her, tilting her energy into his orbit, her scalp heating, the roots of her hair tingling, the hotel corridors, the rows of rooms, movement in the parking lot.

"The other man," she said.

"What?" Millege leaned forward. "You mean the fucking tree-shaker?"

She opened her eyes. "The shadow American is here," she said.

"In San Isidro?"

She nodded, drank her water, and Victor went to the bar for more.

The yellow-walled room was clean and tidy, with one large bed in a basic wooden frame, an open wardrobe with a box television on top, a ceiling fan plus a standing fan, a desk and chair, white tile floor, two framed pastoral scenes, and a bathroom on the outer side of the room, next to a yellow-draped picture window facing the exterior common walkway. Stavo hung his wet shirt on a hanger on the shower rod and pulled his other white shirt out of his duffel bag and shook it vigorously and laid it on the bed. He stood in front of the mirror examining himself, his chest and abs and neck, combing his hair with his fingers. He washed his face and armpits and was toweling himself dry when he heard a light tapping sound. He stepped out into the main room and stood listening, his impression being that someone was either at the door or outside on the walkway. Probably a dinner summons, he thought, expecting a knock. Then he turned and stared at the window, sensing movement out there.

The main light-blocking drapes were still open, bundled by matching yellow-cloth ties on each side, and the inner white liner was partially open, hung up on one side behind the outer drapes, leaving a tall vertical triangle of the window glass visible, illuminated by ambient light from the walkway. With no further movement or sound observed, he approached the window to close the drapes completely.

He reached up to straighten the liner first. He saw himself in the glass, his bare chest, his raised arm, his face imposed on the pharmacy across the parking lot. Then a white-faced clown leaned sideways into the frame and Stavo yelled and flung himself away.

He hit the bed and continued backward over it, fell to the hard floor, mumbling incoherently. Without thinking, he scrambled around, sliding his feet and legs under the frame, covering his head, then his ears against the violent pounding on the window. He hummed for an indeterminate period of time.

When he opened his eyes he was breathing heavily, his cheek pressed against the tile floor, his slot of vision the space under the bed, the room quiet, no pounding, no shouts, his fear like a weight on his back pinning him to the floor. He heard a buzzing and realized his phone was ringing. He was afraid to rise and look at the window, the image there burned onto a blank screen in his mind, not a regular creepy circus clown, but a horror clown, round red nose punctuating a powder-white face, black smudges circling the eyes, and three individual tufts of bright red hair standing out insanely on each side and the top of the head, the scalp between bald, the worst of hair styles, the wide grinning mouth drawn by garish red lips, the yellow teeth sharp and terrifying.

Jesus Christ Almighty. He was trembling, his greatest childhood fear manifested again, more intense than ever. His phone was ringing. Was that the second time? He had no idea how much time had passed. He looked at his watch but couldn't see the dial. His chest was slick against the tile. He felt he might start to slide, like the floor was tilted. He was nauseous, his whole body bunkered under the bed. He stretched his arms out, wanting more surface contact, wanting the cool floor to calm his skin, bring its temperature down.

Millege did not toast anyone or anything. They had moved to a dining table and he was on the verge of instructing Victor to check on the missing team member when Stavo entered the room visibly shaky and sweating.

He apologized and took a seat between Millege and

Liz. His hand shook as he drank water, his eyes darting around at the others watching him, noting his pale face and damp, lank hair.

"Have you just seen a ghost?" Millege said.

Stavo set his glass down. "A clown, sir," he said.

Two other tables now had patrons, a pair of businessmen at one and a group of four at the other, a middle-aged couple with the husband's parents. It was dark outside the louvered windows and wall lamps shone brightly on the tile floor and the white tablecloths. With only marginal lighting from the highway and the hotel itself, the parking lot was practically invisible and Millege felt as if he were sitting in a rectangular fish bowl.

Stavo's face flushed as he explained, his lingering fear compounded by the feeling that he was letting the team down.

Millege gulped his margarita, staring at the opaque windows on two sides of the room, staring at what he couldn't see beyond. He looked at the ice in his glass. He looked at each of his staff in turn. The odd, strikingly marked girl with visions real or conjured. The silent unproven Indian showing no outward allegiance to anything. The earnest young man with—what was it? coulrophobia?—a fear of clowns, for Christ sake, who would fucking believe that?

What sort of stalker would even carry a fucking clown mask in his kit? Obviously, a psychological game-player, a provocateur in dire need of a lesson.

His phone vibrated in his pocket and he pulled it out and cupped it until it stopped. Hiller again. He set the phone beside his plate. They were all watching him now, studying his silence, waiting for his response to the clown.

He stood and pocketed his phone and said, "Go ahead and order. I need to make a call." He stepped away.

"Sir," Liz said. "Do you want some food too?"

Millege hesitated, not certain if he was hungry, then spoke over his shoulder. "Just some"—he wasn't finding the local words—"just some of that typical chicken meal." He went into the bar, got a fresh drink with an extra shot, walked out the front door and around the corner to the parking lot.

The rain had let up. Passing dark room windows he moved casually to the back of the building. He surveyed the few parked cars and heard television voices and a woman's pealing laugh above him on the second level. Diagonally across from the rear of the building was a small fenced soccer field, an artificially turfed practice area. He turned the corner and looked at the dark, deserted swimming pool, then up at the building and its rear spiral staircase.

He swirled the ice in his glass and stood listening. Beyond the pool the land dropped off to another property, a sort of half-manicured backyard of the neighboring business, with thick clusters of banana trees he saw as cover and between them a worn path toward nearby houses, an escape route through the hollow. He downed his drink, stooped to set the glass against the building, felt the tequila's mind-shift.

He continued down the drive past the soccer park to a garage behind it, a refrigeration company. No black Nissan. He held a cigar in his mouth and a box of matches in his hand, picturing as he pressed a match against the striking board a clown sniper, its rubber cheek fast against the stock of the rifle, its unblinking eye at the eyehole waiting for a flame. But there wouldn't be a rifle. He struck the match and puffed until the tip glowed uniformly. He shook the flame out and left a drifting cloud as he headed back.

Second time in San Isidro, no closer to his quarry.

Literally going in circles. As he walked, he searched the upper walkways, the top of the spiral staircase, the parking lot, seeking any kind of signal, an out of place sound, a movement, any clue from this shadow creep. Who almost certainly wasn't staying here. He thought of bringing Liz outside to focus on the problem. But the man would follow again in the morning, looking to be led to the target, all easy-peasy, like a hyena tailing a pride of lions.

Millege climbed the rear staircase, stepping carefully on the wet metal, buzzed and lonely, inhaling thin streams of nicotine lift. Who was he to criticize anyone? His own methods seemed archaic, simplistic, random, sloppy. What kind of bullshit professional stopped calling in? He was a renegade now, a dice-roller, a follower of mystical outsiders, a time-bider, a hoper, a ringleader of misfits. Nothing wrong with playing hunches as long as hard evidence kept them aloft. Inside, team morale would be sinking in his absence. His food would be cold, wasted.

At the second level he moved along the interior walkway toward the front of the building. His left knee ached and his stomach rumbled. As he puffed to rekindle his fire, a door at the end he had just passed opened and he looked back. A woman's head leaned out and looked around, her long dark hair hanging down the doorframe, her television's volume spilling out. She stared at Millege for a prolonged period as he stood immobile, hands at his side, a thread of smoke trailing up his arm, then pulled back inside and withdrew from sight.

He stood at the outer railing looking across at the highway traffic, the granular pyritic light cast across the wet pavement below, hearing diffused voices from the restaurant rising between the irregular wind-rush of passing cars, his mind dipping into Chet Baker's creamy-reedy-fragile voice singing "My Funny Valentine," which made him smile, his bloated face sweating, and softly sing the tune to himself. He threw his hands out one after the other, shuffled his feet forward and back, bobbed his head from side to side, his fists punching the space over the railing to his own sound effect. *Oooff. Oooff.*

He finger-launched his cigar overboard, a blunt tumbler rotating like an unmoored satellite, its spinning engine bursting into orange spangles on impact, life expectancy reached, mission terminated.

Ambling past the rooms, he glanced at window reflections. Halted at an open curtain, the sideshow view inside. The curious long-haired breezeway peeker stood back from her glass, immobile form tinted with light escaping the seams of a closed bathroom door. Long-sleeved white shirt fully unbuttoned, hair cascading over shoulders, black panties and black boots, and Millege was struck by the warmth reaching him, her naked half-hidden breasts and bare thighs radiating sultry energy and her dark eyes daring him.

He walked briskly around to the interior walkway and pushed open the unshut door, saw the window where he had just been, the other side of this inverted dream. She was unmoved. Bed still made, one small bag on the floor, television off, black skirt over the chair, bottle of rum on the desk, cowboy boots, he noticed now. Where the hell did she come from?

He stopped at the threshold, one foot inside, hand on the door knob, about to make the universal hand signal for a drink, along with a shrug, a smile, an intimated question regarding the price backed by any language.

He looked at the bathroom door. She smiled at last. Something was off. The lure was immaculate. She was good, smoldering in place. He held up his index finger, needing a minute, then little finger and thumb held phone-like at mouth and ear, an asinine call he'd forgotten, as he stepped back out and fled.

Nothing happened. He was giddy in his room. Way off his game. Typing.

Dear Dave, phone reception, wifi spotty, trying update again. Frustration goes along with progress. Nice country, by the way. A green beauty mark on the face of the planet. When you get closer, though, some of that green is artificial. The trees are too orderly, if you get my meaning. Some say we're on our way to becoming another Venus. When you're driving do you sometimes suddenly see yourself as a moving speck in the big picture? Do you ever think about the company you work for? Do you consider the phrase, economic growth? The way it implies continual, as in always, forever. Leads you right into capitalism. But I digress. The small picture view is about us doing our jobs and getting paid so we can buy groceries and cars and sunblock. The small picture problem is we have encountered a third party of unknown origin, likely private hire. Motive unclear but counterproductive to our goals. Strange toxic pain in the ass. Need to immobilize before proceeding to target. Momentarily side-tracked but delivery still imminent. You can rest easy, go time-share shopping, but budget for unforeseen hazard, risk pay for support team.

Millege read it again, his room dark but for the computer's blue screen glow. Then he hit Delete.

The little devils were in disarray. Stavo could not eat and Liz insisted he take the boss's meal back to his room since deep sleep was unlikely. She was concerned about Phil Millege too. And physically distracted by Victor, who wondered aloud about her safety, about the clown uncovering Stavo's phobia.

"Could be a coincidence," Liz said. "Many people

are afraid of clowns."

They walked the subdued young man to his room and told him not to worry, that they all looked out for their team. Then Liz and Victor stood outside her door in the breezeway and Victor brought his hands out of his pockets and slipped his arm around her shoulder. He wanted to ask about her life in Sierpe and her family, but his voice was hidden. She understood this but whispered for silence anyway so they could locate their younger selves and find some way to bridge the long interval and feel their memories unspool together. She closed her eyes and summoned a fresh hope to form around them, her arms encircling him and her head like a nervous bird settling upon his wild heart.

17. Petrospheric Harmony and Balance

costa rica
Cheryl Paddington
To: peypad
My dear Peyton, We have been enjoying your messages so much. Your father and I are so proud of you, and so encouraged by what we hear from you lately. It sounds like you girls (women) are having the time of your lives. And learning important life lessons. It's so important to balance the two. Given time, everyone finds their path, the journey they are meant to take. Their life mission, in other words. We never know where we might end up or what successes we may achieve unless we find that special path and follow it. We are always rooting for you and wishing you the best that life can possibly provide.
Your dad is hoping you might take this new interest into veterinary school. No pressure of course. You know he aims high. But seriously, whatever you want to study is fine with us (as long as it's legal. LOL) because it's always good to have your degree. As I guess you've heard me say before. Sigh!

Things are basically fine around here. Simon dislocated his thumb playing baseball but it hasn't slowed him down much. He says, Hey Pey! Yes, a man of so many words. Paula enjoyed hearing about sloths and the danta, and she is making some drawings to give to you. She is quite the budding artist these days and will draw whatever pops into her head just to expand her skills. She likes colored pencils the most.

Snowball got into some oil under the car and your dad had to use mineral spirits to clean her fur, which was a struggle for all concerned, including me. He threatened to have her declawed but was, naturally, just kidding and acting tough.

Please be safe, both of you, and give my love to Chloe too.

We love you, honey, Mom

—

At breakfast Millege gave his "needle in a haystack" speech, focusing on the low odds of finding their man among all the hotels, cabinas, homestays, lodges, shacks, treehouses, and unoccupied homes. And boats, he added. His team had trouble understanding his message and his negative attitude went against their prior experiences with him. He said they had missed their best chance in Sierpe. He said Ellis Hayden might be using an alias and apparently had not been seen enough to be identified despite the reward offered.

"Behind everything is something else," Millege said. "What we see from the road is just the surface. There are places whose signs you don't see until you are upon them. There are other places lacking signs all together."

Liz and Victor looked at each other, not as they had been since the evening before, with curiosity and disbelief and excitement, but with concern, as if the soft emotional ground they occupied had shifted again and structural tremors now ran up through their legs. And silent in his own upturned world, Stavo drank more coffee, having only gotten a couple hours of sleep at best.

Millege walked out behind the hotel and lit a cigar. The morning was clear and he stood squinting at the sky above the trees. A blazing swollen sun had risen into the open blue and he found himself reminded of Circle of Light.

He called Dave Hiller.

"Well it's about fucking time," Hiller said.

"Got a minute?" Millege said.

"I really hope you have some positive news to report."

A black Nissan X-Trail pulled into the parking lot as Millege watched.

"Call you right back," he said, and clicked off, walking toward the hotel. The car looped around in front of the pharmacy and back out the drive to the highway, its driver, the lone occupant, staring at Millege as he trotted forward.

When Hiller answered again he said, "What the hell's going on there? Finally get me on the line and— What are you breathing about, man?"

"If you let me get a word in edgewise, I'll explain what's going on."

"Hey, son, don't forget who's paying your salary."

"If you can learn to listen for just a few minutes you'll get an update."

In the gaping pause, Millege caught his breath and continued.

"We have an interloper here, of uncertain origin and purpose. Feels mercenary in the worst way. That's one part, the other part is a deliberate interference in my mission. This is causing a delay because we must derail this element before proceeding further."

Hiller cut in. "Felipe is expecting—"

"Fucking Felipe can just chill. Okay? Let me finish. We're looking at a threat not only to the target, to the mission, but to our physical selves as well. It's imperative that we nullify this threat before moving ahead."

"Give me a specific instance," Hiller said.

"Weapon aimed at a team member."

"When was this?"

"Yesterday."

"Intimidation tactic, not unheard of. But who's behind him?"

"That's the issue. We don't know. Could be a distraught family member. But I have to protect my team. To be completely clear, I'm talking hazard here."

"So what then, he's trying to scare you off? One guy?"

"It seems that way. Or use us."

"Don't try to play me."

"I'm not playing anything, Hiller. I have a genuine safety concern."

"What's your plan?"

"I can't discuss that."

"What, you think you're being bugged too?"

"I'm giving you the reason for the delay."

There was a long pause. Then Hiller said, "Understood. I'll speak to Felipe. Hazard pay will be wired. Do what you need to do. Use any means."

—

Russet. She mouthed the word again. Russet. "Russet monkey," she whispered. She later supposed that was the trigger. Looking through the spotting scope into the high treetops to watch a spider monkey glance down at the human group, or gaze away into its own world up there, toward other monkeys, nearby family members or outside agitators, distant threats, competitors in the canopy, or a fruit meal or birds or any movement at that level. It was black and russet, supremely fuzzy, the prehensile tail a long fifth limb wrapped around a branch, a safety feature continually reaching out to grip and hold, seeming to operate on its own, the small face alert, sharp-eyed, the smooth skin around eyes and nose and mouth like a black mask, the surrounding hair swept out and away as if combed, standing up punk-style on top. It looked down again, mouth set in concentration, aware of the ground people, then yawned, showed a lack of concern, stark white primate teeth, four formidable incisors, pink tongue, its observant eyes looking at Peyton as its round face relaxed into repose again.

The others moved on, Chloe and Ellis and the guide Rafael, carrying his tripod over his shoulder, following a trickling stream. But Peyton remained under the monkeys, still looking skyward, the fur shapes conducting their own business, several of them now, half hidden in their elevated world of limbs and leaves, languid arms draped loose in the morning warmth, the unexpected russet flooding her mind as she closed her eyes and drifted in the forest realm.

After a time, she heard someone calling and realized she was sitting streamside on a log. She looked up to see Ellis jogging toward her on the trail.

"What are you doing?" he said.

"I don't know," she said. "I just—I just sat down for a second. I guess."

"Are you dizzy or something?"

"No." She stood and smiled at him. "I feel great, actually. I just spaced out for a minute. I couldn't leave this spot right away." She shrugged. "I don't really know how to explain it."

"That's fine," he said. "We were just wondering where you went. Rafa thinks we should head over to the mouth of the river. He saw a danta there last week and thinks we might get lucky again."

She was still smiling at him, like she had something to add, and then wrinkled her nose in a crazy grin. "That would be so cool," she said. "But it's like it doesn't even matter right now. You know? I just had this amazing moment that washed over me like—I don't know, like waves or something. Nirvana."

He stared back into her wide brown eyes, noticed beads of sweat at her hairline, strands of damp dark hair hanging loose at her neck, bits of bark or leaf debris stuck there, her ponytail unraveling, her red cheeks and freckled nose, her smiling mouth, her natural beauty pumped up with joy.

They walked side by side and he told her about a similar experience he had had a few years before.

"I was floating in the sea in St Croix after I swam out over a minefield of black urchins, their spikes almost grazing my chest and thighs. I got to deeper water and was able to forget about certain large fish of an unnamed species"—he glanced over and saw her grinning—"and I was bobbing in perfect ocean water, salty enough to keep me up, the temperature and clarity ideal. The green hillsides were part of the view upward to a flawless blue sky and there was no sound to speak of, no worries that came to mind, the beach and the other people drifted out of my sight and I felt some kind of elation coursing through me. I don't know how long it lasted, but it felt incredibly rare."

She was nodding and he went on.

"There are a few exquisite moments we have at certain points in our lives. Moments that are as unexpected as they are beautiful and wonderful, though those words are not really accurate. Even transcendent seems lame. Maybe for some people they're less rare than for others. And I'd bet that almost always the experience happens in a natural setting. But that's not it either. It's more like some kind of chance alignment, where everything about your concept of life on earth, your place in it, the actual particles of your being, your health and state of mind, your self-awareness, your immediate surroundings, all of this, all of everything, the planet spinning, the weather"—he stopped to laugh at his broad description—"the world in its odd mystery comes together in a splendid instance of you in the world as natural and inevitable as anything you've ever believed."

He paused. "I can't even say what I mean, but it's like a buoyancy, a belonging, a sense of well-being that balloons you up above yourself, out of yourself—not with drugs or any artificial method—and leaves you suspended, not mindful of work or family or problems on the world stage or on your own horizon. Everything clicks for a minute, fits together, makes sense, or just vanishes altogether, because you're not thinking consciously. You're barely even thinking at all. You're just there, feeling that moment, aware of yourself in it but just floating, as I was that day, literally. All your senses are registering a confluence of input that melds into one blissful entity."

He paused again. "So what am I talking about, how can I sum it up? Have you accidently found a moment of purity? What does that even mean? Pure what? Contentment, awareness, understanding? You, in that moment, feeling but not thinking, getting something back, some nugget of treasure from nature, from the nameless void that holds you in an embrace that's only cheesy when you try to explain it back at the bar. It's not any one thing. It's just there, everything. It's enchantment that touches you by chance. A gift that bubbles up through a fissure below the surface of your normal life. It's not God, not the universe, nothing pompous or cosmic in that sense. It's like you took a blind turn and got to an intersection where everything was happening perfectly, and you realized it and felt it for as long as those vibrations lasted. Then it was gone. You didn't seek it and you can't hold it or keep it."

They walked on together. "Maybe certain people," he said, "with enough practice, can go find it whenever they like. But it seems more special if it comes out of nowhere and finds you. If only we knew where nowhere was."

They both laughed and she took his hand for a second and squeezed it.

—

The new plan was to split up, lie low for a few days, allow the annoying shadow to fade away. Stavo would return to his job in Uvita. Nothing personal, Millege assured him, it was just time for a break. Millege would ride with him, out of sight in the rear, as far as Circle of Light, and they would leave after the other vehicle. Victor would drive the Rav4 with Liz and they would pick up Victor's bike in Palmar Norte and canvas the area for sightings of their quarry. Then bring both vehicles and get Millege three days later, unless he overdosed or got assassinated. He was the only one who chuckled at this.

Millege hopped out at the turnoff and ambled down the track as the minivan drove off, Stavo's arm waving wildly from the window. "Christ, don't wave," Millege said, and was soon out of sight of the highway, his bag hefted over one shoulder, his mood lifting as he walked alone, physically clear for the moment of everything troubling him.

At the thatched greeting terrace the sound of the river drifted across the clearing and passed through Millege like a panacea. But instead of Dimaris he found a thin young man named Monty who reeked of patchouli. Millege then suffered his third disappointment in quick succession early in his discourse with the greeter. Monty's brown hair was dyed blue on top and stood up in a crest, his brown eyes were disproportionately close together, his oversized upper lip with its deep philtrum suggested a beak, and the turns of his head were bird-like in their observant, wary manner, but despite these avian movements, including his neck's frequent bobbing retreat, which seemed to help him attain a preferred conversational focal distance, the young man's mind seemed to be running at a lower speed than normal, and Millege felt compelled to ask about Dimaris, who remained imbedded in his memory as a quick-witted and nubile curiosity, because he was curious and also because he felt her name would offer an association and a sounder reason for his presence—something like a verbal coupon—than his sweaty, out of shape appearance would otherwise provoke. His was not the body type likely to be seen on the cover of a yoga magazine.

Monty gazed about the clearing as if listening for the girl, as if a birdcall might announce her arrival, as if it might in fact be time for a shift change. He blinked and tugged gently at the wispy cluster of chin hairs sprouting from his otherwise serenely smooth face. Not the best spokesman, Millege thought, wondering if the young man's dull processing was due to the aftereffects of the very mind-altering treatment the Circle promoted and he now considered. Aside from that, the patchouli oil caused Millege to back away a few steps.

"Are you an acolyte?" Millege asked.

"She is occupied at this time," Monty said.

"Yes, I figured that," Millege said. "Please extend my deepest blessings."

"Very well," the young man said.

"Have you ever worked at a natural foods market?" Millege asked.

"We have the one opening," Monty said, ignoring the question either to confirm that it lacked significance or because it had failed to land and stick.

"I feel like we might have met at a checkout in Asheville," Millege said.

"I'm a door sitter," Monty said. He smiled his welcoming smile. "It will be my pleasure to assist you when you need it most," he said, and Millege did not pursue the meaning of this ominous statement. Monty extended his whole arm and open hand, palm vertically positioned, to point downhill in the manner of a signpost. "You may register at the next station," he said, "to begin your journey." He pointed a long thin forefinger, reminiscent of a peacock's middle toe, at Millege's front pocket, the cigar peeking out. "While here you will want to cleanse yourself of negative habits and energies and prepare your body for a positive redirection with a natural diet. For your own sake please take the preparations seriously. And please, for the sake of group harmony, turn off your phone before proceeding. Technology is desacralized here and you will only be able to untrack successfully without it."

Millege continued slightly downhill, the dirt and gravel track bordered by forest and garden areas, with small cabins in view along the curve ahead. At the next station, a spartan screened hut, he stood at the counter and signed a release and completed a medical form and answered a few questions regarding his expectations and made his payment in cash. He spoke with a middle-aged woman who introduced herself as Juvia, "with a J," she said, though she allowed and even encouraged the confusion with the Spanish word for rain, *lluvia*. "Some people call me Rain," she said. "I don't mind. I'm from California." She was patient and calming in her manner, wore long gray-brown braids with yellow and purple yarns interwoven. A wooden bowl of red hibiscus blossoms sat on the counter next to a clipboard and pen. Beside them were a wine bottle of drinking water and a tray of small glass jars, which must have once contained jelly. They were uniformly faded, the glass worn nearly milky, as if they had been used for decades, an unbroken collection no longer collectable but still someone's fortunate flea market score purposely repurposed, the remaining traces of colored line suggesting cartoon drawings which had now deliquesced into unrecognizable characters. Millege found himself thinking fondly of Huckleberry Hound.

"How have you arrived at this place?" she asked.

"By car and by foot," he said.

"No, no." She smiled patiently. "I meant this decision." She touched her forehead.

He smiled in return. "I desire new ways of looking at old ways."

"Ahh," she said. "Excellent."

She opened a drawer and withdrew a sheet of suggestions entitled "Spirit Mother's Life Review: A Circle Path to Renewal."

"Here is your guide," she said, "and we are all of us here your guides as well. In addition, of course, to the shaman and the sacred plant and your own truth. Open your mind and welcome the spirit of transformation to dwell within. Share your soul."

"I will," he said. "Is there a restroom nearby?"

The Path of the Tapir

"Work on your intentions," she said. "There are several composting toilets between cabin nine and the round house."

Reality began to sink in. He read as he walked. People waved, said welcome, he nodded, smiled. *No alcohol, no coffee, no tobacco, no meat, no salt, no sugar, no dairy. Stay with your breath. Work on your intentions. What do you need to do? What is your totem?*

He dropped his bag in cabin nine and looked at the spartan room. The cushions and blanket, the narrow wooden bed. Desk and chair. Candles. Bundle of sage. He had neglected to bring any food. Or a defined purpose. He read the rest of the guide.

Nestled nearby the clear currents of the Bueno River this transformative exploration of the heart and soul is worthy of deep and triumphant introspection at the height you wish to travel. Surrounded by clean hills laden with exotic fruits and blazing colored birds who turn nature into awareness we invite you to balance your health with environments created to stimulate your senses and transport your essence to mindful destinations both backward and forward and ultimately bring your body to new levels of blissful attainment.

What? He read it again. Had no one—retired teacher or grammatically fortified consultant—volunteered to render the statement in clear language?

Outside, beside the door, a plate-sized round mirror was affixed to the wall. He bent and peered at himself, his fleshy stubbled face floating against a background of leaves and marbled sky above another cabin. A young woman was passing in the road.

"That's to reflect negative energies away from the house," she said.

He straightened and turned. "Where do they go from there?"

She smiled and continued her walk.

The main house was a circular screened room with a high center pole surrounded by twenty-eight perimeter poles. The thatch roof peaked at least twenty feet above the center of the worn wooden floor and sloped downward to extend beyond the interior space by several feet to ward off rain. There was no furniture in the spacious room but stacks of mattress cushions with blue cotton covers were piled around the center support and just inside the entrance stood a column of purple plastic purge buckets that Millege perceived as a tower of warning.

He followed the dirt track past scattered cabins and gardens and signs to the fire pit, the green house, the koi pond, and came to the rushing river and a gathering of boulders with swim-suited clients splayed over their surfaces or standing in the current as if communing with the lifeblood of the region. In the sensory foam of rushing water and voices and mist and sunlight he stood observing the young bodies, primarily female, noticing that he was two decades older than almost everyone there, a lumpen and inert imposter, mainly an asylum seeker, who'd missed the resounding call for early enlightenment and rejuvenation that they had heard and heeded. The air smelled of fruit and soil and the perspiration of the earnest.

A bearded head surfaced midstream and its body advanced swimming to the shore where Millege stood. As the man attained an upright position his familiarity caused a ripple of shock that clenched in the right knee of Phil Millege as he braced himself and tried to place the man's face in his memory. The dripping man stepped out of the river and into the older man's personal space, his hair hanging flat and overlapping his beard which continued down his neck and merged with the splayed hair of his shoulders and chest that in his peripheral vision Millege realized disappeared into the man's board shorts and reappeared undiminished in the furry matting of his legs and the tops of his feet, his overall hirsute appearance along with the sharp pointed expression of his nose and mouth at this range caused his observer to think *badger*.

"Well ain't this a New Age shakeup," the wet man said, smiling. "You're the absolute last unlikely sight I expected to see around here."

With the drawn-out diction, the recollection came to Millege in a flash. One of the four surfers he'd met together in Uvita, the oldest one with the least to say on that occasion.

"I hear you," Millege said. "And I never expected to run into Sasquatch this far south."

The mirthful surfer laughed, showing a mouthful of well-maintained white teeth. "Have you entirely lost your way?" he asked with a wide grin.

"The path is not always the expected one," Millege said.

The surfer leaned back and cocked his head, hands on hips. "Well," he said, "you have got me there. Wisdom is yours for the taking."

Several women were within earshot and one of them, a well-tanned brunette whose wild torrents of hair fell to the middle of her back, stepped closer. She wore a leopard print bikini top and hip-riding white cotton shorts, rolled up high on her thighs. Her right incisor protruded outward against her upper lip and gave her mouth a slightly sardonic snarl.

"Welcome," she said, extending her hand to Millege. "I'm Cassandra."

"Philip," he said, taking her hand.

"You have any questions," she said, "you seek me out. Don't bother with Merlin, he'll just lead you astray." She smiled, nodding at the surfer.

"Merlin?" Millege said, and let the unspoken follow-up speak for itself.

"He's a magical-thinking kind of dude," she said as he stood silently by, as handsomely magisterial as he knew how, exuding whatever intangible power he could without words.

A gong sounded, a single deep rippling reverberation that wobbled through the riverine valley from someplace up on the ridge or within the community or out of the sky, Millege could not determine the direction of its source. People began to exit the river and head back up the track. Cassandra turned away and Millege noted the leopard print pattern broadly stretched beneath her white shorts and observed her lower back tattoo, three linear blue hills without additional color or much detail, the middle rise higher than those on either side, between them deep twin dimples that alternated winks as she walked.

"Three hills," he said, almost to himself.

She turned and looked back at him. "As you like it," she said.

He stood listening to the river, its minimal white noise tumbling through his mind, and breathing the river air until he was alone. He looked at his feet, his sandals and stubby toes and white legs. What was he doing here? His own actions surprised him. Maybe the mission's stagnation called for a reboot, but this was radical. He was rolling the dice at a critical time. It just felt right.

He looked at the swirling water, the rocks, the cobalt flutter of a large butterfly descending, landing on mud, its wings slowly beating open and closed like a heart, blue and brown, blue and brown. One side plain, one side resplendent. So there it was: the famous blue morpho. Would that be a good totem? Didn't he need a spirit animal too? Couldn't they be the same? Maybe an insect was too fragile, not significant enough for a totem. Maybe a badger was better, more substantial.

What was Cassandra's totem? A blue hill? Three blue hills? A morpho flying over a blue hill? Was it okay to ask someone to disclose their totem? Not to copy it or anything, just to know. And what did she mean by "As you like it"? Was that a Shakespearean reference? Was she a reader of plays, a fan of classical comedy dramas? As you like what? Her three hills? Why was the middle one taller? This was a question he could ask her. Regarding symbolism.

The ceremony would be held the following night. Today and tomorrow were preparatory days, meant for cleansing and clarifying intention. He didn't have any secret food so fasting seemed like a good intention. Not total fasting. Simple meals would be provided and if he found some extra fruit he figured it would be okay to eat it to keep from fainting. He didn't want to become completely listless and feeble. In the back of his mind the mission had to remain in focus. Not to be dramatic in a time of purity and spirituality but his physical life might be at stake. How was that for intention? Staying alive.

He planned to get better acquainted with the area, then take a nap. Maybe a series of naps. Intentional naps.

Inside the main house a group of people were stretching as wisps of smoke escaped through the screening and withered into afternoon sunlight. These folks were doing everything in unison as if they had been practicing as a class for a long time or had graduated from the same stretching school. Millege caught the woody disinfectant smell of sage—a natural cleanser of the soul?—and kept walking. He took a turn at a sign that simply showed a circular line coiling in on itself.

Here in the lower folds of the Tinamaste Mountains, amid cloud-cloaked ridges and falls and pools and bamboo and coati and toucans and sloths and peccaries and newts and rain frogs, there were bare roads cut to fish farms and organic plots of jackfruit and rambutan and banana, and here too was created a spiritual improvement farm with its natural embrace of water and air and basic local food and healers illuminating the path to plant spirits, to simplicity and the green source, the gift of ecotopia for as long as you stayed, checking out of the run-of-the-mill machine of your life back home. But short term by agreement, by definition, not just due to cost but also to logic, the way something special and meaningful cannot last beyond its novelty, its intrinsic value linked to brevity, to a unique placemark in the seeker's life.

He came to a labyrinth made of river stones, the whole circular route contained within a space of roughly ten square yards, a maze of convoluted pathways, or actually a single path, he discovered, whose stone walls were less than a foot high. It wasn't a matter of physically finding your way, but an exercise in contemplation or meditation, however you termed it. Several fellow attendees were present but only one was engaged in the act of walking the labyrinth. Merlin the magical surfer, Millege mused. The hairy man seemed to be navigating the path with his eyes closed. Millege assumed he was cheating.

The wild-haired Cassandra appeared out of a

cluster of women and walked toward him. Her smile made him notice his sweating scalp. He took off his safari hat and pushed his fingers through his damp hair.

"Are you here to walk?" she said.

"Just looking around," he said.

"Are you feeling comfortable?" she said.

"I'm okay," he said, watching the slow-moving surfer pause and assume a pose of stillness.

"Merlin's taken a vow of silence," she said.

"For how long, a month or so?" he said.

She laughed, her crooked incisor reaching for him like a fang. He imagined her biting his neck and him trying to isolate the impression of that one tooth. That would be an exercise. Probably difficult to pull off.

"Are you preparing for tomorrow night?" she said. "Do you have your totem together? Your mantra?"

Her smile was killing him. Was she mocking the whole business? Messing with him, or offering help?

"I was wondering if my spirit animal could be my totem," he said.

"It can if you want," she said. "But usually a totem is an item you bring to the ceremony—a rock or a feather or a piece of sea glass, any kind of found object, or a photo of a loved one or a favorite place—some special thing in your life, a sacred object, whatever that means to you."

"So anyone can see your totem"—he almost inadvertently added *pole*—"and it's not a private thing."

She stared at him for a moment, thinking he was playing with her, and said, "You could totally show me your totem, and I'd be cool with that. It's only your mantra you need to keep secret. Do you have a mantra?"

"Almost," he said. "I'm trying to understand the

rules."

She nodded, her blue eyes dancing, her errant tooth breaking the seal of her lips, her torrent of hair cascading, begging to be tied back or braided.

"Forget the rules," she said. "You get yourself a good mantra and don't tell anyone, not even me." She reached out and put her hands on his forearms. "No matter what I do."

"Understood," he said.

She stared into his wide puzzled face and her hands lifted away. "I'll see you later," she said.

He stood motionless as clouds rolled over the river and hunger overtook him, the others drifting away, their voices vanishing, odd birdcalls like random advisories also fading away. A mantra was bubbling up, trying to be born out of his intestines, looking for him as if he were separate from his own mind, some kind of thing he needed but hadn't known he needed until today, until now.

He stepped into the labyrinth, his stomach growling, his head making the silence loud, full of competing strands of dialogue, imagined conversations with Cassandra, his wayward team, conflicted thoughts as warring factions on the subject of his ill-considered quarry, his missing plan of action or any tangible method of recovery, all of which he wanted to escape. The labyrinth was land art, a rock drawing spread before him. How much better, he thought, if the walls were above his head and he was contained within them. Wouldn't his mind be quieter if he wasn't so exposed? There were animals watching his little steps between the rocks, the convoluted path twisting in imitation of his own intestines, as if he were walking into himself. Wasn't that the point? The outer world was encroaching on him as he curled into himself and disappeared for a while. He was a silent embryonic being walking a curved line into himself, into his grumbling guts, his mind skeptical and rebellious.

Walking back to his cabin he tried to empty his mind of burritos and cigar cravings and images of Cassandra and Dimaris coating each other with mud for health reasons as they languished by the river. Why would he assume they even knew each other? He went inside and lay down and plummeted into a cascade of dreams.

In the first one, he found a folded note in the crack of his door. He opened the paper and read shaky blue words spidering upward across a white page—*Not all those who wander are lost. Go easy Mister Blando*—and immediately figured Merlin for the trickster culprit, deducing that he had written left-handed to render his style child-like and unknowable. Millege resolved to observe the man's hands when next they met.

In the following sequence, he was looking for something, possibly his totem, entering the labyrinth again but somehow joining a riverside column of seekers as they each followed the person ahead of them, the whole line seeming to chant a single syllable that sounded to Millege like the word stone—*stone stone stone stone*—then Merlin was waving him out of the line to join a group of breakaways standing off to the side of the meandering line. We think there is a sphere near here, someone said. He realized it was Cassandra who had spoken as she turned and disappeared into a thicket of bush. He had the feeling he was meant to follow but no one else moved so he remained where he stood. She has a thing for the more mature dudes, Merlin said. Millege looked at him and said, More mature than what? Everyone else nodded knowingly.

In the third dream he was driving in an unknown city, scanning the passing scenery of vaguely familiar streets, looking for clues, reading signs as he they flew by his eyes, words and letters and symbols and scrawls of graffiti flashing in his mind as his speed increased along with his anxiety. Billboards were written in gibberish, street signs made no sense, their words foreign to him. He was missing something, not able to see what he should be seeing, unable to know what was right before him. He awoke suddenly, words exiting his mouth.

"*Zwa zom fo.*" He repeated them. "*Zwa zom fo.*" Leaning over, he dug into his bag, withdrew his journal and opened it to the first blank page. Which was the second page, after he'd written his airline details and a few notes on the country. The case details, such as they were, he kept in his head. But now he had a mantra and he wrote it down. It didn't matter what it meant. He'd seen the words somewhere recently, possibly in Miami on his way down here. He could research them later when he was back online. Not now. He was offline until he left, no service here anyway. So, top of page 2—*Zwa zom fo.*

He continued to write.

Observations. Getting acclimated in what is assumed to be a safe haven. As if such a place existed. Change of course, pace, view, approach. Everyone is expecting to experience something new or transforming. Tomorrow night. In the meantime—hang out, talk, share, meditate, eat simply, swim, walk, tend garden, gather your totems? So far I have an elongated rock, bulbous at one end, found by river. Possibly comical. First stone that caught my eye, no need to overthink it. Have learned some ceremonial basics—a candlelit circle, water bottles, sage, purge buckets. Shaman will apparently sing to call in spirits. We will have flashlights, cushions, blankets, totems, insights? Notebook to record revelations. No sign yet of shaman. Dimaris either. Suppress your cynical inclinations. Accept the fresh you inside. Is there one? Confront your fears. I now smoke an air cigar, privately. Shaman will attempt to create a sacred, silent, protected space. He will speak but no one else should. No video, no phones, no talking, no clapping, no chanting, but crying ok. No physical contact during ceremony. Presumably other times are fine. Following day is group sharing. Head count approx 22. Communal lunch was rice, legumes, avocado, salad. Breakfast will be fruit, oatmeal. I await catharsis, renewal. A new direction? Meanwhile, I leave no footprints, my trail goes stone cold. Like the other.

Mantra: zwa zom fo.
Totem: vaguely phallic river rock.
Spirit animal: whatever local badger is called.

18. The Bird's Eye View of Marco Vargas

Costa Rica Courier
Paradise under assault—the bounty hunter and the greenman
Marco Vargas / May 21, 2014
marcovargas@crcourier.com
Paradise is a relative term. But we all feel a sadness when something we love is destroyed. And something we love is destroyed every day. People, animals, trees, jungles, waterways, relationships, agreements, trust, love itself. Sometimes the acts of destruction are criminal and the blame is deflected in another direction, and someone must then point out the misdirection so the full story can be known and understood.
A few weeks ago I reported on two American girls who were burned to death on a property belonging to PPOI. For those unfamiliar with the initials, they stand for Progressive Palm Oil International, a big player along our south-central Pacific coast, meaning a substantial amount of money is generated, a lot of it flowing out of the country to the corporate office in Raleigh, North

Carolina, while a fair number of locals are employed at the nitty-gritty levels of operation.

The story seemed like a simple story. And people like simple stories they can understand and reach a tidy conclusion about and then put behind them, to make room for new stories, much like the police are sometimes accused of doing—grabbing the first potential perpetrator and making that person fit the crime, especially if he is poor and unable to properly defend himself—the better to conclude the inquiry, quiet the outcry if the case is sensational, and move on to the new cases arising.

So here's the simple version. Two subversive tourist girls trespassed on private property at night and died in a fire they either set or caused to happen. Definitely a tragedy but they brought it on themselves for nefarious reasons and got what they deserved. In addition, a third party, an expat male who was with them and got away, was part of their plan but left them to die. After a brief investigation, the police called the deaths accidental without commenting on the cause of the fire or whether they were seeking the third party. There was also some talk of a second man on the scene but this has not been acknowledged or denied by police or the company. PPOI initiated an internal investigation for insurance purposes. Quiet protocol.

That's when the story became another kind of story altogether.

Shortly after my initial article on the fire that destroyed—apart from the lives of the two women—a field maintenance shed in Sierpe, I received an email in which the sender claimed to be planning an attack on the main processing plant up the coast. Even though the scale is obviously greater, you could call it a copycat threat because the intent, the message, is the same as the one generated by the shed fire. The company also received this threat so we can call that a warning even if there is no follow-through. No details or date were provided, but the company was forced to enlist extra security and bear the subsequent cost, along with the unwanted attention to the recent incident and to their operations in general.

The African oil palm industry is coming under harsher scrutiny every day. The worldwide use of vegetable oil, particularly in biofuels, was supposed to help us clean up our dirty addiction to fossil fuels, to benefit the blemished health of our planet by reducing carbon dioxide emissions. So, in Indonesia and other countries across the tropical belt circling our round world, huge swaths of wild uncultivated forest land have been cleared, slashed and burned for palm oil plantations. When you happen to see the mature manufactured forests of these trees standing sixty feet tall in row after symmetrical row, there is a sense of organized beauty, a kind of peaceful acceptance, a sort of soulful weighing of options, a lopsided gratitude that there is no concrete in view, no power plants or power lines or roads or buildings. Instead, there is a nearly natural-feeling green grove where a hawk might fly or a snake might crawl. Yet is not an actual home to biodiversity or a functioning, self-maintained ecosystem, but a place whose sole purpose is to deliver a regular yield of orange nuts, clump after clump after clump, truckloads rolling out day after day. You might forget what was there before, who lived there, or what the process of land change was like, the destruction and carnage leading to the making of a pseudo-forest.

There are many forms and levels of paradise. Your lush

little backyard with its bird feeders and herbs and flowering plants. The park down the road where you enjoy walking and stretching and meeting friends. The preserve you visit on vacation, where the natural land extends beyond the horizon and you feel you've escaped the daily trappings of your mechanized, digital, regulated, information-overloaded life. That place on the other side of the globe with otherworldly mists and primeval trees and great apes in the jungle shadows. If you look closer, all around the edges, you'll see the hacked-out roads, the influx of miners and wood-cutters and land-clearers on the way, a trail of bush meat in their wake, the ashes of progress and money-seeking fluttering in shafts of light, the smoky plumes of profit rising in the distance, signals of our demise, the myriad ways we are screwing up the place. In Borneo, the old men of the forest are dying out, the sad-eyed, intelligent and bewildered orangutans are on the run. Over here, the tapirs and jaguars are driven out by the same cultivation of orange palm nuts.

This is big business, big agro, corporate power, government corruption, the bulldozing of indigenous people, the burning out and banishment of nature and its many denizens. The best way to fight big money is with big money, with watchdogs and lawsuits that delay the assault. But nothing will end it.

Letters will be written, protests held, encampments staged, and yet the drive for profit will overrun all in its path.

So who can fault the subversive groundwork, the flies in the ointment, the anger and guerilla tactics of the green people, the hidden greenmen and greenwomen acting in determined defiance?

Sometimes I feel like I'm floating above it all, struggling

to gain perspective, to see the connections between all the elements at play, the pathways of history intersecting the new roads at more and more points, lines crisscrossing the land below, the frontier towns and gleaming grid cities growing denser in their cross-hatched patterns, their ever-expanding borders, their unstoppable pushing.

And when I zoom in, relentless drone that I am, I see figures moving over the landscape, current stories unfolding. I see the flattened ashes in Sierpe, the nut-cutters and harvesters on bicycles, the earthmovers and planting crews and lumbering trucks and vast tracts of fronds woven through the flatland between mountain and sea. We may be screwed but we still have our stories.

I see an investigator chasing the one that got away, the greenman who lost his greenwomen. I'm interested in this conflict, how it plays out.

Every tale is colored by the teller. Objectivity is an ideal seldom embraced. The voice in a story has an opinion which is either clear or disguised. I've covered protests against the expansion of the pineapple industry, against the loss of family farms, against the treatment of Nicaraguan migrant workers. And yes, against Dole and Del Monte, the heirs of the United Fruit Company's legendary banana empire morphed into fields and fields of other fruits.

I ask questions and I solicit information. I ask for your help now. Again.

My sources tell me the company man is a former bail enforcement agent, a modern title for a bounty hunter. Except no one here has jumped bail. No arrests, no charges, no crime? How can this be? Naturally, certain people want answers, but not publicly. The bounty hunter is now an investigator. He needs the input of the greenman to close the case. He has assembled a team of locals to make inroads in the culture, to overturn clues to the whereabouts of the mysterious missing greenman. And what will happen if the greenman is found? Will the police emerge with renewed interest? Will the immigration authorities instigate deportation proceedings? Or will PPOI handle the matter internally, secretly, in whatever manner they see fit? Will the greenman vanish, along with the story?

Dear readers, these figures are out there moving among you, from San Vito to San Isidro, from Dominical to Sierpe. Please reach out to me if you see or hear anything concerning these characters or this story. All info is confidential. The story is alive, in motion, unresolved.

And listen, Greenman, if you wish to comment on anything at all...

Peace be unto you, marcovargas@crcourier.com

19. Babylon Sky

At the end of the dirt street a flop-eared calf peeked at the approaching car through the gate slats of a small corral shed. Beside the shed a white dog was bent intently to a pile of rice, eyes closed and mouth working. Beyond the shed, the land sloped down to the Térraba River, flowing brown and steady between its green banks.

Victor parked the car apart and across from the house of his landlord. From the kitchen window the landlord's wife watched her tenant and his female passenger exiting the car and her suspicious eye locked onto the girl's face immediately. As he neared the house Victor raised a hand, and the woman nodded almost imperceptibly. Liz felt the heat of her stare as they passed.

They entered the breezeway separating the two parts of the house and Victor unlocked his door. He held the door open for Liz and tossed their bags inside and then went to the end of the breezeway and around the corner. His bike was chained to a tree in the shade of the yard, its wet tarp sagging to the muddy ground. He folded the tarp and wrapped the chain around his arm and wheeled the bike into the breezeway to wipe it down.

They used the bathroom and repacked and lay quietly on the bed with the fan caressing them, her eyes roaming around the room as if to catalog his meager furnishings. They slept briefly under the fan's oscillating drone, their arms touching by their natural proximity. Outside, the dog sniffed at the bottom of the door, and a neighbor's chickens scratched at the dirt around the tree where the bike had been, clucking among themselves.

"Let's take a ride so we can talk," Victor said.

At a curve in the south road to town, he wormed the bike down a rutted, puddled channel through river grass. Behind them a two-story house could be seen above the grass. Victor stopped near the water and killed the motor and leaned the bike to the side so Liz could reach the ground and slide off the back of the seat. A pile of rambutan husks lay on the ground and the grass was matted down into a seating area hidden from the house and the street. The highway bridge was off to their right and cars rumbled regularly across it. A green heron leaned into the shallows a few yards away, its bill as poised as a drawn arrow.

They discussed the meaning of the word gunslinger. Phil Millege had used it once and then never again. Liz had meant to ask for clarification but the moment had passed.

"Someone who is easy with his weapon," Victor said. "Someone who shoots quickly. I remember I saw this in a movie once."

He stood gazing at the bridge, the random passing of vehicles that could be carrying either man, the gunslinger or the target. "This is a strange situation," he said.

She looked at his back, the dark ponytail against

his blue shirt, and then out at the water flowing past them, the inevitability of its motion, and thought again of all the years gone by. "We have changed, of course," she said. "We are not kids."

"Yes, that is true," he said. He turned to see her, to look directly into her dark eyes, her divided face. "But we take money to play a game. We pretend, like kids."

She nodded, meeting his eyes. "I want to help Mr Phil," she said. "And also help Ellis. I know those statements are contradictory. But I was thinking at the beginning that I could influence the outcome if I was part of the pursuit."

"I understand," he said. "An opportunity came and we each took it. An unusual foreign opportunity. And now we are between opposing Americans."

"We are not caught," Liz said.

"Yes, we are," Victor said, "as long as we remain between them."

"And because of this, Victor," she said, "we found each other again."

He did not know how to answer this. Did not know how to proceed with her. He had held her, had felt her heart beating, her life pressed against his again. But he was cautious about her, about the remaining spirit and energy of their childhood crush, about the rising dangers associated with the Americans.

He returned in his mind to their fervent meeting beside another river, an upland stream that descended into this one, and he could still feel the heat in her young hands, her face, her lips, and he said finally, as if in a dream, as if swimming across a river of time, "I'm worried that harm will come to you."

She looked at him and smiled. "We can protect each other."

"Maybe," he said. "If we don't lose our heads, if we

don't forget to stay alert and keep looking around."

Liz made a point of looking around, at the tall river grass, the flowing river and the thick trees opposite, at the distant bridge signifying the world at large, their relative seclusion at the moment. She sat down in the matted grass.

"We can relax for a minute," she said, "and then go back to being alert." Her face was two shades of red. "We can look for Ellis and take our vehicles back to San Isidro and get our rooms and make sure Mr Phil is okay."

Victor looked down at Liz holding her knees, her hair falling across one bright brown eye, her vulnerability, her unique and unlikely presence here with him. He turned for a moment and stared across at the other bank, tracked the treeline and listened hard to hear anything beyond the rushing water, beyond the sound of his deep steady breathing. He turned back and sat beside her.

He remained cross-legged and upright, a seated sentry against a river approach. After a while she took one of his calloused hands and held it in hers. In the transfer of warmth she massaged his knuckles and pressed her grip into the base of his thumb and pushed her own thumb into his palm as if to smooth the roughness there. Tension drained from his shoulders and he lay back and looked at the sky, the blemished gray clouds moving in layers of discolored uncertainty. She reclined on one elbow beside him and he looked at her and reached up and pulled her face to his.

—

● ○ ○ ○ ○ Reviewed May 29, 2014
"Kayaking trip is one long sweaty hunger ordeal"
My girlfriend and I are not naturalists (even if we went to a nude resort one time, which was not actually a great

experience, but that's another story, which my honest review could inform you of if I gave you the name of the place) or high maintenance people. We don't as a rule complain without really good reasons but in this case we both agree the reasons were highly numerous. We are not health freaks or survivalists but we do enjoy getting out of doors when conditions are conducive, like warm, sunny weather and meals included in the price. We were enjoying Costa Rica with relatively few issues when we met this guy serving us beers and whole fish in a restaurant and he talked us into taking a mangrove tour. He arranged our trip with Selva Tours and we met him early the next morning for departure from the same place, which was not even open at that hour. We thought coffee would be served before the long drive in his minivan but sadly he didn't offer this basic service. We fell asleep and woke with stiff necks from the uncomfortable seats in his vehicle. Our guide, whose name was Gustavo but who insisted we call him Stavo, suggested that my girlfriend ride in his kayak because he didn't think she could paddle the whole way which was part jungle tunnels and part open river that was a struggle to navigate when we hit waves coming from the ocean. I'm not a big fan of sweating, even though it comes naturally to me, and our guide never mentioned the great amount that would happen on this trip. I prefer to be alerted to a sharply dropping comfort level beforehand. In this case a motor option would have been helpful and appreciated. I'm sure other tours offer a more complete service. Who hasn't seen a small trolling motor attached to the rear of a kayak? I had a headache from no coffee and he did all the paddling for Beatrice who was just cruising along taking phone pics. I could see they were talking a lot and I was always

catching up just when he finished showing her some small, practically invisible bats on a tree or a sleeping raccoon (to be honest, who hasn't already seen a sleeping raccoon on numerous occasions?) Our guide only brought water and granola bars but no barbecue chips or ham sandwiches or diet cokes to provide us the necessary energy. He showed us a boa constrictor but didn't say how big it was if stretched out or how large an animal it could swallow. His knowledge was underwhelming. Not to mention his accent was heavy and his English vocabulary poor. All in all I was completely exhausted at the end, and super starved. We saw a huge crowd of vultures on our landing beach (weren't there any other landing choices?) and he pointed out what he said were crocodiles in the river but all I saw were ripples of waves. In summation this kayak tour was mostly constant paddling for me and a lot of laughing for my girlfriend, who found our guide to be Mr Entertainment. In my opinion he was way too friendly with her. He made up animal names like bignose bat and boathead heron to cover his lack of information. And as I mentioned, he showed a serious lack of regard for feeding his clients. In all honesty I have to award this company one star. The weather was ok.
rowanbowlers
Date of experience: May 28, 2014

—

Stavo got a call in the stock room of Ballena Bahia. He set down two cases of beer and flipped open his phone. It was Julio Hernandez, the owner of Selva Tours, a company which was actually just him, if you didn't count the extra guides he hired to take on more clients.

"Stavo, did you see that shit review?"

"Julio, brother, those people were crazy."

"Yes, that's probably true, but who brought them out so they could write one? You have to determine who should come out and who should stay by their hotel pool sipping fruity drinks."

"Sipping drinks is not paying us money," Stavo said.

"That asshole made it seem like you were paddling away with his girl."

"She was in my boat, man."

"Of course you weren't flirting with her."

"I was just doing my job. It wasn't easy with that fat guy, but I tried. Look, brother, it won't happen again. I'll be super careful about clients. Right now I have to get the bar ready. Okay?"

"I'll be in touch," Julio said. "Unless you're planning to disappear again."

"That other thing will end soon," Stavo said. "It's just a quick opportunity."

When he came out he saw that a man had taken a seat at the bar. It was the slack afternoon period between lunch and dinner and no one else was around except Henry in the kitchen. Stavo set the cases on the bar and lifted the counter hatch and entered the bartending space. The other man, who was wearing a blue ballcap and aviator sunglasses, was staring at the supermarket parking lot as if expecting someone's arrival.

Stavo put the beer on the floor and opened the cooler. He straightened and said to the customer, "You want a drink, amigo?"

The man looked at him, unsmiling. "I'm waiting for my friend," he said. "He's such a clown, always late, doesn't give a damn about others. A real asshole," he said, "but also terrifying. Fucking scary sometimes."

Stavo stared at the sunglasses turned on him, this

gringo speaking English, not a young tourist but a mature man exuding a professional manner.

The man stared back, then stood, rising taller, and spoke slowly, deliberately. "Fucking clown," he said. And then in Spanish, "*Maldito payaso.*"

Stavo felt a wave of recognition, then a loss of stability, a swirl of turbulence enveloping his inner ear. He put a hand forward on the counter even as he meant to step backward. Sweat erupted at his hairline and crept back across his scalp like condensation moving over glass.

Traffic passed, an amalgamation of noise fragments drifted over from the market, the bar's television mumbled on low, the ceiling fan whirred like a mad bird descending, a monster of some kind. Before he could think of leaving, the man was behind the bar. Stavo took a swing at him, felt his right arm seized, his hand twisted into a wrist lock, his body rotated downward, his muffled cry like a mute straining to sound out the first letter of the alphabet.

They sank to the floor, out of sight, Stavo's knees pressed into the rubber mat, his elbow torqued into pain, his face dripping, his mouth open, his eyelids fluttering, his thumb a lever to stretched tendons, the other man's mouth at his ear, whispering casually.

"You have quit your team," he said. "If you fuck with me I'll snap both your thumbs and dislocate your shoulders and break your knees with a liquor bottle. You understand me? We're going to stand now so you can be the helpful bartender. Does your mother enjoy clowns too? Maybe she'd like a visit and the chance to laugh her fucking head off."

When he rose to standing height and into view again, Stavo was surprised that nothing had changed, that apparently almost no time had passed. The other man stood beside him at the open counter hatch, as if helping the bartender with something, smoothing out a paper on the counter, like an order form or a checklist, but as he focused on the paper, Stavo saw that it was a map with handwritten notes beside a road. He squinted, breathing through his mouth, gulping air and exhaling as if concluding a race. His right arm hung limply at his side, aching in several places. He wanted to ask about reasons for all this but could not speak yet, felt muscles twitching in his legs.

"I will point to places between San Isidro and Dominical," the man said, "and you will confirm the point where your boss got out. *Claro*?"

Stavo leaned forward, wiped his eyes of moisture, thought of calling for Henry, immediately realized the stupidity of that. Nothing should delay this man's departure. He watched the finger slide down the road, Route 243, and without making eye contact saw the man's face turning to look for reactions.

Stavo cleared his throat. "There," he said.

"Don't lie to me," the man said. "You do not want me to drive there and find a mistake. You do not want me to come back here."

"No," Stavo said. "No mistake."

"So down this road then. To where, Circle of Light?"

Stavo nodded. The man folded the map and slid it into his pocket. He glanced around and put his arm on the bartender's shoulder as if to hug him fondly, then pinched a neck nerve hard enough to leave a twinging reminder.

After the clown man drove away, Stavo walked into the sun and wiped his nose, paced the parking lot next door, pulling himself together. He called Phil Millege, got his voicemail, called again, got the same result, hung up. He called Liz and got her voicemail, asked her to call him. He called Victor and the man answered.

"What's up, Stavo?"

"Victor, man. I had a bad visitor just now. He wants Mr Phil."

"What?" Victor said. "I'm on the bike. Speak louder."

"The American," Stavo said louder. "The clown in San Isidro."

Victor waited, air rushing around the phone. "The clown?" he said.

"Tell Phil Millege." Stavo was shouting to be heard over the wind on the other end. "The man is coming."

"The fucking tree-shaker?" Victor asked.

"Yes, man," Stavo said. "I'm sorry. He wants Mr Phil. I don't know why."

Victor thought he heard sobs. "Is he coming to Circle of Light?" he asked.

"Yes," Stavo said. "I couldn't—"

"Don't worry, brother," Victor said. "I'm going there too."

―

On the roof thatch the rain sounded like rattles shaken by medicine men. The shaman, Rapu, needed to raise his voice to be heard clearly. He was dressed in airy white pants rolled up to his shins and a handmade sleeveless cotton tunic of blue and yellow vertical stripes that, in the eyes of some of the attendees, seemed to vibrate. He had left his leather sandals at the door and sat cross-legged upon a low wooden table in the center of the round house. His hair was a lustrous black and long enough to be shaped in the manner of a cowl, his bangs cut in a curve that followed his jawline, giving his face a round, hazelnut shape, along with its hue. In fact, all of his visible skin appeared as uniformly brown as a ripe filbert. A long iridescent green Quetzal tail feather hung over his shoulder from a braid behind his left ear as if to call out his own resplendence. In his physical condition and tribal appearance, he might have walked into their orbit directly from Amazonia and would not seem out of place in a log canoe or wearing a bone nose ornament. Rather than Brazil, though, or any of its South American neighbors, Rapu had come from Tucson, Arizona.

"Examine the value of each individual breath," he said. "Think of yourself in the high country, walking a steep trail in Chirripó, every oxygen molecule a valued friend, a measure of life, every burning step an achievement delivering you to your destination. But what is it? And why must you journey through discomfort to reach it?"

Phil Millege had a cramp in his left calf and his varied movements on his cushion made him seem a restless child, the oldest kid in the room, though he wasn't sure about the shaman, who was lined and weathered, yet youthful.

Millege pushed his leg out straight toward the center and wiggled his toes as if signaling to the man speaking.

"Tonight will be a somatic experience and, of course, a transition," Rapu was saying. "*Madre Aya* goes in and through, she cleans out your unwanted energies, teaches you to see the hidden landscapes in your own mind."

Sage fumes were causing Millege to believe someone was smoking a cigarette outside the room's screening. In his mind a cigar was passing across the afternoon sky, cruising deliberately in the style of a deep space capsule.

Whisking, rustling, rain-beaten thatch obliterated some words. Several people had their eyes closed, some sat upright in a meditative pose, others lay back and looked at the ceiling and let the sounds wash over them.

Mother Ayahuasca. Spirit Vine. Childhood memories. Shadow material. Stay with your breath. Your self-improvement. Find catharsis. Plant spirits will enter the ceremony. Renewal. Affirmation. Simplicity. Truth. Removal of negative energies. Healing. Peace. Only the shaman sings and chants. No clapping, no talking, no physical contact during the ceremony.

Millege stood to relieve his leg cramp, which felt like a walnut lodged in his calf. He walked around his cushion and squatted to stretch his muscles. Several attendees looked up at him. He moved to the wall and began to hobble around the perimeter of the room. Rapu glanced at him, then at his helpers, two local women dressed in white, and one of them—when Millege passed as quietly as he could, his shoulders lifted in pantomime of someone attempting to lessen their body weight through arm movements and tiptoe walking to avoid causing floor boards to creak—held out a directive hand toward the very space he had just vacated. Instead, Millege pushed open the screen door and walked down the steps into the rain.

—

After she got a distress call from her father, Liz Zuniga told Victor to leave without her. She left Phil Millege a voicemail, knowing he probably had no reception but figuring there was at least a reasonable chance that he would leave the natural medicine ranch early and get back on the road.

She drove to Sierpe in the blue Rav4. According to her father, her mother, Isabel, was not doing well. The pressure to move had ramped up, and they had been shown a house in town where they were now supposed to live. This house did not suit her, and her level of anxiety had risen to manifest in repetitive muscle movement and disorientation. Leo did not go into detail on the phone, except to say that his wife kept shrugging her shoulders.

In her floral house dress and old slippers Isabel shuffled from room to room, from the small living room and adjacent dining table to the kitchen to the bedrooms to the bathroom, where she stopped to speak to herself in the discolored mirror. She lifted her braid and shook it, admonishing her reflection.

"You are not going anywhere," she said.

She heard someone calling and turned to see. Maybe it was someone coming to move in alongside her and Leo. Anything could happen now.

Entering the kitchen, she was startled to see a woman standing at the stove. Oh, thank God, her own daughter. "Where have you been?" she asked.

"I've been calling you, Mami. What are you doing? Have you eaten?"

Isabel looked at her and thought about the question but did not know what to say. She went to the front door and peered outside, then shut it.

She turned back to her daughter. "Where's the American girl?" she said.

Liz stared at her mother's innocent wrinkled face, her clouded gray eyes. "I came alone, Mami," she said. "Where's Papi?"

Her mother shrugged, her eyes widening as her lips pursed tight with a look of impish wonder. She shrugged again.

Liz went to the rear door and opened it and looked out back at the long grass and the garden remains, the broken fencing and weeds overrunning, the ancient stone sphere at the edge of the grove. She did not see her father, then noticed a movement in the plumbeous gloom of the palms. She turned back to her mother and said, "Stay here, Mami."

A white hawk flew keening into the grove as she

entered, a guide to her father, she thought, watching her footing in the muddy ruts between the trees. Up ahead, a man riding a bike approached her, a field worker with no work in this section, who could be making better time on the road. He adjusted his hat, staring at her face as he passed, then pointed over his shoulder with a thumb, shaking his head negatively and frowning in comment on what he'd witnessed.

She saw Leo's slick bare back as he leaned his weight into a palm's trunk, his shirt tied around his waist, his pants and shoes mud-speckled, and she heard the high whine of a power drill as she got closer.

"Papi," she called. He looked up and withdrew the drill's long bit and watched as she circled the tree, inspecting the ring of holes he'd made. "What is this?" she said. "What can this possibly accomplish?"

He raised himself erect and lifted his chin defiantly, breathing heavily, his arms covered in bits of wood and dirt. "I'll add poison," he said.

"Poison?" she said. "Poison? What poison? Where did you get the drill?"

"Roberto lent it to me," he said, "to repair the side shed."

"Is this how you spend your time now?" she said, her voice rising, her face growing hot. "Leaving Mami alone in the house?" She moved closer, meeting his eyes. "That worker saw you doing this. Do you think the company will do nothing about their trees? How many have you drilled?"

He looked around, wiped his forehead, his wet scalp. "Maybe eighteen," he said. "I don't know exactly."

"Mother Mary," she said. "You are a man of science, Papi. Look at all these trees. What good will your little acts of destruction do? Do you believe you're hurting these big trees? Will it help Mami if you go to jail? Will it help Mami if you get bitten by a snake?"

He stared off into the infinite orderly forest, the palms with their long lower fronds brown and drooping against the trunk like grass skirts almost to the ground, an army of tall sturdy beings with wild green shocks of stiff hair, rough algal skin, their fruit on the way, endless bunches of oily orange nuts.

"It's just an exercise," he said at last, his voice low in the murky stillness.

"Then take a walk, Papi," she said. "You have to control your frustration."

"What happened to your American friend?" he said. "Have you seen him?"

"He's not around right now," she said.

Leo nodded, set the drill on the ground, wiped his hands on his pants. "He sent a message to the company," he said. "Now they're after him."

"Why do you say that?" she said.

"Everybody knows," he said. "But he is already suffering enough. For the girls. For Chloe." He shook his head. "Your mother liked her," he said.

"She just asked me where the American girl was," Liz said. "Let's go inside now, Papi. You shouldn't leave her alone for so long."

At the house, Leo set the drill on the back steps and slipped off his shoes. They stepped inside and Liz called out for her mother. Silence met them. Leo went through the kitchen and peered out the window into the open shed. He motioned to his daughter and she joined him. Isabel stood under the tin roof hanging laundry from a line that ran diagonally the length of the concrete slab. No water dripped from the clothes. The basin at her feet was dry.

"How can this be?" he said.

Liz put her hand on his shoulder. He heard the back door close and watched his daughter enter the shed with the hose and begin to fill the basin. She measured a cup of soap powder into the water and then hugged her mother, pulled her close, felt the warmth of their cheeks together. She took down a shirt and dropped it in the basin and Isabel took down a dress and put it into the bubbles rising. She looked at her daughter and shrugged sharply several times, her hands hanging loosely at her sides.

Tears ran down Leo's face as he watched. He took off his pants and rolled them up with his shirt and walked out to the shed in his shorts and put his clothes in the foaming basin. He pulled his wife into his thin wiry embrace, one arm around her back and the other holding her head, pressing her face to his. He whispered in her ear, "Thank you for being on this planet with me."

20. Open World

Millege was rain-soaked and side-tracked, hiking up a slippery trail to imagine a stealthy approach from the outside, postponing his preparations for the main event, reading the terrain rising behind his cabin to examine his defensive position. Surrounding ridge altitude roughly 2500 feet, descending sharply. Potential access overland from a neighboring business. Sunrise 0530.

At several places he saw a wooden tree-mounted sign about the size of a legal pad. *Silent is Better*, it said. He acknowledged this and headed back.

He sat at his desk wearing a towel. The cool damp air drifted through his room delivering the fruit smells of trees breathing out their water-quenched breaths. Through his windows the afternoon light was filtered through a screen of silvery rain. He heard light steps on his porch, then a light tap at his door. He rose soundlessly but for the slight creak of the chair, lifted his expandable baton and held it behind his back.

"Yes," he said.

"Hey, it's me," she said. It was Cassandra—another young woman, he thought, with a potential gift of prophecy.

He tossed the baton on the bed and opened the door.

She smiled from under a red umbrella. "Can I come in?" she said.

He stepped back and she collapsed her umbrella, shook it over the porch as she entered, and closed the door behind her. He offered her the chair but she remained standing by the desk. He stood beside the bed.

She glanced at his towel and the steel baton on the bed, took in his fleshy torso, held her dripping umbrella in front of her.

"Since you left early," she said, looking at his face, "I just wanted to make sure you were okay. Chris was going to check on you, but I said I would."

"Who's Chris?" he said.

"Oh, he's that greeter dude. You've met him. And he'll be there tonight."

"You mean Monty, the birdman?"

She giggled. "His name is Chris," she said, "but he calls himself Monty."

"Okay," he said. "My name's Phil, but I call myself Phil."

She smiled. "I guess you're doing okay," she said, "but I wanted to pass along a few words anyway. If you don't mind."

"Anything you like," he said, taking in her snaggletooth as she spoke, her lips, her provocative blue eyes, her fountain of hair.

"Look, no offense, and I'm very glad we met," she said, "but you seem a bit out of place. And distracted, like you have a lot on your mind. Which I guess could be said about any of us. But this stuff we're about to take is a psychoactive brew. You know what I mean? If something's bothering you or lurking just below the surface, it could erupt like a volcano. I mean, like taking disturbing forms. Possibly. You never know. I just want to warn you, not knowing how you've actually prepared yourself for this or what's hounding you. My advice, regarding the elixir, would be to take a moderate taste."

"I appreciate that," he said. "You're very thoughtful."

"I don't want you to have a bad experience," she said. "It's more fun if you have a good one. Then relaxing the day after, the introspection, is much better. The sharing."

"All I have to do is make it through the night," he said.

She laughed. "That's about it."

At the door she glanced down at his desk and saw the oblong stone there. "What's that?" she asked. "Is this smooth little phallus your totem?"

"That's from the river," he said. "Or one of the three hills. I forget which."

She smiled, opened the door and stepped out. "You're on a curious journey," she said. "The fact that I can't figure you out gives me a little tingle."

"A tingle of any size sounds good," he said.

"Oh, it is, it definitely is," she said. She blossomed her umbrella and stepped down to the road and left him in the doorway watching her walk.

—

Like ghost fish, the gray carp flowed back and forth over and among themselves, turning constantly at the close walls of the open tank, weaving as if trying to lace their world into knots. Del Preet lifted his eyes from the tank and gazed out over the valley, the scattered lowland patches of jungle, garden and pasture, the red dirt road, the sweeping curves of a river. A few patrons sat at picnic tables on the wide terrace and several more held positions at the bar beneath the high peaked roof. Del Preet's meal arrived and he took a seat at a table and asked for water.

When his phone buzzed he stepped over to the railing and answered.

"Go ahead," he said.

"News flash," a voice said. It was Reynaldo, his in-country associate.

"Hit me," Del Preet said.

"Your man used an ATM in San Vito today, 1100 hours."

"How much?" Del Preet said.

"Three hundred bucks. In colones."

"Hard times," Del Preet said. "Probably on the move."

"I take it you're not there," Reynaldo said.

"I'm having a meal with a view outside San Isidro."

Reynaldo chuckled. "Not exactly close," he said.

"It's been quiet," Del Preet said. "I've had to amuse myself."

"Sounds like trouble," his friend said. "For someone."

"Let me have a direction when you have one," Del Preet said.

"Roger that, bucko," Reynaldo said.

Del Preet hung up and returned to his food. After he finished, he stopped beside a stone sphere outside the terrace gate and withdrew the folded Missing Person poster he'd taken from a pole in Dominical. He smoothed the paper on the curved surface of the stone and called the number listed.

His anonymous call forwarded to Liz Zuniga and she answered.

Del Preet spoke in a mixture of Spanish and English, using a higher pitch than his normal voice. He said he was certain he'd seen the man in San Vito today at the BCR cash machine. He said he was not calling for a reward.

"I'm a concerned expat," he said. "I only want peace and justice."

She thanked him for calling.

—

A red dirt bike passed the Circle of Light entrance sign, the rider studying other signs and turnoffs and the general undulations of the land. The bike was a Honda CR250, a two-stroke, and its raspy whine echoed off the hills. Any close enthusiast could have attested that the machine, while not a new model, was cared for and well-maintained. The signs told of farms—for tilapia and catfish, for jack fruit and mangosteen—and an ecolodge that appeared inactive, with empty stables and the bare indication of horse trails branching off the ascending driveway.

Victor rode to the top of the drive, cut the engine, removed his half-shell helmet and sat surveying the property as if considering its value. He observed the quiet house and listened, perched above the road, his head turning in the poised, casual manner of a raptor. After fifteen minutes without another vehicle in the vicinity, he dismounted and wheeled his bike behind the house. He chained it to a clothesline pole, stuffed his helmet into his backpack, and walked into the surrounding trees. He estimated his position at roughly two miles from the Circle of Light entrance.

—

Pre-ceremony status: questionable for take-off. Shaman seems sententious, possibly due to this particular attendee's skepticism. Why can't I get onboard? Is it because Solitude and Belonging are opposing forces? It's not too late to change careers either. Shouldn't I be having these insightful thoughts

AFTER the magic vine does its work? Does it work even before you take it? Just by planning to take it? Don't we all need to open our minds to new possibilities? Will I keep asking questions during this entire entry?

When people say, anything can happen, is that almost true? What am I supposed to be working on here? Am I not, like everyone else, in a prison of my own making? A prisoner of my mind and habits, my way of thinking? Is the purpose to break out? See beyond the walls into a new land?

Is Liz actually clairvoyant? Does she possess precognition? No, that would be the future. Maybe she has developed a sensitivity that allows her to guess with more accuracy. She started hot, then cooled off.

All day I've been singing this song of ego and retribution.

I ran forty-two pins through your gabardine heart, and still you pass by my house.

Some kind of country ballad I have to destroy in my head. What if I break out singing tonight?

Here's how it is here. Howler monkeys in the morning. Mantra when remembered. Not really a chanter by nature though. Could it become a useful practice? Hummingbirds. Toucans. Colorful frogs. Maybe get a field guide later? Saw my spirit animal, a glimpse, right by the koi pond, like it was scoping out a meal. Less than badger size, sort of a hefty weasel, white head above the eyes, dark face below. Striking. Monty/Chris called it a grison.

—

Costa Rica Courier
The greenman, New Indian, open world, a quantum entanglement
Marco Vargas / May 30, 2014
marcovargas@crcourier.com

There is a term I recently encountered, one which I had never heard before.
New Indian. Two words, four syllables. They sound solid together.
The name could be a brand, a title applied to a sweat lodge ceremony, the promotion of a shell-sloughing metamorphosis from which a reborn being will emerge, not the stereotype of the noble savage living completely in tune with nature but an enlightened warrior fiercely protective of our good Mother Earth. It has both a New Age sound and a traditional resonance. It suggests the joining of the more recently conceptualized with the old throwback, the reimagining of a well-worn trope.
Those stridently advocating the overhaul of all older cultural labels deemed offensive to any human, living or dead, by current correctness standards, and who support a rigorous updating by those policing the field of language with the pickets and staves of outrage, will want to change the phrase to Modern Indigenous Person. But to me, New Indian is more potent as a concept worth exploring, one whose deeper meaning bears relevance to this story.
New World Indian cultures have been absorbed, almost without exception, into the larger colonial cultures who overtook them, overran them, decimated them, pushed them aside in waves of territorial expansion. They now adhere to the federal laws under which they live, governed by outsiders. They struggle to maintain their language and tribal customs, hunkering down on the meager lands left to them, often descending into poverty and despair, periodically lifting up to showcase the remnants of once proud traditions.
In my view, New Indian signifies a recapturing of the former spirit, the fire and pride of peoples living with and

upon the earth, not as ideal stewards but as respectful independents. Of course we cannot go back to simpler visions of life. Harmony means something smaller today, something only seen in little pockets existing in cultural isolation or within the mechanized societies that rule the world. Open space and wild land are seen strictly in monetary terms, in what and how much can be reaped, squeezed, extracted. Short-term profits always outweigh the big picture concepts—life for its own sake, the right of other beings to exist, the need for forests as planetary oxygen makers, the climate changes we start and are unwilling or unable to stop. For some reason we can't do the right thing. We prefer televised distractions and new cars to decency. While poor people don't even have the luxury to contemplate choices in lifestyle. Whether to use plastic or paper. Whether to care about a section of forest when they need to grow beans or rice. And on it goes.

So what can a New Indian do? Should he cut his hair, put on a suit, and join a big environmental group? Should he be presented as an authentic native spokesman, dressed in skins, paint and feathers? Should she be the archetypal Earth Mother pleading her case before corporate businessmen? Should she be prepared to laugh with them? Drink their drinks and hear their promises and believe they will look into it? Should she lift her skirts and let them penetrate?

No, let the big groups enter the courts and fight there. The New Indian is more shadowy, geared for physical acts, guerilla skirmishes, the sharpening of knives, the honing of tomahawks. Warning by steel and fire.

This is the impasse we have reached and must accept. Which leads me back to the greenman story. You recall the greenman's pursuit by the bounty hunter sent by the palm oil company, the corporate entity bent on some kind of resolution to a thorny PR issue so minor it could have been swept under a thatch rug faster than palm nuts grow—if not for the fact of those inconvenient deaths. The poor girls! They made a point with their lives, even if the final point was unintended. Did they die in vain? No, I can't stomach the thought of that. I can't drop this story, especially since it remains unresolved. We have a real-life allegory for our turbulent times. And we have a New Indian on the loose.

Readers have been weighing in, sharing their opinions on what they know so far, what they've heard from others, what they think will happen. Or should happen. And from a just-in email, blazing new info.

It seems that a third party has joined the chase, without official sanction, my source feels, more in an undercover capacity. To some, this could appear to be a mercenary action. Who is this character, and who sent him to meddle? He is a third particle in the cosmos of this chase. According to my new source, he looks to be in direct conflict with the bounty hunter. Some new details are decidedly confidential, and I always protect my sources, but I feel within my bounds to characterize this mercenary as a demonic comic. Yes, off-kilter. Should you happen to find yourself in the path of any member of this triad, you are advised to take immediate cover. Or better yet, run.

For you physics geeks out there, the case presents us with something similar to a quantum entanglement, whereby each of these three particles is linked to the others, and the action or movement of any one will affect the others, no matter their distance apart. They have lost their independence.

Which brings me, on this path of tangentially linked

ideas, to the open world concept. If you're a gamer (and I am not) you will recognize the concept, the nonlinear, open-walled game. The players make decisions that determine the structure of their world. The outcome is evolving, based on actions that are happening, instead of issuing from an imposed framework that only allows one of several built-in possibilities.

Will justice be served? In this case, what does justice even mean?

This is an opinion piece as well as a local story currently unfolding, and I have always advocated side roads.

Greenman, I'm still here, advocating.

Peace be unto you, marcovargas@crcourier.com

—

The light and the mood were subdued inside the round house, though the world outside still wavered in late afternoon energy and color. The shaman supervised the preparation of the medicine in the communal kitchen adjacent. The ayahuasca vine and the chacruna leaves were harvested on the property and had been brewed together in large aluminum pots, stirred and monitored by helpers throughout the day. Now distilled into glass pitchers, the brown viscous residue had cooled for the ceremony.

Before the opening meditation, Rapu made his way around the maloca, as he called the ceremonial house, visiting each of the participants in turn. He spoke softly to each, held their hands and examined them, asked if they were ready, if they wished to remove negative energies and redirect positive ones. If they would do what they needed to do. It was good to be quiet, he told them, to be open, to work on the self in this protected space.

He was dressed as before. His two facilitators were in white, as were the general assistants, a half dozen door sitters and watchers quietly on hand to assist people to the toilets and help soothe any agitations that might occur. The attendees sat on their mats with personal items arranged around them, various combinations of flashlight, water bottle, blanket, cushion, jacket, notebook, and totem, often a photo. Everyone had a purple purge bucket.

Rapu squatted in front of Millege, whose personal items consisted of a flashlight, a water bottle, and a river stone, and looked him over carefully.

"Are you prepared, Philip?" the shaman asked.

"I think so," Millege said.

"Did you make a spontaneous decision about this?" Rapu said.

"Yes," Millege said. "I didn't do the long-form preparation."

"The more respectful you treat the process," Rapu said, "the better the resulting experience."

"Understood," Millege said. "I'll accept and use the experience I get."

The shaman placed his hands together to indicate that Millege should do the same and extend them in the manner of a forward prayer, then he held the two hands with his own and closed his eyes. Millege closed his too and tried to steady his breathing.

Rapu opened his eyes, separated his hands and rose, all in one fluid movement. He looked down at Millege and said, "We must face our fears and explore them." He smiled, then moved on.

A center table draped in white cloth held the medicine pitchers and the small glasses, a water pitcher, two succulent plants in clay pots, a small brass gong suspended in a wooden frame, several brass singing bowls and mallets, a tuning fork, some bundles of sage, the shaman's pipe and tobacco pouch, matches, candles, sea shells and trogon feathers, along with a framed photo of forest trees supporting vines split through by beams of slanting sunlight. A first aid kit was stored under the table.

All around the smooth planked floor were small portable lanterns. Some participants were already seated in meditative positions, spines straight, while others lay back on their cushions or spoke softly with their neighbors. Everyone was barefoot, dressed comfortably in shorts, T-shirts, skirts, beach dresses, loose pullovers, or linen pants. There was a perceptible current of nervousness in the room, as if they were all approaching the edge of a cliff.

Rapu walked around the edge of the room trailing sage smoke, waving it back and forth, speaking of a protected space, the compassion and unity within it, the healing to come, the connection with the divine. He sang sound words, guttural, repetitive, and soothing, modulated into a meditative rhythm. At the table he filled and lit his pipe and again made his rounds, clasping the extended prayerful hands of each participant, inserting the wedge of a wooden funnel between their pressed palms and gently blowing smoke to form a small cloud over and around their hands, a visual conduit from him to them.

As light drained from the medicine house and the vague outlines of trees in the outside world faded into the background, the floor lanterns were turned on and the facilitators helped form a line to the center table where each voyager was given a shot glass of the dark brown fluid. The shaman extended each glass with both hands, as if the substance were heavier than it appeared, and one after the other they were sniffed and sometimes sipped, most often thrown back quickly to surmount the bitter shock of the vile earthy taste, likened by some to a mushroom cocoa bile, the essence of which had to be kept down until absorbed and not purged too early. There were groans, wincing faces, hard swallows and involuntary heaves that were willfully held in check. Everyone had been cautioned.

Millege, last in line, was handed a half glass which he looked into for a long moment before ingesting. After that, the shaman drank his own dose.

In the lamplight, with everyone seated, including the watcher-helpers, the shaman meditated in alternating words and silences, awaiting the arrival of the plant spirits. Two helpers were positioned outside, one as a night guard in the clearing in front of the round house, the other at the toilets.

Face your shadow. You will get what you need, even if it is not what you want. In our sacred readiness we welcome the plant spirits, the natural doctors who come to heal us so everything becomes one. Stay with your breath. Work on your intentions. Do what you need to do. I will sing to call in the medicine.

This *curandero*, the healer, became silent on his central mat. The stillness was punctuated by sounds of movement, the sliding of feet on mats, by burps, modest coughs, by night calls and cries beyond the screen of the room. A warm glow settled upon the participants, some looking around for reactions or spectral visitors, others with eyes closed, peering inward.

Millege noted Cassandra across the room, cross-legged in a black top and skirt, hair in long twin braids, and he noticed the woman who checked him in, Juvia, sitting by the door in a lotus pose, alert and watchful. Three mats away, Merlin, the hirsute surfer, sat bobbing slowly forward and back, annoyingly, like some kind of metronomic show-off. Millege had not engaged meaningfully with many of the young men and woman around him. His casual interest now collapsed into deepening solitude, a sinking into a vast crater, and he felt he could suddenly roll off his mat and down a slope. He braced himself with both hands on the floor but nausea rose like a serpent into his throat and he lay back to keep from falling sideways.

The girl on his right began to cry. He couldn't look anywhere but up. The stars shone through the thatch as it became thinner and thinner, the distance between the fronds expanding, pieces flying away like wings. His liver was moving, being pushed or entwined. There was puking somewhere. And movement, someone walking. He closed his eyes. Cold shivers ran from his stomach cavity through his blood and out to his skin, which then flushed hot. He might need to purge himself. Once the noise let up. Someone was arriving by motorcycle and people were asking questions. A cat rubbed against his leg but he kept his eyes closed. He was shaking. Was he moaning? Jaguars were growling outside. The shaman whistled and groaned his exhalations.

Millege looked into his bucket and released. Fast, noisy. Parasites and toxins expelled. The emptiness of leaving. Natural sounds absorbed into the fabric of song. Stay with your breath. Your pure colors. Your dark shadows.

He heard the bowls singing but no one was playing them. The lantern beams were starbursts in all directions and the whole wood and thatch sepia-toned space was brighter now, each individual thing being outlined separately, its border expanding in layers of color as he watched, rolling beads of green, purple, and yellow tracing the shapes of poles and screens and figures on mats. The bowls became a voice in the center of the room. The voice was chanting low and steady, words he didn't recognize, beautiful words strung together with a steady, rattling percussion. A few were familiar. *Medicina. Mapacho. Ayahuasca.*

Sagrado. Some were invented, or from other languages. Rapu singing and connecting everything with his rattle and his word sounds.

He saw the boy, Harper, who called himself Harper Reaper, running across the tracks as Millege chased, the culmination of a two-month pursuit. The train hit him. No bells, no lights, no crossing gate, just a horn ignored. He was splattered, thrown in a heap. Now he danced, his form an oscillating red, animated, intact, slinging drops of blood across Millege on his mat. Get out of here, Millege said, you're still fucking things up.

He wiped his face clean. Rapu's face appeared in a cloud of smoke. No pork, no street drugs, no sex. First two, no objection, Millege said. I mean, how long is this supposed to go on? Not that anything is about to happen. I mean, sure, possibilities here and there. But. How long we been in here? I can't even decipher your answer, curandero.

There was a floating sour smell mixed with sage and tobacco and sweat and laughter and tears. What's so funny? someone said. What's so sad? came the reply. There should be a fan system or something, right? Purify the air, then worry about the souls. You get my meaning? Basic stuff.

His parents and his sister, waving. Plus cousins. What is it? he said. You just keep waving. Okay, so long then. Good-bye, they said, you are on your own now. No shit. No hard feelings. Good luck. Detachment runs in the family.

Yeah, it's all loosey-goosey, your system in flux, your bowels upended. Keep your breathing. You can be dizzy and still walk. Get to your knees first. What about the space between here and the door? Do you carry your bucket?

He rose to his feet and stepped off his mat. Yellow flashes ran across the window screens like eels of light. Coils of blue wire rolled over the floor, away from his feet, energy scattering. He moved into a higher state of entropy, feeling more disordered. He looked at the prone bodies, their eyes following his. Juvia rose from her mat and bowed slightly, took his hand and pushed open the door. Led him down the steps. He saw a human form standing nearby.

"Who's that?" he said.

"That's Monty," she said. "Monty's keeping watch."

"For what?"

"For anything. It's just procedure, in case someone goes for a walk."

She turned him the other direction and they moved to the toilet shed.

Another woman was hovering there, her white dress ghostly in the darkness. "This is Dimaris," Juvia said. "She's here to assist, should you need anything."

"Hello," Dimaris said.

She floated before him, her skin luminescent, her pale hair wound up into a disk on top of her head, her round face revealed, her small stature and wide eyes making her seem an ethereal sprite. He stared at her as Juvia vanished and the grounding sounds of the *icaros* issuing from the round house, the tones and vibrations of songs sung in the language of the plants, surrounded him in a bubble of love, all the more comforting out here.

A red beam sprang from her hand and shone on the nearest door. "Do you need to go inside?" she said, pulling the door open and shining her light in.

He looked into the wooden closet, at the box seat with its toilet lid, at the paper roll and the book beside it. "I feel better out here," he said.

She closed the door. "Sometimes just moving around helps," she said.

"What's your last name?" he said.

She tilted her head at him. "Kinsey," she said.

"Kinsey Dimaris," he said. "Could go either way. Reversible."

"I suppose so," she said. "Are you feeling okay?"

He motioned at the door, she opened it again, stepped back as he knelt before the box and vomited violently, without much content, into the opening. He stood and wiped his chin as she aimed her light at the ground, a pool of red particles containing them both.

"I forgot my light," he said.

"No worries," she said.

"I need to lie down now," he said.

"Of course," she said. "I'm here for you. Let's go to the house."

"I came out for another reason," he said.

"To shit?" she asked. "Sometimes you just think you do."

"You know a few things," he said.

"I knew you'd come back here," she said.

"Really?" He looked amused. "For some reason you stayed in my mind." He turned to go, then looked up at the winking star dome. "Are you the shaman's girlfriend?"

She laughed. "If I were, I wouldn't be out here."

The bowls were singing, reverberating in waves through the room. Rapu tapped a mallet against the gong, returned to circling a bowl, and then set the tuning fork on its rim, experimenting with sound healing resonances and tone. A helper was pouring the next round and people were standing to partake.

"Don't fight the medicine," Rapu said. "Discover who you are."

Merlin sat smiling and laughing to himself. Millege stood on his mat as if on an island, casting his gaze around the room, preparing to set sail again. He saw Cassandra in a warrior pose on her mat, stretching her whole body. She smiled at him. Others were smiling at him too. He smiled back. He felt like a poster boy for the unexpected trippers.

After everyone had taken their second dose and settled again and the shaman had blown more smoke and thrown drops of jasmine water to tilt participants out of their expectations, and the calls of owls and frogs had been absorbed into an interior sonic texture that varied from listener to listener, the vomiting commenced in concert with writhing and shaking, and Millege saw Merlin lying in a cramped fetal position that further collapsed into screaming.

The helpers were in motion, assisting those in need to sit up, to take some water, to breathe into their demons, to bring them into the light of recognition and clearance. Everyone wanted to love themselves in the end.

The night's darkness deepened and pressed closer, a force of isolation and bonding. Candles flickered, replacing the glow of lanterns. Millege lay back and closed his eyes, found himself at a bus stop. Both of his ex-wives were there, as friends, apparently, to see him off. No hard feelings he figured. He got on the bus and bent down at the back window and watched the two women talking, wearing similar sundresses and hair styles. He began to weep, still standing, the bus rocking along, his hands gripping the backs of the seats on either side of the aisle, passengers staring at him as he recounted his failures, his selfish behavior, his long absences, his constant pursuit of bail jumpers, days in motels without calling, his ridiculous trysts on the road, his noncommittal attitude toward partnership, his lack of contribution, the shitty gifts he'd bought to make amends, the exemption from steadfastness he applied at home. Hey man, the driver said, his distant face up in the slot of his mirror, you got to sit down. You got to sit down, brother, and love people you don't even know. All these people here. We all got to love one another.

He rolled onto his side and tears ran down his face. In the wet blur and darkness of his vision he saw a grison crouched and tensed to spring, its fur smooth and radiant, its mouth open to reveal sharp white teeth. Millege jerked back and sat up, lifting his hands in defense. The animal was gone.

He drank water and gazed up at the attendant hovering and then lay back down. There was a wind storm and he was blown into the jungle and began walking over roots and pulling on vines that came loose and fell on him. He was covered in ants and had to leap into a river and hold onto a log that sent him over a drop into freefall. He expected the log to kill him but it plunged like a pile driver into the water beside him and he bobbed up and kept flowing with the current. Everything was moving faster than normal and he was desperate to get out of the water and slow down.

His grandfather pulled him out and he was amazed to be young again.

They entered a candy store together and his grandfather's kindly face smiled and wrinkled behind his rimless glasses and he let the little boy Philip choose whatever he wanted. The boy took his time, looking at each of the jars, letting himself control and savor the speed of his experience.

He had just collected his pile on the counter when a young man entered and withdrew a pistol and began to yell at the storekeeper. The boy's grandfather moved to shield the child and was shot in the chest as the storekeeper ducked below the counter. The gunman leaned over and shot the storekeeper in the back and went around and emptied the cash drawer. He paused in leaving to stuff some candy from the counter pile into his pocket and seeing the boy looking up at him from the floor, scraped the rest of the pile off the edge to shower down as if in recompense for the killing.

When the bodies were taken away and the boy was questioned, he said the gunman had unkempt brown hair, crooked teeth, and a sour smell, that he wore an orange flannel shirt and jeans and black boots and was not especially tall. The boy did not take any candy.

Though the boy walked a long dusty road, alone and crying, he heard giggling and outright laughter coming from various places along the route, from clumps of grass and abandoned cars and gravel hills. A man wearing a mask followed him at a distance and he realized he did not have a destination. The sky twisted itself into spectacular strands of color, tall helixes both beautiful and beguiling. The strands were part of a fabric, and in the fabric were worlds and lives and the source of the songs he was hearing again. The vibrations of the man's voice, the unknown words, calmed him and kept him on the ground.

He was relaxing in a chair as dusk settled, counting the handful of stars he could see, isolating every distinct sound he could hear. The breeze through heliconia leaves, a plane's distant rumble overhead, a car passing, some kids next door running in their backyard, squealing in play, a young girl's impatient voice: Dad, how much longer?, a peacock's two-part cat cry down the street, bamboo wind chimes tinkling their hollow winsome melody, the peeper frogs warming up, the nearby wobble call of a screech owl starting its night.

The icaros carried out into the night, the curandero hitting his stride, his mind and voice in tune, his sharp, forced exhalations, air expelled in accent to the chanting of words, also entering the surrounding sonic environment. The round house glowed like a large lantern, a thatch-domed capsule nestled in a jungle clearing, the only source of light to be seen in the area.

—

From where he sat atop a boulder, as cross-legged as a practicing meditator, Victor could observe the site of the proceedings, the comings and goings of figures needing to exit for a short time, as well as the male figure stationed a short distance away, who drank from a bottle and urinated on a regular basis, who occasionally sat and allowed his head to nod downward for minutes at a time, who started a fire in the fire pit, perhaps out of boredom, and then quickly let it die out.

The river's constant running, its turns and falls and whispering rush, always arriving and passing and moving on, supplied the background sound to Victor's listening, the ceremonial songs another layer in the music of the night, which included the usual nocturnal flappings and rustlings, the sudden cries and shrieks of creatures either territorial in origin or signaling the panic of attack.

His senses, having grown accustomed to the dark and the accruing substance of starlight, perceived animals and shadows both real and imagined. Wildcats, small and mid-sized, drank from the river, along with pacas, coatis, and raccoons. During the course of the night, as he changed positions and angles of view, he heard night birds and bats and caught glimpses of swooping flights, and he smelled the long-range odor of skunk. On the ground were the shuffling movements of armadillos, and in the trees the tamandua anteater used its long nose to seek out insect nests. In this tropical terrain, the gray fox prowled. And the tayra, a weasel-type predator, also lurked in darkness. Even the jaguarundi, a short-legged, solid-colored, highly vocal and diurnal cat, had ranged into night. As Victor sat somewhat merged with the panoply of forest life, he recalled something Ellis had said last year: all over the world mammals were becoming nocturnal to avoid the primary activities of humans. Naturally, many humans applied the same strategy. And then in the distance, as if to both validate and contradict the thought, an ocelot's primal growl rippled low and long through the trees, a warning or complaint by a hunting mammal prone to circumventing the human scents spreading so voluminously on common currents of air.

By 2:30 a.m., the round house was empty. Victor watched the last few occupants stagger out and meander away behind their beams. The watchman went inside, extinguished the last of the lights, and after another half hour, every aspect of the ceremonial night that Victor could perceive was quiet.

He made his way through the property, skirting the dwellings and intersecting the main path to the entrance road only when he had passed them. His boots crunched lightly on the dirt. He stopped regularly to regain his stillness—to listen, watch, and smell. He felt more alive being alone than he had for a long time. But he was also getting sleepy and figured that Millege was basically okay, hidden and relatively safe, in his cabin.

At the entrance clearing he stopped again and stepped to the side of the path. He saw the corner of the greeting shelter and six cars parked adjacent to it. He crouched slowly, sinking down to the shape of a shrub. And waited.

A crescent moon had risen over the horizon and above the trees and now cleared a ridge of clouds as he examined the cars, his eyes settling on the one at the end of the row, which looked to be, from his vantage point, a black Nissan X-Trail. Victor stared at the windshield and then cast his eyes beside the car to let his peripheral vision work. He did this repeatedly, knowing he needed to approach the car and look inside. He could see no movement within but, of course, an occupant could be reclining.

The dirt and gravel of the clearing shone feebly in the pale light and he rose and walked to the corner of the shelter and squatted again to peer into the dark space of the open deck, his entire body and his senses wired with the possibility that someone was in there already. But in the grainy shadow of the shelter he saw nothing, and he followed the length of it across the front and paused at the far corner. He heard the river below and looked back at the cars and nothing had changed except his level of suspicion. He grasped the railing and pulled himself up and stepped over into the gloom of the shelter.

From his backpack he withdrew a string hammock and slung it from railing to railing in front of the far corner post. He sat in it watching the black car under the pallid moonlight, drank some water, and after a while climbed back over the front railing and crossed to the nearest car, a silver Civic, and moved along the rear of the vehicles until he was behind a red Kia opposite the Nissan. He withdrew his hunting knife from its sheath and held it against his thigh and squat-walked toward the Nissan's passenger door. Halfway there he noticed the rear window was not entirely closed—it was down about an inch—and he froze in his tracks. He sensed or heard some motion inside the vehicle, a slight stirring, and scuttled crab-like to the front passenger door. He waited, his heart pounding in his ears, his blood rushing, his knife blade vertical.

He steadied himself against the metal, his breaths deep and fast. The car moved against his left palm as the opposite rear door opened and the weight inside shifted to the far side. No interior light came on. He heard the person step away from the car and then the sound of water splattering—a man was peeing. He could hear the man's exhaled breath, relaxation into the act of relief, the fatigue of the hour reflected in sighs of blown out air. Victor braced himself to lunge—the tension gathering in his thighs—if the man came around the car.

The car tilted again as the man reentered. The door closed, the lock clicked down. Leaning against the door, Victor could feel the body inside reclining, its weight shifting into the best position the space afforded, and he remained where he was, holding the same position until his knees and calves were numb. Finally, he leaned forward onto his hands and knees and crawled to the front of the Kia. He crawled the length of the row of cars, then stood behind the Civic and flexed his legs, lifted his knees one after the other. He took a step toward the shelter. Something scampered behind him. He turned toward the road and drew back his weapon, but the animal had vanished. He glanced back at the Nissan, then walked across the clearing to the far corner of the shelter and climbed up and over the railing and sat in his hammock. He was drained, completely exhausted. He lay back with his boots flat on the floor, his knife on his chest, and stared overhead, listening and thinking as much as he could. If not the fucking tree-shaker, then who? He couldn't positively identify the car but knew what made the most sense. Unless it belonged to some other unwelcome visitor, or a flipped-out attendee who had retreated to his own vehicle for whatever reason. Victor didn't know where to find Phil Millege. And if this night pisser was the fucking tree-shaker, he probably didn't know which cabin either and was waiting until daylight to move ahead. Victor felt compelled to rest his eyes.

21. Major Mammals

PPOI, and its subsidiary Palma Central, had a public relations department to deal with bad press as well as good press. But there was a separate branch, an offshoot, created to handle the edgier complaints, the more hostile and potentially dangerous threats, of which there were more and more in these times of a widespread environmental consciousness. Most of the threats were empty, without the intention of actual violence, propagated simply to keep the fraught topic of palm oil in the news. However, the company was structured to take every threat seriously and, to this end, had mandated the preemptive practices and problem-solving capabilities of the surreptitious department quietly known as PRX.

One of the department's main objectives was the cultivation of tips on individuals, on conversations, on associations, on newcomers, on idle boasts. Based on the back-channel recommendations of PRX, the company made donations to surfing schools, to indigenous farming collectives, to private nature preserves, to churches and to daycare centers, and along with the payments came smiles and the friendly sounding chats with new associates.

The department's administrator, Felipe Salas, personally covered the area between Quepos and Sierpe, looking for ways to expand his influence. Returning from the south, he stopped in Dominical at a tiny backroad shop—a raised, rough-planked shack with a tin roof—called SurfBoard Medic. The shop's sign, fastened to a bamboo fence post, was half of a yellow surfboard with the words Ding Repair and, beneath it in smaller letters, Pura Vida, along with a phone number, painted in black. Mangoes lay on the ground around the shop, and two surfers sat on the shaded porch in front of the open door.

They looked at the black Range Rover pulling up and at the middle-aged dude who stepped out and approached. He was dressed in light-brown linen trousers and a white linen shirt, his collar open to reveal a delicate gold crucifix, sunglasses resting atop his thick, gray-streaked hair, his sleeves rolled up casually, his posture, bearing and confident manner exuding vigor and power. His driver, a younger man dressed in a light gray suit, stood in front of the vehicle and smoked, examining his phone and keeping an eye on his boss.

Salas greeted the barefoot men with a raised hand and a smile.

"How's business?" he said.

The men looked at him as if he were selling life insurance and no reply was needed, until his driver straightened and fixed them with an intense look, and then one of them gave the visitor a half-hearted thumbs-up.

"I'm with Palma Central," Salas said. "We've been uniting with local companies to find common ground in our common paradise. We want everyone to enjoy their piece of this beautiful land and live in harmony as best we can. If the small businesses do well, we all do well, including the expats and the tourists, upon which much of our economy depends. You get me?" he said.

The two young surfers looked at each other.

Salas continued. "Surfing is a nice part of this world. It fills a need, it's a clean, renewable commodity that should be supported more than it is."

The surfers shifted in their chairs and looked at Salas.

"Palm oil and surfing have more in common than you might think," he said, "and we need someone from the surfing community to represent that bond." He looked back at his driver, then down the dirt road toward the beach, then back toward town. "Who is this man, this superior surfer and eloquent spokesman?" He stared at the young men. "Who in Dominical fits this role? Who do surfers listen to and respect?"

He stepped forward and placed one brown loafer on the edge of the porch and leaned forward over his knee and looked into their faces. He reached back and drew an envelope out of his pocket and tossed it on the boards before them. "That's a small business incentive," he said, "not a loan. No strings at all."

The thumbs-up surfer leaned down and picked up the envelope and opened the flap so his friend could also see the contents. He thumbed through the hundreds, counted five. The driver watched them, left hand holding his cigarette, his right cocked on his hip, his tie loosened.

"Incentive?" the expressive surfer said.

"That's correct," Salas said. "It's yours. Who's your man in town?"

"Jimmy," the surfer said.

"Jimmy who?"

The surfer looked at his companion, who remained

speechless. "Just Jimmy," the talkative surfer said. "He's called Long Jimmy."

Salas smiled. "And where does Long Jimmy spend his time on land?"

"He's probably over at the Flats," the surfer said, pointing down the lane behind the car. "If he's around."

"Good day, gentlemen," Salas said, sliding his soft shoe off the porch. At the car he turned back and pointed his finger at them. "Invest wisely," he said.

The Tortilla Flats happy hour was under way. Patrons spilled out past the entranceway into the beach lane, standing and drinking and laughing and telling stories and smoking in the sand under the palms. A few brown dogs stood among them, waiting for something to fall their way. Inside, the stools fronting the curved bar were filled, the tables supported colorful blended drinks and factions of brown Imperial and Pilsen bottles, a Baltimore Ravens flag mounted high on the wall.

After consulting with a waitress, Felipe Salas made his way toward a table of four young men at the open edge of the space. He saw the Range Rover creep up the lane past the restaurant and pull over before the row of vendor stalls began. The driver looked back and nodded at his boss as they made eye contact, then adjusted his side mirror's view and remained behind the wheel.

"Los surfers," Salas said to the group, noting the beer bottles and the plate of nachos being consumed. "I'm here to meet the legendary Long Jimmy."

The four friends looked at the well-dressed man and each other. Then Jimmy said, "Will the real Long Jimmy please stand up." The other three were tight-lipped, holding their laughs. They took turns beginning the act of standing and then sitting back down again, a rotation of false starts that went around the table a couple of times. Someone finally laughed, then they all did.

Jimmy looked up and said to the man, "What can I do you for, partner?"

"Believe it or not," Salas said, "I've seen the old version of that show, in black and white. But there were only three players, remember? Two imposters."

"You are correct, sir," Jimmy said. "Very impressive. I did not pick you for an old daytime TV watcher. Must have happened in your stoner phase."

Salas chuckled. "Yes, we all go through our phases," he said. "And now, look at me, public relations at a palm oil company. Felipe Salas, big shot."

Jimmy glanced at his friends, a half smile on his face, and they were totally onboard for a little show in the midst of the music and drinking.

"Well, sir," Jimmy said, "you have come to the right place. We are, in fact, righteous members of the public right here. And if I'm not mistaken, you are, in fact, relating to us right now."

The red-headed kid across from him laughed. "Awesome," he said.

"Let me introduce my crew," Jimmy said, feigning a serious tone. "That young knucklehead over there is Scotty. He's an up-and-coming ladies' man."

Salas smiled at the kid, and said, "Good luck."

Jimmy pointed at the ponytailed colleague on his left. "This long-haired libertine is a former activist, hell, maybe still pays his dues for all I know. His code name is Ian, 'cause he never met a cause he didn't like."

Ian gave Salas a vertical salute, one hand's stiff fingers flying outward from the center of his forehead in the manner of a secret handshake.

"And this hairy howler monkey," Jimmy said, jerking a thumb at Merlin—who did not turn, but kept his back to Salas—"is Merlino, a trippy trustafarian who doesn't need shit from anybody, but keeps us company anyway. Now, sir, how in God's name may we be of service?"

Salas smiled down at Jimmy and said, "You are an amusing fellow, just the sort of fun-loving foreigner I enjoy meeting. I've always loved seeing visitors enjoying themselves in our beautiful country. You've got your nachos *mixtos,* chicken and tomato and black beans all covered with *queso,* and music and drinks, and surf right out there, good consistent wave action. And all these babes. Wow, a guy could really get used to this life. Am I right, guys?"

Scotty, Ian, and Merlin were quietly smirking at each other and at Jimmy. Ian looked up. "What's your point, man?" he said.

"Well, unlike you gentlemen," Salas said, gazing out beyond the columns at the people on the beach road, then turning back to the table, "I'm a local, a citizen." He leaned down between Jimmy and Merlin and addressed the four of them. "I have a lot of connections," he said, "not just locally here, but in the government, the police, immigration, even the military. I'm the sort of friend who could be helpful in a variety of situations."

His tone had grown ominous but a smile sat fixed on his face as he looked at each of the Americans, his head now definitely invading their space.

Jimmy turned and pulled back a bit to address the man. "Sir, are you soliciting our friendship?"

"May I?" Salas said, reaching over the table to pull a layered, cheese-held clump of nachos away from the plate, bringing his other hand under to catch any potential droppings, and straightening as he brought the mass to his face and pried and stuffed it whole into his mouth. He chewed in apparent ecstasy as they watched.

"What I'm suggesting," he said, wiping his mouth with the back of his index finger, "is that we foster a feeling of cooperation as inhabitants of the same region." He looked around and added, "Much like the customers in this fine establishment. If someone were to be harassed by a criminal element or outside agitators," he said, "I feel sure their neighbors would be quick to help them." He bent down again and continued. "I want locals, citizens and expats alike, to know that we will help them if they help us too."

None of the four were looking at him. He leaned over the corner of their table like a man waiting for a sign, a welcome mat, a half-hearted thumbs-up.

"Maybe you have a club," he continued, "an informal distribution center for useful surfing information. Maybe your clubhouse is right here, in this bar, your meetings whenever you feel like having them. Or maybe they're held at Long Jimmy's humble pad and might be mistaken for a party. Who cares? Donations bring options and freedom."

He straightened again and let his message sink in.

"What do you want from us?" Jimmy said.

"I want you to walk with me," Salas said.

"Where?" Jimmy said. His friends were watching him.

"Over to my car," Salas said, gesturing toward it.

"Say what you want to say," Jimmy said.

"I need a show of faith," Salas said.

"Look man," Jimmy said, "I'm right here listening."

Ian glanced around, wondering what other customers were seeing here. Salas smiled. He bent close to Jimmy's ear.

"We want this to end positively," he said. "You can

be polite with an eye toward a peaceful surfing future. Or you can throw my suggestion back in my face. Which of course anyone of my culture would take as an insult."

He stood at the table a minute more, then put his hand on Jimmy's shoulder and said, "Meet me at the car. Two minutes. Max." He nodded to the others and said, "Gentlemen," and walked outside and into the road.

"What a fucking prick," Merlin said.

Jimmy pushed back his chair and rose.

"You're not playing that slippery bitch's game, are you?" Ian said.

"It's a tactical move," Jimmy said. "Insuring your sorry asses."

"Oh, he really got in your head, didn't he?" Ian said.

Jimmy forced a grin, picked up his beer and downed it. "Keep your friends close," he said, "and your enemies closer."

Scotty snapped his fingers. "*The Godfather*," he said, looking pleased.

They watched him cross the lane in his board shorts and flipflops and frayed Hawaiian shirt and pass out of sight behind the black car.

"I don't know, man," Ian said.

They dug into the remaining nachos and finished the beers and ordered another round as Jimmy came strolling back and the car pulled away.

He took his seat and looked at his friends as they stared at him.

"Don't be coy," Ian said. "What the fuck did he want from you?"

"He wanted me to pretend to be interested in his offer," Jimmy said.

"Which was what, exactly?"

"To be grateful enough for what he does for the community to feel like alerting him if we hear anything threatening regarding his operations."

"What the fuck," Ian said. "There's an ongoing worldwide negative vibe."

"I rest my case," Jimmy said. "Impossible request, so just pretend."

Ian sat back and drank some beer. "Did he offer you money?" he said.

"He did," Jimmy said, looking at all of them. "But I said no thanks."

Ian nodded, tilted his beer back, set the bottle down. "Did you really?"

"What the fuck, dude," Jimmy said. "Are you doubting my word now?"

Ian shrugged, then said, "Well, he brought you over there for a reason."

Jimmy smirked. "Yeah, you're right," he said. "He brought me over so I'd be seen alone with him and put doubts in your mind."

"So you took one for the team," Merlin said.

"A team player," Scotty said.

"If you want to put it like that, then fuck yeah. You met the guy. Is that who you want breathing down your neck? Or do you want to appease him a little bit and get back to your hedonistic pleasures?"

"Okay, fair enough," Ian said. "So he didn't give you anything. And you didn't give him anything. So we're back at square one, with a new friend."

Scotty and Merlin laughed.

"He gave me this," Jimmy said, pulling a business card out of his shirt pocket. He set it down on the table and they all saw the PPOI logo. The four brown letters in a row, the interior of the *O* orange-colored, a warm and friendly seed, with green fronds growing out of the *I*, overarching the other letters in a kind of natural unity, a false wholesomeness. Jimmy tapped the card. "A get-out-of-jail-free card," he said, "for all of us. With his cell number."

They sat digesting this and the nachos. Scotty wiped his finger along the rim of the platter to round up the remaining streaks of black bean sauce. They finished their beers. An obvious dark cloud hung over the table.

Merlin shook his head. "Fucking dude spoke some perfect English."

Jimmy nodded. "The dude lived in Dallas, Oakland, and Raleigh."

"No shit," Ian said. "An American-trained, master bullshitter."

"What a freakshow," Scotty said. "Can we get some rum now?"

—

In Greek mythology Cassandra predicted the Trojan Horse, and this thought made him think of tricks. It was still dark but Millege was expecting some kind of trick that would only later seem obvious and his mind was jumping all over the place. Surprisingly, he could see in the dark. The sky was full of tendrils reaching in all directions, moving roots entwined with the clouds, seeking water. In the path beside his porch, a line of mammals was walking single-file, some kind of parade it seemed, and they all looked like cats or foxes or skunks but he couldn't figure out exactly what they were. The last in line looked over at him as it passed and he saw that this one was a limping grison. He almost waved but checked himself and remained still.

Today was all about resting and absorbing lessons. But what lessons? He realized he was probably dreaming and getting that rest. He really wanted to swim though. And be submerged. To stay down under a hollow reed.

—

There was a light click above the river's whispering. Or a scrape that ran counter to the amphibian chorus, the texture of the night. Victor opened his eyes, turned his head, and saw a thin beam on the ground by the cars. He swung his right leg over the hammock, placed his left hand on the floor, and lowered himself and stretched out like a ferret and slid to the edge dragging his backpack. He rolled off the deck and thudded into grass and vines, exhaling a bit too loudly. He saw a piece of light beam lift and splash under and over the deck as he lay on the ground like a corpse. Then the light was gone and he rose to his knees and looked across the surface of the boards. Nothing.

—

The scratchy dawn saw night disintegrating from trees and river and pole and thatch dwellings, calling form into view, illuminating figures randomly roaming the land amid the querulous morning calls crosscutting the encampment of the momentarily enlightened.

A motley band of women and men wandered the main trail as if on a pilgrimage to the greeting shelter and the exit to the outside world. The three women were dressed in halters, scarves and sarongs, the two rangy men clothed in shorts and tattoos. At the sight of the parked cars, they turned back.

A few somnolent attendees stood at the river marveling in communal wonder at yellow butterflies winking over the water, horizontal confetti sent out in celebration of this fresh moment presently happening.

Merlin drew an outline in the soft mud with a stick and pressed stones and leaves and flowers into a coiled pattern that he saw as a sand painting, a flat labyrinth. He walked backward to test the riverside feeling of his creative public offering as he raked away his footprints.

The breakfast call came by word of mouth and shared waves of hunger. A wind-carried olfactory summons did not reach far with porridge and fruit and the absence of coffee. Murmuring bees bounced off the kitchen house screens and moths gripped the material where they had clung after the night. The mood was languorous, the honey of jungle in the air. In a little while the shaman would occupy the ceremony house for post-medicine integration.

Millege lay back soaking like a sponge in an upstream pool. No other people. The sky was a pale and darker blue grid with green parrots streaking in amplified squawks across it. A hawk spiraled far above like a paper blade falling and another perched in a dead tree and observed the man in the river. A procession of peccaries trotted through a hillside opening and vanished again. His breathing was even. There's always a solution, he thought. Savor the details. *Zwa zom fo.* Whatever comes at you, goes in and through.

Then, on the ridge above the piggish mammals, a flash of white caught his eye. He sank lower, his eyes just above the water's surface. A white horse emerged from the trees. He rubbed his eyes and blinked. The animal headed down the slope, following a trail, a pale-skinned, golden-haired rider leaning back for balance.

He slipped underwater, thinking he was hallucinating, and held his breath. When he surfaced, the horse and bareback rider were closer, almost to the riverside trail. The girl looked at him, her flaxen hair hanging in a long ponytail at her side, her feet and legs bare, her hips and upper body revealed, her small quivering breasts pointing the way forward.

Dimaris Kinsey studied him a moment, smiled, and rode on, in his mind a mirage disappearing behind boulders. He swam across the pool and got to his knees among stones and pebbles, pulled himself upright and stepped onto the bank. He slipped into his sandals, grabbed his shirt, and walked dripping to the riverside trail. She was not in view so he strode ahead, then broke into a jog. He looked down the turning trail, across the river, saw no one.

He clambered up a boulder pile and stood surveying the area, sunlight blasting his back and raking the forest on each side, the river flashing and gushing around him, its forward source somewhere within the hidden bends ahead, the day already exhibiting ordinary miracles. He turned to climb down.

Del Preet stood in the river below, pistol in hand, watching the other man. Millege flinched, lost his footing and slipped into a squat, dropped his shirt, steadied himself with one hand, then raised them both. Del Preet motioned with the gun for Millege to come down, then intercepted the sinking shirt as an object floated free of its pocket.

He lifted the shirt and snagged the small black canister. It was pepper spray. He tossed the shirt to shore and put the spray in his pocket.

"I eat that shit for breakfast," he said as Millege slid down into the water. The river enveloped them with white noise and sunlit mist.

"Did you see the horse?" Millege asked.

"I see everything," Del Preet said. His gray travel pants waved underwater from the knees down, his running shoes firmly planted on the gravel bottom. He wore a green polo shirt and his usual ballcap and aviator shades. He had missed a couple of days of shaving, the brown stubble giving him a meaner look.

"Not really a satisfying answer," Millege said.

Del Preet smiled. "I'm not here to satisfy you. Just the opposite."

Millege smiled too. "What are you even doing here?" he said. "The ceremony is over. You'll need to register for the next one."

This did not amuse Del Preet. He raised the 9mm and said, "Get down in the water."

"I already soaked," Millege said.

Del Preet stepped forward with the gun at waist level. His left hand thrust out like a striking snake and smacked Millege in the face. A shadow appeared high on the stone surface behind Millege and Del Preet stepped back and turned with the gun to look upward, sensing a blur in his peripheral vision. He was struck in the head. A hard brown object bounced off the side of his face and landed in the river several yards away. He slumped sideways, stunned, his hat and shades falling off as he shook his head. Glancing upward he saw the Indian's silhouette in motion and started to raise his weapon. He was hit by another hurled yuca root, this one glancing off his left forearm. Millege lunged from behind and knocked the man forward, reaching around to grab his gun hand.

Del Preet's head went underwater. He twisted around as his right arm was pulled, struggling to shoot behind him as the heavier man pushed him down. He fired beside his own body and the bullet streamed out of a bubble cloud in an explosion amplified below the surface, clapping his skull with sonic shock waves, and emitting a muffled punch into the bright morning air above.

Victor dropped into the water and slugged Del Preet's face as he surfaced to breathe. He gripped the pistol with both hands and twisted it away as Millege pushed the man's head to the bottom. Blood streamed around them.

Victor stood looking down at the man struggling underwater, his legs kicking as Millege held him down, both hands around his neck, his own chin straining upward at the surface, drawing sharp breaths, his face clouded red.

"You want to kill him?" Victor said. "You're the one bleeding."

Millege glanced at his left leg, the red water shifting, felt a searing pain.

They dragged Del Preet to the bank and dropped him coughing and gasping for air. He turned to his side and vomited, lay hacking and rasping.

Millege examined the deep groove in his calf, his blood pouring down to pool at his foot. He pointed to his shirt, and Victor tore it in half, and Millege tied a piece tightly around the wound. Then tied the other piece above it as a tourniquet. He looked down at Del Preet and pictured putting the gun to his head, the loud retort heard across the farm and beyond, the splattered brains and dead body, the stain on the place, the myriad resulting difficulties even if a drowned man were found. Besides that, he did not, on this of all days, see himself as an executioner.

Victor retrieved his backpack and stowed the pistol inside. With his arm and body support he helped Millege to limp well enough to walk. After a few steps, Millege stopped and hobbled back to Del Preet. The man lay on his side, facing away, breathing with ragged regularity. Millege pulled at the pepper spray protruding out of the man's pants pocket. Del Preet turned and gripped the other man's wrist. Millege tore his hand away, taking the spray.

He turned to leave the man, then shook the

canister and aimed and kicked Del Preet to get his attention and sprayed him full in the face. Del Preet rolled away, covering his head with his arms, grunting and spitting, rolling over pebbles and mud into the river as Millege followed with the spray streaming.

He left Del Preet on his belly, rubbing his head in the river, ears ringing, pushing up to gasp and breathe and then dunking his face again.

The two men hobbled together along the river, the lower cloth a red flag around Millege's calf. A couple of attendees at the regular swimming hole stood in the water, staring as they passed. Most of the participants were in the round house, and Rapu interrupted his speaking when the attention inside was directed outside. It was clear to all that Millege had suffered an injury.

The shaman came out and saw the leg and stopped Millege.

"What has happened?" he asked.

"Nothing serious," Millege said. "I fell and got a puncture."

"We must treat it," Rapu said. He gestured at Victor. "Who is this man?"

"He was hiking," Millege said, "and offered to take me to a hospital."

The shaman and the stranger stared at each other. Victor kept his arm around the injured man's bare midsection as if in possession of him, the other man's arm across his shoulders, the two bound together in their falsehoods.

Rapu placed his hand on Millege's shoulder. "The medicine is still working, Philip," the shaman said. "It can help you find the truth. If you want it."

"I appreciate your guidance through this experience," Millege said.

Rapu nodded and turned back to his audience

lined up at the screen.

The men resumed their walking. Victor left Millege on his porch and said he'd be back soon on his bike. He took off up the trail and Millege went inside to collect his belongings.

The door was open but Cassandra knocked and he welcomed her in. She looked down at his leg and grimaced. "What is going on with you?" she said.

"Accident," he said.

"Stock answer," she said. "And you're totally missing the bonding day."

"I thought we were already bonded."

"We are," she said. "But there are higher levels you could reach."

"Can we talk later?" he said. "I actually have to get going."

She looked at him, his packed bag, the empty desk. "What can I write on?" she said.

He pulled his notebook out and opened the cover, handed her his pen.

"Here's my email," she said, holding the notebook steady, her hand touching his fingers, writing in large block letters.

He turned the notebook around and memorized the address, bent over the bed and put the book back in his bag. He straightened and she put her arms around his neck and pulled herself against him and held her warmth there, breathing with him for longer than he expected. He wrapped his arms around her back and pulled her closer, cementing her embrace inside him.

"You were the best part of this," he said.

She pulled away and smiled her snaggle smile. "I know you're up to something," she said. "You take care and write soon."

"I might be making some changes," he said. "A

healthier lifestyle, though the words sound weird coming from me." He smiled.

"You could be primed for improvement," she said at the door.

"Approaching a new chapter," he said.

Halfway up the main trail, Millege was limping badly, soaked in sweat, blood running down his lower left leg, flies in pursuit. He was light-headed, craving coffee and Percocet. He needed to quit smoking, get his wind back, revive his keen sense of smell, ditch the cumbersome baggage of his road life.

Engulfed in his engine's whine, Victor throttled down at the Circle of Light entrance, on the lookout for an ambush, the pistol in his waistband. He turned in and killed the motor, coasted up to the cars. With his hand on the gun's grip he surveyed the vehicles, saw no change from the night's line-up.

He walked the bike to the empty shelter, leaned it against the side, stepped up to collect his hammock, his boots resounding on the boards. He rolled it tightly, watching the cars, then stuffed it into his pack and walked to the Nissan. He squatted and knifed one rear tire, then the other, the hissing air sounding like agitated cats. As the car slumped lower to the ground, he looked up at the figure approaching. It was Millege.

—

Once she was on the road driving back toward San Isidro, Liz called Stavo in response to his message from the day before. He did not pick up and she left no message. As she hung up a call came in from Victor. He informed her that he and Millege were heading to Dominical, that Millege had a minor injury and they were going to visit Helen Prentiss at the gift shop where she worked, and Liz should meet them.

Weaving slowly down the rutted road through town, the two men on the bike gathered some curious looks. A boy holding a puppy stared at the man's bloody leg as the bike passed. A young woman outside a scooter rental shouted to her friends and pointed at the injury as if noting a perfectly timed warning that illustrated the danger they were just then considering.

Victor parked so that Millege could remain sitting on the bike with his left leg facing the shop rather than the street. Victor dropped his pack on the ground and bent forward to stretch his back as Helen appeared at the open door of the shop. She looked at Millege, lifting her glasses on their chain, putting them on as she approached. He smiled wanly.

"Look at you," she said. "I wondered when I'd see you again."

"Not the best circumstances," he said, "but good to see you anyway."

"My intuition tells me you need medical attention," she said.

"If you're not too backlogged," he said.

"Why not go to the clinic in San Isidro?" she asked.

"It's a bullet wound," he said. "Better to stay under the radar."

She glanced at his leg, then up and down the sun-soaked street. As before, she wore a style of sundress sold in the store, and sandals, and was aware of her fair skin warming, her freckles blossoming. "Let's get out of the heat," she said.

Beside the coastal road Liz saw three white hawks sitting atop a mostly intact crocodile carcass. She slowed the car and took in the scene, picking up cognitive flashes as she observed the stark tableau. She saw three local helpers feeding off the foreigner Millege. She saw herself, Victor, and Millege feeding on the fugitive. She saw Ellis and the burned girls as martyrs standing on the oil company behemoth. She struggled to see more.

When Liz arrived, Helen put a Closed for Lunch sign on the shop's door and locked up. Millege got in the Rav4's passenger seat and they followed Helen. Victor brought up the rear, fading back a little as Millege requested to make sure they were not tailed. The convoy drove south and turned up a paved road in Uvita that soon became gravel as it rose into the hillside.

They parked in the yard in front of Helen's cottage. Liz and Victor sat in the living room before an expanse of windows looking out on a tropical garden. Helen took Millege into the bathroom to wash and evaluate his leg. He sat on a stool in the shower and she cut the pieces of shirt off. A skylight lit the room.

"Jesus," she said, turning his calf, "you're missing some muscle."

"Where's your bedside manner?" he said. "Don't upset the patient."

"If there's no bed," she said, "I forget all about it."

She turned on the water and positioned his leg under it. He winced and groaned. "Let me find you some painkillers," she said. She rummaged in the cabinet for a minute. "No opiates," she said, "just ibuprofen." He took six.

Avoiding the wound, she washed his leg with soap and water and dried it with a towel. He clamped the towel between his teeth as she poured hydrogen peroxide over the groove, which foamed into a pink slug, then rinsed it away with a saline solution and dried it with another towel.

"It's pretty wide to stitch," she said, applying antibiotic ointment with a cotton swab, "but I can pull it closer together, shorten the healing time if you're not planning to see a doctor."

"Yes, do it," he said.

He pushed the stool against the wall so he could

lean back with his eyes closed. Outside the shower's curb, she placed her table and suture kit beside her stool and positioned his wide foot in her lap. She hummed as she worked, pulling and knotting black silk thread to narrow the gap, the background conversation a murmur from the other room, a few regular bird chirps outside her focus.

When she ripped open a bandage pack, he opened his eyes and looked at the knitted groove. She placed a wide dressing over it, a bandage over that, wrapped gauze around his leg several times, and taped it. "Keep it dry, keep it covered, change it every day," she said, then looked him in the eye. "Make sure it doesn't get infected."

"You are an angel," he said, his face dripping with sweat.

"Looks like the dancing has to be postponed, again," she said. "And by that I mean that you need to keep weight off of it some of the time. Let it heal."

He sat up and placed his foot on the floor, applied some pressure.

She was putting away her kit, still seated across from him. "Who are your friends out there?" she said. "Are they supposed to help you catch Ellis?"

He looked at her and sighed. "I'm reevaluating the assignment."

"What does that mean?" she said.

"It means I haven't been actively pursuing him lately."

She frowned. "So what then, just inactively, you mean?" she said.

"I've been examining my motivation for a few days," he said.

She laughed. "And that got you shot I see."

He smiled. "Separate strands of life overlapping," he said.

She shook her head. "You are Mister Fucking Mysterious, aren't you?"

"It's just the line of work," he said. "Doesn't welcome scrutiny."

"Yeah, that's convenient," she said. "Well, here's something you might want to scrutinize. I know who shot you."

He leaned forward with his hands on his knees. "So, you're a bigger asset than I thought," he said. "What's the man's name?"

"I don't know his name," she said, "but he's the other guy looking for Ellis."

"How do you know that?" he said.

"Well, besides the fact that it's in the freaking Courier," she said, "my friend Grady had a visit from the guy because Ellis rented from him."

"And how did that go?" Millege asked.

"Not well," she said. "Scared the shit out of Grady. And also mentioned my name."

"Why your name?" Millege said. "In what context?"

"I don't know. I think he was just being a smartass, acting like he knew everything going on and intimidating Grady. Which doesn't take that much, to be honest."

"So Grady gave him something," Millege said.

"I assume so."

"And you warned Ellis," Millege said.

"Well, what would you—" she stopped, realizing her mistake.

"It's alright," he said. "Any friend would do the same."

"It's not alright," she said. "What if he comes for me next?"

Millege stood and shifted his weight cautiously from foot to foot. She stood and moved her stool back and took his hand as he stepped out of the shower.

While they were alone, Liz had Victor bring her up to date, which he did, however reluctantly. She said he could have been killed, that things were getting out of control, that they should terminate their association with Millege.

"They might know each other," Victor said. "Otherwise, why is this guy not going after Ellis? Does he need to get Phil Millege out of the way first?"

"Let's just ask him," Liz said. "Tell him we're skeptical about continuing. He'll understand."

Victor was looking out the window at a tall balsa tree being climbed by a philodendron. A flock of green parakeets flickered over the clearing. Near the house, pineapple plants grew in crisscrossed clusters. "I thought you wanted to help Ellis," he said.

"Maybe he won't be found," she said, which made her face feel warm.

Victor looked at her. "Whatever brought these guys here," he said, "is not going away without results."

"We can't be between those forces and Ellis," she said.

"We were hired," he said.

"Not for this," she said. "We didn't know what we were getting into."

"I knew," Victor said. "He employed me to watch his back."

"Yes," she said, "but he got shot. Let's see what he wants to do now."

"He won't quit," Victor said.

—

They were back at the girls' cottage for more holiday ribaldry on the porch, their comradery established, their attractions and passions shared, their common restlessness metamorphizing into a broader purpose.

"I met the lion," Jimmy said, "and I can get a pass

into the lion's den."

"Who is this fucking dude?" Peyton said, bringing out a tray of her travel tapas, crackers with cheddar, turkey and mustard. In the corner Chloe was bikini dancing to a song about a murdering conquistador and still listening to everyone else. Ellis mixed grapefruit and rum, four glasses on the bench railing with an ice bucket, the hedge beyond the porch a colorful variety of crotons, heliconias, red ginger, and red sister, beyond that the papaya and frangipani trees, the gurgling river, and over the river the dense wall of jungle. In the side lot, the usual resident gray roadside hawk and, hovering about the hedge, a garden emerald hummingbird.

"Felipe the fixer," Jimmy said. "Spreading harmony and peaceful money all over the region, smiling and spewing PPOI bullshit wherever he goes."

"Let's hit him," Peyton said.

Ellis gave her a look, and handed her a drink. "What do you mean?"

"I mean let's fuck his place up," she said.

"Which place?" Ellis said. He passed out the other drinks.

"I don't know," she said, "whatever Jimmy is talking about."

"I mean I can probably get a tour of the processing plant," Jimmy said.

Chloe came over and they congregated around the tray, munching on the snacks and washing them down. "And then what?" she said. "You'd take secret pictures or draw a diagram or something?"

"I haven't really thought it out," Jimmy said. "But I'd get an idea of the place, the security and personnel, the layout, that kind of stuff."

Ellis laughed. "Let's get real," he said. "We're talking about taking some kind of covert action against a working facility. Just to be crystal clear."

"Well, sure," Peyton said. "And how could we actually hurt the place?"

"How do you mean?" Ellis said. "Vandalize it, damage it, burn it down?"

"Sounds whimsical," Chloe said. She was scrolling through her phone's playlist.

"Not only that," Ellis said. "It would take planning, supplies, illegal entry, accepting the possibility that someone could get arrested or hurt."

"Or killed," Chloe said.

"Fuck it," Peyton said. "We're talking about helping our natural world. That's what matters."

Chloe found an appropriate song and clicked up the volume. They all began to sing along, getting louder in unison, swaying together.

> Those players we run right into the ground
> The greed they breathe is all around
> Heed us, believe us, we mean the best
> When the game is over, we'll leave you the rest

By the end they were a chorus punching upward on the last word.

Ellis made a fresh round of drinks. "Pretty sure that's not a love song," he said, laughing.

"It's our anthem now," Peyton said.

When Ellis took a seat, Chloe sat in his lap and put her arms around his neck. "We could also scale down the mission," he said, "and still make a statement."

Peyton sat on the bench railing with her back against the center post. "If we're going to do something," she said, "let's go big."

"Look," Jimmy said, standing beside her, "why don't I take the tour, check it out, and then we'll know if that target is feasible or not."

"In the meantime," Ellis said, "I'll figure out a backup plan."

"Don't be pussies," Peyton said.

"You guys are totally fucking crazy," Chloe said, laughing.

"The dude is a bad actor," Jimmy said. "A smug fuck who needs a comeuppance in the worst way."

"It's not personal," Ellis said. "It's the whole industry we want to hit." Chloe leaned back and bit his neck. He chuckled and held his drink steady.

"Whatever, man," Jimmy said. "You get them both either way." He slid his hand down between Peyton's crossed thighs and she squeezed it.

"When can you get the tour?" she asked, looking up with a smile.

"I'll call the dude tomorrow," he said, and leaned down to kiss her.

"You can get a tour of my tits right now," she said.

His lips brushed hers and kept going, kissing the hollow of her throat and continuing down into her cleavage, sucking little pink marks on the curves of her breasts as she squirmed and moaned.

"You guys can have the bed," Chloe said.

"I'll share," Peyton said, grinning with her eyes closed.

"We're outdoorsy types," Chloe said. "You guys are classic studio porn."

Ellis laughed, and then they all did.

Peyton said, "She knows me too well." Then she got up to use the bathroom, and Chloe followed.

"Jimmy," Ellis said, "if you take a tour of the plant and something happens to it, you'll jump to the top of the suspect list. You realize that, right?"

"Yeah, maybe so," Jimmy said.

"Tackling that place would require a military-style operation beyond this group's abilities. No matter how much we drink and wish to bring it down."

"Sobering thoughts," Jimmy said. "So tell that to

Peyton."

"The point is to make a point," Ellis said, "and get the story in the media."

"Okay, something smaller," Jimmy said, "like you suggest."

"I think that's the way to go," Ellis said. "This is only successful if nothing happens to any of us."

—

In the fragmented moonlight that filtered down to the forest floor, among the highlights shifting over leaf and vine, a multitude of little rippling moons and half-moons and parabolas and ellipses, there moved a coat of spots and rosettes, a passing pattern of beauty and stealth, muscle and death concealed, a big cat sniffing the air for prey, prowling its empire of meat.

In the same riverine area, another large mammal trod a well-worn track imbedded into the mud by the splayed hooves of its own kind, its long flexible snout to the ground, picking up traces of urine and feces, the expelled seeds and leaf mulch of a regular group of browsing ungulates, its sensitive white-tipped ears attuned to the open, grassy surroundings, the calf at its flank several months old, its rusty brown coat still white-striped and spotted, its quick steps nervously keeping pace with its mother, its baby prehensile trunk stretching upward and turning to register anything out of the ordinary.

The jaguar, downwind at the edge of the marsh, picked up the tapirs' scent and moved soundlessly through the adjacent woodland cover.

Passing through the grass, the adult tapir was an ovoid shadow, nearly invisible and, when she paused, took on a dark boulder shape. Turning aside to attend her offspring, she nudged her proboscis against its rear like the pat of a guiding hand, and he got in line ahead of her.

The tapirs foraged on sedges, wading through the swampy ground toward the river for its cover and aquatic plants. They scrambled up a rise of trickling rivulets and stood on the riverbank scanning the air with both trunks extended upward, quivering for scents. They found ferns along the shore and walked in the still shallows ripping leaves loose and tucking them into their mouths, broken moonlight rippling away from their legs to merge with the reflecting surface of the current.

From the elevated perspective of a tree limb, the male jaguar watched the pair browsing leisurely along the illuminated stream. Ahead, the river veered away from the treeline.

The mother waded deeper into the current and submerged to grasp clumps of bladderwort suspended in the water. She surfaced chewing and heard her calf whistle for his mother as he swam to her side. They both went down and walked along the bottom, their trunks gathering plant stems in concert.

In the silvery light the grass waved and wobbled as if a steady breeze blew over it and fashioned a slight channel of separation, and then the cat's head appeared as a speckled mask among the riverside stalks, its nose and dilated eyes tracking the path of its riparian prey.

The tapirs moved into a barren rocky bottom and the mother raised her snout to breathe while their bodies remained below the surface. She snorkeled air while smelling the immediate area for signs of danger. Her calf swam upward and she brought her head down and pushed him toward shore. They clambered up the bank between boulders and stood dripping together, the mother turning her head to listen, both of their trunks up at attention. The grass grew high on each side and chutes of white water churned downstream between piles of great round stones.

They walked along the bank brushing against the high grass, moving past the stretch of turbulent water. As they entered the river again, the breeze shifted and the mother turned her head downstream, aligning her ears with the direction her trunk probed. She uttered a coughing alarm just as her poor eyes registered the indistinct flash of fur leaping from the bank.

The predator's extended foreclaws hooked into the thick skin of the tapir's flank while its spotted body splashed into the river, rear legs kicking to propel itself upon the back of the desperate herbivore. The tapir turned and dove, and the jaguar stayed with it, plunging its powerful jaws underwater in an effort to bite into the spine of the sinking beast.

Amid the chaos in the water, with his mother's thrashing motions to drag the cat down and get it off her back, the terrified calf instinctively swam toward the shore, away from calamity. He raised his snout for air and went down again, suddenly unsure where to go, continuing under the surface on a path roughly parallel to the attack on his mother.

The adult tapir rolled to the side, holding its breath to outlast the other mammal, using its bulk to anchor both of them to the bottom. The stream swirled around the jaguar's whiskers and eyes and into its open jaws as he pulled himself downward, his body pushed by the current, his strong claws holding him fast, his formidable incisors finally sinking into the tapir's back. Even as the blood rose into his mouth, bubbles escaped his nose, and the need for air took prominence.

The cat retracted his claws and pushed upward. His head broke the surface and he swam hard to shore, angling downstream with the current, and pulled himself onto the bank and lay crouched and wary, sides heaving, jaws open in a grimace of heavy breathing.

The mother tapir surfaced and called for her calf, hiccupping with anxiety, blood flowing in the current around her. The calf found her, and their trunks touched and briefly held. They swam midstream, their legs and feet kicking in overdrive.

After a time, the female angled to shore and they stood in the shallows as she craned her head upward to listen and smell for any presence of danger. Her calf smelled the blood running down her side and took small steps forward and back, anxiously waiting to move on.

They stepped through gravel and clambered up the bank and trotted onward, the mother's head down, seeking a known trail, veering off toward the cover of forest, the young male bumping into her legs as he quick-stepped too close. She wanted black mud, instinctively, to roll in it or sink into a hole, to coat herself as she did habitually to ward off insects, only now to pack her wounds, the punctures and rips of tooth and claw, and to staunch the blood flow.

Under the canopy of trees she caught familiar scents along the ground and quickened her pace, following an invisible line toward deep puddles and a place to rest. Beside her a bent tree abruptly straightened, tension released, and her right rear foot was snagged and caught, her forward momentum arrested. She stumbled and fell on her left side, one knee buckling, then scrambled upright, turning to see her snared leg lifted, foot held aloft. She surged forward and pressure encircled her trapped limb. Coughs of agitation escaped her open mouth, her proboscis raised and her teeth exposed in fear and confusion. Running to his mother's side, her nervous calf hit the unseen wire with his extended snout and jumped back as if struck in the face.

A motorbike brake cable bound her to the tree. She hobbled back and sniffed at the stakes that had held the wire in her path. The area was covered in an amalgam of dirt and leaves and droppings. She stood silently beside her calf as he pushed his head into her side.

She pulled again, attempting to move forward on three legs, straining against the tree's flexibility until she tired. She bent herself to the rear and tried to bite the cable but failed to find purchase with her teeth. After a while she lay down and rested. Her calf walked ahead on the trail and turned to look back. He stood waiting for a few moments, then came back and lay beside her.

—

Juan Mateo steered his bike with difficulty, the extra weight of Ernesto behind him making the bike's front wheel lift off the ground as the terrain rose, and he grumbled and swore as he drove. They were hoping for a cat, something with value in the pet trade, not a paca or a peccary, cheap jungle meat. But snares were random in their seizure. And often the animal, left too long in the cable's grip, was damaged or dead.

At first light they had left the road and gone fishtailing up the slick forest trail. The day's mood fostered silence. Both men were recent victims of a company house-cleaning. New standards had been declared, which were mainly the old ones newly enforced. Those with below-average records—with poor performance ratings, repeated stains of absence, tardiness, drunkenness, or other reckless behavior with safety violations—had been swept out. Plenty of eager new men wanted the jobs, and the new men had clean records. What appeared to be net loss when the cost of training was factored in, was in fact a profitable position after all the lost labor was deducted, since the low-level jobs at PPOI were not difficult to learn.

The front tire shot up and Ernesto lost his balance. As he slid off the back of the seat, he grabbed Juan Mateo's shoulder and pulled the driver back. The bike rose to a nearly vertical position and fell sideways and landed on the driver's right leg and stalled out as his passenger rolled away in wet leaves.

"You fat fucking asshole," Juan Mateo said, sliding out from under the hot machine, "don't pull me off with you."

Ernesto got to his feet and brushed off his face and pants and shirt sleeves and rubbed his stomach. He was a bit heavy lately but he wouldn't say fat, and in his hungover, hazy state he did not feel anger toward his friend, just a touch of pity that the man was losing his shit so easily. He decided to leave Juan Mateo's unreasonable rebuke hanging unanswered in the jungle gloom.

They pushed the bike up the ridge, grunting in teamwork, and then Juan Mateo started it again and they rode on into the forest following the faint trail toward their two traps. They smelled the first victim before they arrived. Juan Mateo pulled his T-shirt up over his nose and Ernesto pressed his sleeve under his. The skunk looked dead and they rode past, forfeiting the snare until a later occasion.

Juan Mateo stopped in dappled light beside two palms with red cloth markers, the engine still running, and they both looked toward the tree with the rope hanging away at an angle that indicated the engagement of the other snare. It was just past 7:30 a.m. They could see a large motionless shape.

"Is that a danta?" Juan Mateo said.

"Look," Ernesto said, "there's a baby too. Behind it."

Juan Mateo killed his engine and they dismounted. The sudden drop in noise made the area seem as silent as an ancient amphitheater. Juan Mateo leaned his bike against a palm tree and they stood sweating, considering the situation. Without a firearm they were not prepared to deal with an agitated adult danta. All this meat would be wasted unless someone got it soon.

As the men slowly approached, the tapir lifted her head and stood. After a few minutes on three trembling legs she slumped down again. The calf remained behind her, hiccupping his distress, eyes round.

"She's all messed up," Juan Mateo said. "Look at the blood."

"We should just cut her loose," Ernesto said.

"Are you crazy?" Juan Mateo said. "She could attack us."

"She's too weak to attack anyone," Ernesto said.

"I wouldn't bet on that," Juan Mateo said.

Ernesto walked to the hanging rope, the tapir's eyes following him, and traced it with his hand down to the cable, squatting to reach the connection. He was only fifteen feet from the animal, the hair raised along the ridge of its back, and he watched its wide-open mouth, the proboscis lifted to reveal pink gums and a display of sharp yellow teeth.

"Don't do that, man," Juan Mateo said. "I'm telling you right now."

Ernesto slipped his belt knife out of its sheath and sawed at the rope until it separated from the cable. He dropped the rope and stood. The animal kept its mouth open but did not move.

"You asshole," Juan Mateo said. "I should leave you here with her."

"No need to panic," Ernesto said.

The Path of the Tapir

"We should at least get the goddamn baby," Juan Mateo said. "That's a premium pet."

"Go for it," Ernesto said.

"It takes two of us," Juan Mateo said, "one from each side."

He moved in a wide arc to the far side of the animals, the mother and calf following his progress, and stopped when he was opposite Ernesto.

"We move toward them slowly at the same time," he said. "If she gets up, we stop. Once the baby separates from her, we run it down from both sides."

Ernesto didn't think much of the plan—they needed a net—but he wanted to appear helpful since they'd gone to the trouble of setting the traps. And since Juan Mateo had come up with this sideline job, used his bike, and learned from his uncle how to make a snare. It was ironic that Ernesto was a driver by trade and now had nothing to drive and nothing to show for employment except this second-rate illegal activity. This was their first trapping success, but since their profit would probably be zero, the word success was inaccurate, and already Ernesto was inclined to quit. He saw now that the work did not suit him the way it did Juan Mateo, who was comfortable with dubious jobs, had been fired for skirting safety regulations and then lying about his actions.

Juan Mateo raised his hand and made a forward motion and both men took steps toward the animals. At first the calf leaned into his mother as if to disappear in her superior size, as if relying on his inborn sense of camouflage. His mother turned her head and hiccupped at him. As the men got closer the calf stepped backward and stood behind its mother. Each man angled his next step toward the calf and the calf moved farther from its protector. They continued this pattern for a few more steps and the calf seemed caught as the middle point in a triangle between them, still held by the force of its mother.

The men stood immobile, breathing deeply, muscles tense, timing their orchestrated lunge. Juan Mateo looked at Ernesto and nodded minimally, one hand at his side showing three fingers. He curled one closed, then the second.

They dove at the calf, arms reaching wide like bars of the barest cage. The calf darted between them, away from its mother, and the men fell on the forest floor within reach of each other. Ernesto scrambled to his feet as the adult tapir rose and turned toward them. He backed away as Juan Mateo started after the calf, tripped on vines and fell facedown. The lumbering tapir bit into the back of his right ankle, just above his shoe, and he screamed and rolled and kicked with his other foot at her face. The animal released him and sat heavily, fresh blood pouring from her flank as the man pulled himself backward in a sitting position, dragging his legs away from her.

Juan Mateo got to his knees and then stood and cried out as his weight pressed downward. His bitten ankle was bleeding. Ernesto came to his side, taking his friend's arm across his shoulders and holding his other arm around the man's waist to support him as they limped toward the bike.

The calf stood watching from some twenty yards away, nearly invisible in the spots and stripes of the filtered morning light. His mother lay as an unmoving silent mass he could smell. And now he knew the scent of men, his small raised trunk telling him they were receding as imminent threats.

Juan Mateo leaned against a tree and studied his throbbing foot, watching blood drip to the ground. And determining in his mind that he could drive and get himself home. "Thanks a lot," he said.

"Don't mention it," Ernesto said.

"No, asshole, thanks for cutting the animal loose so it could bite me."

"You weren't paying attention," Ernesto said.

"You piece of shit," Juan Mateo said, "you can walk home." He leaned on the handlebars and threw his leg over the seat of the bike.

"No problem," Ernesto said. "I've already been told I should get some new friends."

Juan Mateo made an exaggerated frown. "Who told you that, your freaky little sister?"

Ernesto stepped next to the bike. "Why are you bringing her into this?" he said.

"Because it shows why you're so freaky, man."

Ernesto punched the other man in the side of his face and knocked him off the bike, which fell on his left leg this time.

Juan Mateo pulled himself free and said from the ground, "Yeah, that's about right for you, hitting an injured man. When I get better I'll come find you and settle up." He stood and straightened his vehicle and winced while he got his left foot into position and pushed it down on the kickstart lever. He kicked it again and again until the engine started with a loud whine, gave it gas and throttled as much noise and disturbance as he could, moving around to the other side so he could throw his injured foot over. He looked back as he clicked the gearshift and rolled forward.

"Fuck you, Zuniga," he said, "you fucking loser," and then added something else, possibly about the sister, that Ernesto didn't catch.

He watched the bike roll out of sight between trees and then heard the noise for a long time, growing fainter as he looked back at the dying danta and tried to spot the baby. When he did, he walked toward it and continued to push it farther from its mother. He waited until he no longer saw it, until the silence, aside from distant bird calls, brought back a delicate cloak of remoteness. He stood over the adult danta and waited for something he couldn't name. The hide was ripped along the left side and up on the spine. Her eyes were closed, her breathing light, restless trunk limp. Right rear foot marcescent, discolored below the wire. The foot of some other creature fastened on by mistake. He looked around once more for the offspring, then turned and walked away, thirsty and adrift.

22. Accept No Pardon

At the Alamo office in Dominical, Del Preet was waiting for a Toyota Prado, a big silver 4x4, to be cleaned. He'd managed to find his sunglasses in the river but they did not hide his swollen jaw or the red abrasion under his left eye. Hatless, he stepped outside to make a call.

"Reymo, my brother, can you meet me in San Isidro? It pains deeply me to say this, but I need another weapon."

There was a pause. Then Reynaldo laughed. "Are you shitting me? Someone took your weapon? Or did you drop it in a river? We know which is worse though."

"Hey, Mister funny man. Even a blind pig finds an acorn once in a while."

"What the fuck does that mean?"

"Let me translate it for you. Even a fat civilian gets lucky sometimes."

Rey's voice rose. "Oh no, the poor bastard has kicked a hornet's nest."

"How come you know that phrase but not the other?" Del Preet said.

"One is universal," Rey said, "the other sounds

colloquial."

"Well, aren't you the language analyst today."

"Yes I am," Rey said. "Every day."

"Sorry for the extra bullshit, amigo, but when can you get down there?"

"Not until after dark," Rey said.

"I'll meet you outside the cathedral," Del Preet said. "Around eight."

"Roger that," Rey said.

Forty-five minutes later, Del Preet was having lunch at Tortilla Flats—a dorado filet, a salad, a beer—and watching surfers and tourist girls pass by on Beach Road, when Reynaldo Elizondo called back.

"What have you got, *hermano*?" Del Preet said.

"Finally got some phone records," Rey said. "This Grady you mentioned, he called a woman named Helen Prentiss the same night. Then she made a call. No record, probably a burner. Probably your boy."

"Nice work, bro. Send me that info."

"Coming to you."

—

Unless customers were buying or browsing, Helen tried to close up and leave the shop before sunset. She had a twenty-minute drive and liked to arrive at home while there was still some light in the sky. Millege had offered to stay, but she was used to her privacy and he had his team, so she waved off the offer, deciding that his live-in presence in her small place would make her feel strange and helpless.

Instead, they had agreed to maintain regular phone contact, by text or voice, with Victor as a backup in the event that Millege did not immediately respond. Through her connections, Millege had rented a cottage—three-day minimum—in Ojochal to use as a base while his wound mended. Victor and Liz decided to share a bedroom.

Once Helen got behind the wheel of her little silver Corolla, she texted Millege that she was leaving the shop.

He wrote back, told her to be alert on the road, always vigilant. Then signed his message: Camp Counselor. Which made her smile.

She enjoyed the short drive south, seeing the same stretch of road, the usual places, the daily reminders of her life here, then the climb up through the trees, the leaves still dripping from an afternoon shower, the neighbors' brown dog, Bingo, standing at the road watching her pass, the western sky a pale blue tinged with yellow that darkened as she entered the shade of her own drive. The porch light was on, as she habitually left it. Her lawn chairs were wet but the cushions were inside. She parked and stood outside the car for a moment listening to the birds settling. Then she went inside, dropped her bag, set her phone on the counter and poured a glass of chilled white wine.

She brought a cushion and sat outside as darkness descended, aware of her isolation, and along with that, her independence. She toasted herself amid the natural magic of fireflies. After their last meeting, she thought more warmly of Millege, and now glanced at her phone.

Helen heard a faint rustle and turned her head. A fabric fell over her hair and face and plunged her into claustrophobic darkness, her arms and legs flying outward, wine glass and phone knocked to the ground. The hood was twisted tight and she was pulled backward across the ground like a doll, body elevated, feet scraping, the tourniquet cutting off blood and air, her mind tumbling in blank confusion as she clutched at her throat and choked in motion, dragged headlong into quick oblivion.

She coughed as her eyes fluttered and then opened, the weight of her head pressing her face down, water splattering against the cloth enveloping her sight. She smelled wet ground, the stench of urine, and tried to lift her head away from it. But she was head-heavy, her arms unable to come forward and prop her up. The falling water stopped. She blew her nose clear of moisture and tried to roll over. Her hands were together behind her, bound at the wrists, and her shoulder blocked her turn. She lay blind and immobile.

She gagged against the rank covering and remembered what she could. She moved her legs, felt debris clinging to her skin, couldn't tell how much of her body was wet. She knew she was being watched and was afraid to speak.

Nylon bag, slippery wet hood like artificial skin, her wine breath, mouth dry, tongue coated and thick. Her shoulder going numb. Audible breathing, the cloth's constant movement showing her fear. What plan now? Survival is all.

Ground movement, face-level, a shuffle, her eyes closing tightly before a shock of prodding, a tapping at her forehead, her involuntary whimper as her captor's shoe thumped her repeatedly, an insistent message to her brain.

Okay, she was listening. Wouldn't that be fucking obvious?

She heard a rustle of cloth, the figure lowering, changing position.

There was a sigh from above, the almost tangible manifestation of a mutual dilemma, and in that pause she felt the absurdity, the open acceptance of bad outcomes, poor choices of balance beyond this dark event.

She heard slow even breaths, the man squatting in

control. His measured voice caused a ripple down her back that broke her open.

"Have you used these quiet, reflective moments to grasp the severity of your situation?" he said.

She didn't feel she could speak yet, but a remembrance entered her mind, the idea of engaging in conversation with your captor, finding common humanity wherever you could, any point of leverage to build on. Instead, she nodded her head, then again, to make sure her affirmation was seen.

"You should answer questions," he said, "but don't start talking on your own, don't start thinking you can gain my sympathy. Is that clear?"

She mumbled a sound.

"You're not being clear," he said.

"Yes," she said.

"I'm not a major fan of torture," he said, "but I don't shy away from it either. My goal is simply to get what I want. Man, woman, child, animal, it makes no difference to me. I don't think about ethics or permanent damage. I'm totally in the moment. Understand?"

"Yes," she said into the cloth.

She heard him rise again, felt him standing over her. "I'm not sure you do," he said. She heard him move away and her own bewildered gasp.

She drew her legs up and rocked against the obstacle of her shoulder and then rolled onto her back, her hands pressing hard into her lower spine. She sat up and flexed her knees and leaned forward but was unable to stand. She rolled to the right, intending to use her head as a fulcrum and get to her knees. Her face hit the ground hard, and she blacked out.

She heard her phone ringing and footsteps on the grass. She was lifted roughly by the hood, by her stiff neck, until her knees were under her. From behind, he locked his arms under hers and she was suddenly standing, her legs weak, shaking. He held her steady and led her by the left arm, turned her and eased her down into the cushioned chair. She was chilled, her breath in short spurts, nearly hyperventilating. He patted the side of her face, gently slapping.

"Take it easy," he said. "We'll deal with the phone."

He rolled the hood up over her mouth and nose and she was still, heard the rip of tape from its roll, the piece circling her head, a band of pressure applied under her eyes, a half-hood keeping her blind as she gulped clean air.

"Who just called you?" he said, and read her the number.

"A friend," she said, "expecting me to call."

She heard a light scraping, a normal sound, a common kitchen sound, like a jar being opened, metal turning around glass. Something landed solidly on her leg, slid wriggling down between her thighs, and she instinctively parted them as she opened her mouth to cry out. His hand clamped over her mouth as his other pushed against the back of her head, holding her scream inside as she shook her legs and attempted to shake off whatever thing was crawling under her dress.

"That's a centipede," he said. "It'll bite if you're not careful."

She was shaking her head against the pressure he applied. Sweat ran down her scalp into her eyes and burned them. The many tickling legs twisting over the curve of her inner thigh merged with the arthropod image in her mind, driving her mad. She tried to bite his hand and he squeezed harder, hurting her cheeks and nose.

"When I ask who called, give me a fucking name,"

he said. "If you scream, I'll leave it there to find a moist place to invade."

The hand over her mouth lifted.

"Philip Millege," she said, almost spitting.

He pulled her head close to his and put his free hand under her dress and raked his fingers from her crotch outward along the edge of each thigh and the top of the cushion as she held her breath against an impending bite.

He released her and backed off, and she exhaled as if to stir the trees.

She heard motions at the ground, then the jar being closed. She smelled her sweat, her own urine, tasted snot with the salt of her tears.

"Pull yourself together," he said. "We'll text him back."

She was sniffling, mouth-breathing, exhaling forcefully, calming herself to speak if she had to. "Hi Phil," she said, hearing the words wobble.

"Go ahead, recite it," the man said.

She tried again. "Hi Phil, I was in the shower." Her words wavered, too high-pitched. "Yes, I'm fine. All quiet over here."

"It's mind over matter," he said. "You do not want him coming over here. That would be one of the tragic endings you can't abide."

Her heart slowed down but her thinking was disjointed, her senses unreliable. She thought she heard a car passing way up on the road, thought she heard voices among the frogs, imagined moths landing on her sensitive, jumpy legs, kept stamping her bare muddy feet.

"Okay, I'm playing his message," Del Preet said. And she heard Millege's voice.

Helen, check in with me.

Which brought fresh tears to her eyes.

"So we'll text what you just said," the man said as if they were in it together. "'Hi Phil. I was in the shower. Yes, I'm fine, all quiet over here.' Is that it?"

"And 'Thank you,'" she said.

"Okay," he said, "done."

They waited. She pictured him scrolling through her other messages, searching, invading, taking over her life. Her nose itched and she made extremely wrinkled faces to scratch it, thinking how absurd she must look.

The reply came back: *Call me.*

"Stand up," the man said. "He wants you to call him."

She leaned forward, then farther, and stood. He turned her around and put his fingers between her wrists and pried more space. She heard a click and then he said, "Hold still," and made a slight sawing motion back there. Her hands sprang apart and she brought them around and rubbed each wrist as she scratched her nose.

"I want you to handle the phone," he said, "so it'll be more natural."

"Okay," she said.

"Compose yourself and relax," he said.

"I can't remember ever being more relaxed," she said.

"Good," he said. "You're sounding normal. Let's get a refill on the wine."

He led her inside and she stood at the kitchen counter while he opened the fridge. She heard the pour, and he brought a coffee cup to her hand and she sipped the wine, took several gulps.

"It's time to call," he said. "Do you want to sit?"

She slid down and sat on the floor, her back against the cabinet, and finished the wine. For a moment she felt nauseous. Then it passed.

"All set?" he said.

She ran her hands through the hair hanging below the hood and fluffed it out. She rubbed her cheeks and mouth and nose. "Yes," she said.

"It's on speaker," he said, touching her hand with the ringing phone.

She held it horizontally, almost a foot below her mouth.

Millege answered, "Hello."

"Hello there," she said.

There was a slight pause. "What are you doing?" he said.

"Just making a little bite," she said.

"Is that why you're on speaker?" he said.

"Yeah, sorry. Need both hands." She managed a soft chuckle, similar to a sob, feeling the focus of the figure towering over her.

"What are you making?" Millege said.

She tried to remain steady in her eternal darkness. "Cheese and crackers," she said. "Probably a salad too."

"Simple enough," he said. Then, a moment later, "Sleep well."

"You too," she said. "Good night." The line went dead.

Del Preet took the phone. "He's a bit sweet on you," he said.

She sat still, considering her answer. "Maybe a little," she said.

She heard him step to the door, then cross the room. She tilted her head, unable to tell where he was. Then he was squatting beside her on the concrete floor. "How long will it take him to get over here?"

She shook her head a little. "I don't think—" she said, then changed her mind. "If he did that, straight over, then about twenty minutes."

"Here's how it's going to be," he said. "You've gone straight to bed. The house is dark and quiet. You're secured in your bedroom and I'm out of sight."

He held her wrist as he stood and she pulled herself up.

"You have another call to make," he said.

She bit her bottom lip gently, hesitating, then stopped, thinking he would strike her if she asked who he meant.

"What do you want me to say?" she said.

"We'll get to that in a minute," he said.

—

He'd observed the post-medicine protocol overnight, partly due to his injury, but now Millege returned to habits. He lit a cigar—he still had a small reserve of Padrons—and stood under the stars creating a cloud and watching it branch and reveal invisible night currents. He inhaled a taste, swirled the ice in a glass of Abuelo and chased the tobacco bite with a cool swallow of rum.

His head cleared, and he looked again at the facts. Assuming Helen used the word *cheese* in the manner they agreed to—only if she were being used as bait—it meant she wasn't alone and their phone conversation had been heard by the tree-shaker. She would be coerced into calling Ellis and either he would answer and agree to the demand, or would be unreachable or unamenable. If she'd made a mistake and used the code word innocently, that was another story, but didn't rule out anything.

If the fucking tree-shaker was there, as Millege believed, he would now be prepared for a nocturnal visit, and any intruder should expect a trap. Which would put Helen in greater danger. Millege puffed and pondered, running scenarios in his mind. Of course, the tree-shaker could leave at any time, go anywhere, but he'd have a hostage on the road, and this option struck Millege as riskier, and therefore less likely. Daylight would present opportunities more favorable to both sides. And there was the Ellis Hayden wild card, how he'd act.

Millege smelled rain, watched clouds roll down toward the sea. He looked back at the cottage, the glow coming from the kitchen, where Liz and Victor were preparing chicken and tortillas and beans. His wound ached. Palmate leaves of papaya stood out against the sky and he heard the forward drops tapping them before he was peppered by rain. He stood smoking his cigar and sipping his drink.

It was decided that Victor would get some sleep and head over before dawn to the road near Helen's driveway and position himself so that movement to, from, or around the property could be observed. Liz got up with him and he left with hot coffee, cold tortillas, her prayers, and the weapon he now carried.

—

In the Bar La Confianza, in Cuidad Neily, two elderly Americans were drinking beer and catching up. Grady Gordon's younger brother, Charlie, had driven across from Panama to check on his sibling's state of mind, his overall condition. Because an overdue visit had now become painfully due.

"I resent the fact that my life has been disrupted," Grady said.

"Of course you do," Charlie said. "You came down here get away from stress, mainly, and to enjoy your remaining time. Same as me."

"Look at us," Grady said, "drinking beer for breakfast."

Charlie laughed. "We're semi-retired expats, financially solvent, in good health. We can do whatever we want. Plus, it's almost lunchtime."

"I miss my dogs," Grady said. "I can't even, in good conscience, keep them at the house. Their house too. My whole routine has been upended."

"You're lucky you have friends who don't mind helping out. It's what I love about Boquete too, the expat community. I know you like it better over here but you should definitely come for another visit, bring your dogs too, and look at it in a new light. At least until this problem goes away."

"Charlie, it's not that simple," Grady said. "I have to leave someone in charge of my place. They can't just drop by whenever they feel like it."

"I know, brother, I feel the same in Boquete. Can't just leave it open to temptation. But you can start asking around. You're a nervous wreck and you need to get away."

From their table they could see glimpses of people passing the open front door, a dark man in a wide white hat, a woman holding a basin of fruit, pedestrians mostly hidden by the standing Pilsen sign positioned to give the interior some privacy from the busy intersection. Several locals sat watching flat screens at the three-sided wooden bar against the back wall. A dog stood inside a side door looking up at one of the patrons and a bicycle leaned against a table at the opposite door. Two wall-mounted oscillating fans hummed in opposition as they pushed air around the room, and the simplicity and tranquility of the small establishment gave Grady some temporary peace of mind. Almost anyplace, outside of his own property, could feel like an oasis.

"I've become a victim of random upheaval," he said.

"As long as you have tenants," Charlie said, "you're inviting a degree of risk. But hell, you do that just by getting out of bed." He laughed again, enjoying his advisory role. "Look brother, this is just a passing storm, not a reversal of fortune. You're still good."

Grady finished his beer. "In my head I know you're probably right," he said, "but I feel like I've been robbed of my house. I'm a stranger there."

"Let's get some food," Charlie said, pushing his chair back. "What do you like around here?"

Grady adjusted his ballcap and stood. "I like this little outdoor joint up the street, across from the park."

They walked down the narrow sidewalk, passed a watch shop, a women's clothing store, a karaoke sports bar, and turned into the doorway of Soda Eli. They went out to the covered courtyard and took a cement table facing the park, seen through the restaurant's wrought iron security bars.

The waitress brought them water and they sat hunched over the table, debating whether to have a typical breakfast or a typical lunch. Grady looked up as a car passed and his eyes settled on a figure moving through his view along the park's perimeter sidewalk. He straightened and watched the man, a gringo with a backpack, as a spark of recognition caused his hand to twitch as if he'd touched a hot surface.

"What's the matter?" Charlie said, his eyes moving from his brother's startled expression to the park.

"Jesus Christ," Grady said, "I think that's my tenant."

Charlie lifted his sunglasses and squinted, turning his head to follow the figure following the edge of the park. "You mean the fugitive?"

"Yes, him," Grady said, standing and stepping clear of the table. "Listen, I have to make sure." He backed toward the entrance, his hand moving in a slight chopping motion as if in time with his thoughts. "Get your car, Charlie, and head up this way."

Charlie stood and watched his brother exit. Out on

the sidewalk, Grady spoke through the bars. "I'll call you. Keep your phone handy. I can't lose him."

He was huffing for breath by the time he crossed the street and entered the park, partly from excitement, partly from anxiety or fear, a combination of sensations brought on by the chase, the possibility—the actual dread—of intersecting the man searching for the one he was following. He looked around as he rushed ahead, keeping the younger man in sight between trees and cars.

The imagined fugitive—Grady was not certain of the identity, but the stride, the profile, the height, the general impression, all fit together—made his next left. The man was moving purposely, as if he had a destination, but not hurriedly, not abnormally, not like a man on the run.

Grady's phone rang too loud. He stopped and made a one-eighty, put the phone to his mouth, his hands trembling.

"Where are you?" He scanned the street and saw his brother's green Subaru opposite their intended lunch spot. "Make a left," he said, "I'm heading back to the street." The car pulled over as he got to the curb. He hopped into the passenger seat. "Make the next left," he said, sliding low in the seat.

The car turned south on Calle 1 and Charlie drove slowly, not at all confident he could recognize the man. "You need to sit up and spot him," he told his brother. They were approaching Avenida 2 as Grady lifted his head above the dashboard, then higher as he scanned the sidewalks and the intersection.

"He's in the next block," he said, "on the right. See him?"

"I see him," Charlie said. "What are you going to do?"

"Let's just see where he goes," Grady said, staying

low.

"He's making a right," Charlie said.

"Okay, he's probably going to Highway 2," Grady said, "probably heading north. Same as us. Stay with him but stay back."

"What about your car?"

"We'll get it later. This is a golden opportunity, unbelievable luck."

"For what?" Charlie said. "Maybe it's not even him."

"People are after him," Grady said, "because he got people killed, and he's hiding. There's a reward, for God's sake. Not that I give a rat's ass about that."

In Charlie's view, his brother had aged markedly since they'd last been together, about four months ago. He'd gone from a solid, vibrant retiree in full command of his body and mind, to a florid, shambling, nervous version of himself. Right now, his face was a map of red regions and his hands shook.

"Brother," Charlie said, "this is not good for you. Just let it go," he said, watching their man amble along the curve of the street, "the guy's already got enough trouble, and so do you."

Grady turned on him. "He's the goddamn reason I've got enough trouble. If you want to help your big brother just patronize me a little longer."

He suddenly pointed, banging his elbow on the window frame. "Look, I knew it. He's heading north on the highway. Slow down. I wonder where he's going. Maybe back to the scene of the crime. It wouldn't surprise me if he was racked with guilt." Grady looked at his brother's face and felt chastised. "Look, he's not a bad guy, he just fucked up. Bigtime."

As soon as he'd gone a few dozen paces along the edge of the Pan American Highway, the man they called the fugitive stopped and faced the oncoming traffic and held out his thumb.

"Holy shit," Grady said, sliding down again. "Make a left and go back around the block. Clear yourself but don't look at him."

Charlie waited at the intersection, looking mostly left, occasionally daring to look right at the man maybe forty yards down the road looking his way. If the car sat much longer it would call attention to itself. The man stood calmly in the manner of an accomplished hitchhiker where the shoulder was wide and conducive to a smooth, safe pullover, sometimes waving at passing cars before they got to him. He wore long pants and sandals, but neither hat nor sunglasses. He seemed friendly, even from a distance.

"Hurry up," Grady said, slumped low in the seat, an animated head atop a collapsed body. The Subaru leapt forward and turned left. Charlie lost sight of the hitchhiker on the curve behind, made the next left, stopped at the curb.

Grady flung the door open, stepped out and slammed it shut, then leaned back into the window. "You have to pick him up," he said. He shook his head at his brother's frown. "Look, he wants to get caught. He's on the Pan American Highway, for God's sake. I'll get my car and text you. Be cool. Put your phone on silent, please." He gave his brother a thumbs-up, sanctioning the mission as best he could, and Charlie drove away without another word.

Wiping his face with his shirt sleeve, Grady stepped into the shade of a store's overhang. The midday sun reflected in lancing beams off the chrome and glass of stationary vehicles, and trucks flew past in a cascade of noise on the highway behind him. He pulled his phone out and paused, trying to remember where he'd parked, then began to scroll through his contacts.

Up the road in Uvita, Stavo was in motion behind the bar, handling the lunch crowd at Ballena Bahia. His phone vibrated on a box beside the beer cooler, and he leaned down to see the screen. He'd been informed by Millege of the river fight with Del Preet and the kidnapping of Helen. His scalp tingled. No name and he didn't recognize the number, but he picked it up anyway. A tip could come in anytime.

"Gustavo?" the caller said.

"This is," Stavo said. He held up one finger to a gesturing male tourist.

"I'm a customer," Grady said. "I live in Uvita. We've talked before."

"Okay," Stavo said. "I am busy now."

"You gave me a paper," Grady said, speaking louder over the noise. "It was about the missing man. The two dead girls, okay? I just saw the man."

Stavo turned and ducked under the counter hatch and took a few steps toward the kitchen, plugging his other ear with a finger. "Where?" he said.

"He's getting a ride up the coast from Cuidad Neily. I'm in contact with the driver. He'll be there, in Uvita, in two hours. Understand? Call your boss and call me back."

—

A Subaru Outback was angling to the shoulder, blinker on, and for a moment he felt like he was back in Oregon and a green resident was doing his civic duty, some older hippie who recognized a kindred spirit and was of an age to have once relied on the same mode of transportation. The window was down.

"Where you headed?" Charlie said.

"North," Ellis said. "Where you headed?"

"North," Charlie said, then smiled to cover his stumble, realizing he needed to sound less mysterious, less vague. "Up to Dominical," he added.

Ellis remained at the window, looking at the interior, the stained seat, the driver's generic sunglasses, his leathery neck and arms, Casio watch, silver bracelet, coffee cup, his vaguely familiar bearing. "What are the odds?" he said, "Panama plates, on a Subaru."

"Boquete," Charlie said, wondering now if Grady had ever mentioned him to his tenant, or if this man had actually seen him when he last visited.

Ellis opened the door and got in. "Appreciate you stopping," he said.

"Glad to help," Charlie said. He eased out and accelerated into traffic.

They passed the municipal cemetery, both men looking at the hillside field of tombs, tiled and painted boxes in solid colors, a dense pattern of blocks planted side by side in a sloping march up to the treeline, death's playground of promises kept and sealed.

"I look at that," Charlie said, "and I wonder how close I am to the end." He smiled. "Not that I'm particularly morbid, but there's the future right there."

"Unless they don't find your body," Ellis said.

"They can still put up a little tile house for you," Charlie said.

"I guess so," Ellis said, "if someone wants to pay for a marker so they can visit and talk to their memory of you. And after a while the tile is chipped and mud-stained and no one comes anymore and dogs pee on your marker."

Charlie smiled. "You have a rosy view for a man your age."

"No sugar-coating," Ellis said. "No thrones of gold."

"I felt sort of nostalgic," Charlie said, "seeing a hitchhiker. Don't really see many these days. Unless someone's broken down or out of gas. Even then, usually they're walking along the side of the road not expecting anyone to stop."

Ellis glanced at the driver. "Feels too dangerous on either side of the deal," he said. "I mean, why chance it? Why did either of us take the risk?"

"We just decided on the spot," Charlie said, staring at the road ahead. "It was serendipitous."

After a pause, Ellis said, "I don't think that's been established yet."

Charlie let the comment go, the man's suspicion already revealed.

They passed a horse pulling a man in an empty cart, then crossed a shallow river, and a minute later passed an oddly designed church—an imposing tower joined to a market shed—called The Light of the World.

They were in Rio Claro now—supermarket, equipment rental, the turnoff to Golfito—no reason to stop, nothing to say. Charlie's phone vibrated in his pocket but he ignored it. His passenger looked at him briefly, reached back to lift a water bottle out of his pack, silently offered it.

"I'm good, thanks," Charlie said, relieved to break the silence.

Ellis unscrewed the top and drank, gulping the water with his head back, depleting at least half the bottle. He recapped it and leaned back against the seat and closed his eyes. In a matter of seconds his breathing had slowed and deepened, and Charlie realized the man had fallen asleep.

He dug his phone out of his pocket and lifted it to keep his eyes looking forward, tapped his text button and read Grady's two messages.

Destination? and then *?? Reply when you can.*

Charlie slowed, keeping an eye on a truck in front

of him, and replied: *Domin*. He aimed his phone and took a shot of his motionless passenger, sent the photo to Grady, set his phone in the console slot, and drove onward toward Palmar Norte. A message came back: *That's him.*

As he was crossing the Térraba River, the song he'd been singing in his head escaped and became audible.

> You've heard there's some gold in the jaguar's coat
> And a man in San Vito if you know how to ask
> He sits on the river by the door to the trees
> And he can bring you that cat in an indigo mask

Ellis rose like a diver out of his slumber-trance, wondering if the song was in a dream or issuing from a sound system. He sat up abruptly and looked at the driver looking at him. He was surprised to be moving, in a car, until his mind settled into current time. Into reality. He had been standing on a dock examining a boat and listening to music coming across the water from another boat, the air as thick and wavy as water, everything blurry in his view.

Charlie turned to him. "Sorry, I didn't mean to wake you. That song has a way of breaking out of me."

Ellis stared at the river and noted their location. "So many river songs," he said, "that'll run as long as we do."

"Absolutely," Charlie said. "And after that, we'll write dried-up riverbed songs, and more desert songs, and wasteland songs, until there's nothing left."

"Wow," Ellis said, "I really went out."

"Oh, you were flat gone," Charlie said.

"I dreamed I was hearing music," Ellis said, "coming from a boat."

"Dreams suggest solutions indirectly," Charlie said, "processing our problems. Sometimes they show us a way across the border, even if we don't understand it."

"Do you say that because you drove across a border this morning?"

"It's a metaphor," Charlie said. "But I'm impressed that you converted my singing into music in your sleep. Was it the same song in your dream?"

"I doubt it," Ellis said, "but the details have faded away."

"You should hang on to the details," Charlie said, "and examine what the dream is telling you. Might be the answer you're looking for."

"What makes you think I'm looking for an answer?"

"We all have questions and problems to sort out," Charlie said.

"Sure, and what brings you across the border today?" Ellis asked.

Charlie smiled. "I like road trips," he said, "and I like checking out this area. Pretty cool up here, or down here, depending on your reference."

Ellis nodded. "Are you thinking of moving?" He glanced at the phone buzzing on the console but couldn't see the screen.

"It's a possibility," Charlie said. He tilted the phone so he could see the message. *Stop in Uvita for lunch. Ballena Bahia. See Gustavo.* "I'm pretty happy in Boquete," he said, "but you gotta have a backup plan. Right?"

"Right," Ellis said, "in case things go straight to hell."

"Hey, are you hungry?" Charlie said. "I didn't get around to lunch yet."

"I'm on a tight budget," Ellis said.

"I don't mind buying a fellow expat a sandwich, man," Charlie said. "I'm retired and glad for the company."

Ellis looked at the man's profile, his relaxed jaw, a face of concealment. "I didn't say I was an expat," he said.

Charlie looked surprised. "Well, aren't you?" he said. "You don't usually see a tourist thumbing a ride."

"Fair point. Alright, thanks," Ellis said, "I could eat something. There's a place up here at Ojochal. You like ceviche?"

Charlie frowned. "I was looking forward to a fish sandwich at Ballena Bahia. You know that spot in Uvita?"

"I know it," Ellis said. "Unfortunately I had an altercation last time I was there and currently am not welcome."

"Damn," Charlie said. "I had no idea I was aiding and abetting a known agitator."

Ellis glanced into the side mirror. "How could you know a thing like that?" he said. "I warned you about picking up hitchhikers."

"So you did," Charlie said. "So you did. Ojochal it is then. I don't want any trouble. I'm a peaceful Panamanian." Smiling, he briefly lifted both hands from the wheel in the standard open-palm gesture of surrender.

Ellis smiled too and aimed his index finger at the other man. "Don't ever cross me," he said.

Charlie laughed. "Don't shoot, mister," he said. "I'm unarmed."

"I'll spare you," Ellis said, "if I can charge my phone."

"Sure, go ahead," Charlie said, unplugging his own device.

Ellis got out his cable and read Helen's text as he plugged in. *Hey, left you a message last night. Need your help. Can we please meet this morning?*

—

Just as he reached his car, Grady Gordon got a call back.

"This is Phil Millege," the caller said. "My associate Gustavo told me you called with some information."

"Yes," Grady said. "As I told your man, I have breaking news on Ellis Hayden."

"You might as well introduce yourself," Millege said, "to validate your info and your reason for giving it."

"My reason for giving it," Grady said, "is my civic responsibility."

"How do you know you have the right man?" Millege said.

"Because I recognized him," Grady said.

"So you know him and you got a good look?"

"Correct," Grady said.

"Okay," Millege said, "where is he?"

There was a pause, then Grady said, "He's on his way to Uvita."

"How do you know where he's going?" Millege said.

"Because he's with a friend of mine who I'm in touch with."

"So your friend's giving him a lift," Millege said.

"Correct," Grady said.

"Do you know where in Uvita?" Millege said.

"They're going to stop at Ballena Bahia in less than two hours."

"Okay," Millege said. "What's your friend driving?"

"A green Subaru Outback," Grady said. "Twenty ten."

"Okay," Millege said. "Let me know if anything changes."

"Will do," Grady said.

"Thank you for calling," Millege said.

Having slept poorly, he sat at the front-room window, drinking coffee, shuffling pieces in his mind, leaning back to close his eyes and think. Liz paced the house behind him. No morning text from Helen. Victor reported no visible activity on the property. Her silver Corolla was parked in its usual space. Impossible to tell if anyone was home.

—

Under the metal roof of the Bar Coronado they commanded a view of a grass field spread before a line of coconut palms running along the edge of the Coronado lagoon, its outer border a strip of island corralled between the great Térraba's mouth and the Pacific Ocean. Off to the left, the neighboring property showed a modest apartment building snuggled among trees. A few children and two dogs could be seen exploring the driftwood debris beyond the palms.

In the spacious open-air room the tables were widely separated and Charlie and Ellis took one near the rear railing of the terrace. At the back of the restaurant the ground dropped away significantly and on the south side a staircase descended, its stucco sidewall an open, alternating motif of blue dolphin and white wave.

"Not bad," Charlie said, looking out at the distant water.

"The no-see-ums can find you at night," Ellis said.

They each got a dish of fish and shrimp ceviche, with onion, cilantro, and wedges of lime, on a plate with two large *tostones*, and quickly dug into the morsels, washing down succulent bites with Imperial beer.

Down at the neighbor's place, a boy and a girl were dragging a yellow plastic boat away from the building, pulling it over the grass by its bowline.

Charlie nodded in their direction. "Look, there's your way out."

Ellis looked at the kids, then back at Charlie. "Is this where you come clean?" he said.

"My brother keeps texting me," Charlie said,

"wondering if we're at Ballena Bahia yet."

"Your brother?" Ellis said.

"Good ole Grady," Charlie said. "With friends like him—"

Ellis nodded, smiling slightly. "He was my landlord," he said. "We didn't hang out."

"I need to reply," Charlie said. "What do you want me to tell him?"

"So he saw me in Cuidad Neily and came up with this," Ellis said. "And with someone to meet us in Uvita."

"He called someone," Charlie said.

Ellis stared at the kids standing in their boat at the water's edge, with the two dogs looking on. "I can't get hung up with anyone right now," he said. "I have a pressing errand."

"If we don't show up at Ballena Bahia, they'll start looking around," Charlie said. "I'll tell Grady we pushed on to Dominical, that you were in a hurry and couldn't stop."

Ellis considered this, finishing his meal, watching the other man's face.

"I'll pay up," Charlie said, "and drop you wherever you want." He slid back his chair and stood. "Where's the restroom?"

Ellis pointed. "Behind that mural," he said. The wall painting showed a whale's tail sticking up out of a blue sea, a green island on the horizon line, and a toucan perched on a leafy limb of a tree on the foreground shore, the bird centered over the island and the breaching tail.

Holding his phone, Charlie disappeared behind the mural. Ellis stood and hoisted his pack and went down the stairs. He trotted to the edge of the property and into the trees and walked alongside the apartments toward the water.

Millege and Liz were ready to go when Grady called from his car.

"My friend said they were going on to Dominical without stopping," he said. "To be honest though, he sounded a bit strange."

"How so?" Millege asked.

"First, he hasn't been responding promptly," Grady said, "and he seemed too nonchalant. Like he was in charge, or something."

"Do you have reason to believe he's not telling the truth?" Millege said.

"Not precisely," Grady said, "but he does like to insert himself into situations. So he can, you know, have an effect on the outcome."

"Okay," Millege said. "I appreciate the assessment. Let's keep in touch."

As he locked the house, a message came in from Helen's phone. *Slept late, was really beat. Heading to the shop now. How are you?*

I'm ok, he answered. *Was wondering about you.*

Sorry, no worries, the reply said. *Opening late today.*

—

As he waited among trees at the top of the drive, Victor heard the car start. He scrambled back to the road and into the ditch on the far side, hidden by a row of hibiscus bushes. As the car topped the drive and rolled out to the road, he peered through leaves from his prone position and saw Helen at the wheel. From his low vantage point he saw no one else in the car as it passed.

When Millege got the call, he said, "Follow it. He's in there."

"Easy to spot the bike," Victor said.

"I know. Stay back," Millege said. "And let me know

which direction they take on the highway."

—

He found a paddle against the side of the building and handed the kids some money and said he needed the boat for a while. They pushed him off as one of the dogs barked and he steered into the tidal current and began to move past the apartment property, the opposite shore a couple of hundred yards away.

He played the voicemail he'd heard the night before.

Hi, I hope you're well. I'm in a tough spot and need your help. Please call asap.

In reply to her morning text requesting a meeting, he wrote: *Playa Ojochal.*

—

Millege kept Liz up to speed on every new piece of information. As they drove, he went over certain details again. At the intersection of Calle Perezoso and the highway he stopped the car and consulted her. "Take your time," he said, "but not too much."

She looked north and then south, then closed her eyes. "Left," she said.

He pulled out and in a few minutes turned into the parking lot of the Bar Coronado and saw a man on a cell phone next to a green Subaru. The man hung up when he saw Millege. Two other cars were parked in the lot. From the front of the open restaurant the view extended straight to the back and Liz got out and walked inside and stood at the rear railing looking out over the yard at the lagoon and the next-door property. There were no people in sight.

Millege stepped out of his vehicle and approached the Subaru man.

"Hello," he said. "I'm the one looking for your passenger. Your friend said you were going to

Dominical."

"Hello," Charlie said. "We stopped for a bite and your guy ducked out when I went to the restroom."

"Where do you think he went?" Millege said, stepping closer.

Charlie shrugged. "Either he got another ride real quick or he went out back to the water."

"And what, swam away?" Millege said.

"Some kids had a little boat," Charlie said.

"But you didn't see him get into it," Millege said.

"When I got back to the table, he was just gone," Charlie said.

Millege looked inside the car. "Do you mind opening the hatch?"

Charlie stared at the other man, sizing him up, considering how helpful or cagey he was willing to be. "You know what," he said, "your guy could be hiding in the kitchen. I didn't think of that until just now."

Millege moved close to the driver's door, eye to eye so that he was breathing in the other man's face, and Charlie stepped back a half step. "Let me put it another way," Millege said. "Do you want me to open the hatch, or do you want to do it yourself?"

Charlie chuckled. "Like I said, man," he said, "I got nothing to hide."

"You didn't say that," Millege said.

"My forthright answers to a total stranger certainly implied it," Charlie said. He pulled his keys out of his pocket and pressed the release button. The hatch popped up and Millege walked back and lifted it. There was a tarp with a suitcase under it, a funnel, a small toolbox, a roll of masking tape, and a case of Old Milwaukee beer.

Liz came out staring at the other man as she walked to the car. She got back in the Rav4 and shut the door. Millege walked back and stuck his head down into the window and looked at her. "Well?" he said.

"The next beach," she said. "Playa Ojochal."

Millege turned to Charlie and lifted his hand. Then got into the car and pulled away.

—

In the cramped confines of the Corolla, Del Preet lay with his head on Helen's lap, his torso upward and his lower body twisted sideways, his long legs drawn up so that his knees were pressed against the dash. The gear shift hit his chest as she drove and he could feel her nasal exhalations on his face. Her breasts pressed against the side of his face and he pushed back against the right one with the pistol in his left hand, occasionally forcing the barrel deeper into her soft flesh as a reminder.

She'd taken a shower and a few sips of coffee and a single bite of toast. She'd changed into clean clothes and was incredibly relieved to have the hood removed. Be thankful for every small thing, he'd told her. Life is a game. Some periods are more difficult, but that doesn't preclude our enjoyment of them.

To be polite, she thanked him for illustrating that lesson.

On her phone, a text came in and he said, "Playa Ojochal."

"Okay," she said.

"Accept no pardon," he said then, and she did not respond.

23. Ecocide

For the first recon, Ellis drove the girls' rental car and they parked across the road from the maintenance shed and sat with a map spread over the steering wheel and across the dash. It was midday and the area was hot and quiet, as if the air had been pulled out of the region and even the giant African palms struggled to breathe. Aside from two young boys walking across the soccer field, the adjacent neighborhood appeared deserted.

"Isn't this where the Zunigas live?" Chloe said.

Ellis pointed over the hood. "Yeah, way back in that far corner."

"I don't get it," she said. "How is it even worth it for the palm company to push them out?"

"Look at this chunk," Ellis said, sweeping his hand toward the field and the houses south. "Taking one place is a step toward taking them all."

"Are you speculating?" Peyton asked.

He smiled. "Sort of," he said. "These are historic in a sense, but they're run down and poor people live in them. This town is a jumping off point for tourists to get to Drake and whale watching and all that. Plus, the palm nuts."

Across the road two men led an oxcart out of the darkness of palms. The cart was piled with bulky white sacks and the men stopped outside the shed and opened the old doors and went inside. The beasts stood as if asleep.

"So we swing by and lob a Molotov, or what?" Peyton said.

Chloe laughed. "Spoken like a true slacker arsonist," she said.

"Probably a good idea to get in and make sure no one is around," Ellis said. "I'll come back with Jimmy in a different car and we'll check the access."

They sat in silence for a minute watching the torpid oxen, lumpen shapes and long faces, neck flaps and down-turned ears, sleepy eyes resigned. The pair yoked together by leather straps around forehead and horns and the worn board behind their heads.

Chloe turned to the back seat. "Are we doing this?" she asked.

"Oh yes, my girl, we are doing this," Peyton said. "Any vacation less than life-changing is no longer acceptable."

Chloe smiled at her friend. "Here the woman roar," she said.

At the cottage a week later they plotted over Jimmy's sketch of the shed, which also showed the abutting treeline, the road, the edge of the housing area with a circled notation: NEIGHBORS—BEWARE & Be Aware!

"Obviously, we move late on a weeknight," Ellis said. "Little or no moon."

"And with our stars lining up," Chloe said.

Jimmy laughed. "Yeah, let's make sure of that," he said. "Seriously, we should be in and out. We'll have four cans of gas so we can douse, spark and split. We haven't seen the inside but we can speculate. We saw a tractor parked outside, which could be inside on the day. There'll be sickles and other cutting tools. Let's assume a couple of spray tanks of herbicide, probably insecticide too. Packing bags, an oxcart or two, you get the idea. Plantation stuff. Most likely they use paraquat marketed as Gramoxone, or they use glyphosate, which is what's in the weed killer Roundup, so we'll have to be careful around that toxic shit. Not good for skin or eyes, or lungs or brain for that matter"—he grinned theatrically—"or any organ you don't want damaged."

"And absolutely," Ellis said, "if we see anybody anywhere in the area—"

"We abort," Peyton said.

"There's a lock on the door latch," Ellis said, "we can pop off with a crowbar."

"Okay," Chloe said, "which day looks like our day?"

Ellis pulled a calendar out of his pack and ran his finger over April. "There's a third quarter moon on Tuesday," he said, "so between then and the following Tuesday's new moon, as in no moon, we'll have a waning crescent getting smaller every day. So the best case would be Sunday, Monday, the new moon Tuesday, or the following day, Wednesday. After that we are into May, which means the rainy season starting and the moon growing into its first quarter. We should go for one of the first two so we'll still have backup days."

Chloe lined up juice glasses on the railing and poured shots of tequila and sliced a lime into eighths. "Should we wear ninja clothes?" she said.

"I have my black thong," Peyton said, and they all laughed.

Chloe handed out glasses and lime wedges to the others.

"Here's to subversive holiday nights," she said.

"Fuck the palm oil industry," Peyton said.

"Where's the salt?" Jimmy said.

"Fuck the salt," Peyton said, and raised her glass. "Here's to the creatures of the forest and to the health of the children who gather scattered nuts when they should be in school."

"Hold on," Chloe said. She stepped into the kitchen and brought back the salt shaker. "Here you go," she said.

Jimmy licked the web of his thumb and sprinkled salt there, and they all followed suit. "If you're going to do something—" he said.

"To a smooth operation," Ellis said, and they licked their hands and clinked glasses and downed their shots and bit into their limes, their faces moist with sweat and soured in solidarity.

In the afternoon of the waning-moon Sunday, Jimmy said he wasn't feeling it. "Just the vibe," he said. No one questioned him or his feeling. It was all for one, they agreed.

On Monday, they had a late contemplative dinner at the girls' place and loaded the surfer's Jeep with the gas cans and a few tools, and he and Peyton followed Ellis and Chloe down the semideserted highway to the Palmer Sur turn to the dark country road to Sierpe. At the last jog in the road before the straightaway into town, Ellis took the side road and drove just far enough to pull over and park his gray Ranger under the dark cover of African palms.

A couple of minutes later the Jeep picked them up and turned around, and the four of them continued in a rumbling dream of unity. They drove past the shed and gave it a good look. Dead still. Dark but for a powder of starlight falling across the ground, the wooden sides, the rust-mottled roof. The tractor was outside, hitched to a trailer, all seemingly drawn in illusory lines. Across the way the deep-set homes were feebly indicated as basic shapes without evidence of nighttime illumination.

After a few hundred yards Jimmy slowed to turn around but then kept driving as if town were now the objective even though there would be no place at this hour in which to pause and drink and make certain.

"Are you having second thoughts?" Peyton asked.

"Getting centered," he said.

"Now would be a good time for that," she said.

They passed another playing field, more streets and houses, traveling deeper into the community.

Ellis was regretting his decision not to drive.

"It's the simplest of plans," Peyton said.

"Exactly," Jimmy said. "Do we all need to go inside? Shouldn't someone keep the car running and be the lookout?"

"I thought we were working together to be faster," Chloe said. "But sure, why not, if it makes you feel better."

"This isn't a movie," Ellis said. "The car will be right there, not in an alley around the corner. We're in, we're out, we hop in the car and go."

Jimmy kept driving. More streets, a store, a Methodist church.

"We don't want to get any more exposure," Ellis said. "Just pull over so we can sort this out."

Jimmy cleared his throat. "Seems sort of loose," he said.

Ellis looked out at palms darker than sky, a fenceline, a pale pasture, the obscure forms of two ghost horses bearing witness. "Life is loose," he said. "It's just a shed. Nobody's killing anybody."

"Down in back," Peyton said as the Jeep slid to a stop. "Car coming."

They sat on the shoulder beside the pasture as a car approached from town, Ellis and Chloe reclining in the back seat, Jimmy and Peyton embracing, their faces hidden as the headlights blazed through the vehicle, apparently an impatient couple making out, the woman's long hair easily seen as dark, possibly that of a native.

They sat in silence as the explosion of light evaporated and the tail lights receded into the distance, red points they were meant to follow. Each couple cuddled in their own cocoon, holding and kissing each other as if to infuse their warm human feelings into the floating coldness of uncertainty.

They returned to the shed and parked just beyond it on the same side of the road and facing the direction of their escape. They waited a few minutes to see if anyone or anything would materialize to offset the plan as the stillness of night closed in like an isolating fog and settled them into determination.

In the equality of their democratic protest, they each carried a full two-gallon gas can to the far side of the shed, four penlights waving over the ground in single file, while the adjacent enemy army of palm giants stood in formation.

As Peyton wished, they all had a physical hand in popping the lock, much like a team's players placing their hands together, one atop the other, the dull clink of iron against hasp the game's starting bell. The doors creaked outward and they entered a cavern of odors. The musty mulch of nut was quickly followed by an enveloping chemical mix, the caustic bite of fertilizer prominent, dust particles floating like circus sawdust in the beams of their lights, each conducting a chaotic survey into the depths and up in the rafters, their random intersections like a cheap lightshow. From the open door, night air was drawn inside through gaps and cracks and termite wings lifted away in secondary flight, fluttering down through the probing beams like flecks of glitter in a decomposing club. None of them had brought a bandana.

They went around the oxcarts parked inside the doorway and stopped, as a unit, to survey the contents. Chloe had a coughing fit—she thought she was catching a cold, she said—that reverberated off the metal roof. The plan was simple, a quick exploration, the even spreading of fuel from the back corners forward, the prepared torches—a pair of footlong sticks wrapped on one end with a bulb of white rag like oversized cotton swabs—to be soaked, ignited, and only from the exit, thrown in deep.

The place was full, a jumble of materials stacked and pushed against the walls. Crammed as it was, the shed seemed higher and deeper that it appeared from outside. Piles of field sacks along one wall. Shelves and racks of cleaning solvents and hand tools. Intermingled smells of oil, ammonia, the sulfur of insecticide, an unventilated assault. Haphazard piles of scrap wood. Large blue plastic drums, assorted jugs, sprayer pumps, tanks, and hoses. They stood in amazement, wasting precious time as their lights roamed over the confusing assortment.

The only open space was in the middle, just past the carts inside the door, a center lane reserved, presumably, for tractor storage and access. Beyond this space was an odd center wall that seemed at first glance to divide the room, except that it did not extend to either side, but stood as a rack from floor to rafters. Ellis let his beam roam over this clumsy add-on, wondering about its means of support. The cobbled-together lattice was a framework erected for the tallest tools, long-armed sickles, extension poles, and ladders hung from utility hooks on both sides. The upper edge seemed to be secured to a crossbeam by vertical two-by-fours, the whole assemblage flimsy-looking and hazardous. He saw Peyton and Jimmy moving around it on the right side, and he continued on the left, Chloe still behind him.

Back in the northeast corner, surrounded by decayed, slanted shelving, a small makeshift desk retained the local history of agro-absorption in the scars of its wood, its surface littered with sign-in sheets, timetables, and product pamphlets curled into cylinders. Above it, a dented and darkened kerosene lantern hung from a wall nail.

Ellis poured a trail of gas along the rear wall, over tarps and junk wood, making his way to the west side. He glanced over at Jimmy in the opposite corner, sloshing his way backward, the can flying up and down as he hurried. Chloe was coughing again, a staccato rasp echoing on top of itself. She stood leaning over in the middle, hacking against the fumes, spitting into the pool of her light, her can on the floor beside her. Peyton's light quit, and she banged it against her palm a few times, stuck it in her pocket and looked around for options, the thick air and choking darkness barely dissected by the thin beams now focused on individual endeavors. She stumbled past Jimmy and leaned on the work desk and grabbed the lantern off its nail and raised its glass chimney and struck her lighter and lit the wick. The old lantern flared up and illuminated the corner and swung from her hand as she left the desk.

Jimmy straightened up in alarm and stepped away from her. His foot caught on a coil of wire and he fell backward and slammed into the corner of the center wall, his light jerking upward and his dropped can spilling beside him, the hanging tool rack pushed off its perpendicular plane, its angle to the floor torquing the upper half. A pole dislodged from its hook, fell, and struck Chloe on the back of the head, knocking her facedown on the floor. Peyton called out and leapt to her aid, grasped the wobbling wall for support as she went around it, raising her lantern as she reached her groaning accomplice. Jimmy pulled at the base of the wall to straighten it. At the top, a two-by-four buckled under the pressure and popped free. The sudden weight displacement pulled the nails out of the other insect-eaten brace like rotten teeth and the wall was momentarily free-standing. Then it leaned forward and seemed to fall in slow motion.

Peyton threw herself over Chloe's head and torso as the top end of the falling rack hit the back of an oxcart and cracked apart, the bulk of it covering the girls in layers of latticed wood and smashing the lantern's chimney. Flames shot across the floor and up into the wood and spread beyond the rack as Jimmy got to his feet and shielded his eyes. His open can was engulfed and fire crawled inside and blew it apart, throwing threads of fire and hot plastic onto the side wall and across the floor. His pants were speckled with fire and the fire darted along the erratic trail he had poured and joined the line Ellis had drawn and in no time the fireline surrounded them on three sides, crackling in its swift advance.

Batting his burning pants, he heard his name called and across the debris of the broken framework saw Ellis lifting the shattered far corner, the corner itself bending upward without shifting the weight of the piece. He ran around to the same side and they lifted together, pushing the piece vertical as the fire crackled and grew. Peyton's can blew apart and they dropped the rack as fire raced under the entire structure.

Smoke filled the shed as bags and wood and the

plastic of jugs and their combustible contents ignited and added to the spreading blaze. Coughing and half-blind, Ellis pried a pole into the frame and pushed it side to side, trying to make a hole, then began to smash it into the wood near the girls as they cried out in unison for help. He heard Peyton scream, saw her hand reach up through the wood, and he shouted for Jimmy again. Flames were climbing the walls and moving to the front, everything was fire food. He struck the other can beneath the rack and watched flames licking their way over and around it, his face and arms liquid and searing, the shed's burning materials hissing and spitting all around, the air poisoned.

Outside the door Jimmy rolled on the ground and slapped his legs and got to his knees cramping over with ragged coughing. Smoke flowed from the door and seeped through cracks between side boards and the metal sheets of the roof. He stood and staggered toward the road, eyes adjusting to the eastern darkness. Behind him the shed radiated a glow of vertical orange lines. A girl's howl rose from the fire's rushing crackle and pushed him running to the car.

The can beneath the fire-wrapped lattice exploded and drove splinters into the upper left leg of Ellis Hayden as he turned to escape. He fell backward and rolled and crawled toward the door and dragged himself upright and fell again. The sky was upside down and swimming in waves as he rolled clear of the enclosure and drew fresh air and hacked it out and stood and gagged and limped away from the blaze. Inside, a metal container exploded like a cannon shot and shrapnel whistled and clanged into roof panels. He hung his head, eyes and nose dripping, and limped. He looked both ways and did not see the car. Across the road a light appeared, wavering as if from a mast at sea, and it seemed that he was deaf. He turned around and hobbled past the raging shed and between the flickering pillars of the palms and disappeared into darkness.

Stumbling along in shock and strangled by thirst, he stopped to vomit, purged himself empty, and continued on, heading north to his vehicle, tears falling in streams, drool hanging from his chin. His light jerked over the ground as he navigated the ruts between rows, the glow of the burn gone now, and moved parallel to the road, tree by tree, swallowed in a vast pattern of palms.

He came out on a grass berm and crossed it and stood lightless on the ribbon of road. After a few more steps he stood at the intersection and looked south and saw the movement of lights, like fireflies in a smoke drift, a landscape turned alien. He walked on and came to his truck.

He got in and blasted the AC and drank water in the dark waiting for his mind to calculate something. Unable to pass the shed, unable to proceed into the town itself—a village held in the nocturnal embrace of the serpentine river, but by now full of awakened denizens—his instincts gravitated to Sierpe town anyway. He couldn't see himself on the highway, running blind.

He turned around and drove over the little bridge over the Estero Azul, a connection to the Sierpe River, and put his headlights on and followed the side road parallel to town, past more palm rows, a few dark dwellings, farmland. He knew the road would become nothing but agricultural access and he needed to leave his vehicle and get a boat.

Smoke clung to his clothes, kept his nausea at the top of his throat. He drove slowly down the farm road, head aching, his breaths choppy, open land to his left, and intersected a field track and turned right and saw a glimmering bend of the Estero Azul that separated him from the town side. Across the channel marsh plants waved in the night breeze coming off the wide Sierpe just upstream. He turned off the road and rolled into a thicket of trees and sank into soft ground. He got out and retrieved his pack from the rear and headed toward the water's edge, weaving through the trees into crocodile habitat.

The ground was swampy. Wading through high river grass, his wet shoes sloshing into muddy roots, he couldn't see the opposite bank or the little cove marina on that side. Thoughts of survival kept him going one minute and stopped him cold the next. The reptiles would be in the water hunting, ever watchful at the surface, lurking near the banks for opportunity. He needed a way to float across. Swimming would be ill-advised.

The banks were too thick and perilous with vegetation except where properties with docks gave access. He turned around and backtracked past his truck to the farm lane, his leg bleeding, then found the straight road north visible enough. A possum startled him as it crossed the road. The darkness vibrated with the song-racket of crickets and frogs, and beyond that he heard irregular snatches of traffic across the channel, over on the main road. He used his light as little as possible.

At the edge of the closest developed property he watched the dark house and could not see a car from his side angle. He paused under the trees and dry heaved, bent over in abject misery, his mind replaying the flames and the girls calling his name and Peyton's raised hand and her final scream of life. If he were shot now, or drowned, he had no defense.

Following his pale beam he stumbled like a drunk

between coconut palms and fallen fronds and flowering shrubs to a mud beach. The water was low and a small sloping dock with broken boards extended from the bank down into the exposed mud. A narrow wooden utility boat lay stuck in the viscous shallows, a common scuffed blue color, with a pointed prow and V-shaped transom, secured to a palm with a length of yellow nylon rope. He stepped up on the slippery crossboards and shined his light along the shore and over the water's surface looking for predators, then stepped down into the mud and examined the boat. Dry, some leaves and sticks, no paddle. He dragged his heavy feet to shore and untied the line and pushed the boat against the mud's resistance until it floated high enough to turn, then swung the stern around to face him, dropped his pack inside, stepped in and shoved off.

The boat wobbled into the center as he settled at the bow, leaned across the surface of the triangular deck and paddled with his cupped right hand, then his left, trying to keep the boat midstream, floating quiet and dark, only ripples betraying his passage.

As he approached the tangled point of land where his truck was parked, he noticed a couple of trees growing out into the channel like an appendage and he steered right to keep centered. Out of the corner of his eye he caught a glint of surface movement separating from the trees, flashed his beam and saw red eye reflections gliding toward him, a long narrow head barely noticeable in the dark, eye ridges and nostrils like parts of a log breaking the surface, the rest of the body submerged. He made two more hard paddle strokes and withdrew his hands from the water. The boat was heading into a tight bend and he would need to turn left soon to avoid hitting the bank. He looked to his side again but the croc was no longer visible.

The animal was just curious, he told himself, the boat was too large to be prey. Maybe it was a slow night, and the crocodilian brain is programmed to check out the ripples caused by something the size of a human hand.

He scanned the bank, his light off, and paddled with his right hand, making the slow turn. The main road was close at this point, no reason someone couldn't be parked up there, covering this avenue of escape, waiting to see him pass. Everything now slanted against him, his guilty flight, his character. He rested his head on the deck, kept his hand trailing in the water as bait, testing whatever he was testing. Like what, Russian roulette? To see if he got pulled into the water or was allowed to live, protected by providence.

His eyes were closed and the floating sensation grew fuller, the world pushing him onward without his design, as if he need make no more decisions but simply flow with the tide and continue into the night, into the wide Sierpe and past the town and finally out to sea, taken by nature.

Moonlight—the climbing sliver had just risen—touched his face in brushstrokes passing between trees and rippling over grass. When he looked up, the mouth of the little cove marina beckoned, yawning him into its harbor, the last stop before the wide open Sierpe. He paddled hard with his left hand, made the turn and slipped silently inside the protected circle. No more than a dozen boats lined the floating dock at the inner curve. Small work boats, local skiffs and tour boats. And as he glided closer, he saw the Intrepid, the big dog in this pen. A foreign friend's underused vessel, kept in an arrangement with the dockmaster, a hidden key and a couple of people who could be called upon to move the boat in the event of an emergency.

He paddled around under the walk ramp and tied up along the dock's inner edge. He lay back against the gunwale with his knees up and closed his eyes. Stillness descended under moonlight and exhaustion overtook him, a temporary mask over the choke of reckoning as he waited for dawn.

—

Lunchtime was essentially over and Stavo was wiping down the bar when he got the call he was expecting. "Hello Mister Phil," he said.

"All hands on deck," Millege said. "Can you get down to the Ojochal beach right away?"

"I will leave in one minute," Stavo said.

"Good man," Millege said. "We have a lot of moving parts."

"Okay sir," Stavo said, "I will call you."

He spoke to the manager and walked out into the parking lot and beside the open door of his minivan changed out of his white polo shirt. He paused and selected a black T-shirt in case the mission stretched into the evening, and pulled it over his head, noticing the afternoon clouds massing over the hills.

—

Seen from the air, the Coronado lagoon was shaped like a great supple lizard moving north on the coastline, its head extending beyond the mouth of the river, gulping the wild Pacific, jaws open to swallow a sandbar, its forelegs hugging the body, wiggling into its natural swimming position, its hind legs gripping the green shore—a giant crocodile, made of water instead of living in it. The long meandering tail branched off into tendrils penetrating a maze of mangroves. At about shoulder height on the water lizard's immense body, a tiny yellow speck was moving south.

Fed by the Coronado and Térraba Rivers, and shaped by the ocean currents, sandbars appeared, flat gray-brown islands at the mouth and along both shores of the winding course. Ellis struggled in his flimsy plastic boat, a toy-like vessel that proved difficult to steer in the chop of the river waters. He was close to the northern shore, his ballcap soaked with sweat, watching from the shade of its brim for landmarks and signs of the trouble he came to meet. He noted the buildup of clouds above the ridge, the scattered properties nestled on the slope for reasonable western views, the gray beach of Ojochal running long and ill-defined by shifting silt. A couple of cars were parked among coconut palms and two men were unloading fish from a white, blue-topped boat anchored near the shore, three frigate birds and a gull swooping low over it. The remaining pieces of former docks appeared as dark random boards, standing in warning. After a short rest, he kept going.

—

In the passenger seat of her own car, Helen squeezed her zip-tied wrists between her knees to alleviate the discomfort. Del Preet glanced over and said nothing. The gun lay on the floor behind his feet.

"Here's the first turn coming up," Helen said.

He drove past it, glancing down the road, then checked his rearview.

After a sign that advertised cabins, hiking, and the river itself, Del Preet turned and parked under tree cover, out of sight of the turn. He stepped out of the car and bent down to the window and looked at Helen in her green leaf-print dress, red hair tousled, sweat lining her brow and upper lip, her expression as impassive as she could keep it. He put the barrel to his lips in a gesture of quiet and she nodded.

"Don't even picture me having to run you down," he said.

As Victor approached the sign, his bike screaming its 2-stroke whine, he pulled over and killed the engine and sat listening. A car from the south passed him sitting on his bike and holding his phone. He peered into the trees but the cover was too thick to see anything. He called Phil Millege.

"What happened?" Millege said.

"The man took a turn to the river," Victor said. "I'm on the highway."

"You think he spotted you?"

"Maybe he heard the bike," Victor said. "I had to pass the man when he stopped to take the wheel. Then I had to get behind him again to see the turn."

"You could follow on foot," Millege said.

"The side road goes two ways," Victor said. "The man can come back to the highway and circle behind me."

"He has to park and get to the river," Millege said. "We're parked at the beach and there's a guy paddling by in a little yellow boat, a kid's boat, so he hasn't come far. Has to be our man. He's heading down toward you and will probably stay in the open as long as he can."

"Okay," Victor said, "I'll leave my bike at the turn. You are less than a kilometer from me."

"Okay," Millege said. "I'll follow the shore and track the boat."

Liz wanted to reach for the phone and tell Victor to be careful, to avoid taking any chances, or actually, to just stay on his bike and come pick her up on the highway so she could hop on the back and they could leave the area. But she didn't do that.

"Okay," Victor said. "What about Liz?"

"She'll stay with the car or come with me," Millege

said. "Her choice."

Millege turned to Liz. "You can stay with the car," he said. "You're a great help, but don't do anything you're not comfortable doing. Understand?"

"I'm okay, sir," she said.

Millege spoke into the phone. "We'll see you soon," he said.

They got out and walked between the palms toward the river. Millege wore shorts and had his calf wound wrapped. Liz carried her umbrella. Near the muddy shore they passed a wooden sign nailed to a tree: *Crocodile Habitat*.

At the water's edge a small fishing boat was motoring into deeper water and the man who had pushed it off stepped back, waved to the captain, lifted a cooler to one shoulder and headed to his car.

A screen of rain came rolling over the ridge, drumming down the fronds and hissing across the river's surface in a tight frenzy of miniscule splashes. In another moment the fishing boat and the small yellow boat upstream were both obliterated from view.

In the downpour the plastic boat began to fill with water and Ellis, in a brown poncho, paddled and drifted through a gray haze disguising the land. A few box shapes seemed to be basic houses or shacks falling apart in streaks as he passed. The thick green of trees, the riverside jungle, a drift wreck of broken bamboo like a lost beaver's dam he circumvented and then entered a shallow stream dissecting a sandbar. He felt the bottom rubbing and bailed the bow's well with cupped hands. The boat ran aground and he sat as an island himself, a brown rock with water running down all sides.

—

Rain covered the windows and pounded the roof. Leaves and small limbs stuck to the hood. I'm a nurse,

Helen told herself. Unexpected problems are the norm. Calm, rational thinking carries the day. She had no idea where her captor was. But pictured herself running up to the highway. Waving her bound hands in a wet dress like some crazy woman drunk dancing for cars.

Del Preet had positioned himself behind a tree between the car and the turnoff from the highway and stood still as a crane. He'd removed his ballcap to narrow his profile and he squinted and blinked through the water running down his face. He'd seen the bike and figured the rider to be the Indian. Who might reasonably be expected to wait out the heaviest rain for sound and visibility. Or not.

From an early age Victor had gone along on hunting trips to learn the ways of the forest, at first for food, for curassow and deer and paca, and then later for silent observations with birders and survey takers. Even as an older boy he preferred target shooting to the taking of game. He was reminded of his younger self as he eased down the highway slope to the edge of the side road, stowed his pack and waited in a crouch, listening into the rushing deluge and staring into the liquid shimmering air. The rain draped everything and he advanced across the road through its oblivion.

He saw the big silver car but could not distinguish any details of the interior. Then, behind the car, the American man materialized like a spirit, moved in a crouch to the driver's door and ducked inside. The engine came to life and the car rolled forward, the wipers revealing a view of both occupants.

—

Stavo crept down the highway, wondering if he was missing the action. Only one of his minivan's wipers worked—luckily it was on the driver's side—and he proceeded cautiously. Once he made the beach turn he slowed to a crawl and peered through the tunnel vision of his windshield looking for any trouble already underway. None was evident. The only car there was the boss's Rav4 but he drove around it first, then parked beside it and texted Millege.

—

In the clearing's riverfront circumference, the makeshift structures had the look of a squatter's camp. One was a plain scrap-board house with a tar paper roof. An adjacent laundry line confirmed the dwelling's domesticity. A couple of wet shirts hung dripping in the rain, the dry clothes having been taken in prior to the storm's arrival. The other structure was larger, made of taller boards, the back half enclosed for extra living quarters, the front half open on two sides, the roof covered in black plastic sheeting which draped to the ground like a shroud over most of the open section. In storage were water barrels and fuel cans and pieces of wood to be kept dry. Added to the front end was a framework box holding an exposed system of wide plastic pipes cut into troughs that fed rainwater into the barrels inside.

Sitting shirtless on a stump in the open section, a man named Obayda held a small outboard motor between his knees. The engine cowling was off and he was replacing the pull cord while his son Calvo—so-called because of his close-cropped hair and the roundness of his head—stood beside him and watched. The boy was nine and already an accomplished fisherman. When the rain diminished a bit, he stepped out to look at the sky over the river and noticed, out on the sandbar beyond his father's inverted fishing boat, a small yellow boat with a figure sitting in it. He called his father and they walked out to see if there was a problem.

Ellis stood at their approach and stepped out of the small boat with his pack and sloshed through the water and sand and met them where they waited in the rain on the mudflat where the other boat was beached.

"Good afternoon," Ellis said, raising his hand in greeting.

"Good afternoon," Obayda said. "Do you need help?" He still held the screwdriver he had been using and it appeared to Ellis that repair services were being offered or the man was carrying this basic weapon as a matter of course.

Ellis pulled back the hood of his poncho and said, "There's no problem. I was meeting someone at the beach but went too far in the rain. Sorry to bother you. I'd like to take cover and make a call."

The sky was drawn in murky swaths like a poorly erased chalkboard. They walked into the shed and Ellis removed from his pack a plastic bag with his phone inside. As the man and the boy watched, he dialed Helen's number.

The line connected with no answer.

"I'm here," Ellis said.

"Where?" Del Preet said.

"By the river," Ellis said. "You'll see a small yellow boat."

"Do you need a fucking entourage?"

"I didn't say a word," Ellis said. "It must be your entourage."

"Come up to the road," Del Preet said.

"It's quieter down here," Ellis said. "How's Helen?"

"She's running out of patience," Del Preet said. "And time."

The fisherman looked at his son and nodded toward the house. The boy abruptly left.

Seeing the boy go, Ellis hung up and turned to

Obayda. "Where's the path to the road?" he said.

The man pointed to the river.

"How many people live here?" Ellis said.

The man shrugged. "Five," he said. "Seven. Nine." His voice had become distant, and his eyes were growing detached, and Ellis understood he was meant to leave now. He glanced down at the coverless engine and at a pair of bamboo fish spears in the corner.

"Thanks," he said, meeting the man's eyes. Then he turned and walked back out into the rain.

At the house, the boy was surprised to find his mother speaking with two strangers. There was a woman with a shocking red mark on her face and Calvo stared in fascination, knowing his behavior was rude, wondering if the woman had supernatural powers and was casting a spell on his mother. The other stranger, wearing a droopy hat and a leg bandage, was a foreign man who let the woman do all of the talking. The woman called his mother by her name, Noilyn, as if they were friends.

He thought he should run back to his father with this news but his mother motioned him further inside. He looked at the man who was looking at him, and he could see that his mother was listening intently and trying to hide her concern.

"We live here simply," Noilyn said, "without trouble."

Liz nodded and touched the other woman's arm. "What we want to do in this difficult moment is deflect trouble away from you and your family," she said. And Calvo could sense her knowledge and sincerity.

"How can you do that?" Noilyn asked, feeling suddenly that the surprise visitor had unusual powers and should be heeded without reservation.

Liz let her silence speak first, her dark eyes drifting from the woman's face to her child to the plastic chairs and table and rope beds and drapes and to the window to the kitchen shelter with its simmering pots and wash basin.

"With force," she said. "With righteousness and the tools of conflict. We must use anything at hand to repel evil." The rain beat on the roof and the smell of beans drifted inside and everything normal and balanced in this riverside life teetered on a whim of chance and there was nothing Noilyn could do but place her faith in a salient messenger who could never hide her distinctive gift.

She spread her hands to indicate the whole room, whatever the strangers needed for their task, then looked at her son and knew what he was thinking. She moved behind a curtain and bent down and when she returned she was holding an old rifle in both hands like a household treasure.

Millege stepped forward and put his hand out for the gun and Noilyn passed it to him. It was an Ithaca 49 single shot .22, the same model he had owned as a boy, and he held the weapon in amazement and worked the lever, opening and closing the chamber, bemused by his boyhood memories.

"Bullets?" he said.

"*Balas*," Liz said, and Noilyn went back behind the curtain and returned with three bullets, which she deposited in Millege's outstretched palm.

He waited with his hand open but she shook her head.

"Thank you," he said. And to Liz, "Tell the boy I had the same rifle when I was his age."

She translated his statement and the boy smiled briefly, then said, "It's my father's gun."

The rain continued and its passage off the coast seemed to leach some of the sky's glow from its firmament. At the river's edge, the figures might have materialized from above or below, such was the strange quality of the light and their unlikely appearance in the eyes of Obayda, as if a theatrical production were being presented without notice or weather concerns, the first character in the boat now summoning other players by land. He turned to see his wife and child approaching in the company of two more, and though he was curious, he feared for his family.

With Helen in tow, her face and arms scratched and dirty, her dress wet and torn, Del Preet came forward past the beached fishing boat and motioned to Obayda with his pistol. "Where's the engine?" he said in Spanish, pulling Helen by her wrists to position her body in front of his.

Obayda raised his hands and gestured toward the shed.

"Bring it," Del Preet said. He was laser-focused but did not appear ruffled by the crowd. His clothes, other than being wet, and his general appearance, did not reflect the trials of the day.

The shirtless fisherman kept his hands up and entered the open side of the shed. He picked up the engine and the cowling and stepped out drawing his screwdriver from his back pocket.

Del Preet shot him in the stomach and he dropped everything and collapsed to his knees holding his wound. The gunshot and the scream of the man's wife resounded off the trees and across the water. Noilyn fell upon her husband and cradled him as he sat back. Helen yelled in reflex and Del Preet hit the side of her head with his pistol and in the same motion aimed at Millege, who stood stock-still, the small rifle on the ground just behind him, one bullet in the chamber and the other two in his pants pocket.

The boy ran to his father and squatted in front of

him, saw the pain on his face and his clasped fingers with blood seeping between them. The boy strode into the shed as if he'd suddenly remembered a chore, grabbed one of his bamboo fish spears and stepped out, raising it to throw like he'd done many times before, to plunge it into the flesh of his prey.

"No, no," his mother yelled, lunging for his legs as Del Preet took aim at the boy's head, the barrel weaving slightly as he wrestled Helen into a headlock to keep her still.

Noilyn tackled her son and the spear fell to the ground as he did. She scrambled on top of him like a wrestler and pinned him down as he struggled.

Del Preet spoke over his shoulder. "Mr Hayden, get the engine and put it on before someone gets hurt." He processed the entirety of the scene, the calm investigator and his crimson-stained girl under a purple parasol, the little family in pain and self-preservation, agitated Helen, the missing Indian.

Between the hem of the sky's broad gray drape and the lagoon's low green western arm, a thin ellipse of sun shot forth and sprayed the opposite hills in a preening resurgence. A flock of roseate spoonbills, winging pink in upstream flight, was hit by the sudden blast of rays, wings glowing like bright painted kites, the remaining rain falling through the formation of birds in backlit mercurial lines that disappeared in the half-light below and rippled in small eruptions across the river's slate surface.

As he came forward Ellis watched the unreadable face of Liz for a clue but she gave no sign of recognition. He locked eyes with Millege for a moment, wondering what the man was planning. As he bent down to lift the outboard, he briefly acknowledged Obayda's silent suffering, his stressful breathing and blinking eyes. The gut-shot man stared straight at

Ellis, like one trying to look death in the face, almost like he'd seen it coming, just not this soon, not from a toy boat. His wife held her husband like a child, reaching around him to lay her hands upon his as he pressed his stomach, both of them holding his life inside, while the boy clung to her back like an infant sloth. Ellis wanted to tell her to hold on, that nothing could be done until he left. That they could get help then, and their lives would return to normal. But he said nothing.

He turned around and saw Helen's condition, her red eyes and tear-streaked cheeks, met Del Preet's cold roving glance, then carried the engine to the boat without its cover, set it on the mud and turned the boat over. He positioned the engine, tightened it in place, tilted the prop up, then ran back to the shed for a gas can, wanting to leave these people in whatever peace they had left, as soon as possible. He carried the can and attached the fuel hose and untied the boat and pushed it off the mudbank.

Holding Helen as a shield, Del Preet walked backward to the floating boat. "Let's go," he said.

"As we agreed," Ellis said, "leave the woman."

"I'll leave her upriver when we're clear," Del Preet said.

"That's not the deal," Ellis said.

"The deal changes if there's an audience," Del Preet said. "Start the engine unless you want to take your chances right here."

"We need more depth," Ellis said. "Get in and sit down."

Aggravated by a nagging thirst for revenge, however unprofessional it made him feel, Del Preet took aim at Millege, who half-expected to be shot.

Watching the shooter's body language, Millege dropped to the ground and rolled as two shots were fired, unsure if he was hit or not. Liz fell into a crawl and scurried to the side of the huddled family, wanting to protect them from further harm, the harm she had helped to bring upon them, knowing there was no such thing as a zone of exclusion.

Del Preet was hit in the forearm and dropped his pistol. In one deft motion he slid down and grabbed the gun with his left hand, kept his injured arm encircled around Helen as he rose again, seeking the source of the shot. He saw the Indian leaning out from the corner of the shed, pistol in a two-handed grip.

Pushed against the boat, Helen stepped in and Del Preet, his arm bleeding, held her neck until she got her other leg over and stood balanced. He fired a shot at the shed, then stepped over and dragged her with him to the bow to distribute the weight as Ellis pushed the boat out and hopped on the gunwale and took the stern seat. There was a paddle along the side but the boat had no running lights. The river seemed a rippled steel sheet ahead of them, the rain gone but for its cleansing scent. Birds huddled in clusters on the far shore, the stretch of trees silhouetted against the granular orange residue of the western sky, slowly smothering below a closing dome.

The outboard's kill switch was in place and Ellis lowered the shaft and looked back at shore. The two buildings were raised landmarks in the dusk but the figures were blending into the texture of the clearing even as they moved about. He saw his pack, a lump near the yellow plastic boat, then spotted, on the far left side, a figure moving along the shoreline.

He opened the choke, gripped the handle and pulled the starter cord. It was tight, sluggish upon retraction. The boat was listing south, turning sideways to shore. He pulled harder and the engine fired and the cord ripped free and dangled loose as a thread. He dropped the handle, gripped the tiller and increased the throttle steadily, and the boat headed into the dusk.

Among coconut husks, Millege lay prone on the ground, sighting the moving boat, the small rifle resting on his outstretched fist. He steadied his breathing and stroked the curl of the trigger with his index finger and focused on his target. Stavo ran through his line of sight like an off-course jogger and Millege held the shot and closed his eyes and breathed himself into a new aim. Time was running out. He squeezed off the round, heard a distant clang, ejected the shell, took the next round from between his teeth and pushed it into the chamber. He steadied his sight line again, perpendicular to the receding boat, fired and hit the engine and listened as its whine diminished into nothing.

His third shot hit Del Preet in the chest as he stood to return fire. The small bullet did not exit, and he sat heavily on the bow seat. Ellis ducked and brought up the paddle and pulled alternating strokes to resume their course.

Seeing the small yellow boat, Stavo ran to it in bobbing crouch, looking to use his significant kayaking experience, splashing across the sandbar in the failing light, glad to be wearing his dark clothes, and pushed the plastic boat forward with his momentum, sliding it over the sand to open water. He stepped in and sat on the middle brace and paddled parallel to the fleeing fishing boat.

"Stay low," Millege shouted to Liz, who was rising to meet Victor as he came around the shed. A shot from the river ripped through the plastic sheeting and Victor reached out for her arm and pulled her behind the building and against his body.

"We need to get the man to a hospital," Millege

said. "Liz, help Victor get him to the car." Noilyn was tearing her son's shirt into strips with her teeth and wrapping her husband's bloody middle. The boy sprinted to the house and ran back with a small bottle of alcohol and his mother's purse.

Victor came forward and handed the pistol to Millege, then bent down and lifted Obayda as he would a baby, the man groaning at the movement. Liz took the car keys from Millege and they hurried across the property to the shoreline path, Noilyn and Calvo gripping Obayda's dangling hand.

Millege moved along the edge of the sandbar tracking the slow-moving boats, the yellow one visible, the fishing craft beginning to dissolve in the dark.

Out on the river, Ellis was tiring, and he stopped to rest his lungs and aching back. Del Preet was watching him, recalculating, making decisions on time and place. On his own state of health. His breathing was loud, labored.

"Keep going," he said, aiming left-handed at Ellis.

"Catching my breath," Ellis said. "I need to stand for a minute and stretch my back." He stood and lifted his arms overhead and then bent at the waist, feeling his lower back muscles pulling tight. He looked at Helen as she watched him closely. She sat on the bow seat beside Del Preet, her wrists still bound.

The current turned the boat constantly but kept it going forward as the night darkened and the breeze soothed the occupants in their various states of discomfort. The blossoming starlight reflected off the surface and its pale sheen contrasted with the darker treeline on either side, but they were unable to see any logs or debris in their path.

Silence floated over the river and bats cut the air with barely a trace.

Del Preet suddenly stood. "What the fuck is that?"

Ellis looked to their portside and saw something on the water. He squinted hard and realized it was the little yellow boat, following them, possibly gaining. He picked up the paddle again.

Del Preet braced his legs in a wide stance, leaning on the middle seat, and held his aim left-handed, the barrel wavering, his bandana-bound right arm bleeding through the cloth, pressed against his stomach, a small hole in his upper chest.

Ellis looked at Helen, could tell by her posture that she was alert, and nodded his head to the side, then again, indicating the river. He gripped the paddle as a crossbeam, his arms separated for power, and sprang off the seat at the other man. He hit Del Preet broadside and knocked him against the gunwale and over the side. He rolled backward and splashed into the river and came up quickly with his gun raised to shoot. He reached the gunwale with his right hand, gasping at the shock of pain running like a charge through his arm, and clung to the side, barrel pointed upward.

On the opposite side, Helen slid into the river and Ellis jumped in beside her. He found her arms and slid his hand between them and gripped the plastic band encircling her wrists and swam with his other arm, kicking hard.

"Kick," he said, turning his head. "Take a breath and go under, now." He went down trailing her to his side as they passed the shelter of the boat, expecting shots, bullets penetrating the dark water and biting into him or her or both. He swam completely blind, waving into the water as if to ward off whatever he couldn't see.

She broke the surface drawing air in a rasping shriek, unable to swim so restrained, afraid of drowning and crocodiles, her throat emitting low singing moans and her teeth clacking like rocks rolling under waves. She felt herself pulled as she frog-kicked, her arms out in front, her dress waving around her waist like kelp, her neck straining to keep her chin above water, her mind working in rote, pared to a single word: kick, kick, kick.

Stavo heard the splashes and stood almost upright in the bow of the tiny boat. He saw a line of ripples, a surface disturbance, then a hand waving, and he sat with his paddle and dug into the water with renewed force.

Del Preet dropped his pistol into the boat and clung to the gunwale with both hands, gathering his resolve. He swung his leg up and got his foot over the edge and held his position, his injured arm and chest on fire. He closed his eyes and chanted—"Alpha November Papa"—five times, focusing on the rhythm of the words, then heaved himself up and over and toppled into the bottom of the boat, a high-pitched groan escaping from his throat.

"Take her hands," Ellis shouted. He struggled to raise them higher as he held the side of the plastic boat and Stavo leaned over to reach the woman, the small craft listing precariously. Helen was practically dead weight, and once she had her fingers on the lip of the boat, she did not want to let go.

Ellis put his arm around her waist and tried to lift her, pulling on the side of the lightweight boat, but she was too slippery and heavy. He slid down and put his arm between her legs and tried again to help her upward but each time the boat dipped too far over and Stavo had to move backward for balance.

"Cut her hands loose," Ellis said.

"I got nothing," Stavo said.

Ellis dug into his front pocket and lifted his folding knife and Stavo leaned forward to grasp it. Ellis swam to the other side of the boat and hung on the side and pulled some of his weight up to balance the boat as Stavo looked at Helen's face and showed her the knife and then sawed the zip tie off.

Ellis shifted around to the stern and called Helen and reached out his hand. "Come back here," he said. She moved her hands along the gunwale inch by inch and joined him, her face blank as she looked at him in the dark. "He'll tow us in. Kick if you can. Not far to go."

A vast starfield covered them, a deep velvet infinity of twinkling spots. The breathing of the paddler could be heard, his oar plying the river from side to side, their feet slapping at the surface, the dark shore a jagged rise ahead, their voices absent, their silent common fear the unseen reptilians.

Ellis thought of his moving legs, his hand pressing against Helen's, the fishing boat somewhere behind them, the progress being made. Helen was humming, keeping her mind on sounds, a simple tune she could not name.

From shore, a narrow beam of light flared and darted over the boat, illuminated the paddler, the sides of the vessel, the water's surface around it. Ellis turned and caught a glimpse of the other boat drifting on.

Her feet struck bottom and Helen let out a cry of surprise. The boat ran aground and Stavo stepped out and pulled it up on the sandbar, the towed passengers falling forward and crawling up on the sand like castaways. Ellis got to his hands and knees, unable to proceed, the packed mud a refuge. His arms started shaking as a flood of relief implanted his limbs in the sand.

A pair of running shoes entered his ground view and a hand reached out. He took the hand and was lifted to his feet. He turned to see Helen upright and supported by the starlight paddler. She hugged Stavo's neck and thanked him, then stepped forward and fell into the arms of Millege and sobbed against him as he held her close.

They sat and rested on the strip of dark mud, open to the sky and the river's breeze, the carcass of an embedded tree a nearby night figure waiting to be righted, everything stationary but the river. Millege lit a cigar and stood apart, letting silence sooth the nerves. Stavo sat on the edge of the boat.

"Thanks for helping us," Ellis said.

"It's nothing," Stavo said. "I know this river from my kayak tours."

"No, it's something," Ellis said. "The man in the other boat was armed."

Stavo paused, caught between heroism and foolhardiness. "I met that man," he said. "But I am helping the team of Mr Phil."

"We all have questions and need a drink," Millege said. "Let's get back to the house and clean up." He walked over to Ellis. "But while we're here," he said, "let's take the opportunity to get a verification of your death."

Ellis stared without comprehension. "How's that?" he said.

"Certain people will demand a closing of the deal," Millege said, "some piece of evidence. Depending on the condition of the man who took you boating with our lovely Helen, it could be helpful later to have something tangible, something we can accomplish right now."

"What do you have in mind?" Ellis said.

"A phone pic," Millege said, "of you lying dead in the mangroves."

Ellis surrendered his wet shirt and Millege laid it

on the mudbank and placed the barrel against the center of the chest section and fired a hole into it. Then he pressed the area of the hole into his leaking leg bandage and drew blood into the shirt. Ellis put his shirt back on and they picked a spot and he lay faceup across mangrove roots as if he'd washed up dead or had been killed there. He closed his eyes and Millege made suggestions regarding the position of the dead man's limbs, then bent down and wiped mud on the victim's face and arms. He took photos from several angles, the flash revealing momentary freeze frames of a riverside crime scene.

"If he's conscious," Millege said, "your mercenary friend will have heard that shot and be left to wonder or form a conclusion."

They were dog-tired and trudged along the shallows of the sandbar with Millege periodically sweeping his beam ahead. In their wet and bedraggled state they appeared to be refugees or a sundry band of nocturnal scavengers. But there was no one but owls to see them pass.

After a while Stavo stopped and asked for the light. They saw a lump on the shore and he picked up Ellis's backpack and carried it.

They passed the dark and untended property of the squatter family and the heaviness there only added to the burdens they already carried.

24. Peregrinations

On highway 34, when they were nearly to Dominical and the turn to San Isidro, as Victor drove and Liz sat silently in the passenger seat, Obayda died in the back seat of the Rav4, his head in the lap of his wife Noilyn as she stroked his face and whispered soothing words and reminded him of the time they had first met and he had asked her to go fishing and then promised to teach her to swim when she disclosed that she had never learned.

Calvo, kneeling in the rear compartment and leaning over the seat to be included in his family's tragedy, wept at the sight of his father's passing, his tears falling on his mother's shoulder and running down her arm.

The weeping spread and increased, and under the onslaught of audible chaos, Victor pulled off onto the shoulder to determine what should be done. He cut the engine and stepped out to clear his head.

He could see a white box at the next turn and when he crossed the road and got closer he realized it was a ceviche stand on a trailer. Behind it, some town lights were visible and scattered notes of music floated through the warm air. Traffic was sparse.

He looked at the sky and at the moon rising above the treeline of the adjacent field. In the open part of the field an amorphous white shape, like a low mound of sand, began to move toward him. As he watched, the mound separated into individual beings walking in his direction and they became the rounded, forlorn bodies of Brahman cattle.

The field's fence was made of three strands of barbed wire strung between wooden posts, many of which had grown heads of leaves and become trees again. Victor stood at the fence as the cows formed a semicircle before him, their long, loose dewlaps like unhemmed skirts, their dark almond eyes staring as if he could lead them to a different life.

Liz appeared beside him. She put her arm through his and they stood in communion with the silent cattle.

"I asked her to help us," Liz said, "and now her husband is dead."

Victor pulled her body into his. "Things happen," he said.

"I told her we would direct the trouble away from them," she said.

"Don't carry this," he said. "You were trying to save two other people."

"I will carry this for a long time," she said. All of the cows were watching her, and in their silent witness there was neither condemnation nor absolution. There was nothing but their existence alongside hers, and her fence was just as visible. "The weight is like a hill of dirt," she said.

"I'm with you," he said.

Back at the car, Noilyn was walking around talking on her phone. Calvo remained inside with his father's body. After she hung up, Noilyn told Liz that they would deal with the body themselves, that they wished to be taken to a house in Cuidad Cortes, just south of where the evening trip began.

In Victor's mind, there was no need to get into the particulars of their wishes or the legalities in such a case. None of them wanted to submit the death to the bureaucracy of the authorities in San Isidro.

Victor suggested that the body be placed in the rear compartment and covered but Noilyn wanted more time with her husband's lifeless form and her wishes were respected. The body stayed with her in the back seat as if its state were uncertain while the woman prayed aloud for his recovery, then for his resurrection or eternal care, and then a respectable life for her and Calvo. The smell of blood was pervasive and they drove with the windows open, the salty ocean air seemingly bringing the scent of minerals across the land. The journey took forty-five minutes and during that time no one in the car spoke in actual conversation until they turned off the highway and directions were given.

Liz looked over the seat. "Noilyn, I want to call you tomorrow."

The other woman stared at her, then said, "We have spoken enough."

At a small concrete house on a dark street, a man named Navarro and his wife Xinia came outside to meet the car. He reached inside and pulled the body out of Noilyn's arms and carried it into the house without a word. Xinia helped Noilyn out of the car and they walked across the dirt to the door. Calvo climbed over the seat and into his father's blood. He stepped out and stood looking in the passenger window at Liz and Victor, his small round head poised in wonder, his brown eyes moist and full of disbelief. Then he went through the door and closed it on the lethal strangers.

On the way back, Liz and Victor stopped to get Victor's bike and she followed him to the rental house in Ojochal. The lights were on and Stavo's van was gone. Liz reported the news to Millege, who was drinking rum with Ellis. Helen was asleep.

It was decided that Liz and Victor would spend the night at her apartment in Sierpe and return in the morning. When they went outside to board the bike, Ellis joined them. He was light-headed and fully suffused with joy, confusion, and regret. He stood silently swaying as Victor put his helmet on Liz.

"This is very surreal," he said, "seeing you two." He gestured at the house. "With him."

"I know," Liz said. "I couldn't really understand it at first. But it felt like the best thing to do."

"I trust your instincts," he said, then grinned. "I don't know what's next. But it's cool seeing you two together. Best of luck."

"You too," Victor said. He held out his hand and Ellis stepped up and raised his and brought it down in a sharp slap-hold, and they shook hands with force.

Liz smiled at the warmth she felt among them and climbed on the bike behind Victor.

"Thank you both," Ellis said.

"We're all connected," Victor said.

In the clear fulgor of the morning, after coffee and a silent moment for Obayda's random, senseless death, Millege and Ellis used wet towels and disinfectants they found in the house to clean the car's interior as best they could. Helen refused to ride in it and had a friend pick her up with spare keys and give her a lift to the Ojochal beach location where her Corolla was parked.

The following day Millege stopped by the shop in Dominical where Helen worked. He stood in the doorway until she looked up from her position behind the counter and saw him as a nonpaying customer.

"How are you?" he said.

"I'm hanging in there," she said. Her smile was gone.

"I just wanted to check on you."

"Did they find the guy?" she asked. "The mercenary."

"Not yet. He's the type who vanishes."

"That's a comforting thought," she said. "Is that why you're still here?"

"No, I'm just not in a hurry to leave."

She nodded, noting his long pants and button shirt. "Thinking about some real estate?"

He noticed a bruise on her neck, like a purple rope burn. "I'm only thinking about not smoking," he said.

She smiled, despite herself. "I'm taking it slow," she said. "Making some changes too."

"Yeah? What kind?" The shop looked unchanged to him. On the sill of the open side window he saw what he thought was the same lizard he'd seen the first time.

"Oh, you know, life-improvement stuff. Walk more, lose weight. And I'm going to get a dog too. Probably this week. A rescue."

"That's great," he said.

"And I'm going to try to refocus on the reasons I came down here to begin with."

"What were those?"

"Living a purer, simpler life. More serene and healthier."

"What's the secret?"

"Your associations, to begin with," she said. "Having the right kind of people around you."

"The right kind," he said. "Jesus, I've had the whole thing backward."

"Funny," she said. "But it's not that complicated."

"Everything is complicated," he said.

"As you wish," she said, her hand lifting as a shrug. "How's your leg, by the way?"

"Not half bad. I'll probably be surfing soon."

She paused. "Are you being facetious?"

"Yes. But I'm walking better. And I thank you again."

—

At Bahia Ballena, a middle-aged stranger studied the menu without enthusiasm. He was American, dressed in khakis and polo shirt, but rumpled, his straw-colored hair worn long, his face starting to droop. He looked around as if he'd landed at the wrong place, as if he were meeting someone who would never show up, his body slouched against the bar, his posture crooked. Yet his eyes flashed curiosity, and he seemed to be torn between two minds.

On a post behind the bar a yellow card was tacked up to advertise a drink that was not yet on the menu. All new, it read. Yellow Boat Cocktail.

"What's in it?" the man asked the bartender.

The bartender was Stavo, quite pleased that customers were beginning to take notice of the sign. "You begin with white rum," he said. "Like Bacardi, or some other. Then you put some mango juice, very healthy, from the fresh fruit, and also carambola, the yellow starfruit. The next is a fresh lime squeezed, and add seltzer on top, then stir all together. Very simple and a bold, heroic color." He stood back and spread his arms for emphasis.

"Okay, I'll try one."

"Excellent," Stavo said. "On the rocks."

"Did you create this drink?" the customer asked.

"No, no." Stavo shook his head humbly. "The manager made it," he said. "Yesterday."

"Why is it called Yellow Boat?"

Stavo smiled softly. "I had an adventure in a yellow boat recently."

"I see. So the drink is actually named for you."

"Well, yes," Stavo said. "It is named for me."

He bent down and began to mix the drink, the look of concentration on his face like that of a bomb defuser. He wanted it to be perfect, to become very popular. Plus, he didn't want any yellow spots jumping on his white shirt.

The slouching man sat up straighter when the drink was placed before him. Definitely yellow. For some reason it reminded him of dog medicine.

He sipped and nodded. "Not bad. I thought it would be sweeter."

Stavo smiled. "Yes, you must put enough rum. Then you drink like the hero in your mind."

The man drank it as heroically as he could, rather formally, bringing the glass straight up before directing it to his mouth, as if he were observing military angles. A man in search of truth, it seemed, and he ordered another.

Stavo attended to several tables and returned to the bar and found that the man drinking the Yellow Boat Cocktail had tears in his eyes. Stavo was suddenly afraid the drink had a defect that prompted the consumer to weep.

"Sir," Stavo said, "is everything okay?"

The man looked at him and shook his head. "I was thinking about heroes," he said, "which made me think of my daughter, as everything does."

A little spasm crept up Stavo's spine, and he stood at attention, waiting respectfully. "What is her name, sir?"

The man pressed his lips together and rolled them in and out as if he were deciding what name to say.

"Chloe," he said. "Her name was Chloe."

Tears formed in Stavo's eyes, and he reached across the bar with his open hand. "My name is Stavo. I was a friend of your daughter."

The man's eyes shone as he shook the offered hand. "Jon Summers," he said. "Glad to meet you." He began to cry harder as he smiled at Stavo.

Stavo squeezed the grieving father's hand and released it. "She came here too," he said. "She sat where you are sitting."

Jon Summers held his head with both hands and looked around the open restaurant, at the few afternoon faces turned toward him, to better remember this environment he and his daughter had in common.

"I don't know what I expected," he said. "I just wanted to be where she was. You know what I mean." He paused, and swallowed hard. "At the end." He looked again at Stavo. "Do you know where she died?"

Stavo looked into the man's bloodshot eyes and nodded solemnly. "I can show you the place."

"My God," Summers said. "Would you really?"

They met at the restaurant at nine the next morning and Stavo rode with Summers in his Hyundai rental. The day was clear and hopeful and filled with meaning for the two men. En route, Stavo called Liz and explained the situation and asked her to meet them at the Sierpe burn site.

On the road dissecting the groves, the African palms flew by the car's windows like an epileptic's nightmare, row after row, gap after gap, an alternating pattern of dark and light flitting through Summers' vision and brain as he drove, making him feel a mesmerizing anxiety.

At the site, a bulldozer was grading the ground where the shed had been, and a pair of cattle egrets strutted fastidiously over the fresh dirt in its wake, their beaks jabbing at the arthropods and worms unearthed. A larger, abutting area to the north had already been leveled for building. Across the way, two women walked along the road under a pink umbrella.

Summers parked and got out and stood at the edge of the dirt. The machine operator watched the two men as he turned to grade in the opposite direction. The birds lifted off a few feet and touched down behind the dozer.

Summers looked at the ordinary patch of ground and wanted to find greater meaning there. Stavo described the maintenance shed and its basic function in the palm plantation while Summers stood with his hands in his pockets and tried to picture the building with his daughter inside it.

He leaned back and looked at the sky as the machine rumbled by. Against a blue field, a few stratus clouds drifted low over the great wetlands. One of them held the form of an upright being, and he looked for a sign from his daughter, anything. The being had strong-looking legs, and the structure of the cloud imitated muscle tissue. One arm was by its side and the other was raised, as if pointing ahead or striving to get somewhere faster than it was moving. The head section was the thickest part of the cloud. He struggled to see his girl in its shape but the head did not look human. It was flatter, with rounded fuzzy ears, and a snout more than a nose. As he stared, he could see that it resembled a weasel, maybe, or a standing badger.

A knot of frustration coiled inside him and he said her name aloud. Even as the badger stretched apart and got taller and became a nonfigurative shape, a strip of cotton or an unfurled bandage, he said her name.

Summers walked across the raw dirt. He looked at the ground, the dark earth and chips of glass and rusted metal, and he stood in the confines of the shed his mind had built. "Did you burn it down on purpose?" he said.

He heard the bike arrive and watched the rider get off and remove her helmet and shake her hair loose. At the edge of the graded patch she spoke to Stavo. As she walked toward Summers, he thought she looked, in her jeans and blouse, about the same age as Chloe. When he saw the mark on her face—a fire brand, a tattoo of strife—a wave of empathy struck his chest.

"Hello, Mr Summers," she said.

He shook her hand and tried to smile, and fought the urge to hug her. "Hello, Ms Zuniga," he said. "Is my daughter actually dead?"

Liz searched his falling face, saw the flicker of hope in his eyes, then glanced at the parked bulldozer—its rumbling engine shuddering to silence as if in respect—the sturdy palms, the worn-down houses across the road, Stavo standing as a sentinel for the father's privacy.

She pulled a piece of black cloth from her pocket and placed it on her other palm and turned back the corners to show him its contents.

He stared at the small puddle of glass sparkling in the daylight, its distorted iris looking at him, and he was dumbfounded, choked by certainty.

Liz pulled his hand up next to hers and placed the spilled egg of glass in his palm and closed his fingers around it. She held his fist in her hands and felt the transfer of natant emotion.

Jon Summers sank to his knees, steadied himself with a hand on the ground, and then sat. He lay back in the dirt and held the glass to his heart. He closed his eyes to the overhead sun and tears ran down his face in parallel tracks. After a few minutes he placed his daughter's eye on his forehead and let the warmth of the sun radiate through it and burn gently into his skin.

—

From a distance, the boat looked abandoned, adrift, as if it had been poorly secured at its mooring and was now subject to the capricious weather and changing tides of the vast lagoon fed by the Coronado and Térraba Rivers.

Del Preet lay on his back on the floor, his head to the stern, his legs over the middle seat. He had floated through the night, nodding off and jolting to awareness from a stridor of his own making, his breathing a surprising rattle every few minutes. Now he felt the dawn's slow crawl advancing.

Driven by a Yamaha two-horsepower engine, three men puttered along the tangled bank cutting through wisps of early morning mist. The tillerman spotted the unmanned craft as it materialized like a ghost ship out of the haze clinging to the river's surface. He whistled and pointed, and the other men studied the unusual sight, a boating hazard.

The men seated in the bow and center seats were in their fifties, old friends who frequently fished this river system. They used plastic hand reels and wore slacks and collared shirts. One was light-haired with age spots on his face and hands, and the other was dark-haired and of a darker complexion. They often hired the tillerman, an older man with a gray mustache, to pilot them in his scuffed and multi-colored boat to various offshoots into mangrove tunnels. All three men wore well-used bill caps. The old tillerman's shorts and stained T-shirt showed his ease and standing in the group, and his deep-creased and darkened face reflected his experience at the helm of his craft.

He throttled down and coasted in neutral to the other boat. He recognized its appearance and name—Little Snook—and was all the more puzzled. The light-haired fisherman in the bow leaned forward to grasp the gunwale of the drifting vessel and saw the feet and then the bloody torso of the man inside. The startled fisherman grunted and leaned back so suddenly that only the support of his friend's hands kept him from falling over the seat.

"There's a body in it," he said.

"Get the bow line," the tillerman said, nosing his boat against the other.

The man in front stood again and looked at the motionless body as he grabbed the bow line and pulled the slack into his possession.

The tillerman throttled forward a notch and pushed the other boat so that it turned alongside his and the boats were together in their length. He held his paddle as his stern bumped against the other. At his back, a sheathed filet knife rode on his belt.

"Mister," he said, leaning over the bloody man, whose shirt was dried to a rusty crust.

Del Preet opened his eyes and saw the three men staring at him. He squinted and frowned at them, looked confused and displeased, as if he was being disturbed during a pleasure cruise. He pulled his feet down and turned and struggled to get himself into a sitting position.

The other men observed his damaged arm now.

"Where is the owner of the boat?" the tillerman asked.

"I don't know," Del Preet said.

"Why are you in his boat?"

Del Preet looked behind the men as if he was expecting company. "I was attacked at Ojochal," he said. "I found the boat and took it to get away."

"You were shot," the tillerman said.

"I need to get to the road," Del Preet said. "And get my car."

"You need a hospital."

"When I get my car, I'll drive myself."

"Who shot you?"

"A guy who says I owe him money."

The men leaned together and spoke quietly among themselves. Then the tillerman spoke. "We can tow you to Ojochal and call an ambulance."

"I would appreciate that."

The fishermen pushed the disabled boat back along their gunwale and passed its line back to the tillerman. He secured it to his stern and glanced repeatedly at the wounded man, sitting still in the stolen boat. None of the three locals liked the man's story.

With the line taut between them, the tillerman slowly motored north, his small engine revving high with the other boat in tow. The front fisherman watched the water for debris, and the dark-haired middle fisherman faced the rear to keep an eye on the stranger. To the east, the land rose in silhouette and distant hillside homesteads came into definition as the sky grew bluer.

Far ahead, another boat could be discerned, a speck on the surface. Del Preet breathed himself into an injured calm, off-balance but receptive to his surroundings. Sitting up made his chest throb and he felt a fresh flow starting, the pump of his life draining. His right arm was swollen and his right hand nearly unable to grip.

He saw the front fisherman lean forward with his hand held to his ear, a finger in his opposite ear. He was using a phone. Del Preet reached behind the gas can and brought his 9mm forward and shot the dark-haired middle fisherman in the chest as he yelled out. The front man turned to look and was shot in his left shoulder. He fell back against the bow and the next shot went over his head.

The tillerman rolled sideways over the gunwale and splashed out of sight as Del Preet shot again and struck the front man in the neck. Blood spurted across the boat and the man crumpled to the floor and Del Preet rose quickly in a half-crouch and shot into the ripples of the tillerman's submersion. He squeezed the trigger again and no sound emerged. The magazine was empty, though the weapon's explosive sound waves still rippled through the shore trees and across the river's surface in all directions.

Falling wide of his engine's turning propeller, the tillerman swam out of a murky swirl of bubbles and under the rear boat, felt its rough bottom scraping over his fingers. He grabbed the stem of its prop as the vessel moved above him and pulled himself up for air, busting the surface with his head against the stern plate.

Del Preet could not reach the spare magazine in his pants pocket, could not get his hand to cooperate. With his left hand he withdrew his knife from the other pocket and flipped the blade out with his thumb. With no pilot the forward boat angled toward the starboard shore.

The tillerman clung to the dormant engine as Del Preet leaned over the starboard side, searching for signs of the missing man, then straightened and scanned the water behind the boat, looking for a break at the river's surface. After a few moments he turned to the front, set his knife on the bow seat, leaned forward and reached the taut line between the two boats. He imagined himself pulling the line and closing the gap between the two boats, saw himself stepping into the running boat, cutting the rear boat loose, dumping the bodies and making his run to shore. But it was a two-handed job and the line slid through the weak grip of his right hand. Sweat fell from his face and he sat heavily on the bow seat, knocking his knife to the floor. He pulled with his left hand and bent down to put the line under his foot and hold what he'd gained. The line slipped and he realized he'd have to wait until the forward boat hit the shore and the connecting line lost its tension.

The tillerman reached up and gripped the stern and pulled himself high enough to see the other man's position. In his sanguinary state, Del Preet sat with his eyes shut, breathing heavily, his exhalations raspy. The old tillerman lowered his head and began to hand-walk around the port side, each hand sliding in small increments along the lip of the boat, most of his body dangling in the river.

Del Preet felt a shift in the boat's balance and turned to see the brown hands on the port gunwale like knots of hardwood. He reached down for his knife, his fingers scraping across the bottom of the boat, the forward vessel's puttering engine seeming to mask the sound of low-flying aircraft. With knife in hand he turned and looked north, scanning the sky for incoming, then stood to search the river for other boats.

The tillerman pulled himself up for another quick look, saw the man's forward position, his knife, the pistol on the floor, then dropped into the water and caught the prop again as the boat was pulled forward.

In the day's aching brightness, under a visible sun, Del Preet struggled to regain his equilibrium and focus on the missing hands, the vanished man. He staggered to the center of the boat and leaned over the port side, saw nothing, his knife hand on the gunwale for stability. Then he thought about the stern.

He knelt on the rear seat, pressed his fisted knife hand on the exposed engine to steady himself, leaned out over the uncowled motor. And watched an old man rise out of the undulating surface as a river creature, haul himself upward by the engine, flash a filet knife sideways. Del Preet lost tendons in his arm, felt the hot rush of fresh blood, could not fend off the man's wiry hands on his shirt or the weight pulling him over the stern and headlong into the beckoning river.

The lead boat wedged into the looping embrace of mangroves and pivoted perpendicular to shore and the trailing boat drifted in the current like a buoy. The ongoing vibrations of disturbance reverberated up and down the stream and alerted bird, fish and reptile alike. A resting crocodile roused itself from the dark muddy bottom and rose to investigate. Another one swam out of the shore roots as it sensed the nearby flailings on the surface.

Thrashing through the water the old tillerman caught the rear boat and pulled himself up and over the gunwale in one practiced motion. Drawing upon the bow line he propelled himself to his own vessel, reached across and killed the engine. He rested there, dripping in the shade and silence with dead men.

Del Preet turned on his back and tried to float, moving his arms limply to help keep his body up, not knowing his direction or visibility to boaters. He had to get to his car, sleep, get help. His legs were sinking. Pressure gripped his right arm and pulled him down. His head went under and he was turned against his will, flipped over by a rolling reptile, his lungs filling with water and his mind unconscious before the second predator hit.

—

Costa Rica Courier
The Weight of Rain
Marco Vargas / June 11, 2014
marcovargas@crcourier.com

Readers, I bring you the next installment in the recent greenman story, or maybe its final chapter. A bit of evidence has been shown to indicate that the greenman has perished, that the fugitive was apprehended and dispatched with extreme prejudice. A garish nighttime photo shows the greenman with an apparent bullet hole in his chest and his lifeless body washed up in mangroves, presumably on the bank of a local river.

There's at least one little problem. No body. Was it dragged into the river to be consumed and vanish forever? Or did the greenman perform for the camera and walk away? Does he yet walk among us?

Tragically, with an assassin in the picture, the local deaths piled up. Three men died in the Coronado region simply by being in the wrong place at the wrong time. These we know about. Plus, the two girls. Also, the assassin himself was reported drowned, possibly eaten. Again, no body. So if we add up the victims in this case, we get six, or seven, if the greenman actually died.

I've been reporting on a story about an amateur ecoteur, his crimes and misdemeanors, his deceased associates, the attendant corporate schemes, the backdoor plots and deals, the dogged pursuit of those who choose the greater good over the profit margin, along with peripheral mentions of the mystery of ancient stone spheres, the value of indicator species and biological corridors, the eternal machinations of the greed reflex, the wonder of the cosmos. But what's the story here?

Good girls gone bad? The old "fugitive on the run" tale?

Collateral damage? The trampling of nature, the planet, the harvesting of every single creature who translates into, or stands in the way of, money. The need for victims and villains, indigenous tribes cored out and left in brittle translucence like a split cicada husk clinging to bark. Cultural and cosmic mortalities. The small human picture and the infinite over-arching framework. Where does it lead? What can it all mean? What is the weight of rain?

PPOI has begun the construction of a new maintenance shed, and plans to add a security station and a little country chapel next to it. Across the way, they are proceeding with the eviction of an old couple who has lived in the housing area for decades, whose family has been under of the palm oil umbrella for two generations, so that a few more acres of product can be added to a region that values African palm nuts more than people.

Perhaps this is a good time to employ a Swahili saying:
The story has been told. If it was bad, it was my fault, because I am the storyteller. But if it was good, it belongs to everybody.

We live at the top of the chain, and yet we can't control the tiny mosquito. We can't control microbes or viruses. We can't stop plagues from breaking out. If anyone takes over the place, it will be the smallest, the microscopic swarms acting on their own biological codes. No thought, no AI, no machine takeover. Just the animal running on instinct. Not malign or cruel, or even calculating. Just hungry to replicate and run rampant. The same as us.

Good luck, greenman, in this life or the next.

Peace be unto you, marcovargas@crcourier.com

—

Expanding our worthy praise of new mind journeys,

we embrace various feedbacks to modify our own self-perception of integrations. It is necessary to leave your mountain and clean your organism for conscious growth. Brave and seeking guests who enjoy the nature wonders and contemplate organic nurture rather than picky eater destinations, will awaken and rejoice in the inner self and observe its smallest detail as they balance the beauty and introspection of our spacious atmosphere.
Namaste, Circle of Light, summer 2014

—

● ○ ○ ○ ○ Reviewed June 11, 2014
"Circle of Whatever"
My girlfriend and I frequently have difficult vacation experiences because we are adventure souls who raise our expectations according to our chosen pursuits. We are dedicated to hedonistic and challenging thrills as long as the body fuel is compulsory and there is no danger of losing energy and stamina in the midst of our undertaken quest. We ran across a flyer for something called Circle of Light and I said to Beatrice this must be less than advertised or they would state clearly what they mean to say about the place and if so I feel an obligation to alert other adventure readers. She agreed that we should discover more. So we went to this circular establishment and asked to sign up for a head trip to balance the exhausting rigors we have been putting ourselves through. Apparently we were supposed to know beforehand about certain preparation rituals we were expected to endure such as ridding our bodies of the meatlovers pizzas we had already consumed. I was eating Doritos when we entered and was told rather rudely that this was not part of the improvement program there. The young reception girl acted quite frosty for a

tropical setting and told us we should think about our intentions. Which obviously we had or we would not have driven to an isolated mental health spa in the first place. Then she said they could not squeeze us in which was physically insulting since we are both on weight loss regiments. She had a weird first name I wish I could remember to tell you so you could arrive on her day off. Besides our search for audacious experiences we are regular people like everyone else. If we want to pay for a rustic room and practice river chanting I think anyone should be welcome and not rejected and told to get in a pure condition first. For this reason I have to give this circle of whatever a one star even if we did not participate. The location was ok.
rowanbowlers
Date of experience: June 10, 2014

—

The night of the fire Long Jimmy Finn drove home and sat in his car in the dark, not knowing how he had even driven there, windblown and frazzled and still enveloped by the smell he carried in his clothes, in his hair, in the pores of his skin, the putrid compound of chemicals and wood and plastic and rubber, a stench that registered in no memory he could summon except the one playing a soundtrack of screams. Gripped by heartache, he opened the door and gagged and spit out the taste of despair, unable to see his escape from the twin cells of cowardice and shame.

He stripped in the shower and stood on his clothes, hot water spraying his head and body. He washed himself repeatedly, poured shampoo until the bottle was empty, walked over his soapy garments again and again, the repetitive action bringing him down to a kind of ground level stability.

In the morning he stepped outside and opened the doors and windows of his vehicle and smelled the fabric of the driver's seat. He winced at the clinging odor and left the car open. In the shower he wrung out his wet clothes and bagged his burned pants to be dumped elsewhere. He made coffee and toast and cooked some eggs and sat outside eating, then waxed his board and thought about surfing but was unable to leave in his raw state.

No one dropped by and he did not answer his texts. His mind played images of Peyton from the few weeks of their intersecting lives, flickering visions that danced across the screen of his memory. He saw her without him, drinking and laughing at Tortilla Flats, carrying her rental board on the beach, saw the way she stood out from other tourists, even her friend, though he had entertained thoughts of frolicking between them both and almost suggested it before they ended up at her place and the forthright eroticism of her mind and the revelation of her naked body made him want her alone.

Jimmy did not surf that day or the following three days. He did not reply to questions or share his wounded feelings. He mutely carried his sadness and guilt like a waterlogged chest full of tarnished coins, a dark and crusted mass seemingly beyond salvage.

After the few days of isolation he met his crew at the Flats for ceviche and beer as usual. His morose behavior was perfectly understandable and it was assumed that he would eventually snap out of it and retake his rightful place in the surf.

When he was noticed at the table with his friends, some locals nodded at him or waved timidly or said *Sorry, man,* as they passed him on their way out.

"Good to see you, bro," Ian said, lifting his bottle. "To life after tragedy."

They all clinked their bottles and drank.

"Yeah," Jimmy said, "get back on the horse, right?"

"Back on the board, you mean," Scotty said, grinning.

"Tell him about the guy," Merlin said.

Jimmy looked at him. "What guy?"

Ian waved it off. "Some insurance guy, I guess, asking questions about the girls. About the fire and the missing dude who was with them."

Jimmy drank some beer, ate a piece of shrimp, and let a look of mild puzzlement shape his face. "You mean the dude was at the fire and now he's gone? He made it out?"

"Looks that way," Merlin said, rubbing his neck hair in thought.

"And what, now they're looking for him?"

"Apparently, yeah," Ian said. "It was Ellis, man. You know the dude."

They were all looking at Jimmy, wondering how much he knew, what he'd heard, where he'd been.

"No shit," he said, then shook his head. "Not that surprising, I guess."

"You were hanging out with them, dude," Ian said. "Didn't they clue you in a little bit? They didn't just pull off the road and decide to be arsonists."

"Could have been an accident," Jimmy said. "Anyone think of that?"

"Accident?" Ian laughed. "What were they doing there, conducting a safety demonstration that got out of hand?"

Jimmy looked around at the nearest tables, confirming a nominal sense of public privacy. "Look," he said, "maybe they were scoping the place out, you know, and somehow—" He saw the implausibility and stopped.

"I have another idea," Ian said. "I think the dude

murdered them and then burned up the evidence." He nodded at the others in a serious manner.

Jimmy stared at him, then laughed. "I can see you've given this all kinds of thought. Possibly more than it deserves."

"Right," Ian said, "and you have clearly not given it enough. Let's say someone wants to know where your car was four nights ago."

As if on cue, as if the table had been miked for sound, Jimmy's phone buzzed. He declined to answer but looked at the number and then removed a business card from his wallet and compared the neatly written number on it to the incoming one, his team watching him closely.

"Your old pal Felipe," Ian said. "He just wants to know where you were on a certain night. And why you didn't think to give him a little bitty heads-up."

"Would you shut the fuck up?" Merlin said. "Give the man a break."

But Ian was on a roll. "How'd he get your number, man?"

Jimmy couldn't hide his distaste. "Not from me," he said. "Maybe one of you fuckers gave it to him. Maybe the fucking barmaid did."

Ian stifled his laugh, drank some beer, raised his index finger to mark a thought he was having. "I got it, Long Jimmy," he said. "Give him a call back. Reassure the master bullshitter. Tell you were sitting at home all alone. Tell him even mighty American surfers fall ill sometimes. Even dumbshit stoners can get a bad feeling about things."

Scotty laughed despite himself, and Merlin shot him a stern look.

"I've had enough of your shit," Jimmy said. "You're bumming me out."

"Sorry, man," Ian said. "I feel bad for you, all

tripped up in a bogus story like this."

Jimmy smiled at him. "You feel bad?" he said. "When's the last time you lost someone?" He pushed his chair back and stood and all the noise of the bar surrounded him in a swirl. He felt other eyes probing his face and the laughs and colors took on the form of a carnival as he backed away from the table.

Scotty raised his hand like he was in class, and they all looked at him. "We are your brothers," he said. "That's all."

"True," Ian said, "just tell us you won't call Mr fucking palm oil."

Jimmy stared at each of them. "I won't call Mr fucking palm oil," he said.

He walked down the beach road, out to the cool night sand and the water's edge. The surf was steady and calming, a voice he could depend on. He looked at the dark horizon, the stars, the open world of space.

"Peyton," he said. He turned and saw a couple standing together thirty yards south of him, gazing out to sea, so close together they might have been one wide person.

"Peyton," he said, "I'm clumsy sometimes, can't figure out what to say or when to say it. I should have stopped you. I should have been a greater force. I should have written you a poem." He smiled, imagining her in the surf, teasing him, her feet brushed by waves, her shapely calves getting splashed, her hips and waist, her chest and neck, her hair dark falling around her face, her bright provocative eyes. "And I will," he said. "I'll write you one and read it to you right here, in one week's time. I think it could be about the danta I saw down the beach there"—he gestured to the south—"the one I told you about, the one that made me think of you even more than I already was."

He stood listening to the surf, the measure of waves rolling over a fire's snapping crackle, drowning it out. "I'm sorry," he said.

Back at Tortilla Flats a week later, he sat at a table with Ian while Scotty chatted at the bar with a girl from Memphis. Merlin was out under the palms along the beach road smoking a joint with some surfers he'd met that morning. Jimmy was feeling the old gang, the laughs, the consumption of spirits, the camaraderie.

"So you're out of the equation," Ian said. "Your story squares up."

"I'm straight," Jimmy said, "and no one has asked me squat."

Ian nodded. "Your buddy who you barely know is still on the run."

"The thing is," Jimmy said, "the girls left me out of the plan and I barely had any contact with that dude. Sort of like meeting at a party."

Ian watched his friend. "The thing is, also, the girls meant to do a good thing," he said. "May we never forget them." He raised his bottle.

"Here's to those daring young beauties," Jimmy said.

They drank and observed a moment of silence. Then Jimmy said, "I'm writing a poem for Peyton. To keep her memory alive."

"Cool," Ian said. "How's it going?"

Jimmy was glad they were sharing a pensive moment. "It's coming along, slowly," he said. "It's going to take some time to get it right."

Millege kept his Ojochal rental house for a few more days. His crew was paid and Liz and Victor made the trip by bike to Victor's room in Palmar Norte. He picked up a few items and they continued to her small apartment in Sierpe. She decided to try to find a house for her parents or one they could all live in.

To coincide with his cessation of smoking, Millege began to take morning walks on the beach. He preferred the one at Uvita and there was also a breakfast spot he liked nearby. On his phone were eight messages from Hiller and Millege spent some breakfast time composing his report, which now was never going to happen in person.

Some nights he stopped at Bahia Ballena, and he would see Stavo and order the whole fried snapper and drink rum and ruminate on his first night there and the journey he had taken. Not just this journey, but the whole of his passage through adulthood. It seemed that he had reached a crossroads.

At low tide, the beach was wide and gray and soft on the feet. The blue of the morning sky showed its transitory reflection in the wet sand like a mirror dulled by waves. Small smooth rocks pocked the surface of the beach near the treeline and were absorbed into the tall shadows of coconut palms leaning toward the ocean. Here and there coconuts lay sunk in the sand, arrested capsules stirring to seed inside. Dog tracks ran in lines and tangled patterns of inquisitive scenting. Down the coast a mist rose from the constant barrage of surf, the rising land behind it a distant diluted green. As he walked along in his observant mode, Millege passed crab holes whose thrown trails of sand upon their damp canvas had yielded monochromatic drawings which brought to mind hibiscus flowers and simple renderings of cosmic nebulas.

> Hiller, This is the end of the trail, and the case on my end is concluded.
>
> The target was cornered at a desolate spot on the Coronado river during a conflict with the aforementioned mercenary third party who terminated the target by

gunshot to the chest. The occasion was brought about by the third party kidnapping of a woman known to the target, who subsequently agreed to meet the kidnapper in order to gain the release of the woman. My team was in pursuit and the body was briefly observed and identified before gunfire forced us to take cover. In the ensuing exchange of shots, the third party was wounded. During this interval, the body was removed and is assumed to have been delivered to the river for disposal. The body has not been recovered. In the aftermath, the mercenary, who shot and killed several innocent locals and met with resistance during the course of this action, is presumed dead, drowned in the river. Again, no body has been recovered. An article in a local paper speculates that the target may have walked away but the writer presents no evidence. See attached photo.

At this point I recommend employing a riff on the concept of Occam's razor.

Let's say the target is dead. In one scenario, his dead body is dragged into the river and sinks to the bottom and is consumed by the crocodiles prevalent in the region. In the other scenario, his dead body is not actually dead, but appears to be. And at some opportune moment the target makes his escape without detection. In both cases there is no body and the subject is pronounced deceased. Which then, is the simpler, and most likely, explanation?

Additionally, I received a shot to the leg during the course of the mission, and have been taking some downtime to heal properly and reduce the risk of infection. Millege

Hiller's reply was swift and typical:

I didn't hire fucking Occam, I hired you. But understood,

downtime. Let me know if you can meet with Felipe if he wants to debrief. Hiller

Maintaining his habit of clearing up details and loose ends, Millege went to Helen's street and drove past her house, looking into driveways and turnoffs and checking pullover spots for an out-of-place rental car. He went up the hill as far as he could, to the highest driveway, then drove down, looking again. Nothing stood out. It was an impossible task. Any neighbor could have a visitor with a rental car, or temporarily need one themselves. Maybe the tree-shaker's car had been called in and picked up by the rental company.

Millege drove back to the Ojochal beach and combed the side road, checked driveways, the area around the Punta Mala church, and walked among trees, thinking he might find a stashed backpack or some piece of gear belonging to the mercenary. Again, nothing. It was as if the man's vanishing had taken all traces of him with it.

After his morning walk and breakfast, he read from the books in the house, ate papayas and mangos for lunch, took afternoon drives and naps, ate dinner in Uvita or at one of the restaurants in Ojochal.

One afternoon he wrote to Cassandra.

Perhaps you remember the three hills of Tinamaste. I have been thinking lately about those hills and that unusual journey and a fellow attendee I was lucky to meet. My in-country mission is complete and I'm resting up, still here in CR. I hope this finds you well and happily advising the less knowledgeable. Phil

She replied by nightfall.

Yes, I'm reminded of those hills almost daily. What a coincidence. I was lucky to meet someone there too. Really sort of unexpected. Not what I signed up for, lol.

I hope you've sorted out your totem by now. What are your plans now that the mission is over? If you want to repeat your mantra into the wind of Puget Sound I could arrange a ferry crossing for two. Cassandra

One afternoon Millege got a call from Stavo, who said Chloe's father wanted to meet the investigator and would be at the restaurant that night.

Millege picked the man out at the bar and sat next to him. The television was on, the usual background babble, and a fair breeze rustled under the thatch roof. Helen was at a center table with some of the same friends he'd seen her with that first night. She nodded at him.

Summers said, "Thank you for meeting me," and they shook hands.

"You have every right to know as much as you can," Millege said.

Summers nodded. "Stavo told me a little about you and said he knows the guy who wrote the newspaper articles about the case."

Millege smiled, glanced at Stavo, who was wiping the bar like he wasn't part of the conversation. "He's a talker," Millege said, "but a good man."

"He also showed me where my girl died." Summers looked down and composed himself. "Which really"—his voice caught—"really hit me."

"I can imagine," Millege said.

"I guess you know as much about this as anyone," Summers said. "Can you give me your opinion on how and why Chloe died?"

Millege summoned the bartender. "Stavo, can we get some rum?"

"Of course, Mr Phil. I will buy you both a Yellow Boat."

Millege looked at the grieving father and reached for a cigar that wasn't there. He patted his pocket and took a breath.

"Your daughter and her friend Peyton met a local male and together they decided—for a number of reasons, environmental and personal—to damage something belonging to Palma Central, the subsidiary palm oil company. To send a message, make a statement, that sort of thing. They hatched a simple plan which must have seemed low risk or foolproof."

Stavo set the drinks down and Millege stirred his and tasted it. He nodded to the bartender, who smiled.

"They picked a field shed but the building was in poor repair and they neglected to conduct a thorough recon. The girls were captivated by the natural beauty of the region and wanted to do something meaningful to protect it. They found a willing ally and a friend but the way it went bad that night was purely accidental, bad luck. The place was a firetrap and the group was a bit careless. As it happens, the company is unpopular with many due to the pollution from its rendering plants, in addition to all the land taken for the plantations. Some people consider a small act of ecotage to be heroic."

Summers' eyes had welled up, and he nodded his understanding.

"They were best buds," he said.

"No doubt," Millege said. "I wish I had met them."

"And their friend," Summers said. "Is he dead now too?"

Millege rubbed his goatee, glanced at Stavo, and at two guys taking seats at the end of the bar. He looked at Summers. "Do you want him to be?"

Summers shook his head. "I wish he wasn't. Chloe liked him."

"Well," Millege said, "maybe he's moved on to a better place."

Summers stared at him. "I guess we can let it go at

that," he said. "But let me ask you. Why are you working for the palm company?"

Millege took a drink. "I'm freelance," he said. "Each job comes with its own particular revelations. I no longer work for that company—or any other."

The following day Millege received an email regarding a potential job. The sender was a referral from a client he'd worked for some four years prior. The sender's daughter was missing in northern California. She was thirty-two years of age and had been working on a clandestine farm common in the forests of that region. The sender wanted to know if Millege was interested and available.

Millege wrote back and said he was interested but needed more information and could speak on the phone as soon as the sender was ready.

The sender, a man named Martin Redfern, wrote that he could speak at the investigator's earliest convenience and would also be glad to fly Millege to San Francisco and reserve a car for him if Millege didn't mind driving up to Mendocino to meet in person.

Millege stayed home that night. He walked around the small yard with a glass in one hand and an imaginary cigar in the other. He flexed his damaged calf and drew deep inhalations into his lungs and exhaled at the imperfect oval of sky enclosed by a perimeter of trees. He drank and looked at the house and saw himself as an inquiline, living in someone's rental, a jungle burrow. One temporary home after another.

Inside, he wrote another note to Cassandra.

> My time in the Mesoamerican corridor is up for now, and another mission has come my way. And your way. Could something uncovered in our common circle be directional in nature? I'll be heading to northern CA

shortly. You may think me some sort of flaneur, and that may be the case. But I've heard the drive up the Oregon coast is spectacular. Then there's Seattle for the totem sorting. Phil

---

At the Ojochal rental Ellis stayed out of sight for a few days. He and Millege were friendly and he answered most of the investigator's questions as well as he could, feeling he owed the man at least that.

Millege wanted to get the story details straight in his head and would figure out what to do with them later, how to present his wrap-up of the case. He offered to drive Ellis to Sierpe to see if his abandoned truck was still there.

They drove over the Estero Azul bridge and followed the farm road to the intersection with the dirt trail that jogged toward the channel. In the thicket of trees where he'd left his Ranger, Ellis found no evidence of his vehicle. They continued down the road alongside brown dirt fields and turned around when the road ended and a farm trail kept going to the east.

On the way back up the road, as they passed the property where he'd borrowed the small channel boat on the night of the fire, Ellis asked Millege to stop. Some small reflection had caught his eye and he walked into the driveway and saw his truck parked behind a stand of trees. The house was well-kept but presented no sign of current occupancy.

His battery was dead but he had cables under the seat and enlisted Millege's rental for a jumpstart. His engine turned over and he let it run for a time, wondering about the vehicle's position. Someone here had helped him. For a second, he was tempted to see if they'd gotten their boat back but then quit that wish. He hoped his removed truck would serve as a thank-you.

The next day he drove to Golfito and rented a cheap room and mostly stayed inside listening to birds bathing in pothole puddles and the chatter of the girls at a hair salon upstairs. At dusk he walked down to the bay and looked at the orderly marina boats and watched the local transport vessels bobbing at anchor inside the arm of the Osa Peninsula, a dark ridge etched against the roseate glow of the late setting sun. He brought a beer to create a happy hour, as happy as he could make it.

He considered Drake, a small end-of-the-world sort of place with a flow of tourists passing through on their way to boutique resorts along the coast. So sleepy and busy, the contradiction wouldn't settle. Then there was Rincon, also remote, over in the corner of this bay, the sweet gulf, *Golfo Dulce*, but with little opportunity for work. And he needed work.

In the end he looked behind him, up in the hills, and returned to San Vito because he'd liked it there. The climate was good. The size of the town was favorable. There was a famous botanical garden.

He got a job with a Canadian innkeeper, making breakfast for the guests. He cleaned and bartended. Included with the employment was the use of a furnished room the size of a tool shed. In his spare time he apprenticed with a birding guide and spent the dawn hours around the border of the garden, and within it. He learned to identify different hummingbirds by sight and sound. He spotted trogons and flycatchers, antbirds and woodcreepers, tanagers and warblers. He watched toucans, parrots, and the crested guan.

One day he drove eighteen kilometers to La Union, on the Panama border, and bought supplies for the inn at the duty-free store on the Panama side. After shopping he parked on a grassy ridge overlooking the countryside and ate his lunch on the tailgate of his truck. He had cheese and crackers and a beer and it was the first day he felt free in a long time.

He couldn't quit looking over his shoulder but he worked hard and stayed where he was. Spending more time in the garden he got to know the landscape and the employees and on occasion met visiting scientists. He also met a local woman who worked in the gift shop and began to see her regularly.

She had long thick black hair and smiled at his use of Spanish and gently corrected him. Her dark eyes focused on him like he was the subject of a foreign study but he was careful to avoid details of his recent past. She was close to his age and her name was Marisol. She had an interest in rupestral plants and showed him her favorite areas of the garden. On their first full night together he dreamed he was approaching his small room when it burst into flames. In his horror he saw her at the window as he struggled to pull the door open. It was stuck and he yelled for her to push it as he heard her screams and saw her hair on fire. He awoke in a sweat and she held him and stroked his face and kissed him.

The dreams continued for months but he and Marisol shared nights in his cozy room and strolled in the garden when she finished work and he could time his breaks to match. And after a while they walked through the town as a couple and he was accepted as a man who lived there too.